Jill Paton Walsh

Dorothy L. Sa,

A Presumption
of Death

 St. Martin's Minotaur ♔ New York

A PRESUMPTION OF DEATH. Copyright © 2002 by Jill Paton Walsh and The Trustees of Anthony Fleming, deceased. All rights reserved. Printed in the United States of America. No part of this book may be used or reproduced in any manner whatsoever without written permission except in the case of brief quotations embodied in critical articles or reviews. For information, address St. Martin's Press, 175 Fifth Avenue, New York, N.Y. 10010.

www.minotaurbooks.com

Library of Congress Cataloging-in-Publication Data

Paton Walsh, Jill, 1937–
    A presumption of death / Jill Paton Walsh and Dorothy L. Sayers.—1st U.S. ed.
        p. cm.
    Mystery written by Jill Paton Walsh based on Dorothy L. Sayers's descriptions of the Wimseys coping with wartime conditions in 1940.

    1. Vane, Harriet (Fictitious character)—Fiction.
    2. Wimsey, Peter, Lord (Fictitious character)—Fiction.
    3. World War, 1939–1945—England—London—Fiction.
    4. Women detectives—England—London—Fiction.
    5. Women's Land Army (Great Britain)—Fiction. 6. London (England)—Fiction. I. Sayers, Dorothy L. (Dorothy Leigh), 1893–1957. II. Title.

PR6066.A84 P74 2003
823'.914—dc21   2002036879

First published in Great Britain by Hodder and Stoughton
A division of Hodder Headline
ISBN: 978-1-250-01744-4
First U.S. Edition: March 2003

OCT 3 1 2018

A Presumption of Death

NO LONGER PROPERTY OF
SEATTLE PUBLIC LIBRARY

By Dorothy L. Sayers and Jill Paton Walsh
Thrones, Dominations

Detective stories by Jill Paton Walsh
The Wyndham Case
A Piece of Justice
You can find out more about Jill Paton Walsh's other novels for adults and children on http://www.greenbay.co.uk

Detective stories by Dorothy L. Sayers
Busman's Honeymoon
Clouds of Witness
The Documents in the Case (*with Robert Eustace*)
Five Red Herrings
Gaudy Night
Hangman's Holiday
Have His Carcase
In the Teeth of the Evidence
Lord Peter Views the Body
Murder Must Advertise
The Nine Tailors
Striding Folly
Strong Poison
Unnatural Death
The Unpleasantness at the Bellona Club
Whose Body?

By Barbara Reynolds
Dorothy L. Sayers: Her Life and Soul

For Barbara, who remembers

Prologue

Honoria Lucasta, Dowager Duchess of Denver, to her American friend, Cornelia, wife of Lambert B. Vander-Huysen, of New York.

Bredon Hall,   *12th November, 1939*
Duke's Denver, Norfolk

Dear Cornelia,

I think I had better write you my usual Christmas letter now, because naturally the war has upset the posts a little; and one can't really expect ships to go quickly when they are convoyed about like a school crocodile, so tedious for them, or keep to Grand Geometry, or whatever the straight course is called, when they have to keep darting about like snipe to avoid submarines, and anyway I like to get my correspondence in hand early and not do it at the last moment with one's mind full of Christmas trees – though I suppose there will be a shortage of those this year, but, as I said to our village school-mistress, so long as the children get their presents I don't suppose they'll mind whether you hang them on a conifer or the Siegfried Line, and as a matter of fact Denver is thinning a lot of little firs out of the plantation, and you'd better ask him for one before he sends them all to the hospitals.

And really, Cornelia, I think you must have been listening to Goering or Goebbels or that Haw Haw man or something: the suburbs aren't in ruins and Oxford and Cambridge haven't been invaded by anything worse than a lot of undergraduates from other universities, so good for both sides, I think, though I'm told the plague of bicycles in the streets is quite a menace – still, it never was anything else – and we've got plenty of butter and guns, if it comes to that, though they keep on saying they're going to ration them, just as Hitler keeps on saying he's going to begin, only he doesn't go: like the people in the Pirates *of* Penzance, *and Peter says if he waits much longer the audience will refuse to clap and perhaps the Munich bomb was in the nature of a cat-call, but what I say is, if little Adolf found anything nasty in that beer-cellar he must have brought it with him. And, talking of Peter, I can't really tell you where he is, because he's gone back to his old job, and everything comes without any proper address through the Foreign Office. I rather fancy he may have been in Turkey a little while ago, from something he said about the coffee being good; I can't think of any other place where that would be likely to happen, because he never really likes French coffee (too much chicory), and nobody else seems to have any, except us, and I know he's somewhere abroad, the letters take so long.*

Wherever it was, he isn't there now, and that makes me think it must have been Turkey, because they seem to have settled everything splendidly there. But of course this is only guess-work.

It's very hard on poor Harriet, his being sent off like that, but she is being very sensible; they've shut the London house, and she's gone down to Talboys, that's their farmhouse in Hertfordshire, with the children – I enclose a photograph of little Paul, he's nearly a year old now, and Bredon just three; how time flies! – and my daughter Mary's youngsters are there, too. I think it's very good of Harriet to take care of her sister-in-law's children but she says it's no more trouble than looking after just her own. You'll think it's a doting grandmother speaking, but they are very nice children: Charles Peter, who likes to be called Charlie now he is ten, Mary who gets called Polly just as her mother used to, and little Harriet, who is only three, but very sweet-tempered. However you look at it, I think it must be a lot of work for Harriet, but it frees Mary for war work. She's doing ARP work and looking after her husband – you remember him, Charles Parker, the CID Chief Inspector – naturally he can't leave town. They seem well and happy and very busy. Charles was a little upset the other day over finding two human legs (a very bad match) in a police-post, tied up in brown paper. He said it made him feel he was going to miss Peter. However, it turned out they had only been left there by a man who was taking them to a hospital and had popped them inside out of the rain while he hunted for a taxi in the blackout, and it would all have been cleared up quite quickly, only when the poor man had found the taxi he'd forgotten where the police-post was, and drove wildly round the West End looking for it; so confusing, but one must expect these little inconveniences in war-time. And à propos of sandbags (oh, no, I didn't mention them, but the police-post was built of sandbags, a sort of little hut, you know, like a night-watchman's) you can't think how queer Piccadilly Circus looks with Eros gone and a sort of pyramid like King Cheops on a small scale built up over the fountain – though why they should take all that trouble I can't think; unless it's the water-mains, except that people feel very sentimental about it and if anyone dropped a bomb on it they'd feel the heart of Empire had stopped beating. Peter says we ought to do something constructive in the opposite direction and floodlight the Albert Memorial because the park would be better without it, but poor Queen Victoria would turn in her grave and, as I reminded him, he didn't know Queen Victoria personally: I did.

Yes, my dear, we are all quite all right. My older son Gerald, Duke of Denver, is worried about my grandson Jerry, of course, because he's in the RAF, and naturally that's rather dangerous, but dear boy, how he is enjoying himself, being able to go just as fast as he likes (you remember how he used to terrify us with that big racing-car). His father says he ought to have got married to somebody first so as to provide an heir in case of *accidents. 'Really, Gerald,' I said, 'fancy worrying about that at a time like this. If there's anything left to be heir to when we've finished paying for the war, Peter's got two boys – and, judging by Jerry's present taste in young women, we are mercifully spared.' That was rather tactless, I suppose, because Gerald's fretting quite enough about the estate already; he says we shall be ruined, of course, but he doesn't mind that if only he can do his duty by the land.*

And then we've got a big boys' school in the west wing, and that gets on his nerves sometimes – still, most fortunately, Helen, his wife, isn't here, which relieves the tension. As you know, I never like to criticise my daughter-in-law, but she is a very difficult sort of person and I was devoutly thankful when she took herself off to the Ministry of Instruction and Morale. What she can possibly have to instruct anyone about I don't know, but as the place is packed with everybody's wives and nephews and all the real jobs seem to have been handed over to other departments it's as good a spot as any to intern the nation's trouble-makers, and she's got three secretaries paid by a grateful country to endure her so all is for the best. There was a picture of her in the papers last week, glaring like the wrath of God and when Denver saw it I thought he'd burst a blood vessel or have a blood-bath or something, only fortunately, just at that moment, one of our little evacuees put a cricket ball through the long window of the yellow saloon, and in the strain of trying to swear on two fronts at once the frightfulness blew itself off. They are all elementaries (the evacuees, I mean) from a rather slummy bit of London, and I'm afraid the infant cherub with the cricket bat made pique, repique and capot of Denver before he could score half his vocabulary. Curious and charming, isn't it, how much the peerage and the proletariat have in common once you get down to the raw stuff of life, so to speak. Any nice middle-class foster-parent would have turned purple, but Gerald burst out laughing and has begun to take quite an interest in the school. In fact, he's offered to umpire their end-of-term sports competition, and has lent them a pony for riding lessons.

Well, my dear, I must stop now and see a deputation from the Women's Rural Institute, who are getting up a Nativity Play for Polish refugees, so sweet of them, and most providentially there's a full moon for Christmas, so we shall get a good audience. I have promised to play 'Anna a prophetess' – I'd forgotten there was such a person so I must look her up quickly before they come. We carry on, you see, war or no war: 'we don't take no account of blackouts in these parts,' having never known the bright lights. (Dear me, Cornelia, what would you do with a blackout in New York?) And, as for wars, this is a very old country, and we can remember a great many of them.

My best love and all the good wishes of the season to you and yours.

Your affectionate old friend,
Honoria Denver

Harriet, Lady Peter Wimsey, to Lord Peter Wimsey, somewhere abroad. (extract)

Talboys, Paggleham,   *17th November, 1939*
Nr Great Pagford, Herts

. . . I've been trying to write an article about war-aims and peace-aims, though I'm not at all sure that all this definition doesn't end by darkening counsel, on the principle of 'Mummy, I think I might understand if only you wouldn't explain.' We all know pretty well that something we value is threatened, but when we try to say what, we're left with a bunch of big words like justice, freedom, honour, truth and so on, that embarrass us, because they've been misused so often they sound like platform claptrap. And then there's 'peace'. Peter, I'm terrified by this reiterated demand for 'enduring peace and lasting settlement' – it's far too like the 'war to end war'. Do we really still persuade ourselves that there's some final disposition of things – territory, economic adjustment, political machinery – that will stabilise all human relationships by a stroke of the pen? That the story can end in the old-fashioned way with wedding-bells: 'so they married and lived happy ever after'? If so, we need an Ibsen to deal with public life.

If one looks back at the last twenty years, one sees at how many points we might have prevented this war, if it hadn't been for our inflexible will to peace. We said 'Never again', as though 'never' wasn't the rashest word

in the language. 'River, of thy water will I never drink!'
We will never go to war again, we will revise all treaties
in conference; we will never revise anything for fear of
starting a war; we will never interfere in other people's
wars, we will always keep the peace: – we wooed peace
as a valetudinarian woos health, by brooding over it till
we became really ill. No wonder we couldn't stand by the
Covenant of the League, which set out to enforce peace
by making every local injustice an occasion for total war.
That idea was either too brutal or too heroic, I'm not sure
which. A mistake, anyway. What I want to say is that
there's no hope of getting peace till we stop talking about
it. But I don't suppose that view will be very popular! As
for going into a terrifying conflict under the leadership of
Neville Chamberlain – hoping against hope that he will
be better at war than he was at securing 'peace in our
time' – everyone says he was trying his best, but his best
might not be nearly good enough.

Oh, well! Meanwhile, Paggleham continues to adapt
itself to war conditions. On Wednesday we had a fire-
practice, with Mr Puffett in charge. (His all-round experience in the building and chimney-sweeping way is held
to qualify him to take the lead in emergencies of this
sort.) I said they might hold their demonstration here,
on the strict understanding that little Paul should take
no personal part in the proceedings and that the pouring
of water inside the house should be a purely symbolic act.
We arranged a very fine performance: an incendiary bomb
was to be deemed to have come through your bedroom

ceiling, with the accompaniment of high explosive in the scullery, the maids playing parts as casualties, and the children and I as victims of the fire. We thought it better not to sound the local siren and whistles for fear of misunderstanding, but the vicar kindly gave the signal for the attack by having the church bells rung.

Everything went off beautifully. Miss Twitterton was with us, having come over from Pagford for choir-practice (even in war-time, Wednesday is always choir-practice), and rendered first-aid superbly. I lent her your old tin hat ('for protection from shrapnel and falling brickwork') and her pleasure was indescribable. We evacuated Polly and Bredon from the bedroom window and the other two from the attic in a sheet, and had just got to the pièce de résistance – my own rescue from the roof with a dummy baby under one arm and the family plate under the other – when the Vicarage kitchen-maid arrived panting to say that the Vicarage chimney was afire and would Mr Puffett please come quick. Our gallant fire-captain immediately snatched away the ladder, leaving me marooned on the roof, and pelted up the lane still in his gas mask, and followed by the ARP warden crying that it would be blackout time in half an hour, and if Hitler was to catch sight of that there chimney ablaze there wouldn't half be trouble with the police. So I retired gracefully through the skylight, and we transferred the venue to the Vicarage, getting the fire extinguished in nineteen and a half minutes by the warden's watch – after which the fire-fighters adjourned to the Crown for beer, and I had the vicar and *his wife to dinner, their kitchen being – like Holland – not actually flooded, but pretty well awash . . .*

Honoria Lucasta, Dowager Duchess of Denver, to Lady Peter Wimsey at Talboys.

The Dower House,   *15th December, 1939*
Bredon Hall,
Duke's Denver, Norfolk

Dearest Harriet,

How tiresome for you that Polly should have caught this horrid flu germ! I can't think why the Almighty should have wanted to make such a lot of the nasty little creatures – misplaced ingenuity I should call it in anybody else. Though I read in a book the other day that germs were probably quite well-behaved, originally, but had taken to bad habits and living on other people, like mistletoe. Interesting, if true, and all Adam and Eve's fault, no doubt. Anyway, I saw Mary in town and told her not to worry and she sent love and said how sweet of you to stay at home and look after her erring offspring. I hope you have received all the parcels. I couldn't get a gas-mask case to match the dress-pattern exactly, but the one I sent tones in pretty well, I think. The shoes have had to be specially dyed, I'm afraid – it seems to be rather a difficult colour. I hope the Christmas cards will do. I had a terrible time with the sacred ones; there seems to be nothing this year between things from the British Museum and those sentimental modern ones with the Virgin and angels very thin and willowy and ten feet tall. Such a mistake, too, to imagine that children approve of baby cherubs and little darling boys and girls swarming over everything. At least, I know my children always wanted stories and pictures about proper-sized people, whether it was knights or cavaliers or pirates, and just the same with their dolls and things – I suppose it gave them a grown-up feeling and counteracted their inferiority complexes.

It's only grown-ups who want children to be children; children themselves always want to be real people – do remember that, dear, won't you? But I'm sure you will because you're always most tactful with them, even with your own Bredon; more a friend than a parent, so to speak. All this cult of keeping young as long as possible is a lot of unnatural nonsense; no wonder the world seems to get sillier and sillier. Dear me! when I think of some of the Elizabethan Wimseys: the third Lord Christian, for instance, who could write four languages at eleven, left Oxford at fifteen, married at sixteen and had two wives and twelve children by the time he was thirty (two lots of twins, certainly, but it's all experience), besides producing a book of elegies and a learned disquisition on Leviathans, and he would have done a great deal more, I dare say, if he hadn't unfortunately been killed by savages on Drake's first voyage to the Indies. I sometimes feel that our young people don't get enough out of life these days. However, I hear young Jerry shot down a German bomber last week, and that's something, though I don't think he's likely to do very much with the languages or the Leviathans.

Talking of books, I had a heartfelt outburst from the young woman at the library, who said she really didn't know what to do with some of the subscribers. If there isn't a brand-new book published for them every day they go in, they grumble frightfully, and they won't condescend to take anything that's a couple of months old, even if they haven't read it, which seems quite demented. They seem to spend their time running to catch up with the day after tomorrow – is it the influence of Einstein? The girl asked when there was going to be a new Harriet Vane murder story. I said you thought the dictators were doing quite enough in that way, but she said her readers wanted their minds taken off dictators, though why murders should do that I don't know – you'd think it would remind them. I suppose people like to persuade themselves that death is a thing that only happens in books, and if you come to think of it, that's probably the way they feel about religion, too, hence the pretty-pretty Christmas cards. All the same, I'm sending a few assorted murders to the poor dear men who are being so bored on the balloon barrage and jobs like that. So dull for them, poor things, and nobody seems to take much interest in them. More romantic, of course, to send to the men overseas, but it can't be so solitary out there as sitting up all night with a blimp in darkest England.

Talking of darkest England, what one wants on the shops at night is not just a sign saying 'Open', but something to show what they've got inside. They're allowed a little light on the goods, but if one's driving along one can't possibly see whether a pile of vague little shapes is cigarettes or chocolates or bath buns or something to do with wireless sets; and it doesn't help much to see just 'J. Blogg' or 'Pumpkin and Co.' unless you know what Blogg or Pumpkin is supposed to be selling.

My dear, this letter is full of shopping and nonsense, but I've made up my mind that we just mustn't worry about Peter because he disappeared so many times in the last war and always turned up again more or less safe and sound. He's got quite a good instinct of self-preservation, really. And he's not stupid, which is a comfort, whatever Kingsley has to say about being good and letting who will be clever, though I don't see how you can be clever just by willing. Peter always maintains that Kingsley said 'can', not 'will', and perhaps he did. I only hope he still has Bunter with him, though if he's gone into any queer place in disguise I can't think what he can have done with him, because if ever a man had 'English gentleman's personal gentleman' written all over him, it's Bunter. I had a letter from him yesterday, so discreet it might have been written from Piccadilly, and conveying the compliments of the season to all the Family, with a capital F.

We're looking forward to seeing you all for Christmas, germs permitting. I hope you won't mind our being over-run with evacuees and children's parties – Christmas tree and conjurer in the ballroom, with charades and games after supper – I'm afraid it will be rather noisy and rampageous and not very restful.

Always your affectionate
Mother

PS: I'm sorry my English is so confusing. It was Bunter, not Peter, who wrote the discreet letter, and Peter, not Kingsley, who has Bunter with him – at least, I hope so.

Lady Peter Wimsey to Lord Peter Wimsey, somewhere abroad. (extract)

6th February, 1940
. . . This is the coldest winter anyone can remember. The Pag has frozen solid, and all the children and the land-girls have been skating on the village pond, looking like a scene painted by Brueghel. There is no coal to be had for love nor money, which is more to do with the freeze-up than the enemy. Troops are being used to dig snow off the railway lines. I'm afraid the vine in the glass-house will die, but other than lining the glass with newspaper – it is already elaborately criss-crossed with sticky tape, as are all the windows of the house – I can't think what to do about it. We have no fuel to spare for a heater; as it is we are carrying branches home from Blackden Wood, and spending most of the day in the kitchen, where Mrs Trapp keeps the range going splendidly, and it's always warm.

In all this chill we need a hot topic, and that is provided by the land-girls. Seven of them are working at Datchett's farm and five at Bateson's. John Bateson has lodged them in the outbuildings just beyond our kitchen garden, you know – the range that was the stable yard and tack rooms before this house was split from the farm itself. They all seem rather jolly to me, and incredibly hard-working. John Bateson seems rather hard on them: I heard him the other day saying, 'You've come here to do a man's job, and you'll just have to get on with it!' They have been kitted out for work with awful fawn aertex shirts, grey slacks and green pullovers but they wear silk stockings and lipstick when off duty, and have rapidly acquired a reputation for being 'fast', which has all the young men buzzing round like wasps at a honey pot. There's no shortage of young men to buzz round, because we have two airfields between here and Broxford, and some sort of hush-hush military establishment in the Manor House, requisitioned from the squire, and full of youngsters in mufti fond of dancing and the flicks when off duty. This is all rather a lot to swallow for the older people, who shake their heads over it all till their necks must ache!

The other big news is that the Anderson shelters have arrived – at long last; Broxford and Lopsley have had theirs for weeks – and of course the ground is frozen so hard that nobody can dig the holes in the gardens required to erect them. Mr Gudgeon – you remember him, the landlord of the Crown – has made his cellars available as a public shelter. It turns out the Crown is much older than it looks above ground; it has a warren of vaulted powerfully ancient-looking undercrofts, which surely must have been part of an abbey before the Re-formation, and although the handiest part, down some stairs behind the bar, is full of beer barrels, there are positively spacious catacombs further in. Gudgeon will throw these open to the villagers. The president of the Paggleham Women's Institute was talking of providing comforts – built-in bunks, paraffin heaters, tea-kettles, a library of second-hand books, communal blankets – when, behold and lo! a difficulty arises: the Methodists of Paggleham will on no account be herded into a public house, not even as a matter of life and death. Mr Gudgeon, rather magnanimously I thought, offered to close off his beer barrels so that one could reach the safety of the vaults without even catching sight of a stave or hoop or spigot, but it will not do. In Paggleham not even Hitler will cause a Methodist to be caught sight of entering a public house.

There matters rested for several days until someone remembered 'The Cave', an excavation in the chalk of Spring Hill, used, I am told, in the Napoleonic War as a munitions store, and seemingly deep enough for safety, and large enough for the congregation of the Chapel. Mrs Ruddle's Bert is duly at work fitting it out with primitive bunks; never let it be said that Church folk or the Godless had an easier berth than Chapel folk . . .

I can't help thinking that in practice, when we get an air-raid, everyone will rush to the nearest point of safety, and we shall have ecumenical havens, one each end of the village.

As Hitler has not yet obliged us with an actual peril, our excellent ARP committee has ordered a rehearsal on Saturday night, when an air-raid will be supposed to take place. It has to be Saturday, as everyone is available then, and nobody wants to imitate the horrible inconvenience that might attend a real air-raid.

Since there is to be a dance on Saturday next week in the Village Memorial Hall, and we don't want to disappoint the brave fellows from the airfields all around, the practice is timed for just after the dance, and we shall see if the Methodists' cave is near enough to be reached in time. The cave would be nearer than the Crown for Talboys, of course, but I have promised to help Mrs Goodacre with the refreshments for the dance, so it will be the vaults for us this time. Dear Peter, how petty all this must seem to you, reading this letter, if you ever get it, in the middle of something much more world-shattering, and in danger for which no artificial rehearsal is necessary. But it's all the news there is from our parish pump. God keep us from having anything more interesting to write to you about! . . .

One

It is through chance that, from among the various
individuals of which each of us is composed,
one emerges rather than another.

Henry de Montherlant, *Explicit Mysterium*, 1931

'Whoever, for example, Lady Peter,' said Miss Agnes Twitterton, 'is that?'

'You do have a point, my dear,' said Mrs Goodacre, the vicar's wife, who was standing with the two women behind a trestle table at one end of the Village Hall, pouring out Miss Twitterton's parsnip wine into rows of assorted sherry glasses. 'There was a time, as you say, and not so long ago, when we would have known everybody we could possibly meet here – when any stranger was a seven-day wonder – and now here we are organising a village hop, and we don't know half the people here. They could be anybody; indeed I expect they are.'

Harriet looked around. The shabby little hall, with a dusty dais at one end, had perhaps fifty people in it. About half were young men in uniform, rather outshining the youthful farm workers and shop-boys in civvies. The uniform blotted out whatever they may have been like in peace-time; no better than the rest of the company, most likely, and possibly much worse, but khaki and air-force blue gave them now the status of heroes.

It's Tommy this, an' Tommy that, an' 'Chuck him out, the brute!'
But it's 'Saviour of 'is country' when the guns begin to shoot.

ran through her mind. The notorious land-girls were much in evidence, with their city skills in make-up and nice dresses. Harriet did not in fact know everybody, far from it. Had the assembly gathered the older people of the village she might have done better; she had spent long enough here to know most of them. But unlike the true villagers she didn't expect to know everybody; she was used to the crowded anonymity of London.

'One shouldn't think the worst of newcomers,' she said mildly. 'You don't want to sound like Mrs Ruddle.' She smiled to herself at the memory. 'When Lord Peter and I rolled up here on our very first night as man and wife she took one look at us, and declared we were no better than we should be!'

'You must have been wearing that magnificent fur cloak of yours,' said Mrs Goodacre. 'One associates fur with loose morals very easily these days, because of the cinema.'

'Yes, I was,' said Harriet. 'And I'm glad to say I can tell you who that is, Miss Twitterton. That is Flight Lieutenant Brinklow.'

'Well, if you say so,' said Miss Twitterton. 'But that's just it! We know his name, but we know nothing about him. He could be any sort of villain, for all we know – he could even be a German spy!'

'As a matter of fact I think he's a war hero,' said Harriet. 'He is here recuperating. His fighter plane was shot down and he baled out and was injured slightly. He can't go back on active duty until his shattered ankle has mended, so he has taken Susan Hodge's cottage – the one just opposite the churchyard gate – for a month of quiet in the country.'

'He's very good-looking,' said Miss Twitterton dubiously, as if the officer's looks made this history improbable. She was certainly right in that. Flight Lieutenant Brinklow was tall and blond, with brown eyes and a candid manly address. He was not dancing – presumably his ankle made that impossible – but was standing surrounded by a group of pretty girls and brother officers, looking perfectly at ease.

'You are very well informed, Lady Peter,' said Mrs Goodacre. 'As the vicar's wife I am not often pipped at the post with the gossip. You are becoming quite a villager!'

'You forget I was born here,' said Lady Peter mildly. 'But there's no mystery about it. The poor man is on sticks, and so he needed a bed brought down the stairs to the dining-room, and Susan Hodge asked a couple of the land-girls at Bateson's farm to help her do it, and it got stuck halfway down, and they had to heave it back upstairs again, and take it apart. One of them told Mrs Ruddle all about it, and what Mrs Ruddle knows is soon common knowledge.'

'One of those airmen,' observed Mrs Lugg, who was making up the fourth hand at the refreshment table, 'is even better looking.'

'That,' said Harriet with a mildly triumphant note in her voice, 'is Peter's nephew, Gerald Wimsey, home on leave for three days, and staying with us.'

'Do you mean Lord St George?' asked Miss Twitterton. 'The one who will one day be a duke?' A maiden lady somewhere in her forties, Miss Twitterton had become acquainted with the Wimseys on their very first evening in the village, and was almost too interested in the family, including those she had heard mentioned only once or twice.

'Yes, the very man. But he likes to be plain Flying Officer Wimsey for the moment. He tells me everyone in the RAF just mucks in without distinction. Nothing counts but your service rank. So plain Jerry Wimsey it is.'

At that moment the band-leader struck a chord, and plain Jerry Wimsey stepped up to the microphone, as the band – a rather under-rehearsed group, including most of the Salvation Army's brass players from Pagford – broke into 'Dreamshine'. Jerry began to sing in a light tenor voice of great sweetness, sounding so like his Uncle Peter that Harriet flinched inwardly.

> *Under a shining moon,*
> *And to a tender tune . . .*

Harriet watched the couples foxtrotting round the floor, holding each other as closely as lovers, in an aura of yearning which surely had something to do with the times as much as the people.

> . . . *We danced the night away,*
> *And at the break of day*
> *We found the world had changed . . .*

She was aching to be dancing herself, provided only that she could be dancing with Peter – Peter somewhere far away and in danger – and, cross with herself for being so easily touched by a trivial tune, but Jerry was singing beautifully, she sternly turned her attention to sandwiches and the tea-urn. Obviously yearning made young people hungry, for the plates were emptying fast. The little cornflour cakes that Mrs Trapp had provided had already gone. And now Harriet felt touched by that: all these grown-ups eating cakes like children at a birthday party, when the times ensured that it was only too likely to be a wake for some of them, especially those in uniform, and you could hardly blame them if they snatched things – cakes, girls – while they had the chance.

'Fancy a turn about the room, Aunt Harriet?'

Here was Jerry, having resigned the microphone to a sexy-looking young woman, holding out his arms to her. She allowed herself to be steered away from slicing dense and rubbery fruit cake, and propelled into the throng. Jerry held her just a little too close, pressed his cheek against hers a little too much – the gesture was pointless without Peter there to be stung by it – but Jerry was always living on the edge, pushing his luck.

> *One more dance before we part . . .*

Suddenly singer and band both were drowned out by a horrible cacophonous wailing, eliding sickeningly between two notes. The air-raid warning! The band came to a ragged note-by-note stop. The singer faltered and fell silent. The band-master took the microphone.

'Now don't panic, everyone. As you probably know this is a planned rehearsal to see how quickly we can all get underground. Our friends in uniform must decide for themselves whether to join the civilians in the exercise, or return to their base; but I'm afraid the dance is over. If you are disappointed to miss the last waltz, don't blame me, blame the ARP officer, he's a little quick off the mark. Don't forget your gas masks, everyone. Just make your way quietly either to the cellars of the Crown, or to the Paggleham Cave. If you have left your children at home with Gran, go and fetch them now, exactly as you would do if this were a real emergency. Thank you and goodnight.'

There was a jostle of people in the doorways as everyone took coats and gas-mask holders off the hooks. 'I suppose we can't clear up tonight,' said Mrs Goodacre. 'We'll have to come back in the morning.'

'That's all right, missus,' said the caretaker. 'I'll lock up. Just get yourselves under cover before that blinking Hitler gets to you.'

'Oh dear, are you sure?' said Miss Twitterton. 'Only since it's only a practice, you know, we certainly could stay back and see to things . . .'

'No, you don't, Aggie Twitterton,' said the caretaker.

'You'll spoil the whole thing if you don't co-operate, and it'll have to be done again. Off you go with everyone else.'

Standing in the moonlit road outside the hall, listening to Miss Twitterton apologising repeatedly and explaining that she only thought . . . Harriet found Jerry at her elbow.

'I'll walk you home, Aunt Harriet,' he said, smiling at her from a face half moonlit, half in darkness, 'and help you round up all those kids.'

'There aren't so very many,' said Harriet. 'Only five. But they do seem like a multitude at times!'

They walked towards Talboys under the brilliant light of a full moon. All the warm comfortable lights that used to shine from cottage windows were now blacked out, and the street lamps, all seven of them, were extinguished, but this icy light was bright enough to show every house and tree, every bridge and pillar-box to anyone who had been looking down on it, taking aim.

'We've certainly got a bomber's moon tonight,' Jerry said.

As they passed the church the moonlight showed them, clearly pencilled in silver, the silhouette of Mr Lugg the undertaker perched on the tower under his tin hat, doing his turn at fire-watching. Harriet waved at him, and then felt frivolous. But he briefly waved back.

'Aunt Harriet, I suppose you haven't thought of taking that houseful of yours up to Denver, have you?' asked Jerry.

'We were there at Christmas,' Harriet said. 'We're only just back.'

'I meant have you considered moving there for the duration?'

'No!' she said. 'I have not.'

'There's such a lot of room up there,' he said. 'Bredon Hall is genormous.'

'But they've got an entire boys' school billeted on them,' she said.

'Even so. And Grandmama would be so pleased to have you; I know she would!'

'I'm very fond of my mother-in-law, Jerry,' said Harriet, 'but as to uprooting myself from my own establishment, and plumping myself and all these other people on hers . . .'

'I just thought you might be safer there.'

'But we're as safe here as anywhere. Hasn't the government just billeted several dozen evacuees in the village?'

They walked a few paces further in silence. 'This entire county is covered in airfields,' Jerry said. 'They've got to be a target of attack.'

'But so is the district round Denver,' protested Harriet. 'I can't make any sense of this, Jerry. Are you trying to tell me something?'

'I ought not to be,' he said dejectedly. 'I haven't said a word. I just wish you'd think about it, Aunt Harriet.'

'Think about what you haven't said?'

'Think about moving to Denver.'

'Oh, look,' said Harriet, with some relief, 'here are Sadie and Queenie now, with the children.'

The two maids from Talboys were coming towards them, leading Bredon by the hand, and carrying Paul. Charlie and Polly skipped along beside them. Little Harriet Parker, who was only three, was asleep in the pram.

'We heard the siren, my lady, and we thought best to come along without waiting for you,' said Queenie.

'Quite right,' said Harriet, taking her son by the hand. 'Is Mrs Trapp coming?'

'Not her!' said Sadie. 'She said as she didn't get out of bed for the Kaiser, and she isn't going to do so for Hitler, no matter what that ARP warden says.'

Jerry took his nephew Paul into his arms, and they all turned back towards the village centre.

'Which is the nearest shelter?' asked Jerry. 'Do say it's the Crown, so I can have a pint of beer to drown my sorrows.'

'What sorrows are those, Jerry?' said Harriet. 'Yes, let's go with the sinners to the Crown, rather than with the heathen Methodees in the cave.'

'Are Methodists heathen?' asked Charlie. 'Only I thought—'

Heavens, what am I saying? thought Harriet. 'That was a joke, Charlie,' she said solemnly. 'Methodists are perfectly good Christians.'

'Mummy, will we be allowed to get up in the night all through the war?' asked Bredon. 'I'm in pyjamas under my coat and scarf,' he added. 'A bit like dreaming. Sadie did put on her gas mask, Mummy, like you said, but it frightened Paul so she took it off again.'

But when they reached the village High Street, the

people streaming into the Crown were mostly wearing their gas masks. It gave them a horrific appearance, with socket eyes like skulls and black skin and wide snouts. Firmly holding on to his uncle's jacket, Paul appeared not to mind it this time.

'But what are we actually going to do down here?' enquired Archie Lugg.

Everyone was just standing around on the dusty floors of the crypt. A single electric bulb dangled from the ceiling of each of the four huge rooms. There was nothing to sit on, and the air smelled dusty and cold.

'Well, what would you be doing if you was in your own little dugout, Archie?' asked George Withers.

'Don't ask,' said Mrs Ruddle, sniggering.

'I've got a magazine showing how you make an Anderson shelter really cosy,' said Mrs Puffett. 'With bunks and little curtains, and a cribbage board and a paraffin heater.'

'I seen an Anderson over at Broxford the other day,' someone said. 'All fixed up like as Ma Puffett says. Only that were a foot deep in water what had drained in off the garden. Quite all right apart from that. Bloke has a stirrup pump fixed up to bail her out. They don't say about that in the magazines, I'll be bound. Deep enough to drown a cat that was, being as you had a cat.'

Constable Jack Baker stood up on an orange crate, and clapped his hands for silence. 'I need a bit of a head count,' he said, 'to see how many people got here. We closed the doors eight minutes after the siren; we'll have to do a bit better than that in future. Could everyone stay right where they are while I count you, and then I'll come round and you can let me know if there's anyone you think ought to be here, and who hasn't showed up.'

'Fred Lugg isn't here,' offered someone.

'Well, he's fire-watching, isn't he?' said Archie Lugg. 'Can't spot a fire from down here, can he?'

'He could be anywhere, if you ask me,' said Mrs Hodge.

'He's on the church tower,' said Harriet. 'We saw him there.'

Slowly an atmosphere of dismay was seeping through the company. They stood around with hands in pockets, or leaned against the stone walls. A few people had brought blankets or folding stools, and could make themselves a corner to sit down. A wormy old settle long cast out of the snug and thrust into a corner accommodated a row of three very old gentlemen, and someone had brought a folding table and a pack of cards. But it was plainly going to be very uncomfortable and very boring to stay for long.

It wasn't much consolation, thought Harriet, that this was only practice, when the real thing was looming over them all.

'Tell you something,' said George Withers suddenly. 'Just as soon as we got a thaw, I'm going to put up me own Anderson, and not have to hang around here with all you lot!'

He had caught the mood, and Harriet suddenly became concerned – a whole group of people in the grip of misery locked up together for hours would certainly be bad for morale and could turn really nasty – when, as often happens in this tight little island, a man for the moment, a woman for the moment emerged.

The chairman of the Paggleham Women's Institute got up on Constable Baker's orange crate, and began to speak.

'Well, as you can all see, we've got to do something about this,' she said. 'Even if it's only for a few weeks, and as a matter of fact I don't see why we shouldn't settle in here for the rest of the war, and not bother with Anderson shelters. As some of you already know, I've drawn up an outline plan. We need bunks. People can bring their own blankets. We need a few trestle tables and a primus stove to make tea and hot soup, and some paraffin heaters to get a bit of a fug in here on a cold night. We need coat hooks for all those gas-mask holders, and perhaps the schoolchildren can paint some pictures to cheer up the walls a bit. We need volunteers. Lots of volunteers.'

'Bert Ruddle is doing bunks for the Methodists,' said George Withers.

'I could fix up some bunks,' offered Archie Lugg, 'if I had some help. I've got a lot of spare timber from that row of sheds we took down when they put an airfield on a bit of Datchett farm.'

'I'll give you a hand,' said Mr Puffett. 'We can do as well as that Bert Ruddle, I'm sure.'

'Splendid, both of you. Thank you.'

'I've got quite a few folding chairs,' someone offered. 'And some card tables. We used to have a bridge club days gone by.'

'I'll get in a first-aid kit,' offered Harriet. 'Dr Jellyfield will advise me what to put in it. And how about a shelf of books? I'm sure we could contribute to that.'

'Thank you, Lady Peter.'

'See here, missus,' said Mrs Hodge. 'We got three rooms here. We could have a quiet room with bunks for people to sleep in, and a room with cards and that for them as can't sleep, and a room for the kiddies.'

'And I think I could offer, on behalf of the Women's Institute, to get in emergency supplies: candles, and biscuits and tea . . .'

'Jes' like a picnic!' said Mrs Baker. 'The kiddies will be in the seventh heaven.'

But the kiddies were not enjoying it much now. Bredon, Harriet was glad to see, was quietly playing in a corner with his cousin Charlie, and young Sam Bateson. They were making an airfield in the dust of the floor and landing their toy aeroplanes on it.

They were not making whirring and roaring sounds to go with it.

'It's very quiet, Mummy,' Bredon offered, 'because it's flying secret missions.'

'Good,' said Harriet. 'Good boys.' Paul had fallen asleep on her lap.

But few of the village children were asleep. They were over-excited, and getting cold and fretful. Trying to sleep on the floor with only the odd blanket that had been brought with them was not easy, but the sound of children wailing quickly gets on one's nerves. And those adults who had come straight from the dance in the hall had not even got a blanket. They were left standing, or sitting on the bare floor. The practice appeared to be going on far longer than anyone had expected.

'This is all a bit previous, if you ask me,' Roger Datchett observed. He farmed on the opposite side of the village, and had furthest to come. 'It's like having those pesky London children all over the place. I mean, it's not as if there has been any bombing yet.'

'There was a Heinkel shot down not so far from here, last week,' said Constable Baker.

'And plenty more where that come from,' added the landlord.

'Anyone heard that all-clear yet?' asked Mr Puffett.

Nobody had.

'Only I thought tonight's effort were just to see how quick we could all get down here,' Mr Puffett said. 'Not to keep us here all blooming night. I haven't brought me pipe.'

'You can't smoke a pipe down here, Tom Puffett, even being as if you had remembered it,' said Mrs Ruddle. 'Them pipes smells something horrible, and it won't be safe along of paraffin heaters.'

'Won't be any more dangerous than candles, you silly besom,' retorted Mr Puffett.

Once again the chairman of the Women's Institute came to the rescue. 'That's a good point you are making,' she said, beaming at the two of them. 'We'd better see if there's room in one of these side-caves for a smoking-room. And we'd better see if there's some kind of lantern that works without a naked flame.'

'Davy lamps,' said Constable Baker. 'They use them down mines. Against fire-damp,' he added.

'I wonder where we'd get them?' said the chairman, making notes.

'Isn't that all-clear *ever* going to go?' asked one of the land-girls. 'I'm just busting for a pee . . .'

'You mind your language, my girl!' cried Mrs Hodge. 'There's decent people down here.'

'Well, how are we going to manage in that regard?' asked the vicar. 'I mean, if it were a real air-raid, it might be prolonged beyond what flesh and blood can bear . . .'

'Buckets of earth, vicar,' said someone sitting near the wall. 'Buckets of earth, and a spade. It's what we used behind the front line at Mons. Quite wholesome as long as you shovel a bit of earth in after yourself.'

'I think I'm going to put my head out and see what's happening,' said Mr Gudgeon. 'It'll be closing time in a minute.'

'That's right, landlord. Get us out of here in time to have another drink!' said Mr Puffett.

Mr Gudgeon climbed his steps, and opened the heavy wooden doors to the bar. They heard his footsteps across the flagstone floor, and they heard the street door open, creaking on its hinges. They didn't hear the all-clear. Instead they heard the dull grinding sound of aircraft.

'Gawd-strewth, Baker, are you sure this is just practice?' someone said.

'This is getting a bit out of hand, Simon,' said the vicar's wife softly to her husband. 'Can you do something?'

'What do you suggest, my dear?'

'A sing-song? I'm sure the Methodists are having a sing-song in their cave.'

'Excellent idea. Now who can find us a note?'

'Mr Puffett might have his accordion with him,' Mrs Goodacre suggested. 'That box of his looks rather large for a gas mask.'

An expression of pain crossed the vicar's countenance, but he mastered himself and went across to talk to Tom Puffett.

Tom had indeed got his squeeze-box handy. The vicar stood to beat time. He had hauled his favourite choir-boy to stand up and take the lead.

'*Abide with me; fast falls the eventide . . .*' the boy began.

'No, no, dear!' cried Mrs Goodacre. 'No, Simon – something cheerful!'

'Well I'm not sure that I know—'

'Think of something!' Mrs Goodacre commanded. 'Something you boys sing out of church . . . anything!'

'Anything?' the boy said. A conspiratorial grin of great wickedness lit his countenance. He lifted his heavenly ethereal treble, and sang:

> *Hitler has only got one ball!*
> *Goering has two but rather small . . .*

The company gasped, and then began to laugh. They

roared with laughter; a sort of hysterical mirth possessed them, they swayed and held on to each other, laughing till they cried.

Mr Puffett put huge elbow grease into his horrible harmonium, and the boy's lovely voice soared above the racket:

> *Himmler, is somewhat simmler,*
> *And Dr Goebbels has no balls at all!*

It turned out that this lamentable ditty was rather well known, for when Puffett struck the note again the whole company offered a hearty repeat performance.

'Well,' said Mrs Simcox as the finale died down, 'I'll tell you one thing, vicar. I'll bet my life the Methodists aren't singing *that*!' Whereupon gales of laughter rang round the vaults again.

'I ought to reprove that boy,' said Mr Goodacre. 'What a disgrace.'

'Not this time, vicar,' said Harriet quietly. 'Can't you feel how he's changed the atmosphere down here?'

'Do you really think so, Lady Peter? Can I really let it pass? Such language! And women present!'

'The women laughed too, vicar. And do you know, I rather think that while we laugh we can't be beaten.'

'Ah,' he said. 'Ah.'

And while he was thinking about it, to change the subject, Harriet said, 'Talking of scandals, will somebody point out to me this scandalous land-girl everyone is talking about. Which is she?'

'Wendy Percival, you mean?' said Mrs Goodacre. 'The one they're calling Wicked Wendy?'

'However do you know that, my dear?' exclaimed Mr Goodacre.

'Ways and means, Simon, ways and means. Well, now you come to mention it I can't see her. I haven't seen her at all tonight. That's odd; I would have expected to see her at the dance, now you come to mention it. Rather her sort of occasion with all those good-looking airmen around.'

'Perhaps she's took shelter with the Methodists,' said Mrs Ruddle. 'They'll give 'er a warm welcome, I don't think!' More laughter.

'You know, my dear,' said Mr Goodacre, 'I really don't think it is right to call that young woman wicked. It makes me quite uneasy. She may be a little wild, but when you think what turpitude we do hear about, it really isn't proportional. I don't think either you or I should countenance it.'

'What turpitude do you refer to, vicar?' asked Harriet. 'That sounds interesting.'

'Well, we heard the other day,' said Mrs Goodacre, answering for her husband, 'of a young pilot in a parish in Lincolnshire who did not return from a mission in the North Sea, and they put him down as missing presumed dead, when all the while he had baled out, I think they call it, and been rescued by a fishing boat. And instead of reporting back to base he just went to London and took a job under a false name, only of course he hadn't got a ration-book, and so he got into difficulties and had to confess.'

'Do you think perhaps he was very frightened, and didn't want to have to fly again?' asked Harriet.

'What a charitable view of human nature you have, dear Lady Peter. No, I understand that it was because he was heavily in debt under his real name, and he was hoping to avoid his creditors.'

'If so, that was indeed turpitudinous of him,' Harriet agreed.

'It takes all sorts to make an air force,' said Jerry, looking up from a copy of *Picture Post*, which he had apparently had in his greatcoat pocket. 'I've even encountered this evening the only man I have ever spoken to who was not impressed by a Spitfire. Actually thought the Luftwaffe had better kites. Amazing.'

'Who was that, Jerry?' asked Harriet.

'Didn't catch his name.'

'Quiet, everyone!' said Constable Baker. 'I think I can hear . . .'

And as everyone hushed they could all hear it – the steady triumphant level note of the siren sounding the all-clear.

'And about time too,' said Mrs Ruddle, heaving her substantial bulk up off the floor with the aid of a sharp tug from her son.

'Cheer up, Baker,' said Dr Jellyfield. 'Perhaps we'll never have to do it for real.'

The expression on Constable Baker's face made Harriet

suppose that he would far far rather have the village obliterated by enemy bombs than have his work thus converted to yet another form of labour in vain. But people were pressing towards the door now, all at once, carting their possessions and creating a bottle-neck, which it was Constable Baker's duty to sort out.

Shortly they emerged, burdened by whatever they had brought with them, their gas-mask boxes slung over their shoulders, their sleeping children limp and heavy in their arms, into the still and bitterly cold open air. Suddenly everyone seemed in a good humour. Greetings and goodnights rang out from neighbour to neighbour, and then faltered into silence.

The Crown Inn stood at the widest part of the village street, known as the Square. A horse trough and a couple of flower-boxes graced it, and by day the greengrocer could let his boxes spread over the pavement. The icy moonlight bathed it with an eerie clarity, and now that the moon was high overhead there were no more shadows than at noon. And clearly visible to everyone was a young woman lying on her back in the middle of the street, one hand thrown up, the palm lying empty, her head turned to one side, the taffeta of her slinky dance dress silvered in the moonlight, her gas-mask case beside her as though she had let it go as she fell. She had been carrying a blanket that was still folded over her left arm.

Dr Jellyfield pushed through the little knot of people, and knelt down to take the girl's pulse. Then he passed his hand over the face, to close the eyes, and stood up.

'I thought this was supposed to be a dumb-show. Just for practice,' said Mrs Hodge. She sounded indignant, as if, should there have been any real need for the night's excursion, she had been cheated.

'Well, if it was a real raid . . .' said Mr Gudgeon. Everyone looked round as if to discover the impact of enemy action but not so much as a broken window could be seen. The higgledy-piggledy line of the village houses with their uneven roof lines, crooked chimneys, thatch or slate roofs and pargeted or brick frontages, every detail deeply familiar, stood serenely unchanged. The very idea that they could be at risk, that something could smash such a long-established and ordinary sight as this seemed unreal.

And yet here was someone lying stone still on the cold ground. Harriet knew in her bones who this someone must be. This would be Wicked Wendy, surely; not, after all, safe among the Methodists, but slipping on the icy ground as she ran for shelter, falling, banging her head . . .

Dr Jellyfield got to his feet.

'A bit of shrapnel, was it?' asked Mr Gudgeon, looking at the sky as if he thought a German aircraft might appear and own up.

'Where's Constable Baker?' said Dr Jellyfield. 'No, Mr Gudgeon. This is not enemy action. This is plain old-fashioned murder.'

Two

No one gossips about other people's
secret virtues.
Bertrand Russell, *On Education*, 1926

At eleven o'clock in the morning, three days later, Harriet was not surprised to see Superintendent Kirk coming up the path to her front door, though she was immediately somewhat wary. She broke off her task – she had been making a selection of books from the Talboys shelves that could be donated to the ad hoc-library in the air-raid shelter – and welcomed her visitor in the drawing-room with the offer of sherry and biscuits.

'I know it's a little early for sherry, Mr Kirk,' she said, 'but alas, we have no coffee to offer you, although I'm sure we could rustle up a cup of tea.'

'A sherry would be very welcome, Lady Peter,' Mr Kirk said. 'Thank you.'

'You look rather downcast,' said Harriet as she handed him his glass.

'Downcast?' he said. 'I don't know which way to turn, Lady Peter, and that's the truth. There's no news of Lord Peter, I suppose?'

He sounded so wistful that there was no difficulty reading him at all.

'Will he turn up out of the blue and solve the murder for you, you mean? I wish I thought so. Of course there's never any telling with Peter. But I'm afraid I don't expect him, even if mony a heart would break in twa . . .'

A gloomy silence hung between them while Harriet poured herself a glass of sherry to keep him company.

'Should he no' come back again,' he observed at last.

'Spot on. I'm glad you're not too oppressed to play the game.'

'Not me! Don't know as I've ever known who wrote it, mind.'

'It was someone called Carolina Oliphant,' said Harriet. 'And not many people, I'm sure, know that.' To mollify him, she added, 'Seems harder to note the author if one just knows something out of a song-book.'

'I suppose a song-book might be full of improving sentiments,' he said. 'Specially if it happened to be full of hymns. But a song-book isn't a solitary pleasure, my lady, like the *Golden Treasury*. I can't see myself a-singing in the fireside chair of an evening – Mrs Kirk likes to listen to the wireless.'

'No one will reproach you for not being able to name Carolina Oliphant,' said Harriet, smiling. She really did rather like the Superintendent. 'You may leave the court without a stain on your character.'

'What? Oh, I see what you mean. Very good. But, Lady Peter, I really am at my wits' end. I'm so short-staffed, you see, what with running around looking for blackout failures, and watching the stations and bus-stops for suspicious characters, and checking up on these here new slaughtering licences, and all the black-market control jobs, as well as all the usual things we used to do in peace-time. A murder is the very last thing I need, leave alone the victim being a woman.'

'I'm sorry you're short-staffed,' said Harriet. 'I thought policemen were in a reserved occupation. But why is it worse for you if the victim is a woman?'

'You're quite right that policemen aren't getting called up directly,' said the Superintendent. 'But stopping them as has a mind from resigning and then joining up is another thing. They are more than welcome in the military police, because of their experience. I've lost two young constables that way. And a woman constable too; she had to go home to look after her mother in Scotland, so she applied for a transfer, and I can't replace her. And what chance do you think, Lady Peter, one of my men in uniform would have of getting information about a young woman out of her friends? People just don't confide in police officers about that sort of thing.'

'About what sort of thing, Mr Kirk?'

'Troubles of the heart, you might say. Playing the field. Whatever it was that got someone worked up enough to kill her.'

'What makes you think it was that sort of thing?' asked Harriet.

'What else could it likely be?' he asked. 'When a crime

involves a woman it's nearly always that. I heard about one case what was about the ownership of a plot of land; but that was the exception that proves the rule.'

'Mr Kirk, if Peter were here, I know what he would say. He would say motives are moonshine. When you know how you know who. I've heard him say it over and over again.'

'Well, this time there isn't any mystery about how. I've got a preliminary post-mortem report. Someone met her in the street, and struck a violent blow to her chin, breaking her jaw in two places. Then he spun her round, put his hands round her neck, applied pressure to her carotid arteries, and kicked her in the back. She was dead when he dropped her.'

'She was lying on her back, though?'

'You're a sharp one,' said Kirk appreciatively. 'Her assailant must have rolled her over – perhaps with his foot, like. She was as slack as a sack of potatoes by then, and that's how come she looked quite natural when you got a sight of her.'

'You know,' said Harriet thoughtfully, 'that sounds very expert to me. Not the sort of thing that just anyone could have done.'

'Six months ago I would have agreed with you,' he said. 'Happy days! Only someone trained in the Great War, I would have thought. But now half the population of England is training to kill. ARP units, Home Defence units, hundreds of people. There aren't any guns for them, so they are drilling with wooden rifles, and learning how to use their bare hands. I'm almost sorry for any German parachutist who runs into an average English villager.'

'Well, we can be reasonably sure that Wicked Wendy wasn't a German parachutist,' said Harriet.

'Is "Wicked Wendy" what they were calling her?'

'I'm afraid so.'

'Then it most likely was the sort of thing I was suspecting.'

Harriet couldn't deny it.

'In view of which,' he added, studiously avoiding her eye, 'and seeing as Lord Peter isn't available, I was wondering if you would feel like lending a hand.'

'At a bit of detecting? I'm a very poor substitute for Peter.'

'Your books are very ingenious, my lady. You have the aptitude.'

'Now you have surprised me, Mr Kirk. I never thought to hear a policeman express any sort of admiration for crime fiction. You have made a great concession.'

'Do you think you could help out, as a kind of war work?' he said. 'I mean, we can't let villains get away with murder just because there's a war on.'

'You'd have to be willing to put me completely in the picture, as you see it,' said Harriet doubtfully.

'Agreed,' he said. 'This isn't the usual situation, I'm not a-going to insist on the usual procedures.'

'Then I will stand at your right hand. What precisely do you want me to do?' asked Harriet.

'And keep the bridge with me!' he said. 'Macaulay, Thomas Babington. Oh, quite like old times, Lady Peter.

I'd like you to find out all that you can about the girl. Her friends, boyfriends, background, that sort of thing. Was she walking out with someone? Could you ferret around for me?'

Harriet thought about it. 'I could try. But not if it involves pretending that it wasn't official. I would be open about who had asked me to ferret around.'

'You wouldn't like to be an undercover copper's nark, Lady Peter? Well, I can understand that.'

'Peter himself would never dissemble about that sort of thing,' said Harriet firmly.

'No,' said Mr Kirk, 'I don't suppose he would. And you really have no idea when he will get back?'

'Honestly none.'

'That must be uncommon hard on you, I think.'

'It isn't easy,' said Harriet, grateful for his flash of sympathy. 'Standing in for Peter in various ways is what I seem to be for, at the moment. But I'd much rather he were here to play his roles for himself.'

'And all these kiddies what you have under your wing?' Superintendent Kirk was gazing out of the window at the riotous game being played on the lawn.

'That's my son Bredon, trying to hold the bat – he's just three, and my second son Paul sitting watching in the push-chair. The others are my sister-in-law's three: a boy and two girls. Charlie is quite a little grown-up at ten, and the other two are his sister Polly and his baby sister Harriet, my god-daughter.'

'Have I seen that young Charlie at the Boy Scouts in

Great Pagford? I was there the other day giving a police talk to help out the scout-master.'

'You might well have done. He goes to Scouts with Sam Bateson, the neighbour's little boy. We get them over there when we can, but we don't always manage it.'

'You must have your hands full; perhaps I shouldn't have asked you . . .'

'Rubbish, Mr Kirk, you shouldn't worry on that account. I have a cook and a house-maid, and a nursery-maid, and all these children are in the family, more or less. The women in the village who are coping with the children of perfect strangers without a hand to help them are the ones we should be concerned about.'

'You're only too right there,' he said. 'The war gets into everything, doesn't it? Change and decay in all around we see. You know, Lady Peter, we are fighting for freedom, as I understand it, and yet I'm expected to make sure that Aggie Twitterton doesn't buy herself an egg while she is keeping them hens. I've become such a bully as I hardly recognise myself. Funny sort of freedom, if you ask me.'

'It's a very different kind of war this time,' Harriet said. 'It isn't somewhere over there – the soldiers marching away, and coming back victorious or defeated from elsewhere. This time we're all in it together. And cheer up, not all the news is bad. The news this morning says a whole squadron of the Canadian Air Force have arrived to help us.'

The Superintendent had picked up his hat, and was preparing to leave.

'You're a good trooper, Lady Peter,' he said.

Harriet wondered where to start. She supposed, thinking about the land-girls, working hard all day getting hungry as hunters and far from home, that a cake might improve her welcome, so she wandered into the kitchen to see if Mrs Trapp could rustle something up. Mrs Ruddle's voice at high volume drifted down the hall towards her.

'I suppose, Mrs Trapp, this is the kind of thing we must expect,' Mrs Ruddle was saying.

'Good morning, Mrs Ruddle,' said Harriet. 'What kind of thing must we expect?' Mrs Ruddle had been employed as a charlady when the Wimseys first moved into the house, and had never quite resigned the right to come and go there. She was seldom needed now, although very willing when she was wanted. She was now comfortably ensconced on the Windsor chair at the end of kitchen table nearest the fire, with a cup of tea in her hand. Mrs Trapp was kneading bread, turning and slapping the dough rhythmically on the other end of the table. Not for her a tea-break to keep her visitor company.

'Getting murdered in our beds, Lady Peter!' said Mrs Ruddle.

'Who's been murdered in their bed, Mrs Ruddle?' Harriet asked.

'That poor young woman . . .'

'Murdered in the street, I think.'

'Well, that's even worse, isn't it, if we can't even walk down the middle of the street without being done for.'

'It is horrible,' said Mrs Trapp, cutting up her dough and twisting it neatly into the bread tins. 'I don't envy whoever has to tell her parents.'

'But why should we expect it, Mrs Ruddle? I don't understand you,' said Harriet.

'With all these German spies around,' said Mrs Ruddle gleefully.

'What German spies are those?' asked Harriet. 'Have you heard something I haven't?' Not that that was unlikely, she thought. Mrs Ruddle was at the centre of every web of gossip for twenty miles around – certainly for the entire area served by the local telephone exchange, at which her daughter worked.

'Well, I can't say exactly,' admitted Mrs Ruddle. 'But it stands to reason, Lady Peter. If there aren't any German spies, what for are we taking down all the signposts? How come my Bert has got a job of work to do painting out the name of the village on the railway station? Answer me that!'

Harriet couldn't think of an answer, and Mrs Ruddle continued. 'You want to ask Mrs Spright – she says she's spotted two or three of 'em around already!'

'Do I know Mrs Spright?' asked Harriet.

'P'raps you don't, Lady Peter,' said Mrs Ruddle. 'She used to be a dentist over at Broxford. She retired here to that house down Datchett's Lane. Three year or more ago.'

'If she's seen any spies around, she ought to tell the authorities,' remarked Mrs Trapp, spreading a floured cloth over her loaf tins.

'That's what I told her!' said Mrs Ruddle. 'I said, you ought to go tell one of them officers at the airfield, and get them arrested. She said she would tell who she felt like, when she was good and ready. She said as how you couldn't necessarily trust a body along of 'im wearing a Nar A ef uniform.'

'You should tell her if she knows anything, it's no more than her duty, Mrs Ruddle,' said Mrs Trapp. 'She should tell the police.'

'A lot of good that'ud do, I don't think!' cried Mrs Ruddle. Harriet remembered the Ruddle family's long-lasting grudge against a village policeman who had been replaced some time back.

'I suppose you must be very busy, Mrs Ruddle?' asked Harriet mildly. 'Everyone seems to have such a lot to do.'

'What? Oh, yes, I can't hang around like this gossiping with Mrs Trapp,' said Mrs Ruddle, heaving herself out of her chair. 'I'll bid you good morning, and be off.'

'Did she want anything in particular, Mrs Trapp?' asked Harriet when the door closed safely on Mrs Ruddle's back.

'To borrow a mug of sugar, and to talk about the murder. A dreadful thing, I know, but ... I'm afraid I told her, m'lady, that now sugar is rationed we didn't have any to lend.'

'Quite right, Mrs Trapp. But that didn't get rid of her?'

'Not her!' said Mrs Trapp with emphasis. 'She sat right

in there till I more or less had to make a cup of tea. Sugar, indeed! It was gossip she came for!'

'Talking of sugar,' said Harriet tentatively, 'how hard would it be to rustle up a cake? I need to get on the right side of those land-girls.'

'A fruit cake, Lady Peter?'

'Just the thing. Can we do it?'

'I'll eke the sugar out with grated carrot. You'll not know the difference.'

'Mrs Trapp,' said Harriet with feeling, 'you are a wonderful woman, and I don't know what we would do without you.'

'Go along with you, my lady,' said Mrs Trapp.

With Mrs Trapp's cake in a tartan shortbread tin, Harriet presented herself at five o'clock in the afternoon at the barns where Farmer Bateson had housed his team of land-girls. It was getting dark, and she reckoned they would be home and making a meal. She found a group of eight of them, sitting round an old table, in what had been the tack room, and preparing a supper of potatoes and beans. The room had the rough and ready look of a Girl Guides camp. There were storm lanterns hanging from the roof beams, and clothes drying on a web of lines rigged round the little pot-bellied stove that had kept the stable boys from freezing in winter. A Ministry poster, showing a laughing, healthy young woman tossing a corn-sheaf on to a bright green lorry, and saying 'Lend a hand on the land', had been pasted on the wall opposite the door, and beside it a home-made one said: 'God speed the plough, and the woman that drives it.'

'Can I come in for a moment?' Harriet asked.

A tough-looking red-head responded. 'Cor, look what the cat's brought in!'

But a blonde girl reading a newspaper at the table put it down, and said, 'Don't be rude, Rita. It's Lady Peter, isn't it? Take a seat.'

Harriet pulled out a chair and sat down. She glanced, willy-nilly, at the newspaper headline: NEW SOVIET ATTACK FORCES FINNS BACK.

'Oh, gosh, how posh!' Rita was saying. 'Lady Petaaa! We are honoured.'

'I'm not posh,' said Harriet crisply. 'I married above myself. I'm the local doctor's daughter. I've brought you a cake.' She took the lid off the tin. The cake was still warm, and a wonderful fruity fragrance began to disperse from it. Harriet caught herself hoping that Mrs Trapp had baked another for home consumption as well as this one.

'Now, look here, Rita,' said a third young woman, with a distinct upper cut to her voice, 'don't you say anything – *anything!* – that imperils our chances of getting at that cake. Understand?'

Harriet laughed. 'Don't worry,' she said. 'The cake is an unconditional gift in appreciation of your hard work in the fields.'

'You just won me over, heart and body,' said Rita. 'Did you hear that clunk? That was the sound of the chip falling off my shoulder.'

'Just the same, *timeo Danaos*, and all that,' said the blonde girl. 'You must want something.'

'You do brown me off, Muriel,' said Rita. 'What was that about tim something or other?'

'Beware of the Greeks when they bring gifts,' said Muriel. 'The cake is a Trojan Horse. It's not hard to work out. Lady Peter's husband is a famous detective. A friend of ours has just been murdered. Result – cake.'

'I don't know how you can be so flippant, both of you,' said a dark girl from the other end of the table.

An uneasy silence fell. 'You're right. Sorry,' said Rita.

'Murder is always a serious matter,' said Harriet quietly. 'A life is lost; here we have a young life lost, and others are then at risk.'

'I'm truly sorry,' said Muriel. 'But the fact is, with all that mayhem across the Channel, and all the young men we know, and all the citizens of southern England in danger of violent death, it seems less outrageous than it would in peace-time.'

'Not that that's logical,' observed Rita. 'The truth is, it hasn't sunk in yet, Lady what's-your-name.'

'Call me Harriet. I've come to ask you, semi-officially, whether any of you know any reason why it was Wendy who was attacked.'

'What difference does it make, now she's dead?' someone asked – a stringy-looking girl sitting at the far end of the table.

'That's our barrack-room lawyer,' said Rita. 'Always has a question.'

'It might make a very great difference,' said Harriet. 'If it was a private quarrel of some sort, then most likely, having settled his score – or her score, of course – the murderer will not act against anyone else. Or, alternatively, he might be a threat to any and every one of us. So, the simplest question is, do any of you know of anyone who had a grudge against Wendy? Did she have enemies?'

'She annoyed people,' said Rita, 'but . . .'

'How?' asked Harriet.

'Well, she was a devil of a tease,' said Rita. 'She loved having fun. She would flirt with anybody.'

'And once or twice people thought she was serious,' said Muriel, 'and got very put out when she just laughed it off. I was always telling her it wasn't kind.'

'And she just laughed at you, I suppose?' said Rita. 'We're a mixed bunch here, Lady . . . Harriet, I mean. We've got all sorts of background; up and down the country, rich and poor. You can tell a lot from our voices – that Muriel and me are out of different boxes: she is nicely brought up – we're all different. But Wendy didn't fit with any of us. Don't get me wrong; we rub along all right. We have a good laugh together over it. But . . .'

'Wendy didn't laugh?' prompted Harriet.

'She was quick enough to laugh *at* us,' said Rita.

'About what sort of thing?' asked Harriet.

'Well, she thought of herself as a cut above her company,' said Rita, who seemed to have dropped her hostility and decided to co-operate. 'Not because she was posh – she wasn't as posh as Muriel here, as far as I can tell. Not that

I know about that sort of thing. But she was clever; she was better educated than anyone else here. She'd been to university.'

'Only Reading University,' offered the stringy young woman from the far end of the table. 'It wasn't Oxford. Besides, surely people don't get murdered for having a degree in Modern Languages.'

'Well, I could have murdered her for carrying on about the English being narrow and insular,' said Muriel. 'And name-dropping. Place-name-dropping, that is. Nice, and Grenoble and Madrid, and Zurich.'

'No, you couldn't, Muriel, don't be silly,' said Rita. 'If you were capable of killing anyone, you would have murdered me. Several times. We do get ratty with each other when we're tired and hungry,' she added, turning to Harriet.

'Of course you do,' said Harriet. 'But have I got this right: none of you got on easily with Wendy; none of you liked her?'

'Oh, no, wrong,' said a rather older woman. 'We're giving the wrong impression. Wendy was lovely; she was lots of fun. She could be a bit outrageous, but it was only fooling around. She never *meant* to be unkind. People could take it wrong, that's all.'

'What about boyfriends? Did you say she flirted?'

'All the time. But that was as far as it went. We're all sleeping in a hay-loft here, Lady Peter. We would know if anyone wasn't in their bed.'

'We sleep soundly, though,' said Rita.

'And of course, wickedness is possible in the forenoon, and the tea-break,' said Muriel, 'as well as by night.'

'We work all day except Sundays,' said the older woman. 'And I don't know about anyone else, but I'm too dog-tired for wickedness any time of day from the lunch-break onwards.'

This remark was greeted with rueful laughter.

'Do you know who was upset? Who had taken her more seriously than she meant? Could you give me names?' Harriet was met with an embarrassed silence. 'I know it feels like sneaking to the teacher. But Wendy was killed by someone who could do it with his bare hands, very quickly. He didn't need a weapon. He could strike again any time. So let's start with that dance.'

'She didn't go,' said Rita at once. 'She said she had a headache, ho, ho.'

'You didn't believe her?'

'Well, I thought her headache might have been called Roger.'

'You had better explain that, Rita,' said Muriel.

'Wendy had gone out a couple of times with one or two local fellows: Archie Lugg, for one, and Jake Datchett. They were offering to fight each other over her, and she thought that was positively hilarious. She called them the bumpkins. She had promised both of them a dance on Saturday. But a month ago she met Roger Birdlap – he's an RAF officer over at Steen Manor – and she fell head over heels for him. Really deep stuff. So I rather think the dance was a good opportunity to meet him somewhere quiet; here, for example. We were all going to the dance; he would come over in the vans from the base with all the others, and slip away quietly to meet her. Then when the dance was over the air-raid practice would give them plenty of warning, because you can hear the sirens from here. He would rejoin his mates, and she would scamper along to the shelter.'

'She was dressed for the dance,' remarked Harriet.

'If she hadn't dressed up, we'd all have noticed,' said Rita. 'That was a very nice frock to put on for him, and take off for him.'

'But surely she wouldn't have liked to be quite alone with a man . . .' said a young rather pallid-looking girl, with an Alice band holding back mousy hair.

'Mistake,' said Rita tartly. '*You* wouldn't like to be quite alone with a man. Most of us would grab the chance if we fancied the fellow in question.'

'But . . .'

'It isn't entirely respectable? Your mother wouldn't like it? Gentlemen prefer virgins? For lord's sake, there's a war on.'

'I don't see what the war's got to do with things like that,' said the girl, who was blushing crimson under Rita's assault.

'You don't see what difference it makes that those airmen are about to be slaughtered by the enemy? That none of us may live to see our next birthday? You really don't?'

Rita turned her back on the company and took to stirring

a pan of soup on the primus stove. Harriet thanked them all, including Rita's back, for helpful information, and took her leave. She was followed across the yard by Muriel. 'Lady Peter, could you, I mean if you can, would you keep us abreast with things? With the investigation? Even if we can't help any further?'

'Yes, of course I will,' said Harriet. There was a just perceptible glint of tears in Muriel's pallid blue eyes. Wicked Wendy had had a friend after all.

Returning to her house, Harriet found her nephew Charlie Parker and Lord St George, heads bent, absorbed in a task which had covered the sofa table in the drawing-room with bits and pieces. Charlie looked up with shining eyes.

'Aunt Harriet, guess what!' he cried. 'Uncle Jerry has bought me a crystal set kit and we're just putting it together now! Wait till I show Sam Bateson – he'll be green with envy!'

'Don't gloat over your friends, young Charles,' said Jerry firmly. 'The best people don't do that. Besides, you might need his help. I'm not putting it together for you, I'm just showing you how it goes and how to work it. You'll have to assemble it yourself.'

'But you'll help me?'

'Sorry, chum, I have to be off in a mo. As soon as I've said goodbye to your aunt here.'

'Oh, Uncle Jerry,' groaned Charlie. 'Can't you stay till tomorrow?'

'Wish I could, old man, but duty calls,' said Jerry. 'You

just clear all this stuff off the table back into the box, and take it upstairs and get going on it.'

When the boy had departed, arms full, and shunted the door closed behind him with his left foot, Jerry said to Harriet, 'Are you getting involved with this murder, Aunt Harriet?'

'Somewhat, Jerry. Do you think I shouldn't?'

'Well, if Uncle Peter were here . . .'

'Precisely.'

'You don't think it might be dangerous?'

'A village mystery? Hardly . . . Compared to the general danger . . .'

'It might not be unrelated.'

'Well, the victim wouldn't have been here apart from the war. The land would have been worked by Peter Gurney, Harry Hawk, Old Uncle Tom Cobleigh and all, and Wicked Wendy would have been – I wonder what she would have been? Working as a school-teacher perhaps?'

'Hardly. She wasn't the type. She was drinking in the Crown last time I was here on leave, and vamping all the chaps, Aunt Harriet,' he said. 'If I weren't hopelessly infatuated with my aunt by marriage, I would have been taken for a ride myself.'

'But it's funny how often, when the murder victim is a woman, it turns out to have been mostly her fault. She was too cold, or too enticing, or flirtatious or chilly, but somehow . . .'

'She is made out to deserve her fate. I see what you mean.

It's very unfair to the fairer sex. And the dead can't defend themselves. Just the same, take care.'

'I might rather say the same to you. If fighter pilots can take care.'

'I can take care that if I go down I'll take one of the bastards with me. You can be sure of that.'

'Come back alive. Or you'll break your father's heart.'

'Not really. It's not me he's so sold on, it's an heir. Now if I would break *your* heart, that would be an inducement.'

'Jerry, don't you ever stop fooling? Of course I would grieve for you, deeply; but I'd rather have you living, and giving me cheek.'

'Alive or dead, I'm breaking my father's heart, you know,' he said, suddenly sombre. 'If I inherit the title and the land and all that, I shall sell it all at once, and set myself up in a nice bachelor pad in West One.'

'So you think now. You might surprise yourself.'

'I've got to go,' he said, flushing slightly, and looking at his watch. 'Kiss me goodbye?'

Harriet kissed him on both cheeks, and watched him run away, swinging his case into the passenger seat of his sports car, and roaring off down the drive.

'Oh, Jerry,' she said softly to herself, sighing.

Three

We're being led to the altar this spring: its flowers
will I suppose nod and yellow and redden the garden
with the bombs falling – oh, it's a queer sense of
suspense being led up to the spring of 1940.
Virginia Woolf, *Diary*, 8th February, 1940

Harriet spent Tuesday morning at the Vicarage, help-ing Mrs Goodacre. The Vicarage was even more crowded than Talboys, since the Goodacres had taken in an assorted crew of refugees, ranging from three Czechs of Jewish descent to a Polish chicken-farmer who was trying to enlist in the air force or the army and lying robustly about his age. The Pole was busy in the kitchen when Harriet arrived, expertly plucking a fowl and putting the feathers in a sack.

'Jan is very good at cooking,' Mrs Goodacre told her visitor. 'Although he would rather be fighting, if we would let him.'

'How old I look?' Jan asked Harriet.

She contemplated him. His round and friendly face was not heavily lined, except on smile lines, but his hair was greying.

'Forty?' she guessed. 'Forty-five?'

'Is fifty,' he said sorrowfully. 'They say no good for army. Less good even for air force.'

'I'm sorry,' said Harriet, as though she had herself formulated the policy. 'But surely they will find you something else to do. Some sort of war work.'

'Farm work is all,' he said.

'Cheer up,' said Harriet. 'Food is a munition of war, they keep telling us.'

The vicar's wife had undertaken the contentious task of billeting officer for Paggleham, and was organising visits of inspection to every family that had taken in evacuees. Many of them had been taken home again by their London families, for a variety of reasons. Now Mrs Goodacre needed an up-to-date survey of who had still got their evacuees, who had now got spare rooms, who was willing and who would be difficult when the next wave of displaced mothers and children had to be accommodated. It was all too clear that the German advance across northern France was bringing bomber bases ever nearer English targets, and as soon as the long feared and awaited attacks on cities began, it was very likely that the evacuees would be back in the countryside in large numbers.

Mrs Goodacre settled down with Harriet at her kitchen table, and sorted out a bunch of cards from her index of families and addresses. She gave Harriet nine cards to direct her part of the task. Glancing through them Harriet saw to her amazement the letters VD against some of the children's names, and one VD against the address of Mr Maggs.

'Good lord, Mrs Goodacre!' she exclaimed. 'I've heard of bed-wetting and head-lice among the children, but VD?'

'Well, a lot of them were, when they arrived, and as for that Mrs Maggs, you should have seen her kitchen, Harriet . . .'

'A lot of them were what?' asked Harriet faintly. 'And what was in the kitchen?'

'Very dirty,' said Mrs Goodacre. 'It's my shorthand for very dirty. And what was in the kitchen was cockroaches.'

'Well, thank heavens for that!' said Harriet.

'Thank heavens?' said Mrs Goodacre in surprise.

'That it was nothing worse,' said Harriet solemnly.

'I suppose things could have been worse,' said Mrs Goodacre doubtfully. 'But I do rather feel that the government have been a little unimaginative about some things: dislocation of commerce, and evacuation and that kind of thing. They seem, the government, I mean, to have thought out the beginning of everything very well, and then to have rather stopped thinking! Like the schoolchildren for example: I expect it was necessary to get them out without any books or pencils or anything to the nearest available place; but I do think the government might have helped the subsequent arrangements rather more, and got the schools together and organised the distribution of equipment and things.'

'Well, if they thought we could be relied on to just get on and manage, they might not be so wrong, Mrs Goodacre,' said Harriet, smiling at her friend.

'But it's a dreadful pity that so many of the children are

being taken home again; it's so good for them to get a bit of air and exercise, and find out how country people live. Someone told me the other day that her little London boy had piped up suddenly and asked if sheep laid eggs! Did you ever!'

'I suppose it's natural for parents to want their children with them,' said Harriet. 'When large-scale bombing begins—'

'Paggleham at least will have an up-to-date register of billets,' said Mrs Goodacre.

Harriet's tour of duty revealed nothing that surprised her. Mrs Marbleham, billeted above the greengrocer's shop in pleasant sunny rooms, was very far from grateful. She complained to Harriet that she was woken every morning by the greengrocer setting up shop at an unearthly hour, clattering his boxes as he spread out across the pavement, and whistling to himself as he worked. Harriet wondered if she could ask him not to whistle, and decided against it.

'It must be nice to have his shop just down the stairs, though,' she offered.

'Not really. We don't eat vegetables. Not being pigs. Not like some,' the woman replied.

'Vegetables are good for you,' suggested Harriet, rather dismayed on behalf of the Marbleham boys.

'Well, we don't eat them. Only chips,' was the reply. 'What I wouldn't give to be back right near a good fish and chip shop . . .'

Harriet couldn't help that. She was more useful at Mrs Maggs's cottage. The Maggses had a rambling set of bedrooms up a second stair that had once housed the blacksmith's apprentices. They had taken in six boys, aged from ten to fourteen, from two different families. One family had sent enough warm clothes, and the other had sent nothing. One family paid up their ten and six for the first child, and eight and sixpence a week for the others very regularly; the second family had sent nothing. At least the clothes could be sorted out; Harriet wrote out a ticket to the clothes exchange organised by the WVS.

The third family she visited was very crowded, with the daughter sharing her bedroom with a little London girl who cried for her mother at night. And billets in Paggleham were not plentiful.

Passing the end of Church Lane on her way back to the Vicarage, it occurred to Harriet that Susan Hodge's cottage, rented out to Flight Lieutenant Brinklow, would become available when he went back to his unit. She walked down to it. It stood four-square a little apart from its neighbours in an overgrown garden that was mostly old apple trees. The garden abutted an arm of Blackden Wood. Peter had bought the wood a couple of years back to stop it being clear-felled, because the hillside it stood on was in plain view from the bedroom windows of Talboys. At the time Harriet had thought it extravagant of him, and she had been amused when he said woodland always came in handy, but now it was providing firewood for Talboys, and most of the villagers, she couldn't dispute it. It was handy to own it. Peter said there was an implied permission for anyone to take sticks for firewood – anything they could get 'by hook or by crook' – but no gathering with axe or saw.

Harriet knocked at the cottage door, waited and knocked again. The officer must be out. It was rather an isolated dwelling, she thought, but it looked as though you could put a whole family in it, which would certainly cheer it up a bit, and it would be nice for a London family to have the run of the wood. She must find out tactfully about the condition of the house, and the rent. She didn't want to suggest the requisitioning of something that was essential to a local family's income.

Later that day Harriet went into Great Pagford to shop. Paul needed larger clothes every week, it seemed, and it was getting very difficult to find things. She dropped in on Mr Kirk at the police station and gave him the names she had elicited. He thanked her in an abstracted way.

'I'll check up on these men as soon as I can,' he said. 'I'm being driven up the wall, my lady, by reports of spies. Everywhere. You wouldn't have been able to see the moon for parachutes if the half of these tales were true. They all turn out to be Polish or Jewish refugees or fellows from Scotland whose funny accents hail from Glasgow rather than Berlin. But I can't risk not investigating.'

'There was a real one in the paper this morning,' said Harriet. 'A couple who turned up at Largo asking for the train to London, and aroused suspicion by not knowing where they were.'

'See what I mean? We have to check however barmy it sounds. Look, we obviously have to follow up this Birdlap person. If I gave you a note to his commanding officer, you wouldn't care to do that for me, would you?'

'I'll do what I can,' said Harriet, carefully folding the hastily scribbled note into her handbag. 'If he won't talk to anyone unofficial, I'll hand it back to you.'

As she reached the door of his office it occurred to her to ask, 'What about Wendy's parents?'

'In Brighton!' he cried, as though it had been Timbuktu.

'We have a friend who might be able to help,' said Harriet. 'I couldn't go myself, I'm afraid; but the friend in question has been very useful to Peter in several enquiries.'

'Lady Peter,' said Mr Kirk, 'you are the answer to a maiden's prayer, in a manner of speaking, of course. Just a minute while I find the parents' address.'

Getting in to Steen Manor proved to be a little difficult. Harriet drove herself there, since it was rather too far to walk, even for an able-bodied and healthy woman. The road ran for two miles alongside a six-foot-high wall of mellow brick, topped with rolls of barbed-wire. She had to wait for ages at the guard post at the entrance. The lovely wrought-iron gates of what had clearly been the drive to a substantial gentleman's house had been opened wide, and in the space between them a wooden hut had been erected, together with a red and white pole barrier. The sentry rang for instructions, which took some time to come.

Harriet stood quietly, leaning on her car bonnet, listening to the sweetly unaware birdsong. It comforted her, like the flowers in the banks. Eventually an airman in uniform came marching down the drive, and escorted Harriet up to the house. Surprisingly for a house built in Hertfordshire it was of a stone, grey, ashlar under a tiled roof, a bold plain Georgian building with Victorian additions and grand bay windows along the front. Her escort led her into a large hall with an elaborate oak staircase, and into a room that had once been the drawing-room, but was now lined with filing cabinets. The man behind the half-acre desk who rose to meet her was not in uniform. Harriet's escort introduced her as: 'The plain-clothes police officer, sir!' saluted, and departed, closing the door behind him.

'I'm sorry to say I may be here under false pretences,' said Harriet at once. 'I am not a police officer. I am simply a private citizen helping the police.' She handed Superintendent Kirk's note across the desk.

'Do sit down,' said the officer. He read the note carefully, twice.

'Well, Lady Peter,' he said eventually, 'this is irregular, very irregular, but then these are not normal times. I think I met your husband once. It was some years back.'

'Before I met him myself, I expect,' said Harriet.

'Yes, no doubt,' he replied. 'My name is Baldock. I am in charge of this establishment, which is, Lady Peter, very hush-hush. I am afraid we should not have admitted you, and having done so we must limit the damage.'

'There isn't any damage so far,' said Harriet quietly, 'unless English domestic architecture is part of the secret.'

'Fine house, isn't it?' he said. 'Glad you noticed. Well now, I am to understand that you need to question one of my staff. A valuable man, if somewhat temperamental. My own concern is twofold. First I must attempt to conceal from you in every way possible the nature of the work going forward here. And second I must try to protect Birdlap from any upset that might take his mind off his work.'

'You need have no concern about the first of those things,' said Harriet. 'It is about incidents in the village of Paggleham that I wish to ask him. I need not, and will not ask him anything about his war work. You have my assurance.'

'Thank you, Lady Peter.'

'About your second concern, however, I cannot be so emollient. It concerns the brutal murder of a young woman with whom he is said to have been involved. I am afraid he may find it very upsetting indeed.'

'I see. Does he already know of this death?'

'I don't know. He may well do. What he may not realise is that he seems to have been the last person to see her alive.'

'And if I refuse your request to interview him, I shall shortly be confronted with one Superintendent Kirk bearing an arrest warrant?'

'Very likely, yes.'

Brigadier Baldock rose, walked to the window, and stood looking out of it, rocking on his heels. Then he turned to Harriet. 'You appear to be the lesser of two evils, Lady Peter,' he said. He rang a bell on his desk, and a uniformed sergeant appeared.

'Fetch Birdlap,' he said.

Baldock sat down again. 'I shall be present throughout this interview,' he stated.

Harriet did not demur. A silence grew in the room. She heard the clock ticking ponderously in the corner. A self-dramatising clock, making the most of ticking off the seconds.

'Lord Peter must have changed a good deal since I knew him,' the Brigadier suddenly observed.

'Why do you think so?' said Harriet, anger flickering in her heart. 'You find me rather unexpected as his wife?'

'Well, I . . . goodness me, dear lady, I didn't mean . . .'

'What you did mean, I imagine,' said Harriet, 'is that I have neither the beauty nor the class that you would have thought necessary to capture him. I take it that you did not know Lord Peter very well.'

'It would be brains, of course,' said the Brigadier imperturbably. 'Brains would do it.'

Harriet was spared the need to answer this by the arrival of Birdlap.

He proved to be a very young, very dishevelled, RAF officer, who had left his jacket unbuttoned, and his dark hair unbrushed. The knot of his tie hung below his unbuttoned shirt collar and he looked not quite sleepy, but very much preoccupied. He was dazzlingly handsome in a vulnerable-looking way, with a long sensitive mouth, and a bony, boyish frame. Harriet thought he would appeal deeply to the mothering instinct in many young women.

She watched him carefully while the Brigadier explained

70

the situation to him, and saw the colour drain from his face when he understood that Wendy Percival was dead.

'I heard something . . . I didn't know it was her,' he said, very quietly.

'But you did know the young woman?' said the Brigadier.

'Yes, sir.'

'Then I think it would be best if you would answer the questions Lady Peter wishes to put to you.'

'There was a dance in the village last Saturday,' Harriet said. 'Were you there?'

He hesitated. Glanced at his commanding officer and away again.

'I have been told that your name was on the list of those who went from here to attend it. Your name was checked off when the party returned here,' Harriet prompted. 'But were you actually at the dance?'

'No,' he said quietly.

'It has been suggested to me that the reason why Wendy was not at the dance was that she was with you. Is that true?'

'Yes.'

'It might help very much if you would tell me about it.'

'It was just such a good chance,' he said miserably. 'Wendy's quarters would be empty, because all the girls were going to the dance. Transport there, transport back again . . . You're going to think me an awful heel, I know, but it wasn't like that. She wanted me to . . . to find a way to . . .' His voice began to shake, and suddenly he was looking at Harriet wide-eyed and desperate. 'It was for me,' he said. 'In case I was going to die – we thought there might never be a chance again. We couldn't wait to make it respectable, we were jumping the gun, but we thought one of us might die at any moment . . . and we hadn't expected – and we thought it would be me – of course we thought it would be me!'

'But you are trying to tell us the young woman was previously of good character?' the Brigadier interposed.

'She was – of course she was! But we were in love, and we didn't know how long we had got; it was first time for both of us, and of course I would have married her if I got back safely . . .'

'About any danger your work entails, least said soonest mended,' said the Brigadier.

'I am so sorry,' said Harriet gently. 'And I do understand that you are under very great pressure. Peace-time rules seem hardly to apply. Could you tell me, however, exactly how you parted from Wendy and got back here undetected?'

'It was easy,' he said. 'It went like a dream. We could hear the air-raid warning from Wendy's bunk, and it gave us time to dress, and get back where we ought to have been. I just joined the press of people getting on to our truck. She stayed back so that the trucks would have driven off, and the locals would all be in the shelters, and nobody would see her, and she was going to get down to the shelter almost last, and say she had gone back for a blanket to keep her dress from getting scruffy sitting on the ground.'

'And did you see anyone else around as you made your way to the truck? Did anyone see you?'

'Not that I can remember. I wasn't watching. I was in a sort of daze . . . I'll tell you one thing,' he added, suddenly sounding collected and emphatic. 'You're going to have more than one murder on your hands if I get to know who killed her. I'll get them myself. And I'm trained to kill, trust me for it.'

'Don't be a silly chump,' said the Brigadier. 'You'll talk yourself into a scrape that might be hard to talk you out of. I'm confining you to barracks, understand? Off with you now, and back to work.'

Birdlap saluted and took himself off.

'I shouldn't think for a minute the poor chap means it,' said the Brigadier. 'But there might be more than one kind of peace-time rule that hardly seems to apply.'

Later Harriet settled down to her desk to write to Miss Climpson. She didn't exactly know why she had not spelled out to Mr Kirk that she, under the aegis of Peter, had a private agency at her command. Miss Climpson had worked ingeniously for Peter for some years. 'Putting questions,' he had said, 'which a young man could not put without a blush.' He had used her, and a little bevy of super-fluous otherwise unoccupied ladies answering suspect advertisements placed by fraudsters and money-lenders and tricksters, and gathering the evidence that convicted them, and rescued their victims. A job without end. And now she had diverted the efforts of her team of 'hens' to keeping an eye on public opinion, the sort of women's underground public opinion that Mass Observation might find impenetrable. Women under stress might grumble to each other, whereas they would put a good face on things in the public world. When she had heard from Miss Climpson recently, she had sounded rather fully occupied. Harriet opened the letter.

. . . Sunday evening is my quietest time now – of course we have to have Evensong in the middle of the afternoon, what with the blackout and winter-time, and the choir-school has been evacuated and two of the assistant priests have gone to be army chaplains, so we have to have Low Mass instead of High Mass, and what with an air-raid shelter in the crypt and one thing and another, we are beginning to feel quite persecuted like early Christians in catacombs! Though indeed I oughtn't to talk in that light-hearted way when Christians in Germany and Austria are being really persecuted – so subtly and wickedly, too, the older people being allowed to go to church, and all the CHILDREN being kept away by Hitler-Jugend meetings on Sundays, and being taught to insult Christ and despise their parents for believing in religion. It must be terrible to be a father or mother and feel that the government is deliberately ALIENATING one's children and BREAKING UP the family and encouraging quite little boys and girls to read horrible, dirty stories about Jews and priests in that dreadful Stuermer. I believe they even teach those

horrible things in schools. But I suppose a totalitarian
state can't afford to allow any group of people to have
interests and ideas of its own – not even the FAMILY!
And when one thinks how deeply the nicest Germans
have always been attached to their gemütlich *(isn't that*
the word?) home-life, it seems quite heart-breaking . . .

Miss Climpson was clearly keeping herself busy. Nevertheless, she might like a little trip down memory lane in the form of an investigation related to a murder enquiry, even if she was asked by Harriet rather than by dear Lord Peter. But pen in hand, and sheet of paper at the ready, Harriet was overwhelmed with the emotion of missing Peter. She, Harriet, had been involved before in murder enquiries, but never without Peter at her side or somewhere in the background. She was missing him desperately, on every front. But how ridiculous to be reduced to tears by writing to Miss Climpson!

Harriet pulled herself together, and looked again at the three names: Jake Datchett; Archie Lugg; John Birdlap. Birdlap she had dealt with. She wondered what she herself knew about either of the others. Archie Lugg was a handyman, and he had put up some rough-and-ready bookcases for her only a week or so back, using old floorboards. A good-looking man, who seemed to live and work in a musing calm she associated with true craftsmen, and who smelled faintly of wood-shavings. She tried, and failed, to imagine him driven mad with love, and killing in a jealous rage; it wasn't easy to imagine, but then she didn't know much about him. If they had been looking for a blunt instrument, Archie's toolbox would have contained plenty. Looking for a man with expertly homicidal hands was quite another thing. Disconcertingly, Harriet found she had quite a good mental picture of Archie Lugg's hands: broad hands with rather spoon-shaped flattened fingers and thumbs. He would have the muscular strength, of course.

She turned back to her letter.

But the letter was out of luck this morning. She heard a child sobbing quietly on the way up the stairs, and put her head round the door to find Charlie in tears.

'What's wrong?' she asked.

'Uncle Jerry's gone!' he wailed.

She held out her arms to him, and briefly hugged him. At ten did he still want to be hugged? Yes, it seemed he did, for he held on to her. Lord, thought Harriet, what can I say? I can't tell him Jerry won't come to any harm when it's only too likely that he will. I don't believe in lying to children. The news was horribly depressing. An increasingly vicious air battle was developing over the North Sea. German planes and German U-boats were attacking neutral shipping and even little inshore fishing boats. The British government had decided to arm merchant ships, and the Nazis had announced that British merchant ships would count as warships. Of course that meant fighter pilots like Jerry flying sorties over the Channel and the North Sea. Anyone could see how dangerous that was. And that the need for seaborne supplies was Britain's Achilles' heel.

'He's gone,' said Charlie, muffled in her loose embrace,

'and I can't make it work! And Sam can't either,' he added, in a normal tone, extricating himself.

'Can't make what work, Charlie?'

'My crystal set!' he cried.

'Are you sure you've put it together right?' she asked, stalling.

'I'm pretty sure,' he said. 'But it keeps picking up the wrong wavelengths.'

'I don't suppose I can help in person, Charlie,' she said. 'It's not my field. But your father and mother are coming at the weekend. Perhaps your father can help.'

'That's ages!' lamented Charlie. But he wandered away, and when Harriet looked up from her letter a few minutes later she saw him with Bredon and Polly, playing French cricket on the lawn, and looking perfectly happy. She finished her letter to Miss Climpson, and began one to Peter.

She had no recent letter from him to respond to, but was still hungrily reading over his last, perfectly discreet letter, in the form of an official letter-gram, reduced to the size of a postcard, closely typed in tiny letters, and bearing an official stamp from the censor.

> . . . *Like the gentleman in the carol, I have seen a wonder sight – the Catholic padre and the refugee Lutheran minister having a drink together and discussing, in very bad Latin, the persecution of the Orthodox Church in Russia. I have seldom heard so much religious toleration or so many false quantities . . .*

Peter's light and ironical tones came clearly off the paper,

77

as though he were in the room, conversing with someone. The letter was censored, but he had managed to make her smile with it. Then the post-script: In case of accident I will write my own epitaph now: HERE LIES AN ANACHRONISM IN THE VAGUE EXPECTATION OF ETERNITY.

Harriet put the letter away in her desk, alongside others, and began to compose a letter for him. The uncertainties of the correspondence made a smoothly alternating sequence of letters and replies impossible. But she could write in hope of reaching him, like Noah sending out a dove.

If one wanted gossip in Paggleham, thought Harriet, one only had to bump into Mrs Ruddle. Not that Mr Kirk had actually asked her to find out about the two local young men, beyond getting their names from the land-girls, but, Harriet thought, either one was doing something or one wasn't. And once involved she couldn't be not involved. Writing to Peter caused her heart-ache, and there was no certainty that any letter would ever reach him. She laid it aside, put on her coat, and having asked Mrs Trapp if anything was needed at the village shop, and put the ration-book into her gas-mask case, she went out for a walk.

Her way took her past the undertaker's shop, and she went in.

'Are you looking for Archie?' enquired Fred Lugg, who was behind the counter, with his spectacles pushed up on his forehead, and his folding rule in his hand. 'Or have you come to have a chat with me?'

'I wasn't hoping to be a customer of yours just yet,' said Harriet.

'Of course not, my lady, heaven forfend,' he said. 'But I thought you might want to ask me a question or two, seeing as you've taken over the murder from Superintendent Kirk.'

'Goodness, who told you that?' asked Harriet.

'Isn't it true, then?' he asked. 'It's all over the village.'

'I agreed to help with one or two simple enquiries,' she said.

'Well, then, how can I help?' he asked. 'Or were you after asking Archie about that young besom who was done to death?'

'Would Archie be able to help, do you think?' said Harriet, stalling.

'No doubt he could tell you how she got her nickname tormenting young men,' said Fred bitterly. 'But isn't anyone going to ask me anything? I mean, Lady Peter, there was I, the only citizen in the whole place who was supposed to be out in the open, and a murder was committed right under my feet, so to speak, and nobody asks me a blamed thing about it!'

'Of course, Mr Lugg, you were on the church tower!' said Harriet. 'In the moonlight. Well, did you see anything?'

'The tree is the problem,' he said. 'You know, that big yew tree by the lych gate. It blanks off just that bit of the Square where it happened. So I didn't see it happen, no. But I saw people walking about, one side of the tree, and the other side of the tree, passing it by on the other side. When everyone was supposed to be in the shelter.'

'You'd better tell me who you saw, Mr Lugg. Or if you don't want to tell me, you could tell the police.'

'I don't mind telling you, Lady Peter. I saw all your people from Talboys, making their way along to the shelter. Not Mrs Trapp, now I come to think of it. She must have decided to absent herself. And I saw you and that young pilot who has being staying with you, coming along and meeting them; well, no, I ought to be strictly accurate, I saw you going towards them, and then I saw you all turn back towards the Crown. Except for your pilot friend, he went off by himself, after he saw you safe inside. There were RAF men walking about everywhere. There were several cars and two RAF trucks went off, one towards Lopseley, and one towards the Broxford aerodrome, and then that Wendy came running along in a big hurry.'

'She wasn't at the dance, so she was coming from the farm to join the air-raid practice,' said Harriet. 'Or so I have been told.'

'Hmph.' He said, 'The thing is, I saw her going behind the tree from the right, and I didn't see her coming out from behind it to the left.'

'Well, no,' said Harriet. 'She would have been struck down behind the tree, from a viewpoint on the tower. So the very important thing, Mr Lugg, is who else did you see moving around there?'

'I wasn't keeping a watch on the street,' he said. 'I was

supposed to be watching the rooftops, and the sky, in case of fires or parachutes.'

'So you didn't see everything – you couldn't if you were doing your job?'

'Just so. When I didn't see the wretched girl coming out from behind the tree, I just thought she had moved on while I had my eyes elsewhere.'

'That's very natural,' said Harriet. But she was mystified, because he was so clearly het up about something. 'So did you see anyone else around after most of us had taken shelter?' she asked.

'I certainly didn't see my son Archie!' he said. 'But I did see that dentist woman – Mrs Spright. She never went down any shelter that night; she was wandering around all over the place. You should try asking her what she was up to.'

'I will do that.'

'It got very cold up there, Lady Peter,' he said lugubriously. 'And I didn't see the murder and I didn't see any enemy action.'

'It's awfully frustrating, isn't it?' she said sympathetically. 'All these preparations going on, and everyone's life disrupted, and all this extra work like ARP precautions, and fire-watching and blackout—'

'And for all that we can tell,' he completed the sentence for her, 'there's nothing in the way of enemy action at all.'

'There seem to have been a couple of spies arrested in Largo,' she said. 'It was in the paper.'

'That's a long way from here,' he said. 'The only thing different around here apart from upheavals which we have organised ourselves without help from the enemy is this murder; and that can't have anything to do it with it, as far as I can see.'

'It's murder just the same,' said Harriet, 'and nobody seems very upset. I can find hardly a good word spoken on behalf of the victim.'

'Well, there you are,' he said. 'The most I shall ever know about her is her size for a coffin. You can't care about strangers the way you would for somebody you've known all your life, can you?'

'Didn't Archie know her a bit?' asked Harriet. 'Why did you think it might be Archie I was wanting to talk to?'

'I supposed you might need some more shelves, my lady,' he said.

'As a matter of fact, Mr Lugg, I do,' said Harriet.

Four

Oh, come and live with me my love
And share my war-time dinner
Who eats the least at this our feast
Shall make John Bull the winner

Here is a plate of cabbage soup
With caterpillars in.
How good they taste! (Avoid all waste
If you the war would win.)

We've no unpatriotic joint
No sugar and no bread
Eat nothing sweet, no rolls, no meat
The Food Controller said.

Aelfrida Tillyard, *The Garden and the Fire*, 1916

In spite of Mrs Trapp's severity with her over bor-
rowing sugar, Mrs Ruddle was sitting comfortably in
the kitchen of Talboys when Harriet got back with the
shopping. She put the string bag down on the deal table,
and said, 'Is there any more tea in the pot, Mrs Trapp?'

'I'll make some fresh, my lady, and bring it up to you,'
said Mrs Trapp.

'No need,' said Harriet, sitting down in the big Windsor chair at one end of the table. 'I'll have what's there. What's the news?'

'Such a carry on!' said Mrs Trapp. 'But I don't blame you, Mrs Ruddle!'

'It's one of them new families from London, Lady Peter,' said Mrs Ruddle, launching joyfully into the account, 'what the billeting officer has put in the flat above the greengrocer's shop.'

'Mrs Marbleham, you mean?' said Harriet.

'That's her. Asked if she could join the pig club. Well, Joan Wagget more or less runs that, so she asks how can you join the pig club when you haven't got anywhere to keep a pig? Oh, says she, do you have to have a pig? I would of thought I could pay my share. Well, you can't, says Joan, the pig club is for them as keeps pigs. Well, says this Mrs Marbleham, I heard as how you need a licence to slaughter a pig, and if I can't join you'd better watch out, she says. Because I'm living right in the middle of this horrible village, she says, and I keeps my eyes skinned. Now what do you make of that?'

'Fascinating,' said Harriet. 'I didn't know there was a pig club. Should we join it, Mrs Trapp?'

'We have done, my lady, and been promised a piglet to fatten as soon as Mr Bateson's sow has her litter.'

'How does it work, Mrs Trapp?'

'Well, it wouldn't make sense in a place this size if everyone who was rearing a pig happened to be killing them in the same week or fortnight. There's only so much you can make into bacon, and people like the fresh pork. So the pig club get together to share the meat out when a pig gets slaughtered and then share in their turn when their own pig is ready. We joined up to it as soon as I heard about it.'

'And very welcome you are,' said Mrs Ruddle. 'You aren't going to be one what feeds the pig onion skins and such as taints the meat. We have thrown someone out of the club, Lady Peter, before now because they growed the most horrible-tasting meat. Now the vicar's autumn pigs are always beautiful, because he lets 'em into his orchard to get all the windfall apples and pears. But Mr Puffett's is best of all. He gives 'em windfall peaches from his kitchen garden, along of all the peelings, and do they taste different! Gorgeous, they are. I had a hand and spring off of Mr Puffett last time we had a share-out what was a real meal to remember . . . I done it with prunes soaked in a little tonic wine, Mrs Trapp, and you couldn't guess how good that was! Even my Bert was pleased, and he always wants the trotters.'

'Is this part of the war effort?' asked Harriet.

'Bless you, no!' said Mrs Ruddle. 'Been going on for years and years. The war effort is what's trying to stop it, making us have a licence to get a pig slaughtered – in your own back yard, too! What next, I says to Bert, whatever next? That stupid Jack Baker what calls hisself a policeman – he isn't any better than Joe Sellon uster be if you ask me – going all around asking people about who was walking out with that land-girl, and might of done her in, and all the people what he was asking about was down the shelter with about a hundred witnesses to as how they weren't available to murder anyone. I ask you. It's just as well you got your finger in that pie, my lady, or it'd be real dog's dinner. Course, it's a shame Lord Peter ain't around to sort it – he'd have it worked out in no time. Well, well, I can't sit around here all day. I better love you and leave you.'

Mrs Trapp waited until the door was firmly shut behind the visitor before saying to Harriet, 'I'm sorry I hadn't mentioned the pig club, my lady; we seem always to have to discuss the rationing.'

'Oh, don't worry,' said Harriet. 'It's a bit of a compliment that we're allowed to join it, since it sounds as if it's insiders only.'

'I don't think it's so much a compliment, my lady, as necessity. It seems that the hoist is in one of our outhouses. They would need us involved.'

'What is a hoist?' asked Harriet.

'An arrangement of ropes and pulleys, my lady, I understand. I haven't been to look myself. Can't say as I'd want to. The butcher at Duke's Denver used to come up when there was a beast to kill on the home farm, but by the time I saw what he was up to it was all nicely jointed.'

Just at that point Polly and Charlie burst in through the garden door, panting and hot and asking for drinks. Harriet hastily changed the subject. 'What can the youngsters drink, Mrs Trapp? Have we got anything for them?'

'The finest drink that man can drink is water from the

spring,' said Mrs Trapp. 'Straight from the tap. Good for your teeth.'

'Can we have it poured from a jug, Mrs Trapp, even if it is just water?' asked Polly. 'Then we can pretend it's something nice.'

'You can have it out of this lovely Staffordshire jug, Miss Polly, as though you were the Queen of Sheba,' said Mrs Trapp, with a flourish. Harriet saw that she was fetching from the pantry a jug with a strange brown fluid in it the colour of watered beer.

'Wow!' cried Charlie. 'Liquorice water! Gosh, Mrs Trapp, I love you!'

'Cupboard love, you young scamp,' said Mrs Trapp, smiling. 'It won't fool me. You won't get round me that way! Now how's that thingummyjig that your uncle gave you? Have you got it working yet?'

'Well,' said Charlie, 'it is working. But I don't think it was me, Mrs Trapp, I think it was Sam Bateson. He's a whiz at it; he got it to pick up the Home Service straight away.'

'I'm glad to hear it,' said Mrs Trapp. 'Now, out of my kitchen all of you, if you want any supper tonight. Right away.'

Harriet felt herself included in the general dismissal. But before she followed her flock out of the kitchen she picked up the glass that Polly had been drinking from, and sipped it. It had a faint and pleasant flavour of liquorice.

'It's only a penny a root,' said Mrs Trapp. 'And that makes a gallon. And it isn't rationed, nor yet on points.'

'It's quite nice,' said Harriet, wondering how she had escaped it in her own childhood.

Her own childhood, as an adored only child, had offered her very little preparation for the life she was now leading, she mused later. She was comfortably curled up on her large soft bed, with Paul beside her, falling asleep over his goodnight story about Babar the elephant. This story, one of those provided by Aunt Mary, Peter's sister, had a distinctly communist tinge, Harriet realised, reading it for the umpteenth time. In a minute Sadie would come, take the boy from Harriet's arms and settle him in his cot for the night. But for the moment Harriet was enjoying the cosy feeling of his heavy head lying against her arm. She had time to make a mental audit of her situation. She was, alas, not living with Peter this week, or next week, and yet now her entire life was living with Peter and that included this week, this day, this hour. It was Peter's money that kept the roof over her head, that paid the servants' wages – admittedly only three compared to the eight it had needed to run the London house, but enough pairs of willing hands to manage caring for the children and keeping the household clean, warm and fed. The cartoon in this morning's paper had made her laugh: it showed a snooty young woman interviewing a stout matron. 'So, actually, all you're doing at the moment,' read the caption, 'is the housework, arranging and cooking meals for your husband, children and evacuees, canteen work, and voluntary fire-watching?'

Harriet's laughter had been tinged with guilt. She was doing everything she was asked to do for the WVS, she had taken a St John's Ambulance Brigade First-Aid course, and had a certificate to prove it, she was contributing 'think pieces' to various newspapers when asked, she had served briefly on a writers' planning committee, and now she was helping Mr Kirk as a stand-in detective. Should she be able to do more?

And yet how could she do more? Mrs Trapp, she knew instinctively, would stay with her through hell and high water, and was far too elderly to be requisitioned for war work. But the housemaids must find working in the country very boring compared to their lives in the London house, and surely they would soon be working in a factory or as land-girls. And if not that, working hard enough as fire-watchers, or in the WVS to compromise the energy they could give to the household. If by then she herself had undertaken other work, there could be real difficulties keeping things going. She had to face it that her primary duties were here, even if at the moment she was only the fall-back for most of the work.

It wasn't the work she had thought to devote her life to, that Peter had expected his wife to be engaged in. How firmly he had briefed the servants in Audley Square about her working hours, how carefully he had arranged for her study to be furnished! The war, which had seemed so slow to start, was now a gradually intensifying whirl-wind blowing the lives of everyone before it. It would be preposterous of her to complain that the war stopped her writing detective stories, when it was stopping so many people from more important work, stopping many people over the Channel even from drawing breath.

Harriet looked ruefully across the room at the bookcase containing the published works of husband and wife: *A Murderer's Vade Mecum* by Lord Peter Wimsey, *Notes on the Collection of Incunabula* by the same author, a row of narrow paper spines representing monographs on various subjects to which Peter had given his attention at one time or another. Her own work was relatively brazen, having been wrapped by her publisher in dust-jackets intended to catch the eye in a crowded bookshop: *Death in the Pot, Murder by Degrees, The Fountain Pen Mystery* – a gaudy row of titles by Harriet Vane. But how frivolous the whole preoccupation seemed compared to the dangers of the present hour. Frivolous? But Peter had once energetically refused to call them that. He had said that they put before the public a world the way it ought to be, and kept alive a dream of justice. And where was justice now? How could it survive in war? Domestic justice now was like a wall of sand in the face of a raging full-flood tide. She saw suddenly that far from making a small injustice, a single domestic murder, less important, the general danger made it even more important. We cannot abandon what we are fighting to defend; that would make our self-defence indefensible.

Peter's last letter – weeks ago now – had suggested she might use her skills to inspire the public with solidarity and heart for the tasks and suffering ahead of them, but the public were behaving by and large very much better than that stupid Ministry of Morale had expected of them. And Harriet's skills were not really those of a propagandist; or not directly. Surely she was right to think that making a skirt for her niece Polly was a more important occupation. Faced with the awful possibility that hardship and death lay ahead of the happy gaggle of children under her care, it seemed overwhelmingly important to keep them carefree for as long as possible.

And that might be difficult. Only yesterday Bredon, who was not quite four, spotting a collapsed section of garden wall in the High Street, had asked her if that was war damage. In a way it was, since old Mr Critch had driven into it, after missing the road in the blackout, but how did Bredon know to ask, when she never listened to news broadcasts till the children were in bed, or playing out of earshot?

Sadie had appeared to fetch Paul to bed. Harriet gently eased her supporting arm from under her sleeping son's head, and handed him over. She tried to gather her thoughts. The children were having a wonderful time, in one way, running almost wild, making friends with village children, always having others to play with. How lonely, by comparison, she herself had been as a child! How lonely, on one level, she was herself now. Missing Peter was something she couldn't afford to think about, it was too painful, too full of hideous dread. But the fact was, she was also missing her profession. Writing scrappily, constantly interrupted, at a little bureau in the sitting-room certainly wasn't the deeply absorbing and consoling thing that work used to be. Was that why she had agreed to help Superintendent Kirk? To have something to think about that was not domestic, and asked for powers of reasoning?

If that were the case, then being desultory about it would not do. It wouldn't do at all. Lord Peter's consort would have to live up to the challenge.

Harriet felt very disinclined to pursue and interview the local young men without an explicit request from Mr Kirk, and he had apparently set his local constable, Jack Baker, to the task. There was a slight sense of impropriety in asking young people about their dating or their love lives directly, except in some official capacity. She did not herself seem to possess Peter's wonderful talent for getting people to talk fluently and indiscreetly. Until Miss Climpson had done her stuff and reported back to Harriet, there didn't seem any way of taking up the gauntlet, except following up the gossamer lead offered by Fred Lugg's sighting of the mysterious Mrs Spright.

The green banks of Datchett's Lane were full of primroses, like clots of curdled cream in the grass, and with a receding glimpse of wild violets here and there. The hedgerows on either side were unfurling tiny leaves on every twig, and cheerful with birdsong. Walking down it lightened Harriet's mood, until the sound of a solitary aircraft overhead reminded her how fragile a peace this was. 'Be reasonable,' she rebuked herself. 'Nothing, not even Hitler victorious, could ever stop an English lane from sprouting wild flowers.' Mrs Spright's cottage was the last in the lane, and backed on to fields. Beyond it was a little wood. Seeing the owner in the garden, Harriet lifted the latch of the gate and went in.

Mrs Spright was rather dishevelled, but then she was busy digging over her vegetable plot. She was a large, rather muscular woman, wearing a cross-over pinafore in flowered cotton over her clothes, and with her grey hair restrained by an Alice band which looked as though it belonged on a child's head rather than a grown woman's.

'What a beautiful day!' said Harriet. 'That looks like warm work.'

Mrs Spright stood upright, and leaned on her garden fork. 'We are enjoined to grow vegetables,' she said.

'But of course,' said Harriet. 'What are you planting?'

'Beans and cabbages first,' said Mrs Spright. 'And carrots, of course, since they help one see in the dark.'

'I have heard that,' said Harriet. 'Is it true?'

'The dark,' remarked Mrs Spright portentously, 'is best for seeing some things that are hidden by day. Yes, Lady Peter, it is true. Also they clean the teeth even better than the proverbial apples.'

'May I ask you what you have seen in the dark, Mrs Spright?' said Harriet boldly. 'On the night of the 17th of last month, in particular. You did not take shelter that night.'

'Wasn't a real raid, was there?' replied Mrs Spright. 'Come in and have a cup of tea. It's too damn cold to stand around out here talking.'

93

The cottage was clean and rather bleak. A number of certificates for achievements in dentistry hung in the hallway, which was also decorated with a display of dark green plates. The sitting-room had brown leather chairs, and a fireplace swept clean and empty. A certain chill about the room, and a number of old newspapers stacked on a pouf, suggested to Harriet that the room's owner spent little time there, and had little attention to spare for it.

'Take a seat,' her hostess said, adding, 'I don't usually sit in here. I prefer the kitchen which isn't overlooked from the road.'

'Is being overlooked a problem?' asked Harriet, surprised. 'Isn't this the last house? There can't be many passers-by, surely.'

'I like to keep out of sight of my enemies,' said Mrs Spright. 'I like them not to know if I am in or out, or around and about. Not to know where I am.'

'What enemies are those?' asked Harriet. She was getting a distinct uneasy feeling.

'Spies,' said Mrs Spright simply, 'and fifth columnists. They know I'm on to them. And since the authorities don't do anything about it, Lady Peter, I have to look out for myself. Mark my words, when the Germans invade they'll be coming for me before many who think themselves too important to act on my information. They'll have a grudge against me for keeping an eye on them when nobody else believed me.'

'Are there many spies in Paggleham?' Harriet asked.

Surely this woman was a loony – and yet she might have seen something.

'Well, if they aren't spying, I'd like to know what they are up to,' said Mrs Spright. 'Sugar, Lady Peter? I've stopped taking it myself, but . . .'

'No, no,' said Harriet hastily, as a laden spoon was held over her cup. 'Thank you, but I don't take sugar in tea. You were saying? What are who up to?'

'I can't trust you,' said Mrs Spright. 'Half the aristocracy are on Hitler's side you know.'

'Not me, I assure you,' said Harriet. 'Nor my husband.' But what form, exactly, did the woman's evident lunacy take?

'There's Aggie Twitterton, for one,' said Mrs Spright.

'Good Lord!' said Harriet, nearly dropping her cup. 'You don't suppose Miss Twitterton to be a German spy?'

'She goes out at night a lot. She's over here rather a lot, for one who doesn't live in the village.'

'Well, she doesn't live far away. Her little cottage is just outside Pagford, on the Paggleham road. An easy walk in fine weather.'

'Friend of yours, is she? Someone should ask her what she's doing after dark, just the same. Then there's Bert Ruddle. Says he's poaching when he goes by at night, but I've seen lights in the woods, and when did a poacher ever show a light? There are people here claiming to be what they aren't, and they think nobody can see through them, but I can spot them. That Brinklow fellow. And what about the vicar? Why has he got an iron cross on the kitchen dresser if he isn't a German? Why does he have Germans living in his house? Answer me that.'

'I think I can, Mrs Spright,' said Harriet indignantly. 'The vicar has the iron cross because it was given to him by a dying German soldier at the Battle of the Somme. He was serving as a stretcher-bearer, behind the lines, being too old for any more active service. The man's courage made a deep impression on him, and he has kept the cross all these years for that reason. As for the strangers living in the Vicarage, he has taken in some refugees.'

'He's taken people in, indeed he has. And then there's that land-girl. Why was she murdered if she wasn't a spy?'

'Did you see who murdered her?' asked Harriet. Not that anything this woman said could be thought reliable.

'I could have murdered her myself,' observed Mrs Spright. 'I don't like spies. They are the foulest of the enemy, and the most cowardly, don't you think? Hanging is too good for them. I saw her running along the street in her tarty dress, but I didn't see who killed her. No. Can't help you there.'

'Did you see anyone else around that night?' asked Harriet, hope against hope.

'And if I did who would believe me? The half of the country are in the pockets of the enemy. If you've finished your tea, Lady Peter, I'll get back to my carrots.'

Harriet walked back to Talboys feeling troubled. There was such a poisonous tinge to Mrs Spright's conversation. Could Aggie Twitterton really have taken to night prowling? And if so what could it be about? More likely a lover than a bout of spying in aid of the enemy. Not that the one was hugely more likely than the other in the case of poor Miss Twitterton. Such a lonely person. Brought up too refined for her station in life, and left high and dry with ideas and manners and aspirations that made her poverty really painful to her. A sort of latter-day version of Miss Bates in Jane Austen's *Emma*. But however unhappy she was, Harriet was sure Agnes Twitterton was not a German spy. She would stake her life on it.

In that case, of course, there would have to be another explanation for the Twitters' night wandering. And the simplest thing to do would be to ask her about it. Surely she was enough of a friend to meet the question without taking offence? She and Harriet had got to know one another quite well, and very quickly when Agnes Twitterton's disappearing Uncle Noakes had turned up in the cellar at Talboys, and disrupted Harriet's honeymoon. Harriet smiled to herself as this recollection brought into her mind a string of images of Peter: most particularly of Peter calling her Queen Aholibah, and riding a chair wildly like a rocking-horse, then a moment of such depth and stillness between them; and poor Miss Twitterton had burst in upon them, wailing that she could not bear it; a happiness so intense had suffused that moment that it was unbearable both to those it excluded and to those it included and enclosed. Once in a lifetime would be enough for such a moment.

Harriet's reverie was broken as she turned into the

home-stretch towards Talboys by finding Polly waiting for her, swinging on the gate. Polly was a pretty child, much more Wimsey than Parker, with her mother's fair hair and china-blue eyes, and would-be-firm expression, quite unlike her father's broad-browed, dark-haired appearance. She was teetering on the brink between baby-childhood and child-childhood. And she was a new experience for Harriet, who couldn't help noticing, although she tried not to, that Charles and Mary's daughter had a line to her understanding not available to her own sons. Daughters are different, evidently.

'Aunt Harriet, couldn't you help Charlie with his crystal set? Couldn't you really?'

'Has it gone wrong again?' asked Harriet. 'Bother! Well, I'll try, but I'm more likely to make it worse than better I'm afraid.'

'He gets so upset,' offered Polly, 'and he isn't any fun when he's upset. We want to look for mushrooms in the wood, and Sadie says we can't go unless Charlie will come to look after us, and Charlie . . .'

'I'll see what I can do,' said Harriet.

It turned out that she couldn't do anything with the receiver, because it had mysteriously righted itself by the time she got to it. And of course, she realised, if Charlie was tuning in to the Home Service, that could explain why Bredon knew about bomb damage. Should she confiscate the set? What grief she would inflict, if she did such a thing as that. No. Should she try to make sure that

98

Charlie didn't play the scary bits of news to the younger children? But did they realise what was scary? Could they possibly realise how serious the situation was? Probably it would be more frightening if she tried to prevent them from listening than if she left well alone.

All the same she tried to offer a bit of moral support. 'Are you listening to much news, Charlie?' she asked him.

'Not much,' he said. 'Only about once a day.'

'You know we are going to win this war, Charlie, however grim the news might be on a given day.'

'I know,' he said serenely.

She had come as near to lying to him as a hair's breadth, though. The trouble with living with children wasn't what she had thought it would be. They were on the whole as interesting to her as a group of adults; she wasn't in the least bored with them, although one could see that if one had no helping hands and could never get an uninterrupted moment for oneself it would be very wearing. But they were liable to present one without any warning at all with acute moral dilemmas, like a fatal cosmic game in which the stake was one's integrity – not truth or dare, but truth or comfort, like this chat with Charlie; justice for all or protection for the weakest, like the other day when Bredon had retaliated against baby Paul throwing bricks.

At least she could look forward to the weekend, when the Parker children could present their moral challenges to their own parents for a couple of days.

Harriet's visit to Miss Twitterton proved surprising. Miss

Twitterton was in the kitchen of her little cottage, carefully weighing out grain into brown paper bags.

'I used to give them more than this each day,' she said sorrowfully to Harriet, 'but now the grain is rationed . . . I don't know what I shall do, Lady Peter, when they go off laying, unless we can have our egg rations back when that happens. Mrs Ruddle says we should give up keeping them, that the game won't be worth the candle by the time the Ministry of Food has tied us all up in knots, but I can't do without my bantams, eggs or no eggs. I'm used to having them, and they're company for me.'

'I brought you a little bacon to go with some of those eggs,' said Harriet. 'Mrs Trapp has a whole side of bacon sent down from the Duke's farm at Denver last week, and she wishes to repay favours with a few rashers while she has some to spare.'

'Oh, oh!' cried Miss Twitterton, clasping her hands together in evident delight. 'Oh, she shouldn't have, Lady Peter! I only gave her an old hen past its day for laying; just once. I suppose the Duke can get a slaughtering licence any time he wants. But the bacon ration is so mean, isn't it? Just four ounces for a whole week! I am most grateful.'

'I haven't asked about licences,' said Harriet, 'and I don't think I will enquire. The Duke raises prize pigs, and I suppose he has to kill one of them now and then.'

'Oh, quite so. Least said soonest mended. I don't think those people in London making up the regulations have the least idea what usually goes on in the country. And you know, Lady Peter, if they try to stop country people keeping the food they raise themselves, and grow themselves, they won't have piles of country produce going off into the cities; they'll just have less food all round. Calling it the black market, when it's only what has been going on since well before the Kaiser won't help – it just gets up people's noses.'

'I suppose you're right, Miss Twitterton. But before I go I did have something to ask you. Mrs Spright tells me she sees you going past her place late at night. I am sure there is an innocent explanation.' Harriet saw in astonishment that bright red patches had appeared on Aggie Twitterton's cheeks. She was wringing her hands in agitation. 'I was sure I had only to ask . . .'

'I'm afraid that's where you're wrong!' cried Miss Twitterton. 'It isn't any business of that Spright woman, it isn't anybody's business, not even yours! It's completely secret.' Then she added, more calmly, 'It's confidential. I gave my word not to tell anyone, and I won't. Not *anyone*. It isn't against the law to go walking down the lanes and in the woods. I'm not breaking blackout; nobody can tell you they've seen me with a torch. I shall keep my counsel, and that's that.'

'Well of course,' said Harriet, both surprised and embarrassed. 'I'm sure you have your reasons. I won't press you about it.'

'What does that old fool say about me?' asked Miss Twitterton. 'Does she say I murdered Wendy Percival? You know that I didn't, Lady Peter, because we were down the shelter together. I suppose she thinks I'm a German spy.

Let her, say I; she's saying that about anyone and everyone, even the dear vicar. Right off her head, she is.'

'Yes, I rather think she is,' said Harriet ruefully. If Mrs Spright was obviously potty, what was she doing asking Agnes Twitterton about her allegations? And yet Miss Twitterton had not denied going up to the woods after dark, had indeed confirmed it.

'She used to be a very good dentist,' said Miss Twitterton. 'I never went to her myself; I always go to Mr Pargeter at Broxford for my teeth. But so I have been told. You won't be cross with me, Lady Peter, for keeping a secret from you? I quite hate not being able to tell you, but you see, I did give my word of honour.'

'Of course I won't be cross,' said Harriet. 'A promise is a promise; I do understand that. I'll see you at choir-practice on Wednesday.'

And indeed, Harriet was not cross with her friend, just severely puzzled. Could Miss Twitterton have remembered the awful crisis during the investigation of the Noakes murder, when Harriet had told Peter about the Twitters' involvement with Crutchley, and Peter had told the police? Miss Twitterton had not asked for secrecy on that occasion, but confidentiality had been implied, and the confidence was misplaced. But that was nearly four years ago, and seemed never to have cast a shadow on friendly relations so far. Indeed Miss Twitterton had seemed overjoyed when Harriet arrived in the village complete with family and appendages, to stay for the duration.

Harriet's meditation on this subject was interrupted by

meeting Mrs Ruddle, coming laden from the village shop, and falling in with Harriet since their way lay together as far as the Talboys gate.

'I've been saying to Mr Willis while he weighed my bit of cheese,' offered Mrs Ruddle, 'as how there's some people really are *perculiar*. There was Mrs Hodge's Susan in the shop with me, buying her bacon ration, what lets out her cottage to that Lieutenant Brinklow, and she says he's got the most horrible toothache, been going on for days, she says, and she told him last Tuesday as how he did ought to go to the dentist, and he wouldn't hear of it, and now she says his poor face is all swoll up as how you'd hardly reconise him. And he must be in agony, Mrs Ruddle, she tells me, in pure agony, and she says to him, well, now surely you'll go to the dentist, and he says to her as how he can't bring himself, along of being terrified of dentists so as he'd rather have the pain. So I says to her, Susan, I says, it isn't just pain you're talking about there, but you can get poisoned blood off of a rotting tooth, I said, like my cousin's sister's hubby over Lopsley way what nearly died of it. Well, I know that, Mrs Ruddle, she said, but what can I do? I can't make him go, can I? He says as how he wouldn't trust a dentist except down in London. I ask you, I says. Him a pilot what flies off to fight with them Messysmiths, brave as a lion in a plane, and afraid of a dentist, what can you say?'

'What indeed, Mrs Ruddle?' said Harriet.

Five

He that hath wife and children hath
given hostages to fortune.
Francis Bacon, 'Of Marriage and Single Life',
Essays, 1625

When she got home she heard laughter coming from the kitchen – adult laughter – and she found her sister-in-law, Lady Mary Parker, formerly Lady Mary Wimsey, sitting at the kitchen table being plied with tea and talk by Mrs Trapp. Mrs Trapp, she realised, must have known Lady Mary from a babe in arms, and as was the way with family servants (the things that marrying Peter had enabled Harriet to know about!) spoke with deep familiarity and scant courtesy to the grown people the family children had become.

'What a set of young savages you've billeted on her ladyship!' Mrs Trapp was saying. 'Greedy as gannets; always hungry and running wild. I'm surprised you're not ashamed to show your face here as their mother.'

'Oh, come, Mrs Trapp,' said Mary. 'At least they weren't sewn into their vests for the winter and full of head-lice like the evacuees we read about in the newspapers.'

'I'll give you that, m'lady,' said Mrs Trapp. 'The poor little mites. Perhaps this'll open people's eyes to what has been going on. My niece in the Salvation Army has tales to tell as would make your blood run cold. Working in the East End is worse than missions in Africa, she says. She says the more of the slums Hitler knocks down the better it will be, as long as the people are down the Underground at the time, of course.'

'Mary!' said Harriet. 'How good to see you.'

'I'm missing the children so much Charles sent me up a day early,' said Mary, rising to embrace her. 'And I haven't had sight or sound of them yet. They're out and about somewhere.'

'They've gone for mushrooms, so they say,' said Mrs Trapp. 'To help out the housekeeping.'

'Goodness, is that safe?' asked Harriet. 'Or shall we find we've been done to death by toadstools supplied by our loving families?'

'Bless you, I won't cook what they bring,' said Mrs Trapp. 'I've got a nice punnet of mushrooms in the larder that Bert Ruddle let me have, and I'll cook those instead.'

'There I go, underestimating you again, Mrs Trapp. It's impossible to overestimate you, I think.'

'Flattery will get you everywhere,' said Mrs Trapp contentedly. 'Off you go, Miss Mary, and take your tea in the drawing-room as if you'd been properly invited!'

There wasn't time to talk to Mary at once though. The children came home from the fields in a hand-holding group, with Sadie shepherding them, and offered to Harriet's fascinated gaze a little family drama. Charlie ran to his mother, offered his cheeks to be kissed, and began at once to tell her about the piglet that would be coming from Bateson's sow's litter, and how Sam—

'Who's Sam, Charlie?' asked Mary.

But Charlie's explanation was long and detailed, and kept falling over itself with his excitement, so that Mary broke into it. Polly was standing in the doorway, seeming almost shy, as though her mother had been a stranger. How long was it, Harriet wondered, since she had seen Mary? Well, it might be eight weeks, and that was a very long time in a life of only seven years.

'How's my little girl?' asked Mary. 'Is there a kiss for Mother?'

But Polly did not move. She said, 'Sadie bathes me, and Aunt Harriet reads my bednight story.'

If Mary flinched, Harriet did not see her. She said, 'Perhaps tonight I could help them?'

Meanwhile little Harriet toddled straight across the room, climbed into Mary's lap, leaned her head against her mother's shoulder, and put her thumb peaceably into her mouth.

Big Harriet intercepted her own two, and carried them away to her bedroom, offering stories and sweets, to give the Parker family time to re-form itself. Would Bredon be just like Charlie in six years' time? she wondered. Was he a mirage of the future of her sons? They could do worse: he was a nice little boy with a kindly disposition towards the babies. And Bredon adored him, and imitated his every move. Only she hoped Bredon would be more light-hearted; Charlie took everything so seriously. But then look at their respective fathers . . .

Later, when the children were asleep, the two women sat comfortably by the fire to talk.

'Polly's still a bit strange with me,' said Mary. 'I ought to get up here more often.'

'It's hardly your fault, when we are sternly enjoined not to travel more than necessary,' Harriet reminded her. 'She'll be all right with you by lunch-time tomorrow.'

'And she's been all right here? Not pining?'

'I'm afraid not. She's been fine. It's only when she saw you . . .'

'And at least mine are with family,' said Mary. 'Think what it must be like to have your children with strangers. One of Charles's officers had to borrow a police car and go and fetch his son home, and the boy had red weals all over his backside. He was being beaten for not eating. Think of it, Harriet, when this war is long over there will be people still alive in the next century who will bear the psychological marks of all this. War damage, so to speak.'

'Well, I expect there are children who are better cared for than they were at home, too.'

'Yes, of course. And if bombing were to really start . . .'

'That would be different, wouldn't it?'

'You know, Harriet, London is really strange at the moment. There are sandbags everywhere, and the other day there was an air-raid warning, I think it was another false alarm, and people were trekking through the streets at dusk to get down Underground stations. Air-raid wardens were trying to stop them and direct them to official shelters, but of course they only had to buy a ticket for the Tube, so they couldn't be stopped, and the surface shelters look pretty flimsy. And at the same time as all this there are still bright young things in posh frocks going to night-clubs and bars, and you can still get a slap-up meal in the big hotels if you have the money, although the Ministry has just forbidden the fish course if you have the main course. And then in the morning all the people stream out of the shelters and trudge home at the same time as the toffs come out of the clubs. It's like a London-wide version of coming out of the opera as the Covent Garden market got going – you remember what fun that was!'

Harriet, who had not been able to afford opera tickets before her marriage, had not had that particular kind of fun. After her marriage Peter had taken her to the opera, of course, but Bunter had always brought the Daimler to the opera house steps to take them home.

Lady Mary was smiling to herself. 'All the coster-mongers and vegetable stall-holders and barrow-boys would stop unloading the farm lorries and stand around waiting for us,' she said. 'They would cat-call, and yell, "Likes your frock, ducks!" Or, "Cor, that's cut a bit low that is. That's a lovely pair of melons, 'ow much do you want for them?"'

Harriet laughed.

'You'd be picking up your hem to step over cabbage leaves and squashed tomatoes, and the cockneys would yell, "Don't touch the fruit now! No prodding, just looking afore you buy!" Sometimes your escort would get annoyed,' said Mary, 'but the awful truth is, I liked it. Nothing like a wolf-whistle for a woman's morale!'

'I don't know what I've been missing,' said Harriet. Though she was not the kind that got whistled at in the street. 'So how is Charles?' she asked.

'He's working far too hard. When the bombs start falling in earnest a lot will be expected of the police. I don't see much of him, so I've volunteered as an ambulance driver. But now I wonder if I shouldn't be here with the children. Or take them to Denver.'

'I wouldn't move them again just yet,' said Harriet.

'I suppose you're missing old Peter?'

'Yes. It makes it harder somehow not knowing where he is.'

'I expect he's in Sweden,' said Mary.

'Whyever? I don't think he's in a neutral country; I believe it's very dangerous.'

'I think Sweden might be a way in to Finland. And we have family in Sweden. Delagardies.'

'But Uncle Paul Delagardie is French!'

'Likes to pretend so, yes.'

'Well, if he's in Finland . . .' said Harriet, with a sinking heart. The Finns had yesterday signed a treaty of capitulation, ceding a large part of their territory to Soviet Russia. They had exacted a terrible price – maybe as many as a million Russian dead – but they had been overwhelmed by sheer weight of numbers. There was no comfort in this. Her unfinished sentence hung in the air between them.

'Look, I haven't a clue really where Peter is,' said Mary. 'It was just an idle guess.'

'I wish he were here,' said Harriet, 'for all sorts of reasons, but not least because in the middle of all this the local police have a squalid ordinary murder on their hands, and I've been asked to help, and of course . . .'

'That's a bit much,' said Lady Mary. 'Do you want me to ask Charles to get at the Chief Constable of Hertfordshire, and have them called off? Although, of course, you have done quite a bit of detecting yourself, one way and another, haven't you?'

'I don't in the least mind being asked to help. But always before I could talk it over with Peter.'

'Can't you write to him?'

'Of course I can write, care of someone – I'd better not say who; and I've even had one or two brief replies, and one transcribed from a telegraph message. But, Mary, think about it; Peter is in hiding and in danger, and when he gets a letter from home he surely doesn't want reams of stuff about land-girls and villagers and who was fire-watching and who was flirting with whom. He just wants to know that we are all safe and we love him. And even if he could reply, do I want a contribution to cracking a sordid mystery in Paggleham? I don't want him thinking about that, I want him thinking about how to accomplish his mission and get home safe and sound.'

'Yes, I see. I do see.'

'And yet telling him about things was always the great clarifier of thought processes. I'm lost without it.'

'Then I think you'd better write to him anyway. Just write; don't send the letters. If you haven't got it solved when he turns up again he can read them then.'

'Mary, that's a very good idea. That's just what I should do. Would you like a glass of Peter's brandy as a night-cap?'

The morrow brought both bright sunlight, and Charles. Mrs Trapp put up a picnic – bread and ham and bread and jam – and the family made up a straggling expedition to the wood, carting the picnic basket and old blankets, and a flask of hot tea, and a huge stoneware jar of lemonade. Harriet pushed Paul's pram as far as the gate to the field below the wood, and Sadie carried him the rest of the way. The holiday atmosphere infected all the children, who were skipping and dancing around the steadily trudging adults, all except Charlie who seemed rather out of sorts.

He tried several times to stop the march: 'Here will do! Wouldn't it be nice right here?' before saying anxiously, 'We aren't going right into the wood, are we, Aunt Harriet?'

'Not right in, Charlie, because some of us like the sunshine. Just on the edge, where we can choose between sun and shade.'

'Okay,' he said, visibly relaxing. 'As long as we don't go right in.'

'We won't,' said Harriet. 'But why shouldn't we?'

'It's forbidden,' he said.

'No, it's not. The wood belongs to your Uncle Peter. He bought it from Bateson's farm last year.'

'Oh, well, it's just that it is very dangerous. Not forbidden, just dangerous.'

'Who told you that?'

'Someone. Can't remember. Might have been Sam.'

Harriet was briefly mystified. She made a mental note to find out more about Sam Bateson, since he seemed such a strong influence on Charlie, but their arrival on the verge of the woodland, and the setting up of the picnic distracted her.

'This is such a treat,' said Charles. 'You can't imagine. Just a sight of green fields after months in London.'

'The peaceful scene belies its appearance though,' said Mary. 'Harriet tells me there has been a local murder. Police baffled. What to do when Lord Peter is absent? Call in wife of famous sleuth.'

'If I had a pound for every time I've been told the police are baffled,' said Charles mildly, 'we'd have a place in the country of our own. What's it about, Harriet?'

Harriet waited until the children were playing a little way off before beginning to explain to Charles what had happened. She put him in the picture as well as she could. 'It's deeply mystifying,' she said in conclusion, 'because nobody knows much about the poor girl, though I've put Miss Climpson on to that. And because all – and I mean all – the people whose feelings she had hurt, or outraged might be a better word, you know what village people are like, Charles, very conservative. Where was I? Yes, all the possible probable and improbable suspects were down one of the shelters when it happened. You could hardly think of a more solid alibi. Besides—'

'Besides what?' he said. He was propped up on one elbow, lounging on the picnic blanket, with Mary stretched out beside him. She looked as contented and sleepy as a cat in a warm spot, but Charles was giving Harriet his full attention with an expression of brotherly concern.

'However infuriating she may have been, however tarty people here found her, I don't somehow think it would add up to the way she died. The way she was killed was so violent – so hands-on violent. That's a lot of hatred. So that a wandering maniac who just encountered her by accident in the street seems the only possibility, and it can't be a very likely one, besides offering no leads to the police at all.'

Charles reached round his wife for the pocket of the jacket that lay beside her, and pulled pencil and a little note-pad out of it.

'Well, let's try an orderly approach to it,' he said. 'If everybody in the village who had any motive based on knowing the woman was in the shelters, then either, one, the murderer knew her before she got here, and came to find her. Or, two, there is in fact a way out of one or other of those shelters. Or, three, one or other of the very few people who were outside – fire-watching or on ARP duties or what have you – is the one you want. Or, four, she wasn't killed because of who she was, but because of where she was.'

'She was in the middle of a village high street, under a bright moon,' said Harriet. 'And just seconds before, nearly the entire population of the village and half the airmen posted in East Anglia had been scurrying about.'

'Perhaps she saw something being done by someone who had supposed that they would not be seen, precisely because everyone would be in the shelter.'

'I don't think a wandering maniac can be the right option, Charles,' Mary chipped in, 'because how would a wandering maniac have known about a dance for the airmen, and then a practice air-raid?'

'The wandering maniac doesn't need to have known about anything; he isn't planning his crime, he just in a mad way does it at a moment's notice,' said Harriet. 'That's what makes him such an enticing possibility. Perhaps the only possibility.'

'Hold on,' said Charles. 'I know our dear Peter has a mind that hops all over the place, and I know how often his is the method that delivers the goods. But like most policemen I can't do detecting by jumping to conclusions. Dogged is what I have to be. Tempting as he is, I wouldn't go for the wandering maniac until I had carefully excluded the other possibilities.' He tore the page he had been writing on out of his notebook, and handed it to her.

'Your Superintendent Kirk is a good man,' he added. 'I expect he's dogged too, but he gets results. I rather admire a policeman who doesn't mind asking for help. Most of us can use it from time to time.'

They were interrupted by Charlie, leaving the game of

rolling down the sloping field below them to come and ask his father, 'Dad, when we get home could you have a look at my crystal set?'

Charles Parker promised his son that he would.

Miss Climpson's letter came on the following Monday. The house was very quiet, saying goodbye to their parents again having visibly depressed the Parker children, and a thin drizzling rain having ruled out cricket on the lawn. They were upstairs reading, or model making, and Harriet sat down to read Miss Climpson carefully.

My dear Lady Peter,

What a pleasure to be able to be of assistance in quite the old way, when life seems so much CHANGED from everything we were used to. And of course with Lord Peter away – Oh, I do so hope he's looking after himself in any way he can! It must be quite terrible for you to be married to a man like that, and have to do without him for months. I know that many people are in the same boat, but you would be surprised, Lady Peter, you really would, at how many of the women we interview for our surveys are quite glad of a little breathing space while their menfolk are away. Women keep telling us how they find they can do things they didn't think they could manage. I spoke to one young lady, quite a girl still, and a peaky-looking little thing, who had taken on a job in an armaments factory which was short-handed, standing in for her brother when he got called up. 'And do you know?' she said to me. 'It's quite easy! Of course I get tired at the end of the shift, but he used to make such a fuss about hard work and doing a man's job, and I find I can do it easy. It isn't as hard work as bringing up children on the dole like my mum did, nor yet as cleaning a house. I can tell you,' she said, 'when things get back to normal after we've seen off blooming Hitler, I'm not going to run around waiting hand and foot on anybody, not even if they are doing factory work. It's opened my eyes,' she said. I couldn't help wondering what sort of upheaval there would be in households up and down the land when the men get back expecting the old life, and all the women have become quite DIFFERENT while they were away.

I went down to Brighton last week, as soon as I got your letter, and I found Wendy Percival's parents quite easily, by asking at the offices of the local newspaper. Even in these days the murder of a local girl is headline news. The Percivals did not want to talk to me at first, although I tried my most SYMPATHETIC manner, but when I explained that Lord Peter had sent me to help in the hunt for the murderer they changed their minds, and asked me in, and helped me with all my questions. I hope you don't think it very SHOCKING of me, Lady Peter to say that Lord Peter had sent me, but it's very close to the truth, because I'm sure if he were at home he would have sent me, and I'm afraid I get used to telling little white lies in my line of work.

Anyway, they are a very respectable pair. Mr Percival is

a bank-manager, and a local councillor, and Mrs Percival has a colourful past – she used to be an actress, and has very glamorous pictures of herself in different roles all round the house. It's a nice Regency house at a good address, and very well furnished, in a fashion, Lady Peter, that one could call modest means with good taste. They have three daughters, but I gathered that Wendy was the favourite. I think Mrs Percival would have liked her daughter to follow her on to the stage, but Wendy didn't like the thought of the discipline of appearing every night; she liked dancing, and she liked travel and excitement.

'My daughter was a gay girl, Miss Climpson,' Mr Percival said, 'fun-loving and a little headstrong. But you see, she was so clever. She got a very good degree, and then she couldn't settle down to life at home.'

Well, the long and the short of it is, Lady Peter, that Wendy wanted to travel, and the Percivals felt that she should stand on her own feet and let them help her younger sisters find theirs. They hoped Wendy would get a good job, but she kept getting short-term work in hotels, or in shops to fund trips abroad. When the war came Mr Percival told her she should offer her language skills to the secret service, and he was disappointed when she volunteered as a land-girl. She had attended an exclusive girls' school, and some of her old friends were going into the Women's Land Army. Now I'm sure what you most wanted to know about was BOYFRIENDS. The trouble is that there were dozens of them, and the parents *couldn't keep up with them. Wendy didn't confide in them; and, Lady Peter, I can see WHY. I think it would be very trying to have parents who at one and the same time were PROUD of one, and DISAPPROVING.*

'She broke a lot of hearts,' the father told me, rather as though he were saying of a cricketer, 'He scored a lot of runs.'

I asked about letters home, but Wendy doesn't seem to have been a great letter-writer, so that they were few and far between. Mrs Percival obviously didn't want to let a stranger look at them, but she said there really was nothing in them that could possibly help the investigation. And I'm afraid there doesn't seem to have been a steady boyfriend in Brighton at whom you could point the finger of suspicion.

I must just tell you something QUITE beside the point, dear Lady Peter: Mrs Percival told me with great indignation that in the first week of the war last September troops arrived in the town, and put barbed-wire rolls along all the beaches, and those concrete tank obstacles on the promenade in case of enemy invasion. And very shortly afterwards train-loads of evacuees arrived, to take refuge in a place of safety. 'I ask you!' she said. I told her it wasn't our place to ask, really, but it does make you wonder who is in charge, Lady Peter, doesn't it!

Ever your sincere friend, and do please give my salutations and good wishes to dear Lord Peter, if you are able to write.

K. Climpson.

And, well, thought Harriet, who *was* in charge? People like her sister-in-law, Helen, Duchess of Denver, who thought, or so she had said, that it would take only one bomb falling on a seaside resort packed with children from London and the industrial towns to create a total collapse of morale, and civic disobedience. Meanwhile their grip on their own duties was such that they could fortify a beach and send hundreds of children to play on it in the same week . . .

Setting herself to expound the case of Wendy Percival, including everything she knew about it, in an orderly manner was an interesting discipline. Also it brought Peter's presence almost palpably into the room; it was for him she was writing, and to his thought patterns, his likely questions and reactions that she was addressing herself. And this process brought before her very lucidly and immediately a pre-eminent difficulty. She could hear Peter's light and rapid tones, with that undertow of seriousness audible to her when he discussed a crime; how had she ever managed to believe that he took these matters lightly, as a game of some kind? How hard it was now to remember how little she had once known and understood him! She could hear him saying that motives were a distraction. Never mind why, he used always to say, when you know how you know who. But, Peter, this time, she told him, writing rapidly in her large scrawling hand, there just isn't any mystery about how. You could ask the pathologist if you were here, and he would tell you in rather sickening detail about a lethal assault. *Why* is the problem – it just is. When we know why we'll know who, or when we know who we'll know why. And so far attempts to find a motive are failures. Of course people are muttering about the victim's morals, but if every young woman who behaved like that were murdered we'd have bodies piled up like haystacks. It's just not *substantial* enough a reason. We must be looking for something much more personal. And the dead can't tell us, can they?

She began to enter Charles's four possibilities into the account. 1) Someone knew her before. 2) There is in fact a way out of one of the shelters. 3) Someone who was above ground, fire-watching, etc. 4) It's not who she was but where she was.

Miss Climpson's letter, interesting though it was, gave no help with number one. In fact one was not susceptible to further investigation by any means Harriet could think of.

Would number three point the finger at Fred Lugg? Well, hardly. He would have had to scamper down the church tower spiral steps at high speed and up again, and there were 142 steps. She should find out as exhaustively as possible who else was on duty above ground that night. There was also of course Mrs Spright and anyone else who took French leave. Heavens! That would include even her own Mrs Trapp! How ridiculous; and yet the hard-headed truth was that anyone who didn't participate in the shelter exercise but just went peacefully to bed . . .

Harriet stared at Charles's point two. *There is in fact a way out of one of the shelters.* She hadn't even clapped eyes on the Methodists' cave. And that at least suggested a practical move. She could do some legwork on that one. She took from her desk drawer a plain brown folder, labelled it *PETER re Wendy Percival. To await return* and put in it carefully her own letter and Miss Climpson's. Then she put her hat on, and went out.

Six

O had she been a country maid,
And I the happy country swain!
Robert Burns, 'The Lass o' Ballochmyle', 1786

The Methodists had made use of the Paggleham Cave, a curious feature of which Harriet had heard, but which she had never seen. She went to find a battered *History of Paggleham*, written by one of Revered Goodacre's predecessors as vicar, which had been among the few books Harriet had inherited from her father. The cave had not, she discovered, been built as a munitions store, though doubtless it had been used as one. It had been discovered during an excavation in 1740, when the churchyard was extended to enable the construction of a mausoleum for the Wyndham family. Clearing the ground for the elaborate proposed monument the workmen had discovered a millstone, and on moving it found beneath it a gaping hole, which turned out be a deep shaft. Further investigation – carried out in the first place by lowering a farmer's boy down into the depths on a rope – had revealed a large bell-shaped cavern cut into the chalk, and half full of loose earth. A treasure-hunting frenzy soon got rid of the earth, and when nothing but a few shards and animal bones had been revealed, attention turned to the strange carvings on the solid chalk of the walls.

The Very Reverend Montague Brown, writing in 1760, had identified the figures incised in the chalk in shallow relief as early Christian saints, a selection from the multitudes of ancients with strange names like St Neot, St Uny, St Chad, and St Erth, and strange stories like a capacity to cross oceans on floating leaves, and turn cattle into parishioners. His account however, by way of indignant refutation, revealed a proponent of quite a different theory, which was that the figures and symbols were much older, were pre-Christian and deeply pagan and Druidical. In the eighteenth century a vogue for antiquarianism had brought about a demand to visit the cave, and, it being clearly impractical to lower fashionable ladies and gentlemen into the bowels of the earth on ropes, a local landowner had financed the cutting of a passage into the cave, descending at a slope. He had recouped the expense by charging a fee to enter.

The sensational interest aroused by the controversy about who the figures on the walls represented had long since died down, and now the parish council maintained the hole, keeping the sides of the passageway fenced and the original hole safely capped, and the whole thing had been very largely forgotten until the present need. Harriet obtained the keys without difficulty from the town clerk, descended the sloping ramp, and let herself in. The reason for Harriet's presence – the need to check the possibility of a sneak exit

– was satisfied at once. It was impossible. The roof of the hole loomed high above her, and the walls were vertical for about sixteen feet, before tapering in a conical shape like a beehive to the shaft at the crest. If the door made to the eighteenth-century exit were closed, then nobody could possibly have left without everyone else who was sheltering there being aware of it. The bunks that Bert Ruddle was supposedly making were in evidence along the back wall; but even using the top one as a foothold would not get a climber anywhere near the exit through the shaft above.

So that was that. But Harriet lingered, shining her torch on the walls, looking at the mysterious figures. She was struck with solemnity by them. It was not particularly in her line of thinking to be impressed by something merely on account of its being old, and it was not the dizzying antiquity of these figures that moved her now, except in the context of the present. Everything she thought of as English, the buildings of Paggleham, and the towns around, the landscape still in use largely as it was laid out and farmed by Anglo-Saxons in the Dark Ages, the beloved, gritty, earthy and lyrical tongue spoken around her, the present generation of people in all their oddity and villainy and common kindness – everything that seemed threatened with obliteration by the looming conflict – was all put in a different context by this. These mysterious figures, made in England, cut in the bones of the local modest, scarcely palpable chalk hills, had survived many conquests, many convulsions, innumerable deaths and changes, had survived their own significance, so that nobody knew what they meant, and they were still here. Still a part of things. Whatever terrible fate awaits us, she told herself inwardly, we must not overestimate it. In another thousand years somebody will stand here, looking baffled, and roused as I am to an unfocused love of country by a few bumps and scratches on a subterranean wall. I wonder why they made this massive hole, with only stag bones and horns as shovels and picks? What labour! Perhaps even then it was a shelter. She noticed that the sign on the door, worn nearly past legibility, had mentioned 'ritual worship'. Ritual worship, she thought smiling to herself, was a translation of 'The archaeologist hasn't a clue what this was for.'

She was roused from reverie by a clatter of boots, and the arrival of Bert Ruddle.

'Morning, mum. Wasn't expecting anyone down here,' he said cheerfully. 'You won't mind if I gets on? Only I got to get this saw back to that old misery-guts George Withers. Said he would put up 'is Anderson in 'is own garden, and keep 'is own company, and that's what he's a-doing.' Bert gave Harriet a gap-toothed grin. 'Ground's as hard as concrete in 'is garden, and nobody wants to lend the old blighter a hand, so he's got his work cut out.'

'But you're helping him, Bert?'

'Fair exchange. I'm agreed to cut the timber for his bunk when I takes back 'is saw. That's a lovely saw he's got. Runs a treat. And I got to get done here before I takes it back.' He was carrying a handsaw and a length of wood. 'Makes a row when I get sawing,' he remarked.

'Oh, I'm going now, Bert. I was just checking up that there isn't any other way out.'

'You want to try the other shelter for that,' he said.

'The cellars of the Crown? I thought . . .'

'There's a lot of beer what's kept down there, mum,' he said, 'and people have been known to get thirsty when they didn't have money to spend. Not that I done it myself,' he added, seeming suddenly to see what he had let slip, 'but I've heard of it.'

'I see,' she said. 'Thank you for the tip-off, Bert.'

'It'd more likely be a Church matter than a Chapel matter, anyways,' he said.

'What would? Pinching beer?'

'Murdering wenches,' he said. 'Not a Methodist way of carrying on, if you ask me. Now I've got to get on, mum, if you don't mind.'

Harriet's next call, obviously, must be to the Crown. Harriet walked across there, enjoying the fine morning, and found a shining powerful motor-bike parked beside the horse trough in the Square. A young airman seated astride it hailed her.

'I say, can you help me?'

Harriet walked across to him. 'I heard a wild rumour that my pal Brinklow was hanging around here somewhere,' he said. 'Do you know where I might find him?'

'He's got a cottage just up the lane on your right,' Harriet said.

'Been there,' the officer said. 'He's not at home. And I've

only got an hour left for a two-hour drive. I seem to have missed him.'

'Can I give him a message?' asked Harriet.

'Good thinking. It's a bit rich of him not to let us know where he is. We've all been worried sick about him. Tell him to show a leg and come and chat to his mess-mates.'

'I will tell him that,' said Harriet. 'I understand he's recuperating, from injuries sustained when he baled out. I don't think he can drive, he has a broken ankle. That's probably why he hasn't visited base.'

'Hum,' said her interlocutor. 'Can't make a phone call, either? It's the merest chance I heard he was here. Fellow mentioned hearing his name at some dance or other. I'll post it up on the mess notice-board now, though, so tell him to drop us a line.'

'I will when I see him,' said Harriet. 'Who shall I say was asking for him?'

'Er, Mike Newcastle. I'm glad the old beggar's all right; I've been missing him. He's got a good line in wise-cracks.'

With that the stranger revved up the engine, and with a squeal of brakes on the bend in the street was off at alarming speed.

Mr Gudgeon welcomed her, and offered her an out-of-hours beer, so long as she would step into the sitting-room; it was more than his licence was worth to have anyone drinking in the bar before opening time. Harriet thanked him and declined. She would drink beer very gladly when she was on a long walk, or thirsty from gardening, but to drink it in cold blood, so to speak, in the middle of the morning did not appeal to her.

'Mrs Gudgeon would make a pot of tea, my lady, if I asks her,' said Mr Gudgeon. 'She's just washing glasses, and the kettle is quite handy.'

'No, please don't put her to any trouble, Mr Gudgeon. I'm here on a particular errand, and I don't need tea. I have heard a rumour that there is more than one way in to the cellars of the Crown, and I feel honour-bound to follow it up.'

'It's news to me, m'lady,' said Mr Gudgeon.

'Well then, I expect it's wrong.'

'Mind you, I have just wondered, now and then . . .'

'Wondered?'

'It has happened that a barrel has run dry before I expected it to. I thought the brewery had given short measure, but it's hard to be sure. If someone had been taking off a pint or so behind my back, that would explain it. But I haven't any idea how they would get in.'

'There isn't a back door, or a ventilation shaft somewhere?'

'No back door. But there is a chimney sort of thing that lets a bit of air in; I'll show you if you like.'

He led the way down the stone steps into the vaults. There were signs of activity since Harriet had last been down here: folding chairs, a shelf of books, a beginning on building bunks. Mr Puffett had been quicker off the mark than Bert Ruddle, and the Church people would be cosy sooner than the Chapel people. Mr Gudgeon led the way through the cellars under the vaulted arches right to the far end, where he had a pair of enormous barrels lying on their sides on trestles. Between them a column of grey pallid light full of floating motes of dust stood on a disc of light cast on the floor. Looking up, Harriet saw a roundel of sky at the head of the shaft, criss-crossed with brambles. Mr Gudgeon's torch lit a few rungs of a set of metal footholds in the sides of the shaft, all rusted, and some missing.

'You would have to be very thirsty, I would think,' said Harriet.

'You'd need a rope lowered from above to use this, seems to me,' said Mr Gudgeon. 'We could have a look outside.'

Outside, in the overgrown orchard behind the pub, the head of the shaft took quite a bit of finding. It came up into a thick bramble patch, in which it was barely visible. Rather to Harriet's surprise, however, there was a coil of rope, lying partly concealed in the nettles under a leaning apple tree.

'When did you last miss any beer, Mr Gudgeon?' asked Harriet.

'Quite a bit ago. Before the war,' he said.

Harriet was rather at a loss. Could the coil of rope have been used recently? She looked to see the tell-tale ring of bleached grass that it would have left if moved slightly, and could not see it. Grass grew quickly at this time of year, however. There were no fallen leaves on the rope, no grass pushing up through the loops of the coil. Obviously it was not completely impossible that the rope had been tied round the trunk of the tree a fortnight ago, and used for somebody's ascent from the shelter. Even, conceivably, their ascent and return. But how could someone have been certain that they would not be seen, climbing up a rope between the barrels?

Only in a certain kind of detection fiction, she reflected, could such a device be used. It would be part of a murder that could have been carried out, but which could not possibly have been planned. Several people who were in the vaults of the Crown could have realised, in theory, that Wendy Percival was not present, and therefore might be on her way there, and in that case would have been moving around alone above ground. But they could have had only a few minutes' notice of that, and the rope would have needed to be provided ahead. There was no sense in this.

'I think I'll take this with me,' said Mr Gudgeon, looping the coil of rope over his arm. 'Safety first.'

'Talking of safety,' she said, as they walked back across the orchard, 'is that shaft safe? Could someone fall in?'

'After they pushed through all those brambles I suppose they could,' said Mr Gudgeon. 'They'd have some scratches to show for it.'

'Has it always been overgrown like that?'

'It's got more so since Clive Martin's joined up,' said Mr Gudgeon. 'He used to scythe it off for me once in a while.'

'And does everyone know about it?'

'Well, local lads would know. I've heard of it being a bit of a dare, when I was a boy.'

Harriet thanked him and left it at that. The murderer, if he had used that method of being in two places at once, however, would obviously have scratched his hands and face. He must also have been thin and agile. Charles's point two didn't lead anywhere. She could cross it off the list.

The next morning Archie Lugg presented himself in the kitchen at Talboys, saying as how he understood some shelves were wanted. Harriet escorted him up the stairs to the landing where she showed him an alcove which could take some more of the London books if it had shelves across it, top to bottom. Archie said, 'The job itself is no problem – a cinch, m'lady. But the timber is another thing. I can't get a good bit of timber for love nor money.'

'Oh, well then, we'll have to manage without,' said Harriet. 'Pity, but it isn't the end of the world.'

'What I could do,' said Archie musingly, 'is use the shelves out of that old wardrobe I got at the sales the other day. There's six good mahogany shelves in there that might be long enough. I'd have to measure.'

'Mahogany is a bit too grand, isn't it, Archie?' said Harriet. 'I was thinking of painting them white. Isn't it a pity to vandalise an old wardrobe?'

'Nope,' he said. 'That's got two broken doors and the back stove in. I paid one an' six for that only on account of the shelves. And it's what I've got to hand, m'lady. We can't pick and choose no more.'

'Okay, Archie. But we won't actually paint them in that case.'

'They'll look lovely with a coat or two of yacht varnish,' he said.

'Fine. Archie, before you go there is something I would like to ask you about. I believe you knew Wendy Percival?'

'I thought you'd get round to that. You didn't have to order shelves from me to bring that up. I'd' a told you anyway.'

'We need the shelves anyway. How well did you know her?'

'Not well enough,' he said bitterly. 'Not enough to tell when she was having me on, and when she meant it.'

'Meant what?'

'Oh, you know,' he said, shrugging his shoulders. 'She made out she thought you were the cat's whiskers, and then you found someone else was getting buttered up just the same. Me and Jake nearly came to blows over her, and we're old friends. Jake had even put down the deposit on a ring. It was that bad.'

'You were both very angry?' said Harriet quietly.

'Not so much angry as miserable,' he said. 'I didn't kill her, lady, and I'll call you to witness that I didn't, since I was down the shelter with my mum, and you saw me there. And I was right at the back when we was leaving, and you'd found her lying there before I got up the steps. But wherever I might have been, I couldn't have harmed her, not to save my life.'

His tone of voice carried a clear message to Harriet. The poor man had really loved Wendy. However foolishly.

'All right, Archie. But you understand questions have to be asked.'

'Oh, you go asking around till you find him that did it,' said Archie. 'I'm all in favour. But one thing I will say, and that's when you find him, you get him safely locked away before I know his name, because if I get my hands on him he won't swing – as God's my witness I'll kill him with my two hands and take the consequences!'

'And the awful thing is,' wrote Harriet to Peter that evening, 'that I believed him.'

Finding Jake Datchett was the obvious next step. Harriet went in search of him, and found him in the barn at Datchett's farm, with his father, checking up supplies of animal feed.

Jake did not react well. He was a gangly youth, with a shock of very red hair. 'I'm not talking to you!' he said, when she asked how well he knew Wendy. 'Why should I? If that Superintendent Kirk wants to ask me things, he can come and ask me himself, not send his la-di-da friends along. You're not even a policewoman. Push off.'

Datchett senior said, 'He's very upset, and it makes him angry. Everyone's asking him about the blasted girl, and he can't have a drink in peace, or get it out of his head of an evening.' To his son he said, 'Have a bit of sense, son. You wasn't involved and the quicker everyone realises that the better. You tell the lady what she wants to know.'

Harriet said to Jake's sullen silence, 'I'll make it quick.

Do you know anything about Wendy's whereabouts on the evening of her death? Before the all-clear?'

'No I don't. She promised me a dance. Two dances, to put Archie Lugg in his place. And then she didn't show up at all. I could have killed her!'

'She'd have led you a pretty dance as a wife, boy,' observed Roger Datchett.

'But you did think she might marry you?' prompted Harriet.

'Well, what would *you* think?' Jake demanded. 'If a girl will walk up the lane with you, have a roll in the hay with you, let you kiss her and feel her a bit? Our country girls may be rough and ready, but they don't do that unless they means to have you. They'd be a scandal all the way to Broxford if they did. Their mothers would have something to say. I didn't expect she was a whore. I thought Archie was lying when he said she'd a been doing the same with him, and I clopped him one.'

'The long and the short of this,' said Roger Datchett, 'is that everyone's running round asking about Archie and Jake here, and neither of them could have done it, because of that blessed air-raid. Thank heavens for that, I say. I thought it was stupid at the time, keeping us out of our beds for nothing when we have to be up early in the morning, but it's turned out a blessing and no mistake.'

'You are right to be angry,' said Harriet to Jake. 'It isn't kind, to put it mildly, I agree, to flirt like that.'

'I suppose it's what they do in towns,' he said dejectedly. 'She said so. She laughed at me for having bumpkin ideas.

She said' – his voice rising to a pitch of indignation – 'that most of the men she knew would have been grateful to have a bit of a snog and get away with it, instead of expecting you were theirs for life because of a kiss and a cuddle.'

'And you don't know anything that might throw light on this?' said Harriet, addressing Jake. 'You know Wendy wasn't at the dance, and you don't know why?'

'Along of having promised the last waltz to more than one man, I thought,' he said. 'Perhaps more than two of us, for all I know. Perhaps she couldn't show her face because she'd promised to dance with the whole blooming lot of us! Someone lost his rag with her,' he added sombrely, 'but it wasn't me.'

Harriet believed him. He looked too slight and stringy to be the brutal assailant they were after. But then as she turned to go, he picked up a huge bale of hay from the floor of the barn, stepped up a ladder, and heaved his burden up into the hay-loft as though it had been as light as chaff. And she noticed the backs of his hands were covered in scratches.

But there didn't seem to be anything of consequence to report to Superintendent Kirk.

It was nothing but idle curiosity that moved Harriet a few days later to look for the pig-killing apparatus. Her curiosity had been triggered by the astonishing appearance on the dinner table of a splendid array of pork chops – a feast no less. This unexpectedly spectacular dinner made

Harriet realise that although nobody in her household was actually going short, they were not exactly *hungry*, yet even so the sensation of being really full and satisfied, so that you couldn't eat another mouthful, had become an unusual one. It had made Harriet very sleepy. However had one managed in peace-time to digest so much food? But the explanation for the plenty must be that someone in the pig club had slaughtered an animal that week, and there had been a share-out. Something about the indignation expressed by Mrs Ruddle over Ministry regulations meddling with what goes on in people's own back yards made Harriet think better of asking questions; but the piglet who was coming their way had already been chosen and named Goering, and would be arriving to the joy of the children quite soon, and Harriet just thought she would inspect its future exit before it made an entry.

Talboys had once been the house for an ample farm, with barns and byres and sheds in two courtyards extending beside it. Peter had bought the yard nearer to the house three years ago, mentioning garaging for the Daimler, stabling for ponies for the children, and a desire to keep the threshing machines a little way removed from his windows. John Bateson had readily agreed – when was a farmer not short of cash? He had kept the more distant yard, which is where he had billeted his land-girls, and he was using all his range of buildings. But quite accidentally Talboys had acquired the shed used for pig-killing. Nobody, as far as Harriet could remember, had mentioned this at the time, or perhaps Peter had known and given permission? More likely the villagers had continued to use the shed as from time immemorial, and assumed permission.

Harriet found it easily, because it had a hasp and ring for a padlock, although there wasn't one there. She felt a tremor of dread at stepping into it, but there was nothing to see at first as she blinked in the darkness. It smelled quite sweet and clean, because it was full of straw, baled up, and stacked against a wall. There were a number of buckets, and a wide shallow half-barrel lined up along the back wall. Her eyes got used to the dimness, and a twittering of disturbed bats made her look up. The shed had robust roof timbers and crossbeams, and the equipment was overhead. It was an elaborate rig-up and it took Harriet a moment to understand it. A hefty, yard-square chunk of concrete with a ring in the top of it was standing on a wooden platform. A rope knotted firmly to the ring ran over a large pulley attached to the ridge beam; the surplus rope then hung slack over a hook in the lowest beam in the roof space. Harriet reached up and unhooked the loops of rope, which uncoiled and reached the floor. A running noose now lay on the shed floor at her feet, and she saw that a ring had been painted on the bricks of the floor, marking the spot where the noose fell. If something dislodged the concrete block it would come crashing down, and anything caught in the noose would be hoisted suddenly upwards and left hanging. Upside down, if it was a pig, presumably.

And sure enough, in the gloom of the roof-space she could now see that the platform supporting the block was hinged, and wedged. If you knocked the wedge out . . . she shuddered, and stepped away from the noose.

'We ought to put that back out of reach,' observed a voice behind her. 'There's little children playing here.' Harriet looked round and saw that Sam Bateson had appeared in the shed door, and was watching her.

'Oh, Sam,' she said.

'I thought I'd see you didn't hurt yourself,' he said. 'We're not allowed in here.'

'I should think not!' she said, gathering up the rope in loops and hooking it back on the beam, out of reach of the younger children. 'I'll get a padlock for that door.'

'It isn't *that* dangerous,' he said. 'It makes a noise. Someone would come.'

'Would we hear it at Talboys?' she asked. 'Mightn't it upset the children if they had got fond of the pig?'

'It makes a crash and a rumble,' he told her. 'You never hear the pig. He shoots up off the ground hanging by his hind legs, and the butcher leans round from behind him, and cuts his throat before he can squeal. That don't feel a thing. Promise.'

He was looking anxious, and Harriet realised that he was afraid she might veto piglet Goering if she thought the creature would suffer. But she was obviously looking unconvinced, because he continued chatting. 'We had a butcher once when we heard the pig squealing, and Dad was furious. Said it wasn't humane and it wasn't needful. We're never going to have that one again. We have a friend of our uncle who farms up at Louth. He gets a lift on a vegetable truck when he's needed, and he does it quick as a flash.'

'All right, Sam, I believe you,' said Harriet, amused at this child's protective instinct. Sam had made sure she didn't get tangled in the rope, and now he was making sure she didn't have nightmares. And he could fix crystal sets too! How old was this paragon? Twelve? He might even be younger; farm children were better fed than most of the evacuees and now they were all in the village school together you could make the comparison. 'Thank you for helping fix Charlie's crystal set,' she said.

'Oh, I didn't fix that,' he said. 'That's like Dad's awful harvester machine – works and then doesn't and then does. That's always broke when we need it, and that's mended itself when we call Jake Datchett to fix it, and as soon as he's gone home that's broke again.'

'It's devilish, isn't it?' said Harriet sympathetically. Sam seemed intent on walking her home to the front door.

'I've got a book about how to spot enemy aircraft,' he said, changing the subject. 'I've learned it all up although I'm too young to do the sky-watching. And I haven't seen a single enemy aircraft yet. I can't wait!'

'Oh yes, you can, Sam,' she said. 'The longer the better.'

Sam Bateson, Harriet concluded, thinking over her day as she sat with a mug of Ovaltine beside the last glow of the living-room fire, was a sensible sort of boy, with a well-developed sense of responsibility. Young Charlie was not likely to come to harm playing with him. Why had she wondered about him? She couldn't remember. And she put it out of her mind to think of other things.

Seven

I have often admired the mystical way of Pythagoras,
and the secret magic of numbers.

Sir Thomas Browne, *Religio Medici*, 1643

Harriet reached home around noon, and as she entered her drawing-room found someone waiting for her. Someone who rose as she entered. Someone pin-striped, sleek, and with that ominous look of the official.

She stopped in her tracks, arrested as she pulled off her left glove, with fear raising her heartbeat, and constricting her throat. 'Peter?' she said.

'Yes,' he said. 'Don't be alarmed.'

She could feel a strange sensation on her cheeks which must be her colour draining from them, and it must be visible as well as palpable.

'You had better sit down, Lady Peter,' the stranger said. 'Can I get you a glass of water? Can I ring for someone?'

She did sit down. 'Excuse me,' she said, 'but who are you?'

'Call me Bungo,' he said. The silly name rang a distant bell with her, but she couldn't place it.

'With news of Peter?'

'Perhaps. There is an indecipherable in from him.'

'A what?'

'Sorry. An encoded message that our people cannot decode. He knows as much. There are four words in clear: "Donne undone – only Harriet."'

'What does he mean?' she asked.

'Almost certainly that only you can guess his cipher text. The established one was John Donne's *Songs and Sonnets*, used at random.'

'I would have guessed that,' Harriet said.

'Someone has, I'm afraid. So for that, or some other reason, he has chosen something else, something we do not know about. And he thinks you will know. May I ask how much you understand about codes, Lady Peter?'

'Very little. I was once involved in a case in which there was a letter to be decoded. It was a thing with a grid and a key-word.'

'There are various ways of using grids,' he said. 'That sounds like a Playfair cipher of some sort. This is a different idea – a book code. May I tell you how it works?'

'Is Peter in danger?' she asked. 'Will this help Peter?'

'I cannot tell you for certain. I can only say that he might be, and that it might.'

'Then I must give it all the strength of mind I can command,' she said.

'Good girl,' said Bungo. 'The difficulty with many codes is that you have to send the key at some time. Or, worse, your agent has to carry the key. I need hardly spell out the dangers. Whereas if you use an agreed text as a key, then the agent can memorise it, and if he or she is captured there is nothing that can be discovered.'

'I see. But how does a book work as a key?'

'First you number all the words in the key text; it needs to be a certain minimum length, although even with quite a chunky one some letters – q, x – can be difficult. Then you use the number assigned to the word to stand for the initial letter of the word. Or sometimes another letter – third, last, or whatever. It's a fairly robust code, because you can usually use several different numbers for each letter of the alphabet, so the frequency decode doesn't work very well.'

'You'll have to explain some more. What is a frequency decode?'

'Basically a method of guessing and trying based on the idea that whatever symbol is the most frequent in the encoded message is likely to represent E, the next most frequent T and so on. But look, don't bother about that, just take my word for it. Book codes are difficult to crack quickly unless you know the key text, although one can sit patiently with a copy of the *Oxford Anthology of English Verse*, and the complete works of Shakespeare, or Magna Carta or something. But if you know the key text it's a piece of cake. And your husband thinks you, and you alone, will be able to guess it.'

'Let me think, let me think about this. It's an emergency, otherwise he would use his established key.'

'It would seem so.'

Harriet gazed at the stranger with a sudden wave of

loathing. How could he talk calmly about this? Didn't he know that without Peter the world would be at an end? Well, no, she thought, struggling to get a grip on herself, he might not even have met Peter.

'This is the message,' he said. He held out a flimsy loose-leaf sheet of paper, and Harriet took it.

It said: 'Donne undone. Only Harriet.' Then:

78 17 38 104 75
3 91 87 106 49
114 17 83 49 10
20 62 27 55 49
5 42 32 63 10
36 62 2 1 26 68
99 106 3 79 11
121 94 37 106 99
18 84 53 62 20
69 63 114 40 58
44 101 117 77 29
101 112 38 64 34
81 99 94 35 38
32 102 110 21 49
6 9 88 18 19
81 7 49 61 8
18 62 6 3 56
19 68 7 20 21
49 59 1 32 9
20 69 68 20 68
55 64 42 64 24 41 102

119 118 32 112 50 3
36 105 121 69 33
62 15 108 69 121
64 53 13 49 11
21 51 68 7 106
25 62 7 32 5
72 20 11 3 31 61

'But what sort of message is this? Did somebody bring it? Did they see Peter?'

'Oh, no. It's a radio message sent in Morse code. And rather dangerous, because all the time they are transmitting they can be detected by the enemy. Our radio operators move about a lot, and never send twice from the same location. So these numbers have been taken down as a series of blips on a radio receiver.'

'I see. What do I have to do?' she asked.

'You suggest things that might be the cipher text, and we try them till something makes sense.'

'Leave it with me and I'll do what I can.'

'Okay,' he said. 'You've grasped how to try it? I'll wait in your very pretty garden, if I may.'

He appalled her. She had thought he would go back to London and she would send news by and by. However long it took. But if he was going to wait in the garden . . .

'It's that urgent?' she said.

'It might be,' he said. 'We need to crack it before an enemy could. Do your best, for everyone's sake.'

Harriet took the paper upstairs to her bedroom. She

was trembling. This was no mood in which to try to climb intellectual monkey puzzles. But the room contained memories. Peter wildly riding a chair like a rocking-horse, crying out to her while she recited: '*I am the Queen Aholibah*', and she had broken in to implore Peter not to break the chair. She had called him a madman. Could Aholibah be what he meant? She took a pencil and began to number the words as she wrote them down.

> I^1 *am*^{2} *the*^{3} *Queen*^{4} *Aholibah*^{5},
> *My*^{6} *lips*^{7} *kissed*^{8} *the*^{9} *dumb*^{10} *word*^{11} *of*^{12} *Ah*^{13},
> *Sighed*^{14} *on*^{15} *strange*^{16} *lips*^{17} *grown*^{18} *sick*^{19}
>   *thereby*^{20}.
> *God*^{21} *wrought*^{22} *to*^{23} *me*^{24} *my*^{25} *royal*^{26} *bed*^{27},
> *The inner work thereof was red,*
> *The outer work was ivory*
> *My mouth's heat was the heat of flame*
> *With lust towards the kings that came*
> *With horsemen riding royally –*

She put the indecipherable page down beside it, and began to work. But there were not enough words. The first line of the message contained the number 104. There were – she counted quickly to the end – only fifty-six words in the stanza. How did it go on? In the great sequence of ghostly queens, who came next? Herodias, Aholibah, Cleopatra; could Peter know all this by heart? She herself could not remember Cleopatra, and had to go downstairs to fetch Swinburne from the shelf. Bungo was visible at the end of the garden as she glanced through the window, peacefully holding *The Times*, apparently at work on the crossword.

Harriet found herself unable to hate him now, because she was inwardly alight with memory, with the horseman riding a chair, and her horseman had called for Aholibah, not Cleopatra. Well, she could hardly have figured as Cleopatra even in Peter's inflamed nuptial vision! She returned to the bedroom and began to number the words in 'Cleopatra'. Even in this emergency she couldn't help noticing that it was a horribly bad stanza:

> *I am the Queen of Ethiope*
> *Love bade my kissing eyelids ope*
> *That men beholding might praise love*
> *My hair was wonderful and curled –*

Oh, really! It simply beggared belief that Peter, who had stuffed away somewhere in his head a vast conspectus of English poetry, should choose to hang his fate on this. She was on the wrong track surely.

So what was the right track? What about '*Auprès de ma Blonde.*'? He had sung that, rather scandalously, on their honeymoon, and Bunter had had to shush him, because there was, after all, a dead body hauled out of the cellar and requiring to have notice taken of it, and due respect paid.

She stared again at the encoded message. Only Harriet. Only she. Nobody else would be able to crack it, and so logically it wasn't Swinburne or anyone else in the corpus of English literature. However unlikely any obscure poem might be, Peter could not be absolutely sure that a code-breaker would not try it. There might be, there probably were, teams of code-breakers working day and night on these things, trying one text after another. That would take time, of course. Could he have been relying on her for a short cut to something that might be found by others, but would not be found quickly? But he could have said 'Try Harriet' or something like that.

'Let's take him literally,' she told herself. 'He doesn't use words sloppily, even when nothing depends on it. So assume that the code text isn't published; it really is something only I would know.' What about the wonderful Donne autograph letter on sacred and profane love which she had ingeniously contrived to buy for his wedding present? That wasn't published anywhere; but no, the other two of his four words said it wasn't Donne. They didn't say it wasn't the *Songs and Sonnets* which he had been using, but that it wasn't Donne. So all right, it wasn't.

Harriet felt as though she were blundering about in the mist. She was so frightened for Peter she simply couldn't see straight. How much time had she already wasted on the harlot Aholibah? The shadows on the lawn were lengthening, and Bungo had retreated from the garden seat. Was Sadie or Mrs Trapp offering him tea? Should she go down and make sure he had been offered tea?

'Hell!' she told herself angrily. 'This isn't a social call! Keep your mind on it, Harriet.' But the thought of tea had started another memory. Tea in a punt, a punt moored up under a willow tree, containing a lord who was then her suitor, but not her husband. She had handed him a dossier of everything she had recorded about the poison-pen menace at Shrewsbury College, and she had accidentally left in it a page containing an incomplete sonnet. When he had given the dossier back to her the octet had sprouted a sestet – rather a good one.

Suddenly certain, Harriet went to her filing cabinet to look for the notes. Were they here? Most of the paperwork had been brought up from London lest it be incinerated by enemy action. The sitting-room at Talboys wasn't a place for filing cabinets, even handsome ones with art deco handles bought on the Tottenham Court Road, so they were in a cupboard in the back hallway. But the dossier was there; whatever you thought of the secretary, Miss Bracey, who had left rather than be dragged into Hertfordshire, she had been a whizz at filing.

Harriet retrieved the dossier with a growing sense of triumph. This would be it. Of course it would. She found the poem, sat down to her desk again, and began to number the words.

Here[1] then[2] at[3] home[4], by[5] no[6] more[7] storms[8]
     distrest[9],
Folding[10] laborious[11] hands[12] we[13] sit[14], wings[15]
     furled[16];
Here[17] in[18] close[19] perfume[20] lies[21] the[22] rose-leaf[23]
     curled[24],
Here[25] the[26] sun[27] stands[28] and[29] knows[30] not[31]
     east[32] nor[33] west[34],

*Here[35] no[36] tide[37] runs[38]; we[39] have[40] come[41], last[42]
and[43] best[44],*
*From[45] the[46] wide[47] zone[48] in[49] dizzying[50] circles[51]
hurled[52]*
*To[53] that[54] still[55] centre[56] where[57] the[58] spinning[59]
world[60]*
*Sleeps[61] on[62] its[63] axis[64], to[65] the[66] heart[67] of[68]
rest[69].*

*Lay[70] on[71] thy[72] whips[73], O[74] Love[75], that[76] we[77]
upright[78],*
*Poised[79] on[80] the[81] perilous[82] point[83], in[84] no[85] lax[86]
bed[87]*
*May[88] sleep[89], as[90] tension[91] at[92] the[93] verberant[94]
core[95]*
*Of[96] music[97] sleeps[98]; for[99], if[100] thou[101] spare[102]
to[103] smite[104],*
*Staggering[105], we[106] stoop[107], stooping[108], fall[109]
dumb[110] and[111] dead[112],*
*And[113], dying[114], so[115], sleep[116] our[117] sweet[118]
sleep[119] no[120] more[121].*

One hundred and twenty-one words. She looked, rapidly. Yes, there was no number higher than 121 in the cipher. She began to decrypt it:

78 17 38 104 75 – uhrsl
3 91 87 106 49 – atbwi
114 17 83 49 10 – shpif

She looked at the result in despair. However she shuffled

these letters, however she ran them together to re-divide them into words, they didn't make sense. This wasn't, after all, the key? Or the coding method wasn't what Bungo had described? Should she ask him for help? Wait – he had said, hadn't he? you used the first or the last or the second or third letter, etc. What if the letter being used was not after all the first of the word? What about the last? She tried again.

78 17 38 104 75 – tesee
3 91 87 106 49 – ttdwn

This wasn't coming out any better. She stared angrily at the jumble. The only set of letters that looked at all like the shape of a word was that one: tesee. Of course there was no certainty that the numbers were the actual words; they had been re-arranged in groups of five throughout. She was about to move on when a thought struck her: she could think of one common five-letter word in the English language which ended in double e – three. Could she have transcribed the second and the third letters wrongly? She looked again and it jumped out at her: the last letter of word 17 was e, but the first letter was h; the last letter of word 38 was s, but the first letter was r – presto! She had the word 'three' using a combination of first and last letters, and she saw at once that the first letters were in the first and the last letters were in the second and last stanza.

She began to work with furious concentration: 'three and eight if possible'. Well, it clearly wasn't possible for that to be a coincidence – she had cracked it.' If not H should read letter in top right bureau drawer. Three blind mice.'

Whatever was that doing? Oh, of course, the Wimsey Arms, three mice courant. That was the end of the message then, and it would move on to the beginning. In fifteen minutes she had it.

> Mission accomplished. Proposal accepted.
> Danger now great. Will come home by plans
> three and eight if possible. If not H to read
> letter in top right bureau drawer. Three
> blind mice.

She wrote it out carefully, as legibly as her energetic handwriting would permit, and carried it downstairs to find Bungo. He was sitting in the drawing-room with a tea tray on a table in front of him, and a large piece of Mrs Trapp's cake on a little Royal Derby plate. 'He came to the party, and ate just as heartily as if he'd been really invited, Harriet thought; but why be so hard on him? She must try not to shoot the messenger. She held the paper out to him.

He jumped up and took it, and scanned it rapidly. 'Ah, yes,' he said.

'Is it very bad?' she asked him.

'Well, they're coming home separately,' he answered. 'Look, may I check this?'

'It was a private thing,' she said obstinately. 'You'll have to trust me.' He hesitated and she said, 'If Peter can trust me for his life, surely you can.'

He folded the paper into his breast pocket, and said, 'Well, I'd better rush. Plans three and eight will need initiating.'

'Of course. Do you need a lift to the station at Paggleford?'

'I have my driver waiting in the lane,' he said. 'I'll let you know if I can. If there's anything. Thank you for tea. Oh, and – look, don't worry too much. Old Wimbles has a habit of survival.' And he was gone.

Harriet went slowly upstairs again, and moved as if hypnotised to the little dressing-room which contained Peter's bureau. A large, handsomely veneered thing with a flap-down writing surface, and numerous drawers and secret drawers. She had never opened it, nor ever looked at anything of his that he kept shut away. But with a sense of trespass she opened it now. It was not locked. Her hand moved as if of itself to the top right drawer. It contained a letter in an envelope of thick laid paper, sealed with his distinctive dark red sealing wax, pressed with the signet ring he wore on the third finger of his right hand. He was not wearing the ring now; it was there in the drawer. Harriet took the letter, and went to sit quietly in the window seat holding it. Turning it over she saw it was addressed to: *Harriet, after my death, or presumed death.*

At once the urge to open it, the human curiosity, the aching need for words from him which must have been what led to this, to her having it in her hand, abruptly and totally left her. 'I will presume no such thing,' she said, aloud. 'And this is not addressed to me. Because I am not who I would be after his death. I am not his widow, I am his wife.' And with that thought came a kind of muted astonishment. She was Peter's wife, she who had fought him off for so long, who had led him a pretty dance for all those years; what she would give now for even an hour or two of all that wasted time, in which she could have been with him, and would not! She could have settled, though it would have been on the wrong terms, and with that her mind jumped to the perilous state of the world. The country she was sitting in now, late, with the one lamp lighted in the room, and the owl hooting somewhere outside, this fortress built by nature for herself, this blessed plot, this earth, this realm, this England could likewise settle, though it would be on the wrong terms. There wasn't any doubt, really, about the need for the right terms, and so she should not harbour regrets.

And with wry amusement she remembered how appalling to her in prospect had been the wealth and privilege of being Peter's wife, how she had withstood it, stiff-necked, how she might well have run off with him and seized their happiness at once if he had been a pauper, or any sort of under-dog, and how brief in the event had been the enjoyment of wealth and comfort, how swiftly the war was levelling everyone, casting down the mighty so that not even crowns and coronets got you more than four ounces of butter a week, and a large house with space and air meant you got strangers billeted on you, and an end of peace and privacy. She should have known it would be fool's gold, all that status and luxury, so very much not what she was born for. She couldn't blame life for taking her down a peg. And she didn't mind, not *really*. The only thing she minded about all this was being parted from Peter, and fearing for his safety. Fearing for the safety of the children . . .

When he comes home, she thought, putting his letter unopened back in the bureau drawer, I shall never complain about any hardship. And it occurred to her then that her life had prepared her for the endurance of a fairly rough existence, for all the make do and mend going on round her, even for barely sufficient amounts to eat. It was Peter who would find the going tough. Peter who was used to the goose-feather bed . . . and then the thought corrected itself. Peter had taken with astonishing calm the disastrous first night in this very house, when the grates were cold, he had to wash under a cold pump, there had been only a scratch supper. What had that incredible man called Bungo just told her: 'Wimbles has a habit of survival'? That would apply, presumably, in peace as well as war. She slipped Peter's ring on to her own finger, closed the bureau, switched off the lamp in the dressing-room and went to her solitary bed.

Eight

If thou beest he; but O how fall'n, how changed
From him who in the happy realms of light
Clothed with transcendent brightness did outshine
Myriads, though bright . . .
John Milton, *Paradise Lost*, 1667

E veryone was being enjoined not to travel: 'Is your journey really necessary?' enquired government posters.
And people were being told that visiting their displaced
children wasn't necessary, or not very often. But Harriet
had a message from Mr Murbles, the family solicitor,
asking her to call at her earliest convenience, so she
intended to ignore the posters, dreamed up by someone
in the Ministry of Instruction and Morale, if not Helen
then someone just like her. There were a number of small
errands that she could do on the same trip: several books
she needed, a little work-box that Mrs Trapp had left in
the housekeeper's room in the London house, and would
be glad to have again, and she had arranged to have lunch
with her old friend Eiluned Price. She was looking forward
to the trip, she thought. And yet she wasn't quite. It was
one thing to have got used to the absence of her husband

at Talboys. Experiencing his absence in the London house would be another thing. So she had hedged the visit to the house all about with Eiluned and Hatchard's, in case it pained her.

She noticed with a sort of detached interest that these days she had to manage her emotions as though they were a dog that might bite, or a turbulent child. She used to have to do that, long ago, before she married Peter. She had had a lot of practice in a troubled life. But marriage had left her unaccustomed to it, and she was relearning something. No doubt she would manage London. She loved London as only those brought up in a village can love it, taking nothing about it for granted. She was getting a very early train from Great Paggleham.

The train was packed with men and women in uniform, or with the ubiquitous armbands – WAS, HDV, WRVS, ARW – which stood in for uniform. Kit-bags and gas-mask cases in the luggage racks loomed dangerously above people's heads. The windows were dirty, and the modestly beautiful Hertfordshire landscape rolled past unseen. A shower of rain washed the glass enough for Harriet to see Hackney Marshes as the train approached Liverpool Street. Harriet thought she should leave taxis for those with urgent business, so she thrust her way through the crowd and got on a bus to the solicitor's office.

The bus too was crowded, and the windows were covered in a mesh of scrim with only a little diamond left in the middle to help you peer out and see where you were. Harriet peered. She saw the sandbagged shop-fronts, the queues at bakers' shops, the air-raid wardens' posts that had sprung up on every corner, the window glass criss-crossed with tape, or boarded up. The city had a sombre and businesslike air, bracing itself for the ordeal to come. Her bus swung round Piccadilly Circus, round the swathed plinth minus its Eros, and up Regent Street, past the Café Royal. A crowd of ball-gowned girls and men in evening dress were emerging on the pavement, blinking at the bright morning.

'Strewth!' said a man sitting beside Harriet. 'Don't they know there's a war on?'

'That lot don't know they're born!' said the bus conductor, swaying on his feet as the bus swept round the curve of the Quadrant.

'Ah, don't be mean,' said the woman sitting beside Harriet. 'Let 'em have fun while they can. They'll learn soon enough.'

Harriet got off the bus full of amazement. Since when did Londoners talk to each other on the buses?

The business with Murbles was quickly accomplished. He needed her signature on some documents, acting as Peter's proxy. Harriet went from his office to Hatchard's, chose books for herself and for the children and arranged to have them sent up to Hertfordshire. She stood amazed on the pavement outside Hatchard's, while the horse-drawn delivery van of a famous hatter trotted past, at first sight everything about it just as usual: immaculate varnish, immaculately turned-out matching greys between the shafts, superbly turned-out liveried coachmen; the only thing that had changed was that they were wearing tin hats instead of toppers. Harriet laughed. And then she walked along to present herself at a little café in Mayfair where she had arranged to meet Eiluned.

'Goodness, Harriet!' said Eiluned, as she sat down. 'You'll get lynched walking round London dressed like that!'

'Like what?' said Harriet, who was wearing her practical country tweeds.

'No uniform? No armband? Don't you know there's a war on?'

'I'm not sure about it. It has a sort of theatrical quality – yes, that's just it – it's like a school play, with everyone very serious about making it work, and the illusion not quite achieved.'

'The *Midsummer Night's Dream* with the gym mistress playing Theseus, because everyone else is too short?'

'That sort of thing.'

'Well, London is a stage set, all right, but I'm not sure I like the prospect of curtains up,' said Eiluned.

'Do you have to stay? With all the masterpieces in the National Gallery going off to Wales, it must be much safer there. You could go home.'

'I'm training as an ambulance driver,' said Eiluned. 'And doing a bit of first-aid training.'

'Good for you. How are all of your crowd doing?'

'Scattered to the four winds. Sylvia has gone to America. Joan – did you know Joan? – has taken over her studio. She's doing posters for the war effort: "Dig for Victory", and "Be like Dad, Keep Mum", all very Soviet. Now, tell me. Is England alive and well and living in Hertfordshire?'

'More or less,' said Harriet. She launched into an account of life in Paggleham, complete with murder.

'It's just as well we're tough, Harry, isn't it?' Eiluned remarked as they were finishing their meal. 'The "little women" act that used to make you and me look like the odd ones out has gone quite out of fashion. Suddenly it's quite the thing to wear mannish clothes and be able to do things. It'll be a terrible shock to the men when they get home – and they might be home sooner than we bargained for!'

'Things look pretty ominous, don't they?' Harriet agreed. 'But I would give my eye-teeth to be a shock to Peter, if he would be shocked, that is.'

'Oh, Peter!' said Eiluned. 'He's so intuitive he's an honorary woman!'

'That idea really might shock him,' said Harriet, smiling.

And now she would have to go to the house, and fetch Mrs Trapp's work-box, and just see that all was well. She walked slowly on sunlit pavements towards Audley Square, full of home thoughts. The house looked blankly at her, with all its windows shuttered. She mounted the steps. Was the key always so stiff in the door? She blinked at the gloomy hallway, coming in from the bright street. The console tables in the hall were all covered in dust-sheets. She mounted the uncarpeted stairs to the drawing-room, and found it likewise wrapped in shrouds. Dusty pillow-cases cocooned the chandeliers, dusty calico covered sofas and chairs, the pictures were draped in lengths of sacking, the carpets rolled up and stacked against the walls. The closed and barred window shutters let in cracks of light in which specks of dust hovered like tiny stars.

It all looked so strange and unexpected that at least Harriet was spared the hard kick of nostalgia that she had feared. The very idea that this house in all its unswathed glory could have been hers lacked plausibility now the Prince had gone from her life. So, likewise of course, had anything like glass slippers and golden gowns.

'Pumpkin time,' Harriet told herself. She found Mrs Trapp's work-box quite easily because it was exactly where Mrs Trapp had said it would be, in the left-hand bottom drawer of the kitchen dresser, along with tea-towels and glass-cloths. It was a charming little thing in Winchester work, a present from the Dowager Duchess to mark Mrs Trapp's twenty-fifth year of service at Denver. But finding the books she wanted was a challenge, since the bookcases in her study were sheeted too. She had to remember where things were, lift the sheet, wriggle under it, and find the book with her nose almost against the spines, squinting at the titles. It turned out that her visual memory for where a book was was pretty good, and she had nearly finished assembling the little pile and putting them in the string bag in which they were to go to Talboys when the sirens began to sound an air-raid warning.

Hell, thought Harriet, what do I do now? She hadn't a clue what to do. Where was the nearest street shelter?

There was nobody to ask. Should she go out into the open and look for one? She opened the shutters a crack and looked out. The street was deserted, there was no such thing as a hurrying crowd she could join. She found that she had decided to stay put and take the risks. But she would concede to Hitler this far, that she would descend the servants' stair and sit out the raid in the basement. Once down there she looked ruefully through the garden door towards the little mews cottage that had been done up so recently, and with such goodwill as married quarters for Bunter and his new wife. The Bunters had a baby now, which was being cared for by Hope's parents, while Hope herself had been recruited for some kind of war work connected with photography, so the mews cottage too was shuttered and silent.

Harriet felt a gust of anger. How dare anyone so threaten and disrupt other people's lives? How monstrous the situation was! Then sadness engulfed her, and she settled quietly in Mrs Trapp's armchair beside the cold kitchen range, with a book in her hand to pass the time. A lot of time passed. She hadn't heard the all-clear, and she was obviously going to miss the train home if it didn't go soon. Would there be another train tonight? The timetables had become skimpy and unreliable. But she wouldn't be able to get a taxi in the middle of an air-raid surely, and she didn't know if the buses kept running. The truth is she had lost her familiarity with London, as the city had changed rapidly. Perhaps she should just walk the two miles or so to Liverpool Street station? That seemed unattractive in an air-raid. She had a recent letter from Peter's Uncle Paul in her handbag, to remind her that London was dangerous territory. Poor prurient, querulous Uncle Paul, displaced from his beloved France, and living in chilly London. She got the letter out, and looked it over again.

> . . . I lunched last week at the House of Lords with your brother-in-law Gerald and his wife. Since she is in the Ministry of Instruction and Morale – Dieu sait pourquoi! – I suggested to her that some attempt should be made by that body to instruct the urban population in the science of walking in the dark. Needless to say, I got no satisfaction. (I do not suppose that any man has ever got satisfaction out of Helen, least of all her husband. As I warned him thirty years ago, she has neither the figure nor the temperament.) On this occasion she replied that the Ministry saw no need to issue propaganda; the public was accepting the blackout well, and the spirit of the nation was excellent. I replied that I was not concerned for its spirit but for its body and brain, of which the one was being mutilated and the other neglected – my objection was not to the blackout (which provides a refreshing relief from the vulgarity which normally disfigures the streets of the metropolis), but only to accidents. I added that the spirit of any nation, however good, was liable to be depressed by an expectation of death which at present stood higher in Great Britain than on the Western Front . . .

She had been warned! And she felt hungry; not surprising

since it was now more than seven hours since lunch with Eiluned. She opened the pantry door, a thing which as mistress of this house she had never done, and saw, as she would have expected, nearly bare, remorselessly orderly shelves, stripped of all perishable foods. All she could find was two tins of sardines, a jar of Shippam's meat paste, a packet of Quaker oats and a tin of treacle. Hunger withered on the bough like blasted fruit. And, of course, with the electricity turned off and the range cold there would be no means of heating porridge. Harriet returned to her chair and fell asleep.

She woke, cold and stiff, at nine o'clock. Could she have slept through the all-clear? Surely not. She decided to run off the stiffness by trotting up and down the house, and set off two steps at a time ascending the elegantly curving stairs. Right at the top of the house there was a little sash window lighting the top landing, left unshuttered because it was only an attic floor. Harriet, slightly breathless, stooped to look out. London lay before her bathed in the cool moonlight, perfectly though faintly clear in every lovely and unlovely detail. Chimneys and fire-escapes, and roofs and spires; dark treetops rising in the parks, the church tower of St James's, the slightly improper exoticism of the Italianate tower of Westminster Cathedral rising above the rooftops beyond the park. And the moon had it all to itself, without a single street light or window light, and drew it all in silver highlight and blue shadow. Overhead she heard a droning sound, and from some little way off a pair of searchlight beams sprang suddenly upright and began to tilt and sweep the sky. When they intersected a soft-edged diamond of double brightness was briefly painted and erased. How naked and vulnerable London lay in view; one might think the moon was a traitor, in league with the enemy.

Harriet felt dizzy, and realised that she was now light-headed with hunger; she must eat the oats dry if need be, or wet and raw, but she must eat something. And then as she descended the stairs on this quest she saw a chink of light showing at a window of the mews house beyond the garden – someone was there!

She moved swiftly. The key to the mews cottage was taken from the hook behind the garden door, the three bolts were swiftly drawn, and she went softly and quickly down the garden, under the apple tree standing like a Japanese print in the papery light, and opened the door to the other house. The stairs up to the living-room were in darkness, but there was light under the door on her right, between hall and kitchen. She listened to unbroken silence. Very gently and quietly she opened the door. What had she expected? Looters? Squatters? Certainly not what she saw by the light of three candles on the table. It was Bunter, slumped forward in a kitchen chair, his head on his arms. Bunter fast asleep. Bunter fast asleep, wearing filthy clothes, and with a three-day beard.

She could not have been more astonished had he been the angel Gabriel in mufti. She could not have been more pleased to see him had he been the dove with an olive branch returning to the ark. Although she had not made a sound some sixth sense suddenly woke him; he leaped to his feet, backed away into a corner, and pointed a revolver at her.

'Bunter, it's me,' she said.

'My lady?' He was blinking at her in the dim light as though she were as unlikely an apparition as he was himself.

'Where is Peter?' she asked him, her heart pounding.

'I don't know, my lady. We had to go separate ways. I had thought . . .' He thought better of what he was going to say. He was swaying on his feet. She understood his silenced sentence all too well, but this was an emergency.

With a blissful sense of turning the tables, Harriet took charge. This was the only time in her life when she was remotely likely to be more on the ball than he was.

'When did you last eat?' she asked him.

'I'm not sure,' he said. 'It was in Holland, I think.'

'Can you manage the stairs?'

'I think so, my lady.'

'Then get up there and get those clothes off. I'll bring some hot water, and find something to eat.'

He hesitated. He too, she saw, exhausted and disorientated as he was, realised that the natural order of things was inverted.

'That's an order, Bunter,' she said crisply, and he went.

Thank the lord they had put a sensible kitchen in here. Harriet found the gas and turned it on, and lit all the burners on the enamel New World cooker. Then she found the water main under the sink and turned that on too, filled all the three largest pans she could find and put them to heat. Then she tackled the electricity. Either the supply was down or all the fuses were blown. She brought the Quaker oats and the treacle from the other kitchen, and made up a pan of porridge. She ate three spoonfuls of it rapidly herself, to deal with her own light head. It tasted impossibly bland, like baby food. Then she filled a ewer with hot water, took one of the candles, and went in search of the intended beneficiary.

He hadn't got far. He had put out some clean clothes on the bed, he had taken off the filthy overcoat, and then fallen asleep again in the bedroom chair. Beneath the overcoat he was wearing workmen's dungarees blackened with motor oil, as though he had been disguised as a mechanic. Harriet contemplated him, seeing him in the light of a problem for the first time since she had known him. A natural deep reticence, a due respect inhibited her. Then common sense and kindness took over. She hauled him to his feet by the straps on his overalls, and helped him undress. It was like putting Bredon to bed, only on a larger scale. The little boy, just like the grown man, could sleep through the process standing. She finished by pushing him over on to the bed, sponging his face and hands, and pulling the coverlet over him. She would have fed him the porridge spoon by spoon if he had not been so deeply asleep. As it was she ate it ravenously herself, found herself a bare mattress in the spare room, and fell deeply and swiftly asleep.

The all-clear woke her. The light of morning was streaming

through the uncurtained windows of the little room, glowing pink on the sloping ceiling above her head. She looked at her watch. Five o'clock. She felt scruffy herself now, having slept in her clothes. Through the open door of the main bedroom she saw Bunter still asleep, and she descended to the kitchen, and returned quietly to her own mothballed house. There she picked up the telephone, more than half expecting to find it had been disconnected 'for the duration', like so many of the conveniences of life, but the operator answered. Harriet asked to be connected to Mrs Bunter, and woke her with the good news. Hope was overjoyed, and would come at once. Harriet made just one more call, to Mrs Trapp at Talboys, to explain why she hadn't returned the previous evening, and put any worry to rest.

Then she contemplated turning on the water, finding the gas main, trying for the minimum necessities in her own house, and thought it would be too much trouble. On the other hand if she went across to Bunter's house, she might wake him before nature would have done, which seemed unkind, or make a third when his wife arrived, which seemed tactless. She felt far too scruffy and underfed to make the journey home as she was. So she remembered the privilege of wealth – she had never entirely got the hang of it – and went to have a bath and breakfast at the Ritz.

When at nine in the morning she returned to Audley Square to pick up that string bag of books, and get over to Liverpool Street for the train home, she was confronted with the astonishing sight of the old Bunter restored to her: Bunter immaculately turned out, scrubbed and shaved and kempt, and clearly lying in wait for her to open the front door.

'Good morning, my lady,' this incredible apparition said to her. 'I trust you slept well?'

'Thank you, Bunter, yes,' she said, 'if less soundly than you.' Did the ghost of a blush appear on Bunter's imperturbable countenance? She noticed with a pang of affection for him that, although spruced up, he looked haggard and exhausted, and older than before.

'I am very afraid, my lady,' he said, 'that I perpetrated an indiscretion last night, which I hope you will be kind enough to overlook, indeed put right out of your mind in the circumstances.'

Perhaps the ghost of a blush was now appearing on her own face. While she wondered what to say, he added, 'I think when you were kind enough to ask me when I last ate, I replied by giving you not the hour of the meal in question, but the location in which it had been consumed. That was officially secret information.'

'Oh, of course, Bunter. I've forgotten it already. I won't mention it to anyone. The entire family have been consoling themselves with the thought that you and Lord Peter were together. You have a reputation for being able to get him out of a hole.'

'Thank you, my lady. That was a very different war. This one has asked of us considerably less digging, and considerably more cunning.'

'I imagine I am not allowed to ask you about the circumstances in which you and Lord Peter went separate ways.'

'Better not, my lady. But I would like you to know that I left him on an order from him, which I would much rather not have obeyed.'

'I believe you.'

'There were two ways home, my lady, of which one was safer than the other. He sent me by the safer one. I now believe that he practised deception on me, my lady, but I did not think of that in the heat of the moment. There were only a few minutes in which to decide.'

'He *tricked* you?' There was amazement in her voice. The relationship between man and master which she had observed for so long, and sometimes even with a pang of jealousy, seemed to make such a thing nearly impossible.

'He suggested that we chose who went by which route by tossing a coin, my lady. I called tails, and he told me it had come up tails. But I did not see the coin myself. Only later did it occur to me . . .'

'It was a very fair way of making the decision, as between two men both with children, Bunter. I am sure Peter didn't cheat. Am I allowed to ask you how he was when you last saw him in whatever country?'

'He was in remarkably cheerful spirits, my lady. He observed that you were an exceptionally clever woman, that he had turned the tables on you at last, and the score was now, so to speak, love all.'

'Whatever . . . ?'

'I think he was adverting, my lady, to the difficulties

173

which can arise when people save each other's lives. May I take this opportunity, my lady, of thanking you on my own behalf, and, of course, on behalf of my wife and son?'

'Oh, rubbish, Bunter. No, you may not.'

'One other thing, my lady. I do not clearly recall how I came to be undressed and asleep in my own bed last night.'

'Neither do I, Bunter,' said Harriet coolly, meeting his eye. 'Neither do I. I am returning to Talboys now. Keep in touch.'

Liverpool Street station was besieged with people. A crowd of uniforms all seething around urgently. Harriet was reminded of anthills, and instantly in a huge hurry, since the departures board was announcing her train in only a few minutes, and unburdened with anything more than a string bag and a gas-mask case, Harriet pushed through the throng and found a seat in the first-class carriage. All the class carriages were packed. Faded posters in the carriage she sat in offered wildly unlikely holidays: in sunny Bournemouth, on the Norfolk Broads, or hunting in France. *Hunting in France!* Did nobody think to bring these things up to date?

Harriet loosened the window-strap in her compartment, and lowered the window so that she could lean out and take a last look at London sliding away behind her. A lot of people were missing, or only just catching, the train. And among them she saw a face she knew: that of Flight Lieutenant Brinklow, racing along the platform when the train had already shuddered, and started to move very slowly. He pulled a door open right at the back of the last carriage, after the guard's flag had dropped and his whistle had blown, and pulled himself aboard. Hadn't Mrs Ruddle said he wouldn't have any but a London dentist? Harriet hoped the posh dentist had fixed his now legendary toothache. She settled into her seat and began to read.

She couldn't concentrate. She couldn't get rid of an expectation that she would open a door at Talboys and find Peter home again. That she would be in her husband's arms again just about at the same time as Hope Bunter arrived in Audley Square. *Jack shall have Jill, Nought shall go ill . . .*

Unfortunately a lot could go ill in these unhappy days. On the station at Great Pagford Harriet bought a newspaper. The first civilian to be killed on British soil by enemy action had died in an air-raid in Scotland. And when she reached home there was no Peter, nor any word from him or about him.

Mrs Trapp was plainly very pleased to hear about Bunter. 'He's a good servant, my lady, in a world that hasn't got any too many of them. And what's even more unusual he's appreciated for what he does. I'll be very glad to have him back in the household.'

'Oh, I don't think so, Mrs Trapp. Surely he'll want to be with his own family at a time like this.'

'He has a living to earn, same as most of us,' she said. Harriet looked at her in surprise, but she didn't seem to mean it pointedly, it was just plain statement of fact. 'Mark my words, my lady, he'll find a way to be back in harness with Lord Peter if he possibly can.'

'Well, as to Lord Peter . . .'

'Have faith, my lady,' said Mrs Trapp. 'It doesn't do a body a might of good to be fretting as you're fretting.'

'I'll try,' said Harriet.

Mrs Trapp was certainly right. If Harriet succumbed to alarm and despondency, where would the household be? There was plenty of distraction however. It was Sadie's day off. Queenie had last week gone to work in a munitions factory in Birmingham, and was ever so sorry to let Harriet down, but could she go without notice? Harriet had of course let her go. It was raining, and the children were fighting air-battles with and over paper planes down the stairs and through the hallway. Charlie kept asking for paper. He didn't seem willing to make his planes out of her scrawled-over rough papers, but wanted virgin sheets each time.

'Couldn't you buy a nice pad of paper with your pocket money?' she asked him, mildly annoyed.

'I did, but it's all used up,' he said, so mournfully that she gave in, and let him have a stack of new writing paper.

Then she returned to the task in hand. There were numerous bills to pay, and Harriet was doggedly ploughing through the desk-work with the study door ajar in case the joyful uproar in the hall turned to tears of outrage or injury. When Mrs Trapp appeared to announce Superintendent

Kirk, and chase the children into the kitchen to play Ludo and help make apple pie, Harriet was relieved.

'The inquest will be next Tuesday, my lady,' said Superintendent Kirk. 'Can't hold it off any longer, even if we haven't got very far. So I thought we had better compare notes.'

'You won't want me as a witness, I think?'

'No, my lady. I'll have all the principals you identified speak for themselves. You have been a great help.'

'I can't have been, I haven't found anything out.'

'Well, it's only in novels that detective work is fascinating and leads quickly to the villain,' he told her. 'In real life it's often as not just plodding. When it isn't obvious, that is. It's a serious disadvantage of the war, Lady Peter, that it gives everyone in sight a cast-iron alibi.'

'Well, if they have cast-iron alibis then they didn't commit the crime, Mr Kirk. It saves you wasting your time on those who didn't do it, but can't remember where they were, or who were wandering about not meeting anyone, or asleep in bed alone, but only a short trot from the scene of the crime. All that sort of thing.'

'Of course you're right, Lady Peter. But when we have eliminated all these people who didn't do it, who is there left? Tell me that.'

'I can't. There's the theory of the passing maniac . . .'

He shrugged his shoulders eloquently.

'There's the theory of the person scrambling up the ventilation shaft out of the vaults below the Crown . . .'

'And this person somehow *knowed* ahead of time that

they would meet Wendy Percival coming down the High Street and nobody else in sight? Or acting on impulse like the passing maniac?'

'Being, in effect, a passing maniac.'

'The trouble with detective stories,' he said solemnly, 'is that—'

'Real murderers have to have more than opportunity. They have to have been able to *foresee* the opportunity,' said Harriet. 'I've thought of that. But one thing I did wonder about, Mr Kirk: did anyone check that all those airmen got back to their barracks after the dance, exactly as they should have done?'

'Oh, yes. First thing we thought about. It's rock solid; they had to have permission to take the RAF lorry to get over here, and there was a roll-call when they got back. All present and correct. You'll hear the commanding officer tell the coroner so.'

'You would like me to be present, then, Mr Kirk, even though you don't want to call me?'

'In case something strikes a woman's eye in the demeanour of witnesses, Lady Peter, yes I would. If you wouldn't mind.'

'What do I hear?' she said. 'What's this about a woman's eye?'

'I'd have to admit,' he said, 'that women are doing very surprising things these days. You'd be amazed what work is being done by the wives of my band of coppers, Lady Peter. We've been seriously underestimating the fair sex, I think.'

'So what has Mrs Kirk been up to?' asked Harriet, smiling.

'She's been organising all those evacuees, Lady Peter. Getting things going for them so the host families have a break one day a week. Running a clothes exchange. You wouldn't believe how few clothes the little perishers have got with them. Some of them are stitched into strips of old sheets instead of underwear. And some of the host families haven't got the funds to buy clothes.'

'Please tell Mrs Kirk that we will sort out everything any of ours have grown out of. I'll gladly contribute.'

'Thank you, my lady. See you next Tuesday, at the Crown.'

Harriet returned to her household accounts. Something was niggling in the back of her mind, some small thing which she should have noticed and hadn't quite registered. To do with Bunter? No, she thought not. But her attention was diverted by the imperious ringing of the telephone. Since the household was now shorter by one pair of hands Harriet went into the hallway to answer it herself. It was the unwelcome voice of her sister-in-law. She would be driving up to Denver at the weekend, and would call at Talboys for lunch on Saturday. She did not ask, she simply declared herself. Harriet did not venture to repel boarders, but meekly accepted her.

Nine

It was a maxim with Foxey –
our revered father, gentlemen –
'Always suspect everybody.'
Charles Dickens, *The Old Curiosity Shop*,
1841

Helen appeared in a kind of ersatz uniform: a dark brown suit with squared shoulders and a military cut. She was very brisk, and evinced such ill-concealed dismay at the appearance of her colony of nephews and nieces at the family lunch table that Harriet dismissed them all to eat in the kitchen.

'Hooray!' said Charlie, with maximum tactlessness. 'Mrs Trapp and Sadie are *good fun*.'

'Heavens!' said Helen. 'Whatever is happening to their manners, Harriet?'

But Harriet, considering that her nephew had been provoked, made no reply.

'Those Parker children must be a bad influence on Bredon; Paul's too young, I suppose . . .'

'Whatever makes you think them a bad influence?' enquired Harriet, serving out the cheese omelette that Mrs

Trapp had provided for lunch. The sight of the omelette briefly diverted Helen.

'Heavens!' she said. 'However many eggs are in this? And just for the two of us.'

'Dried eggs,' said Harriet serenely.

'Look, since I'm here, could you give me a reaction to one or two of these slogans?' Helen asked. 'We just can't get the sort of people we need to dream up nice crisp wording for public information posters, and since you are a writer . . .'

'I'll give you a reaction, gladly,' said Harriet. 'But I'm not the sort of writer you need. You need someone who works in advertising.'

Helen looked at Harriet, horrified. 'Do you really think so? Wouldn't people like that feel a bit uncomfortable? They could hardly fit in . . .'

'What have you got to try on me?' said Harriet, hoping to divert the conversation from the social acceptability of advertising men or women.

'Which is better, do you think: "Saving food saves ships" or, "Better pot luck today with Chamberlain, than humble pie under Hitler tomorrow. Don't waste food!"'

'Hmm,' said Harriet. 'I think I prefer the second, although it is rather wordy for a poster.'

'Well, what about "The squander bug helps Hitler." How does that strike you?'

'It's a bit limp, really, isn't it?'

'I was afraid you would say that. Someone in the department suggested "Make your shopping save our shipping."'

'That's much better – it's got a bit of bite to it, and a memorable word-tune, like a jingle. It jollies us along.'

'I am told the public will resent being jollied along. You don't think they will feel patronised?'

'That is a danger, certainly. Whoever thought up "*Your* courage, *your* cheerfulness, *your* resolution will bring *us* victory" needed a rapid secondment to other work.'

'Really?' said Helen. 'I don't see what's wrong with it, myself. Now, about Bredon . . .'

'What about him?' said Harriet warily.

'Well, that's what I came to talk about,' said Helen. 'Didn't I say? I've been wondering about his schooling. Peter was at Eton of course, but then Peter—'

'Helen, don't you think that's rather a matter for the child's own parents to decide?'

'You have to arrange a boarding school well in advance, Harriet.'

'I'll mention it to Peter when he gets home, Helen. But I don't think we were thinking of boarding schools when he's very young.'

'Look, let's not beat about the bush. You've got to have him educated as Denver's heir, Harriet, in case he *is* Denver's heir.'

Harriet's flash of anger died quickly. 'Helen, we all hope Jerry is taking care of himself. He's full of bravado, I know, but perhaps he isn't as reckless as he likes to make out.'

'Do you think so?' she said. 'I hadn't thought of that. Perhaps you're right, Harriet, but all the same . . .'

'All the same what? What are you asking me to do?'

'Put the boys' names down for a decent prep school, bring them to Denver now and then so that they get to know the place. Keep them away from those rather insolent Parker cousins.'

Harriet considered, her fork poised above the last morsel of omelette on her plate. 'Put their names down for a prep school? Perhaps in due course. Bring them to Denver now and then? Yes, gladly, whenever there's a chance. Keep them away from their cousins? No,' she said, and left Helen to think about it while she cut slices of cold apple pie.

'Now that I'm here, you wouldn't mind my consulting you about something else?' Helen said. 'Only it's difficult for me to work out how ordinary people might react to things—'

'I am the only ordinary person of your acquaintance?' said Harriet, dryly.

Helen missed the tone. 'Well, I don't know many,' she said, 'but then you wouldn't expect—'

'How can I help?' asked Harriet.

'We are being bombarded with letters in the papers, and addressed to us directly, about making some sort of broadcast answer to this wretched Haw-Haw person. Look, I brought just a few from the top of the pile to show you.'

She passed a sheaf of paper across to Harriet. Harriet began to look through them.

Dear Sirs,

I welcome the suggestion to reply to the German propaganda from Hamburg. Anything for a change from the everlasting drone of cinema organs.

184

Dear Lord Beetle,

Do try and stop this suggestion that the BBC should broadcast an answer to Haw-Haw. It would merely encourage my husband to turn the man on, and the creature's voice gets on my nerves, so monotonous and genteel, like a shop-walker. We need not, surely, add to the horrors of war!

Dear Sirs,

I see Mr Harold Nicolson wants to run a series of replies to Haw-Haw. This is all very well and a fine idea, but for pity's sake don't make it one of your college professors but somebody as understands what is a good debating speech. There is nothing like a good controversy for entertainment but it must be good lively stuff. I am a working man myself and wireless is my hobby. I have a set gets all the foreign stations. I think Haw-Haw is very dangerous for ignorant people and there's plenty with posh wireless sets more ignorant than the working class by a long chalk.

Dear Beetle,

What's the good of complaining about the publicity given to Haw-Haw? Do you imagine anything is going to stop the British public from taking cock-shies at an enemy alien? By all means answer the fellow and give the nation its money's worth. Undignified be damned!

Dear Sirs,

Since the identity of the German broadcaster known as 'Haw-Haw' seems to be arousing some public interest, may I offer a suggestion? His accent seems to me to resemble very closely (particularly in the vowel sounds) that used by (a) an actor of insufficient breeding and experience when impersonating an English aristocrat, or (b) (more subtly) an experienced actor of good social standing impersonating a man of inferior breeding aping the speech of the English aristocracy. It is, in fact, very like the accent I use myself in the character of the self-made Stanton in Dangerous Corner, *which I have played with marked success in the West End and in the provinces (photograph and press cuttings enclosed, with stamped addressed envelope for return). If it is decided to broadcast a reply to this propaganda, would you consider me for the part?*

Harriet laughed.

'I think the public are bearing up remarkably,' said Helen, 'and no action or reply is required. What do you think, Harriet?'

Harriet took a moment to reply; this was, after all, the first time her sister-in-law had asked her opinion about anything whatever. 'Better no answer than a badly made one; a pompous one, for example,' she said. 'I don't think he's doing any actual harm at the moment. His scriptwriters seem to think that the British working classes go around saying "honest injun" and calling each other "old chap"; he mostly just arouses derision. The other day, when he had been telling us to ask "Where is HMS *Daring*?" I heard people in the queue at the butcher's saying in his hee-haw tones, "Where is the Isle of Wight?"'

'I don't understand you,' said Helen. 'Everybody knows where the Isle of Wight is; it's at the mouth of Southampton Water.'

'Never mind, Helen,' said Harriet. 'I'm agreeing with you. At the moment Lord Haw-Haw is just a harmless entertainment.'

'Yes. Good,' said Helen. 'You ought to reconsider the schooling,' she added, suddenly returning to the attack. 'There's an excellent little prep school at Duke's Denver that takes boarders from seven. And he would be near his grandmother for weekend outings.'

'Look, Helen, I do see that the situation gives you an interest in how Peter and I raise our children. But it doesn't put you in charge. I think a child is far too young for boarding school at seven. But I'm not making decisions about that kind of thing without Peter.'

'You may have to,' Helen said.

Harriet let silence lengthen between them.

Then: 'I only thought, since your own background was rather different, you might like a little help and advice.'

'I am half my children's background,' said Harriet, 'and the other half is not the Duke of Denver, but the wildly unconventional younger brother.'

'Well, I've said my piece,' said Helen, rising abruptly. 'I must be going. I've got a lot of work to do. I'll just say a word to Mrs Trapp. I must get her recipe for omelette with dried egg – that was absolutely first class. My friend in the Ministry of Food is urgently seeking palatable recipes.'

She strode down the hallway and into the kitchen, where she found the children, with the addition of Sam Bateson, all happily eating chocolate custard.

Mrs Trapp, straight-faced, gave her a recipe for making an omelette with reconstituted dried egg. Then Helen left, saying as she went, 'I hope that other child brings a ration-book when he eats here!'

Charlie thumbed his nose at the back of his departing aunt. Both Harriet and Mrs Trapp saw him do it, but neither of them reproached him.

'Where did those eggs come from?' asked Harriet, when Helen had departed. 'Ought I to ask?'

'Miss Twitterton let me have two dozen of her bantams' eggs the day before yesterday, m'lady.'

'Did we pay for them? I didn't notice them in the accounts for the week.'

'Fair exchange,' said Mrs Trapp. 'She had bought a beautiful silk blouse at a WVS sale, which was far too big for her, and she wondered if it could be taken in. Ivory crêpe-de-chine – gorgeous to wear, but slippery to work with.'

'You managed it for her?'

'She's thin as a stick, that woman. I had to cut each piece of the shirt out of the seams, and make it again.'

'So we won't be short of eggs for a while? All completely against the regulations, Mrs Trapp.'

'People who make regulations,' Mrs Trapp observed, 'should have a firm grasp of human nature.'

And Harriet couldn't argue with that. She looked forward to seeing Miss Twitterton resplendent in ivory silk. But whatever Miss Twitterton had wanted the gorgeous shirt for, it wasn't to wear to church on Sunday. She appeared as usual to play the organ at the communion service, wearing her navy Viyella dress.

An inquest held by Mr Perkins, the coroner, and featuring evidence of the cause and time of death given by the local pathologist, Dr Craven, was bound to take Harriet's mind back to the inquest that had interrupted her honeymoon. This one was not likely to be as lively as the earlier one, surely. But perhaps there is a pattern to village inquests, for, as on the previous occasion, the back room at the Crown was packed. Somehow a lot of people had contrived to be available to attend in the middle of the working morning. A hum of excitement filled the room, and Mr Perkins had to hammer hard with his gavel to obtain the necessary silence. There were some similarities in the proceedings. Evidence of identification was given by Rita Smith, working at Bateson's farm for the Women's Land Army. The murdered girl's next of kin, Superintendent Kirk told the jury, lived a distance off, and were understandably too distressed to make the identification. Rita Smith had lived and worked with the deceased for some months. Miss Smith gave evidence in a firm voice, although she was visibly distressed herself.

Harriet thought that many people in the room were for the first time perceiving Wendy as a real person with grieving parents and friends; her reality had been masked in the eyes of many by the miasma of disapproval which surrounded her dashing conduct. Harriet herself had once been wrapped in notoriety – admittedly much more extreme. Nobody had been able to see her clearly through the fog of condemnation. It had seemed to most people that a woman who would live in sin with a man would do anything, even murder him. Only Peter had seen her clearly, and he had done so on first sight! She wrenched her attention back to the present moment.

Dr Craven described the results of the post-mortem he had carried out. There had been a sequence of hard blows which had overpowered and killed the deceased: a blow to the front of the throat which had crushed the vocal cords, a hard blow to the side of the neck, sufficient to interrupt the flow of blood through the jugular vein, a blow to the kidneys from the back, probably caused by the assailant's knee, minor injuries consistent with falling to the ground as the attack concluded.

'In your experience as a pathologist, have you ever encountered injuries such as these before?' enquired Mr Perkins.

'Never. A killing without a weapon of somebody who resists is usually a prolonged and messy affair. This was expertly and rapidly done.'

'Can we draw conclusions as to the identity of the assailant, do you think, Dr Craven?'

'Hardly, Mr Perkins. May I draw your attention to the training booklet for unarmed conflict that was issued to

Home Defence instructors last year? There must now be many people with the requisite knowledge.'

Dr Jellyfield gave evidence of the warmth of the body when he knelt to take the pulse of the deceased as the crowd dispersed from the Crown. The corpse had been warm to the touch. His own hands had been cold from the chill of the underground vault, and he had experienced the woman's wrist as warmer than his own fingers. He concluded that she had been dead only for a very short time; a conclusion which was consistent with the body temperature taken by thermometer half an hour later in the police cell to which the body had been taken.

Police Constable Jack Baker gave evidence that he had been at the scene of the crime very quickly, since he and his wife were among those taking shelter in the vaults of the Crown. He had come forward in the crowd, and had reached the body while Dr Jellyfield was still holding the victim's wrist, and trying to take a pulse. He had asked the crowd to stand back, and he had telephoned Superintendent Kirk at Pagford who was senior enough to take charge. Then he had stood beside the body until he could hand over to the Superintendent.

Superintendent Kirk gave evidence confirming Constable Baker's account, and embarking briefly on the investigation that he had conducted. Because of the dance at the Crown the village had been full of strangers on the evening in question. The first thing he had put in hand was interviewing the commanding officers of all the air-bases whose men had attended the dance. He had satisfied himself that all the air force personnel had arrived and departed in official transport, and that nobody had failed to return in the truck in which he had left the base.

'That is to say,' interposed Mr Perkins, 'that although many men in uniform attended the dance, they had all departed upon the sirens announcing the practice air-raid, and are all accounted for?'

'Quite so, Mr Perkins. The enlisted men cannot leave their bases without signing themselves out with the duty sergeant at the gates, and they have to sign in when they return. The times are given in the books, and this is all in order for the evening in question.'

The coroner proceeded to interview Fred Lugg as to what he had seen from his vantage point on the church tower, which led to the calling of Mrs Spright, who had been seen walking around during the air-raid practice.

'Why were you walking about after dark?' enquired the coroner. 'Were you on your way to one or other of the shelters?'

'I was just looking around.'

'Late at night?'

'I'm not the only one who walks about at night in this village. You should ask Miss Twitterton what she is doing, up and down the lane all the time.'

'I am interviewing you at the moment. Did you encounter any other person in the streets while you were looking around?' asked Mr Perkins.

Mrs Spright had encountered several. The party from Talboys, for example. She had also observed a young woman, whom she now knew to have been Wendy Percival, running down the street in a great hurry towards the Crown. She had not seen what happened to the deceased, because she had crouched down behind the garden wall of a nearby house so as not to be seen.

'And from this vantage point, while you could not see anything, you might easily have heard something? A cry, for example?'

'I heard her stop running. Those silly high heels she was wearing made a tap-tap sound. And I heard her say, "Great heavens, what are you doing here?"'

'And then? What was the reply?'

'Not another thing. She didn't get an answer, as far as I could hear.'

'You didn't see who she was talking to?'

'As I told you, no.'

'You didn't see what it was that someone was doing that occasioned the deceased such surprise?'

'No, I kept my head down.'

At this point the foreman of the jury raised his hand. 'Can the witness be asked, Mr Perkins, what *she* was doing, hiding in the bushes in the middle of the night instead of joining in the air-raid practice?'

The coroner thought about it. 'Is that to the point?' he mused aloud.

'The witness has a reputation for odd behaviour, sir. It might help us assess her evidence.'

'Very well, I shall put the question.'

Mrs Spright replied, 'I was keeping a watch out for

spies. If the authorities won't act on information, then the private citizen has to. It's a scandal – and it ought to be in the papers. Some people need showing up for what they are. Fifth columnists everywhere, and it's no good telling that Superintendent Kirk what is going on, because—'

'That will do, thank you,' said Mr Perkins.

'Oh, it will, will it?' cried Mrs Spright. 'I have family and friends in Norway, and I can tell you that there must be enemies among us everywhere. Half the upper classes are fascists, like that man Oswald Mosley. And there's someone walking around this very village that you can tell isn't who he says he is, every time he opens his mouth. When someone came asking for *him*, I sent him packing right away. "Gone to Cornwall," I said. "You won't find him still here." I thought, why should I help a couple of spies make contact with each other—'

'I take it that you have nothing further to tell us that is to the point?' Mr Perkins interrupted. His voice had taken on the unmistakable timbre of saintly patience.

'You don't want to hear me out, either, I see,' said Mrs Spright, flouncing out.

'Members of the jury, I should advise you to weigh carefully what witnesses say, without prejudice, as far as you are able,' Mr Perkins said. To Superintendent Kirk he said, 'Do you wish to request an adjournment while you pursue further enquiries?'

'With respect, Mr Perkins,' said Superintendent Kirk, 'in present circumstances I think it would be helpful if we got as far as we can this morning. Things being unpredictable, and manpower short, sir. And the witnesses – the young airmen who were present in the village for the dance, for example, or any local man who is liable to be called up, or directed into war work somewhere else – may be scattered to the four winds before we are in a position to resume.'

'I take your point. Very well, the jury must do what they can with what evidence they have.' Scrupulously Mr Perkins proceeded to tell the jury that a charge of murder would require the Crown to prove malice, intention, and the sanity of the accused. In the absence of any evidence as to the identity of the killer, let alone of his state of mind, the useful verdict of unlawful killing would be available, which would represent the present state of knowledge of the affair.

The jury would have none of it. They took less than an hour to bring in a verdict of murder by person or persons unknown.

'Well, Superintendent Kirk, if you take Mrs Spright seriously you should be looking for a Nazi spy,' said Mr Perkins, pulling on his coat as the public dispersed, most of them heading to the bar downstairs. Harriet, who overheard this remark, judged from Superintendent Kirk's expression that he was not inclined to take Mrs Spright seriously. Very far from it.

It was a week after the inquest that Bunter presented himself at Talboys. He arrived from the station in John Bateson's horse-drawn farm cart, and Harriet noticed the moment she saw him descending that he had two very large suitcases with him, made of brown leather and liberally covered with the destination labels of a much travelled man.

'Leave those in the hall, and come and talk to me in here, Bunter,' she said, leading the way to the sitting-room. 'And please sit down.'

'You have no word from his lordship, my lady?'

'None, Bunter. Have you?'

'No, my lady.'

'You have come with your luggage, I see.'

'With your ladyship's permission I have come to resume my employment with Lord Peter's household.'

Harriet hesitated. It would be wonderful to have Bunter smoothing her path in every detail, as he had done in the past. 'Oh, Bunter, that would be splendid, but—'

'It seems to you that to have a gentleman's gentleman in the middle of a war, even if the gentleman himself were here to be served, would be extravagant, my lady?'

'Exactly. You understand me perfectly.'

'May I attempt to put your mind at rest on that point? Since you saw me last I have made repeated and very urgent attempts to enlist in the services. I have almost unscrupulously used every contact that years of service with his lordship have given me. I have not succeeded. My age is against me. It has been strongly suggested to me that I would best be employed in some rural district assisting the local authorities in the organisation of Home Defence. And since at present my family are residing in a rural district, I am putting myself at the disposal of the Pagford district war committee, and of you, my lady.'

'Bunter, I am very touched that you should regard us as your family. But shouldn't you be with your own wife and baby?'

'The powers that be have elected to move Mrs Bunter,' he said. 'She has been sent to work not far from here, at Lopsley Manor. I am hoping to see her from time to time.'

'She is working as a photographer?'

'Her talent is being employed in the interpretation of aerial reconnaissance photographs, my lady.'

'You must be glad that she is out of London. But surely, with a baby to look after she isn't in the category they are describing as "a mobile woman"?'

'Her mother is happy to continue looking after our little boy, my lady. I believe the work Hope is engaged on is technical and urgent and they are very short of trained people.'

'Well then, Bunter, the only question is where we are going to put you. You need to be private and comfortable. Queenie has left us to work in a munitions factory in Stevenage, but her room was very small . . .'

'This house has extensive attics, my lady. I shall make myself quarters.'

'Adequate for Hope to come and join you when she has leave? The ideal, really, would be to find you somewhere independent but nearby. But the village is packed with evacuees. Although when I come to think of it there is a cottage which should be available before very long. I can ask about it.'

'I shall be quite comfortable here,' he said.

'Bunter, I don't know if I am being tactful in saying this, and I am sure that your little son Peter is well cared for by his Fanshaw grandparents. But we are looking after five children here already, and Harriet Parker must be roughly the same age as your son. I can't think that one more child about the house would make any difference; as far as keeping the peace is concerned, all is already lost. In short if you would like to have him here with you it would not be any bother to us at all.'

'Thank you, my lady. I will consult my wife at the earliest opportunity.'

'Mrs Trapp will be glad to have you back. She told me you would return to us, but I didn't see how she could be right.'

'Mrs Trapp is a woman of very sound views.'

'Quite so, Bunter. Oh, and Bunter – welcome home.'

Ten

'What's that, young sirs? **Stole** *a pig?*
Where are your licences?' said the policeman.
Beatrix Potter, *The Tale of Pigling Bland*, 1913

A household with Bunter in it appeared to run on
wheels, even in war-time.

Mrs Trapp could take an afternoon off, leaving supper
in capable hands. Sadie could have a break from looking
after children, while Bunter firmly whisked Charlie and
Polly off to catch rabbits, or construct a look-out post, and
Harriet looked after the toddlers. Suddenly her working
time was restored to her; at odd hours, it was true, but reli-
ably. Bunter got Rita and Muriel to plough up a plot at the
nearer end of the field beyond the outhouses, and planted
lettuce and beans and carrots. Harriet could sit down in
the afternoon to write an account of the inquest and add
it to the piles of unposted letters to Peter. Whatever, she
wondered, writing it down, had Mrs Spright meant about
not helping spies get in touch with each other? She had
thrown another pot-shot at Aggie Twitterton, too. What
an unpleasant woman!

When the account was written down as clearly and

fully as she could, Harriet wandered into the kitchen in search of a cup of tea, and offered Mrs Trapp a helping hand. Bunter, she understood, was in the village, at the blacksmith's.

'What is he doing there?' asked Harriet, picking up the paring knife she had been offered and sitting down to the task of peeling carrots and turnips.

'He's getting a new tyre on one of the wheels of a little cart he found, parked in the garage, m'dear,' said Mrs Trapp. 'He's fixing it all up.'

'Mysteries all around,' said Harriet. 'Why do we need a cart? I didn't know carts had tyres. A tyre goes to a garage, doesn't it?'

'There's no mystery about any of that,' said Mrs Trapp. 'Now mind you get that peel off very thin; the best bit of the veg is just below the skin. We need a cart to bring sensible amounts of firewood out of his lordship's wood, to save coal. Cart wheels do have tyres, m'lady, I'm surprised at you for not noticing that. And the tyres they have are bands of iron, so it's the forge, and not the garage that's wanted.'

'Thank you, Mrs Trapp. Is this peeled thinly enough? And while you are putting me right, can you tell me what Miss Twitterton might be doing, wandering around at night and getting that awful Spright woman sniping at her?'

'No; can't say as I can,' said Mrs Trapp. 'But, bless you, it won't be spying for the Nazis. It'll be to do with the pig club, more like.'

'Is Miss Twitterton in the pig club? How can she be? She hasn't even got space enough for more hens!'

'She is an honorary member, you might say. She contributes old hens past their laying, and sometimes eggs to help out between pigs. And peelings and kitchen waste for the pigswill, same as everyone else. And she gets a cut of meat in exchange when a pig is killed. Mrs Wagget, the club secretary, works out how much value Miss Twitterton has put in the kitty, and she takes it back as pork. All very fair and reasonable.'

'I'm glad to know that. But do pig club members have to walk the lanes at night?'

'Well,' said Mrs Trapp, vigorously rolling out the pastry for her Woolton pie, 'let's just say there are occasions when they might. Now if you've finished that, m'lady, why don't you get the older children together and walk them down to the blacksmith's to see that tyre put on the wheel? That makes a bit of a show. Young Charlie will like to see that.'

On the way they encountered Flight Lieutenant Brinklow coming from the village shops, hobbling along with his purchases. She called to him. 'You missed a friend the other morning. He gave me a message for you.'

Brinklow stopped and she had an uncanny feeling that her words had caused an instant of dismay before he answered her. 'Oh?' he said.

'Mike Newcastle,' she said.

'I don't think I know—'

'He's from your unit,' she prompted. 'Red hair, freckles,

dimpled smile. He said they had been concerned about you. You ought to be in touch.'

'Yes, of course. I'll give him a bell,' he said.

Harriet was left slightly baffled. Had Mike Newcastle said Brinklow had a good line in wisecracks? Somehow that seemed unlikely. Perhaps the poor man's tooth was still hurting him. But Bredon was tugging at her hand, in a hurry to get to the show.

And it was indeed a show. Mr Puffett was in attendance: 'On account of there being a thatch near enough for those sparks,' as he explained.

'Of course, Mr Puffett, you are on duty as the fire-officer,' said Harriet.

'Wouldn't take Hitler to have me here when Maggs 'as got a big job on,' Mr Puffett told her. 'He 'as a lot of soot in that chimbley of his, and that can burn something shocking.'

Mr Maggs in his leather apron and shirt-sleeves was hammering out a thick red-hot girder on his anvil, while Mr Puffett trod the bellows to get a brilliant white glow on the coals. Bunter was standing by, and one wheel of the cart was leaning against the wall of the forge. Sparks were flying and ascending on the column of smoke into the blackened roof of the forge, and out of the chimney.

Bunter said, 'May I respectfully suggest, my lady, that the children should watch from the other side of the lane?'

'Good idea,' said Mr Maggs. 'When the wheel rolls it

can be hard to steer it straight. Don't want no accidents.'

Puzzled, but learning, Harriet led Charlie and Polly across the lane, and picked up Bredon to carry him. On the other side of the lane was a little brook, which widened to a small pond opposite the forge door. The milkman left a bottle of milk standing in a clay pipe there each morning, so that the trickle of water kept it cool, and the section of footpath with a hand-rail ran behind the pond, to give dry footing when the pond brimmed over in winter and covered the road. On this path Harriet lined up her little band of spectators. Through the open door of the forge they could see the bright girder being dragged out of the fire first white, and then red, and then on the anvil fading to a web of orange under a grey skin with a pewter-coloured sheen as it cooled and lengthened under the blows.

Charlie was in ecstasy, and Polly was watching with concentration; Bredon resisted being put down, but held on hard to his mother with his thumb in his mouth. Suddenly everything was ready. Mr Maggs and Mr Puffett thrust a rod through the wheel hub to make a temporary axle. They trundled the wheel up to the anvil, and Mr Maggs brought an end of the sullenly glowing iron bar to rest on the rim of the wheel. He struck a single long nail through buttery metal into wood. Smoke rose from the point of contact, and a scorched smell drifted across the lane. Then the two men seized the axle rod and wheeled the wheel away. As they did it picked up the metal and wrapped it round itself. When it overlapped, a very small overlap Maggs swung his hammer, and hammered the join flat, and all the while the wheel was moving slowly, smoking, across the road. Mr Maggs pulled out the temporary axle, and used it like the stick with a child's hoop to drive the wheel onwards. It toppled, rolled, shed sparks, toppled, and rolled into the pond where it sank in an explosion of steam and hissing.

'Oh, smashing!' said Charlie joyfully. 'Oh, gosh!' Then he added, conversationally, 'Mr Maggs, will one nail be enough to hold it on?'

Mr Maggs was leaning on his makeshift axle, breathing hard. The pond had settled, and the wheel was visible, lying on the gravel in a foot of running water.

'More than enough,' he said, answering Charlie's question. 'The iron shrinks in the water, young man, it shrinks on to the wheel, and bites on hard. Doesn't need a nail. That'll be on that wheel until the wheel's broke or the iron's wore through.'

Charlie heaved a satisfied sigh. 'Can I help you, next time?' he asked.

'When you can lift my anvil you can help me,' said Mr Maggs.

'That won't be just yet, Charlie,' said Harriet, smiling.

'Look a-here, Puffett,' said Mr Maggs, 'there isn't much depth of water in the pond. We'd better leave that wheel in the wet a minute or two longer.'

'Where does this stream come from, then, Mr Maggs?' asked Bunter.

'Down from that wood of yours. Yours in a manner of speaking, I mean, since the owner is your employer, Mr Bunter. There's a spring right by the old pig-pens up there. Then round behind the row of cottages in Simpkins Street, and through a culvert into the Pag below the bridge,' said Mr Maggs.

'Most of us as were boys here can remember that running right down the middle of the High Street, open to the air,' said Mr Puffett. 'We uster catch tiddlers in that when we were boys, and the landlord of the Crown uster put his glasses in baskets down in it to have the brook wash them out for him. Then they wanted the street wider, so they put it in a pipe.'

'So where would the firemen get water from, if there were a house on fire in the High Street?' asked Harriet.

'Couple of manhole covers in the middle of the road,' said Mr Puffett. 'Local knowledge, m'lady, is what you need for fires.'

'Now if you'd stand back a bit, Mr Bunter, Maggs and I will fetch that wheel up out of the drink for you, and you can put it on the cart as good as new. Just don't nobody touch it for an hour or two – that'll take a while to cool right off.'

'Thank you, Mr Maggs,' said Bunter. 'I think we'll play safe and walk the children home. I'll return to fetch the cart tomorrow.'

As they walked back up the High Street, Harriet spotted

Susan Hodge, buying fish from the back of the Grimsby van, which parked by the horse trough every Tuesday. She walked across to speak to her. 'I was wondering, Miss Hodge, if your cottage would shortly be available? We are very crowded at Talboys, and we would be glad to rent it from you.'

'Sorry, my lady,' said Susan Hodge, 'but I've just now taken the down payment for the next month. Otherwise you'd have been welcome. I was surprised that he took it again, to be honest, but he's a good tenant. Keeps himself to himself, and everything spotless. Couldn't ask for better.'

'Well, would you let me know when it becomes free?' said Harriet. 'We might still be glad to take it in four weeks.'

'I will indeed. Rather you than the billeting officer and a crowd of kids what wet their beds and have head-lice,' said Miss Hodge.

It was a bright, still, April evening. Harriet paced about her room, finding things to do. She could hear the children still awake in the nursery, Polly's voice, Charlie reading to her, Bredon who had just learned to count going up to twelve and getting stuck again and again. Sometimes he hit seven, sometimes he skipped it. Harriet was humming tunelessly. Baby Paul was fast asleep in his cot in the corner of her room, his tousled blond hair and flushed plump cheeks reminding her of Mabel Lucie Attwell postcards from before the war. The sweet light of the lingering dusk persuaded Harriet to put her coat on and go for a late walk. It seemed lighter out of doors than it had through the windows, as though the darkness filled the houses first, and left the open air for later. Harriet walked through the old farmyard, past all the barns, noticing the refurbished cart standing ready for use. Had Bunter wheeled it up the hill himself?

She badly needed the walk, to throw off her deeply apprehensive mood. It was easy to read between the lines and discern an unfolding disaster in Norway. The Germans had easily taken the centres of population, and the allies were steadily retreating northwards into the snows. The wireless news tonight had made much of the cost to German shipping of the naval battles off the Norwegian coast. Hitler would find it hard to assemble ships for another sea-borne invasion. Harriet thought that sounded uncomfortably like whistling in the dark.

She went between the Talboys barns and Bateson's barns, and up the track to the wood. Slowly above her head the stars became visible, very softly, and with them a sliver of moon. The edge of the wood was infiltrated already with the blackness of night, and when she reached the top of the swelling field she was not tempted to go further. Instead she turned and looked at Paggleham below her. In peace-time this view would be twinkling with lights in cottage windows, and the church clock would be lit up. A line of lamp-posts would prick out the track of the High Street. Now it was all in rapidly darkening shadow. Someone opened a door in the street below her, and she saw the oblong of light appear, to be swiftly closed off again. The news from France was very bad, and it was hard not to see the darkness as a metaphor.

And yet there was enough residual light for her to see her way by. And as she drew nearer home she could hear voices rising towards her. A conversation in the street was audible, although she could not make out what was being said. She heard a rumble and a thud that puzzled her until she remembered the pig-killing set-up. The fate of another poor pig promised another lovely pork dinner. Sam had said it was quick and silent. She could hear the land-girls singing in their barn as she passed their doors; it sounded very jolly:

> *My mother said*
> *Always look under the bed*
> *Before you put the candle out,*
> *In case there is A MAN about . . .*

The barnyard was now very dark. Harriet nearly collided with the cart, having forgotten it was standing there. That cartwheel! She thought she recalled reading of iron rims on the Celtic chariots in which the chieftains rode to battle who had defeated the tribes who made the carvings in the chalk in the Paggleham Cave. The thing had been done that way, no doubt, since centuries before Julius Caesar scrambled up the shingle on the Channel shore. In the deep past the beloved island had been conquered again and again, and always absorbed its conquerors. But at the moment, Harriet thought, quietly lifting the latch of the back door, and going in to her peaceful household, that was not an entirely comforting thought.

Bunter was sitting at the kitchen table in his shirt-sleeves, reading a book. She had the feeling at once that he had been waiting for her.

'A pleasant walk, my lady?' he said, rising as she came in.

'Yes thank you, Bunter.'

'May I lock up now?'

'Of course. Goodnight.'

And in her bedroom she found hot water waiting in an enamel jug. A little bunch of wild flowers on the dressing-table. The bed turned down and ready. Everything the heart could desire – except her husband.

The bad news was getting steadily worse. Someone called Quisling – may his name be cursed for centuries – had appointed himself head of the Norwegian state and ordered resistance to cease. It hadn't ceased; presumably Britain would retaliate, but you didn't need to be much of a strategist to see how bad this looked. You didn't even have to have a husband out there somewhere, and in danger. You only had to know that Germany needed the iron ore that was shipped out of Narvik.

Bunter had set up a map over the kitchen mantelpiece on which little rows of pins marked German and allied positions. Watching him, Harriet saw him moving the pins to mark yet another retreat.

'Bunter, what can happen?' she asked him.

'We don't want to frighten the horses, my lady,' he said, and she realised that Charlie and Polly had entered the kitchen.

'Later,' she said. But she didn't need Bunter to tell her that it looked as if the Germans were irresistible. Everything they attacked went down like ninepins.

What Bunter thought was even plainer when she found him engaged in a curious operation in the old hay-loft. There was an upper door there that had been used to raise the hay and swing it into the loft. Harriet, finding the house empty, had gone in search of everyone, and found them all, with the usual addition of Sam Bateson, watching Bunter. Sadie and Mrs Trapp between them were hanging on to the tiny children, well out of the way of Bunter's activity. He had an old iron preserving pan suspended from the beam above his head, a garden sieve at his feet, and a barrel of water on the ground below him. Using a pair of tongs he was gingerly tipping the pan, and something molten was falling through the sieve to land in hissing droplets in the water.

'Whatever is Bunter doing?' Harriet asked Mrs Trapp.

'He's making bullets!' cried Charlie.

'Out of gutter pipe. I didn't know you could do that,' said Sam.

'Neither did I,' said Harriet tersely.

'Ammunition for shotguns,' Bunter told her, when she challenged him later. 'Lead shot; well, I didn't have enough height to get nice round shot. It would be more truthful to say they were pellets.'

'But, Bunter . . .'

'We have nine shotguns available to the Local Defence Volunteers, my lady, but nothing like enough shot. I was hoping to mitigate the deficiency.'

'But, Bunter, aren't lead bullets against the Geneva Convention?'

'Dum-dum bullets are, my lady, yes.'

'Explain the difference to me.'

'Lead shot is very small, my lady. It penetrates without spreading enough on impact to make a really nasty exit wound.'

'Your home-made pellets wouldn't spread?'

'We are not facing a sporting contest, my lady.'

The freezing winter, and the sense of crisis that had accompanied the move to Talboys had shifted the heart of the house permanently. Now that early spring made it possible to sit with open windows, and the sunlight made the sitting-room comfortable even with no fire in the grate, Harriet was not quite sure why the adults and children alike gravitated to the long scrubbed deal table in the kitchen, and an ingrained habit of getting under Mrs Trapp's feet. But so it seemed. Mrs Trapp was often exercised about the menus of the day. And Mrs Ruddle was very often to be found 'dropping in' for a chat, a cup of tea, a scrounge for something, and, to do her justice, the offer of a hand with this or that.

'It will be a sight different next time there's one of them there air-raids,' Harriet heard her telling Bunter one morning. 'For the Methodists, that is. My Bert has fixed up the cave something lovely. Snug as bugs in rugs, that's what we'll be.'

'You said it, Mrs Ruddle,' observed Bunter.

'Unless you can shoot me a rabbit or two, Mr Bunter,' said Mrs Trapp unhappily, 'we shall have to make do tonight with cheese and potatoes.'

'That will be very nice, Mrs Trapp,' said Harriet. 'We aren't going hungry so far. But cheer us up – we have a prospect of pork don't we? I was going to ask you what cut we would get this time.'

'Who's getting pork?' cried Mrs Ruddle. 'No one as far as I know! And if I don't know, I'd like to know who does!'

'Calm down, Martha,' said Mrs Trapp. 'Nobody has offered us a pork share. Her ladyship is mistaken, that's all.'

'Very likely,' said Harriet. 'I thought I heard that thingummy in the shed come rumbling down, but I must have been mistaken.'

'When?' cried Mrs Ruddle. 'When was that?'

'Two nights ago – or three. When I went out for a moonlight walk.'

'Lawks!' cried Mrs Ruddle. 'Someone has stolen one of our pigs! One of them will be found gorn, and nothing to be done! Oh, blimey, I'm going to get Bert to have a looksee.'

'Here's the rota, Mrs Ruddle,' said Mrs Trapp. 'The next one due is Joan Raikes's; then Mrs Simcox . . .'

'It won't be a rota one!' wailed Mrs Ruddle. 'Too easy checked up on, it'll be . . . oops!' She stopped. 'I'm off!' she declared.

'I'll go,' said Sam, looking up from the pile of comics he had been reading with Charlie, sprawled on the rug by the window. 'I can run faster than that Ma Ruddle, any day!'

'Well, whatcha waiting for?' cried Mrs Ruddle. 'Sooner you go sooner you get back again!'

'Bunter, would you go and look in the shed?' said Harriet. To Mrs Ruddle she said, 'Would you like me to call the police?'

'Oh, no, mum, don't do that!' cried Mrs Ruddle. 'Please don't. Just leave it to me and Bert and the locals. We'll sort it out. And we'll sort out ooever done it.'

'I don't like the sound of this at all,' said Harriet. 'If a pig has been stolen, why shouldn't we tell the police? And come to that whoever is missing a pig has probably told Constable Baker already.'

'Well, that's just it!' cried Mrs Ruddle. 'It won't be one of *those* pigs, it'll be one of the extra ones . . .'

Bunter was lingering at the back door, on his way out. 'Explain yourself, woman!' he said, in terrible tones.

'You need a licence to slaughter a pig,' said Mrs Ruddle, not meeting his eyes. 'But not if they don't know you've got one. There's some club pigs that aren't on the rota. It's all square,' she added defiantly. 'Everyone gets a cut just the same, as long as they can be trusted to keep it dark.'

'And where are these extra-curricular pigs being kept, Mrs Ruddle?' asked Bunter sternly.

'I didn't oughter tell,' she said.

'I could deploy the Home Guard to find them,' said Bunter.

'They've got more sense, most of them, than to look very 'ard,' she said defiantly.

'I think Sam is already looking,' said Harriet. She was remembering how anxious young Charlie had been on the day of the picnic with Charles and Mary that they should not enter the wood, and she thought she could make a good guess where Sam, his confederate, was looking. And was that what took Miss Twitterton up to the wood in the dusk? A turn at taking pigswill?

'If we can't keep a few things hid, we'll be right down to what they say we can have on the rations,' said Mrs Ruddle sadly. 'And my Bert says if they feed us like pigeons, we'll have the 'earts of pigeons.'

'Feeding us *on* pigeons would be more practical,' said Harriet solemnly. 'Mrs Trapp makes an excellent pigeon pie.'

Bunter said, 'I think the first step is to go and inspect the suspect equipment.'

'Of course, Bunter.'

Harriet followed Bunter out into the yard. He unbolted the pig-shed door, and they looked in. Harriet saw at once that the great block of concrete was on the floor; the gadget had been sprung, and she was right, she *had* heard it go. Bunter took a torch from his pocket and played it round the

214

shed; there were no windows, and they were standing in the light of the door. Harriet frowned deeply as she looked. The end of the rope now hung halfway from ridge to floor. It had been cut, leaving a rough end. Why? Wouldn't one lower the pig again, slacken the loop, and remove it? Now a new one would need to be made and the rope would be shortened a bit.

'Don't go in, my lady,' said Bunter. 'You'll get blood on your shoes.'

And indeed his torch showed the straw on the floor to be thickly fouled with dried blood. The whole shed had the smell of it. Bunter stepped in to shine his torch into the roof, and disturbed a cloud of flies from the straw. He moved around. 'The blood buckets are empty,' he said. 'What a waste! What a wicked waste! The clowns who did this, m'lady, can never have heard of blood sausage, or black pudding. A bad business. It must have been a case of taking the meat, and making a run for it. I can't imagine Mrs Ruddle and her like having a hand in such a botch.'

'Well, that's a relief,' said Harriet. 'I wouldn't like to condone the black market, but I don't want to pick a quarrel with village people who are all our neighbours, and some of them our friends.'

Bunter was shining his torch all round the shed. 'Country people are usually so thrifty,' he said thoughtfully. 'I imagine this is the work of a town's person. But it would have to be someone who had lived here long enough to know how this works. And, of course, to know about the whereabouts of the pig.'

'We have lots of Londoners here. But they're women and children. Of course their menfolk come to visit sometimes, the ones that aren't in the forces. But perhaps it's simply that there wasn't time to do it properly?'

'The meat is inedible, my lady, unless it is drained,' he said.

'Well, I for one didn't know that, Bunter.'

Mrs Ruddle must have been niftier than she looked in a crisis, for she had raised a widespread hue and cry, and various people were arriving: John Bateson, and Mr Puffett, and Archie Lugg, and Aggie Twitterton, and even Mrs Goodacre. Indignant voices filled the yard.

'Well, but what can we do about it?'

'We've been stung. Had. That's what it amounts to,' Mr Puffett was saying. 'And we can't complain to nobody.'

'Just let me get my hands on whoever . . .'

'Funny thing though. One or two people couldn't hardly eat a whole pig, could they?' asked Mr Puffett. 'So I'd like to bet it's gone down to London for the black market. Must have.'

'Instead of being for our own black market, right here?' That was Mrs Goodacre.

'It's not to sell, Mrs Goodacre. It's only to eat,' said John Bateson. 'And it's a damn fool regulation that makes a crime out of what has been going on peacefully for centuries.'

'Don't you know there's a war on?' Mrs Goodacre said sadly.

'Well, let's get things clear,' said John Bateson. 'There's

a pig been slaughtered here that none of us knows a thing about. Is that it?'

'It seems so,' said Harriet. Behind her she heard Bunter close the shed door. She heard the hasp pushed home on the hoop of the latch. He took a padlock from his pocket, and she heard it click shut.

'So most likely,' Bert Ruddles said, 'one of our hidden pigs 'as been took.'

'Whatever next?' said Mrs Simcox. 'Whatever next?'

'Serves us right, really, doesn't it?' said Mrs Raikes.

And then Sam Bateson came running into the yard, bright-eyed and breathless. 'It's all right, everyone!' he cried. 'They're both there! Kaiser and Führer, they're both alive and rooting around just where they oughter be!'

Bunter said quietly to Harriet, 'We'd better get the police. Whatever these good people say. At once.'

Hope Fanshaw, Mrs Mervyn Bunter, turned up unexpectedly, tapping at the front door, which was standing ajar, and stepping into the hall while Harriet was calling the police. She stood looking quizzical while Harriet briefly explained, and said, as soon as Harriet put the receiver down, 'Not again!'

'Oh, Hope!' cried Harriet, 'I am so glad to see you! I have been missing you badly!'

'So what's all this about the police?' said Hope. 'Has Mervyn been up to something again? I'm surprised at him, I always thought it was Lord Peter who led him into mischief.'

'I'll go and fetch him,' said Harriet. 'He's just outside in the stable yards.'

'Dealing with a crisis, I gather.'

'Someone has been making use of our premises to butcher an animal without our knowledge,' said Harriet, 'and therefore, we assume, without a licence. But most likely with the connivance of somebody in the village.'

'Is that all?' said Hope. 'Then I suppose Mervyn will have some time to spare. I've got forty-eight hours' leave.'

Harriet said, 'I've just remembered an errand. I'll leave you to it.'

She went through the kitchen, asked Mrs Trapp to put the kettle on, and returned to the yard. Nobody was there now except Bunter.

'People were not exceptionally keen to stay to talk to the police, my lady,' he said. 'They all remembered some chores they had to do, or an urgent errand of some kind.'

'Funny thing, Bunter, I've just remembered an errand myself. And there's an unexpected visitor in the house. Would you deal with it, please? I'll wait here for the police officer.'

Harriet sat down on the mounting block at the stable door on the other side of the yard from the pig-shed. She closed her eyes in the warmth of the sun. Surely there was some way of finding room for Bunter and Hope? And preferably room for their baby son. Bunter said he was comfortable in the attic, but for a family you would need at least three rooms. How extensive were the attics, anyway? They were full of stuff moved up from the London house, but that could be shoved in a shed somewhere. How good it would be to recreate at Talboys the comfortable situation they had constructed in London, with the Bunters in the mews behind the house, and a pleasant friendship between herself and Hope. Harriet did feel lonely here. Surrounded by people and with three servants and all the children in the house she nevertheless had no friend of her own class. Miss Twitterton was the nearest to an independent and equal friend she had here. Perhaps that was why she had been so stung by Miss Twitterton's refusal of confidence. There was the vicar and his wife, of course, excellent people. They reminded Harriet in many ways of her own parents. But London friends were out of reach now, Oxford friends even more distant.

There were letters, of course – everyone was diligently writing to each other. But a sort of official good cheer and uplift had taken over from intimacy, and the war had driven other subjects to the margins. Even Miss Martin, the dean of Harriet's old college, and a close friend, wrote such letters now. What had she written about last week? Harriet rehearsed the letter in memory.

. . . If Sir John Simon would only explain how exactly one is to spend hard to win the Economic War, and at the same time save hard to win the Economic Peace, he would confer a benefit on mere narrow-minded logicians like me – but I suppose the answer is that in war-time one has to do the impossible, and will end by doing it . . . 'This is a funny war,' people say, and I know

what they mean. When everything happens at sea, it's rather like two people playing chess. There's a deathly silence, and you don't know quite what they're up to; you only see one piece after another swept off the board and accounted for – a destroyer here, a merchantman there, a black knight exchanged for a white bishop – all queerly impersonal and worked out in terms of things – pieces – so many taken and so many left . . . Look here, I do think somebody ought to do something to throttle that Haw-Haw creature. I don't mind his having said that half Oxford was in flames, and that the soldiers had to be protected by pickets from the unwelcome attentions of the women students. That gave us much harmless pleasure, but . . .

Harriet couldn't remember what had followed the 'but'. But how good it would be to hear from Letitia Martin about some arcane point of scholarship, or some completely trivial conflict in the senior common room, or some owlish comment about men, women and love! Harriet was homesick for normality. It would be very good to see more of Hope when she could get leave.

If only that cottage of Susan Hodge's would come vacant! It was a short enough step away; but perhaps even better would be to arrange a swap: to put Bateson's land-girls in the cottage, and take over their quarters as an annex to Talboys. It was a great pity the Yew Tree Lane cottage was not soon to be free, as well as surprising – she had a strong impression that Flight Lieutenant Brinklow was recovering well. Yet hadn't Susan Hodge said he had taken it for another month? Perhaps, thought Harriet, the poor man was skiving, postponing his return to active duty. It must take a bit of manly courage having been shot down once to offer oneself for the same ordeal again. Perhaps it would be natural of him, if not admirable, to take his time.

'Shame on you, Harriet,' she told herself. Thinking of the poor chap as skiving, when – and then suddenly he snapped into focus in her mind, like one of those lantern slides the children played with in the nursery: he came into her mind's eye running for the train. And yet hadn't she seen him the other day, limping along on sticks just the same as before? A man of contradictions: a fighter hero afraid to get his teeth fixed. Very odd. And then something else occurred to her about Brinklow. He had been at the dance, standing talking, the night Wendy was murdered. He had not been down in the shelter below the Crown. Was he accounted for? Because he was the only man in uniform who would not have been going back to barracks that night. Kirk's men had checked that every airman who came from the surrounding bases had got back again. What about an airman living in Susan Hodge's cottage, right here? And another thought came to her: standing on the tower Fred Lugg had told her he had seen the Talboys party pass out of view behind the yew tree at the churchyard gate; surely that tree would also mask from view the junction of Yew Tree Lane with the High Street? If Wendy had met someone coming down the lane as she ran towards the shelter, Fred Lugg wouldn't have seen that.

'Oh, but this is ridiculous,' she told herself. There hadn't been the breath of a suggestion from anyone that Wendy and Brinklow had even clapped eyes on each other. Why would he strike her down in the street? But a quotation from the inimitable Sherlock Holmes came into her mind: 'When you have eliminated the impossible, whatever remains, however improbable, must be the truth.' At the very least, she should ask Superintendent Kirk to follow it up and get Brinklow to account for his movements on the night of the crime.

And here, as if called by her thought, came Superintendent Kirk with Jack Baker into the yard.

'I'm glad of the excuse to come myself, Lady Peter,' he said. 'Now, what's all this about a pig?'

Eleven

So shalt thou feed on Death, that feeds on men,
And Death once dead, there's no more dying then.
William Shakespeare, sonnet 146, 1609

The Superintendent dealt briskly with the pig. He told Jack Baker to lock the shed behind him, and put an official police seal on the door. Then he was to tour every registered pig in the village, and satisfy himself that it was still alive.

'As for unregistered pigs . . . I expect that's what we have here, Lady Peter, and a bother and trouble it is likely to be.'

'I think you're right, Superintendent. Come indoors, and we can talk quietly. I've thought of something. Or someone, rather; someone we haven't checked.'

'You are quite right!' Superintendent Kirk exclaimed, after she'd told him who was on her mind. 'He wasn't a villager, so we didn't check up on him as one of them, and he wouldn't have been one of the officers returning to base. We just plain overlooked him.'

'I haven't a clue why he might have been a danger to Wendy,' Harriet said. 'He seems only marginally more

likely than the notorious wandering maniac. But I think
we should ask him where he was, don't you?'

'I'll get on to it right away,' said Kirk. 'May I use your
phone?'

'It's very interesting work,' Hope told Harriet and Bunter.
They were having mugs of Ovaltine, sitting in the kitchen,
after everyone else was in bed. Harriet was resolved to
go soon to bed herself, but she was indulging herself
in catching up a bit with Hope. 'Of course I can't tell
you much; the interesting thing about it is how unlike
it is from the photography we used to do, Mervyn. I
would have chucked out any blurry negative I got, just
reproached myself, and tried to focus better next time.
But now I have to really look hard at them, however
technically faulty they are. You have to have an eye for
detail; Suffolk and Essex are full of ancient farmhouses
with the same footprint as this one, for instance; you'd
have to study outbuildings and road junctions to place
things. But you'd be surprised how much small things can
show, when it really matters to decipher them. You can
spot troop movements, and changes in buildings. When
they camouflage something you can see them doing it,
from one picture to another, and wonder why. What they
are hiding. It can even be funny. AS sorties lose people,
and a little light relief is very welcome.'

'What's an AS sortie, Hope?' asked Harriet.

'Aerial Surveillance. Hazardous, very often. Although
not as bad as fighter squadrons. One of the units picked

up a dummy airfield being built. They kept an eye on it, and we could see them making makeshift runways, and all these shacks to look like hangars. They even put some mock-up planes on it, would you believe. All intended to draw our fire from something else. Then when it was ready and complete we bombed it – with wooden bombs!'

Harriet laughed. 'Hope, I do miss having you nearby. I'm keeping a close eye on that cottage I wrote to you about.'

'The one with the downed airman in it?'

'The very one. He must be well enough to return to active service soon. The cottage is just up the lane to Blackden Wood. Five minutes from here. You could have the baby with you.'

'Sounds rather too good to be true,' said Hope. 'But I wish the airman well. What do you think, Mervyn?'

Harriet left them to it. She went to bed, stopping to look into the nursery on the way. All was well. Charlie's crystal set was carefully set on a shelf above his bed. That tale about wooden bombs sounded exactly the sort of thing Jerry would get up to.

Jack Baker appeared in the Talboys kitchen quite early the next morning, important with news.

'Superintendent Kirk says to tell you, m'lady, that Lieutenant Brinklow isn't to be found. He would like to know when you last saw him. He's not answering the door.'

Bunter was in his shirt-sleeves, putting Hope's breakfast on a tray, since she had slept late that morning.

'I'll come,' said Harriet, getting up at once.

Superintendent Kirk was standing at the gate of Yew Tree Cottage. He greeted her gloomily. 'Seems that nobody has actually seen him for several days,' he said. 'Susan Hodge says it wouldn't be unusual, he kept himself to himself.'

'The obvious thing would be that he has gone back to his unit,' Harriet said.

'Do you happen to know which unit that is?'

'I'm afraid not, Superintendent. Has he taken all his things?'

'I can't get in to look. I haven't broken the door down. I'd need a warrant for that, and grounds for asking for one. Whereas all I've got is instinct. I don't like the feel of this at all.'

'Something is rotten in the state of Denmark?'

'*Hamlet*,' he said glumly. 'Yes, that's about it.'

'I hope no harm has come to him,' said Harriet. 'I hope it isn't the wandering maniac strikes again.'

'My guess would be that he cottoned on to it that we were catching up with him to ask about Wendy Percival, and he's done a bunk. You'd be amazed how often a suspect bolts for it when there's hardly a thread of evidence, and then you've got him. If you haven't anything to hide, you ask 'em, why did you scarper?'

'You don't think he might be a second victim?'

'It's one thing to attack a defenceless woman,' said Kirk. 'Quite another to have a go at a man in the prime of life, trained, fit, tall. Even if he did have a gammy ankle.'

'That ankle!' she said. 'But I saw him running for a train!'

226

'Did you indeed? When, exactly?'

'A fortnight ago; the day I was in London. And now I come to think of it that was before he took this cottage for another month. Now the plot thickens very much upon us . . .'

'That's a tough one, Lady Peter. I don't have enough eddication for that one. And I do think as how we've got to get in to this cottage.'

'It is rather obscure, Mr Kirk. The Duke of Buckingham, in a play. Miss Hodge would let you have a key.'

'To sneak a look? Against the rules.'

'I'll get the key,' said Harriet. 'And if anyone objects I shall say with perfect truth that I was looking over the place because I want to rent it as soon as it's available. You just happened to be with me.'

She left him standing in the garden and went to look for Susan Hodge.

Brinklow hadn't taken his things. His shirts were in the wardrobe, there was food in the larder – bread, curdled milk, some rather grey-green-looking sausages – his ration-book was propped behind the clock on the kitchen mantel-piece. A game of chess was laid out to be played solitaire, with a chess problem book open on the table beside it. It was the ration-book that was conclusive; to leave it was to risk starvation. A little discreet rummaging in a chest of drawers produced a wodge of banknotes in an elastic band. A lot of money.

'He's coming back,' suggested Harriet.

'Looks as though he meant to,' Kirk agreed. 'I still don't like the look of this. I'm going to get a warrant, and search properly. I could do with fingerprinting the scene, just in case. I suppose Mr Bunter wouldn't care to assist?'

'I'll ask him,' said Harriet. 'But his wife is with us just for two days, so don't keep him too long, will you?'

This led to a briefing of Bunter, who was very willing to help out, and put on his jacket at once. He borrowed talcum powder from Harriet, and set off. She went to her desk, and opened her notebook to work.

Perhaps an hour later Hope began to play the piano in the room below. Harriet laid down her pencil and listened. She loved the sound of the piano being played in another room, the sense of the house shared with music. Her mother had played, though mostly hymn tunes. Peter played, mostly Bach. Hope was playing Chopin: a nocturne. And it was a piece that Harriet knew from long ago, because the German music teacher at her school had loved it, played it often, played it with intense feeling. The Fräulein had not succeeded in teaching Harriet to play; she had managed in the course of that failure to teach her to listen. So now the Fräulein was back in Harriet's mind: her blunted features, dark straight hair, strong square hands on the keyboard. A couple of years back Harriet had suddenly and unexpectedly had a letter from her, forwarded by the school. The Fräulein remembered England with much affection. She had heard that Harriet was a writer; she would like to read something Harriet had written. Would Harriet, for old time's sake, send her a copy? Ordering books from England cost more than she could afford. Times were hard; it was very hard indeed for musicians to live in Germany nowadays. 'Of course,' she had added, 'I am an ardent Nazi.'

Harriet had sent the book. And now she sat wondering what becomes of ageing women whose skill is rooted in the wrong memories, when times turn murderous? It might well be that ardent Nazis were not encouraged to play Polish music. Had the Fräulein been playing Chopin when the bombs fell on Warsaw, or did the nocturne ring out for the last time on the last night of August last year?

If Chopin and the old school hall were out in force taking messages to the Fräulein, Harriet would not have cried halt. Deeply troubled, seeing suddenly how deadly the virtues of England were, she began at the climax of the music to weep. Quite silently. She did not hear the light step on the stair. She heard, with the zany inconsequential quality of a dream, Peter's voice behind her saying: 'And sorrow proud to be advanced so . . . what's amiss, Domina? I hope you're not regretting your skills as a code-breaker; never was a wife presented with so elegant a chance to disembarrass herself of a husband without the trouble and expense of a divorce . . .' But his voice was shaking. She pushed back the chair from her desk and went straight to his arms.

The house had fallen quite silent. Not another note, not a step on the stairs, not a voice in the hallway. It was

229

as if the two of them had boarded the *Marie Celeste* alone. Some time later, Peter said, 'This can't be true, can it? Aren't you going to produce Miss Twitterton from a closet, or a body from the cellar to locate us on solid ground?'

'Yearning for pumpkin-time? Not charming of you, my lord. I don't need stage props to find you real. Although perhaps you are rather unbelievably kempt and clean. Bunter was more than scruffy when he showed up again.'

'Scruffy? Bunter? Oh frabjous day! I wish I had seen that.'

And as if on cue a tap on the door announced Bunter. 'Very sorry indeed to disturb you, my lord, my lady, but Superintendent Kirk is downstairs in a somewhat agitated state, asking to see Lady Peter. I did not take the liberty, my lord, of informing him that you had returned. I thought you might like to tell him yourself.'

'Peter, if you laugh as hysterically as that he will hear you, and the cat will be out of the bag.'

'And what kind of a cat, may I ask, do you take me for? Pedigree Persian? Siamese?'

'A common sort of a ranging tom, I think, with a tabby coat like a garden tiger.'

'Mewing to be stroked,' he said.

'You shall have milk and fish and infinite caresses. But first we must assist the police. Our ordinary duty in peace and in war.'

'But, Harriet, I haven't an idea what is going on. I am quite clueless. Have you been doing a bit of sleuthing on the side, to fill in long hours of idleness while I have been away?'

'What makes you think I am idle in your absence? I wrote it all down for you, Peter, you can read it up tonight.'

Superintendent Kirk was not as amazed to see Peter as Harriet had expected. He did say warmly, 'Glad to see you back, my lord,' but he was deeply preoccupied with the matter in hand.

'We've called off the search for Brinklow, Lady Peter,' he said. 'We have, in a manner of speaking, run him to earth. And guess what—'

'Brinklow?' said Peter. 'A Flight Lieutenant Brinklow? *Alan* Brinklow?'

'That's him,' said Kirk.

'He's dead,' said Peter.

'Now, however did you know that, my lord?' said Kirk.

The question hung in the air between them like an undetonated bombshell. Peter opened his mouth and shut it again.

'We only found him an hour ago,' said Kirk.

'You can't have,' said Peter. 'He's dead.'

'You're right there, my lord,' said Kirk. 'He's as dead as any corpse I've ever seen. But what I want to know is, how do you know that?'

'Peter must be guessing, Superintendent,' said Harriet. But she was looking at her husband with an expression of astonishment. He had gone very white, she saw. He was definitely in earnest.

'Guessing, my arm!' said Kirk.

'Hell,' said Peter. 'Hell, hell, hell. Look, Kirk, where did you find this corpse whoever it is, and why were you looking for him?'

'As to why, my lord,' said Kirk, 'your good lady knows all about it. She will fill you in. He was wanted for questioning in connection with the events of the night of the 17th of February. As to where, buried in a pile of loose earth in George Withers's back garden. A pile of earth thrown up beside the hole he was digging to plant his Anderson shelter. Says it's been there for days and days. He dug the hole, and then he went down with flu and hasn't been near the job for more than a fortnight. Then this morning he was feeling up to it again, he got the metal bit bolted together and standing ready, and when he went to shovel the earth back on top of it like the Ministry pamphlet says to do he had a nasty surprise.'

'Cause of death?' asked Peter.

'Throat cut. The pathologist is there now, and I must get back there. I have left Mr Bunter standing guard over the cottage in Yew Tree Lane, and I have just called in to ask Lady Peter to send someone up there to tell him not to bother. Contents of the cottage can wait.'

'I'll go,' said Peter. 'Haven't seen Bunter in weeks. But look here, Superintendent, whoever you've got laid out in Mr Withers's garden, it isn't Alan Brinklow, believe me.'

'But how do you *know*, my lord?' cried Kirk in exasperation.

'Because, as I said, he was dead already,' said Peter

mysteriously. 'Look, Kirk old chap, you'll have to wait a couple of hours for an explanation.'

There would be a man-to-man reunion between Peter and Bunter. Harriet thought she had best leave them to it. She would round up the children and take them off somewhere. It was a hot afternoon; perhaps they would like a dip in the Pag. There was a swimming hole across the meadow from Talboys with a shallow bank of gravel for the little ones to splash on if they were carefully watched. A cheerful chaos broke out in the boot room behind the kitchen and spilled into the hall while the children collected rugs and towels and drinks and biscuits.

Sitting on the river bank, keeping an eye on the children, and then in due course shedding her shoes and stockings and paddling herself, looking, under Polly's instructions, to see her feet 'wobble' on the submerged shingle, and admiring one after another the pebbles chosen by the children as special, Harriet was possessed by joy. Joy and guilt. She might have been going to share the terrible pain of the bereaved, the threadbare consolations of those whose dear ones had died for their country. Peter's name might have been destined to be written in gold in Balliol College chapel, and on the walls of the church in Denver – in blessed memory, at the going down of the sun; greater love hath no man; in proud and grateful memory – and at least for the moment he was spared, she was spared. It wasn't fair. But how good it made the cool water, the gentle sun, the children's laughter.

At tea-time they came trailing home through the ankle-high grasses – the hay would be ready to cut early this year – a little gaggle of them, and the children at once besieged Mrs Trapp demanding their tea. Harriet found Peter reading the letters she had written to him all about Wendy Percival.

'Thank you, Harriet, for writing all this. It must have been frustrating to have had no reply.'

'It kept you in mind, Peter. It helped me think.'

'It's invaluable now. I've given Bunter the afternoon off. He's taken Hope on a walk to Broxley. I've asked Bungo to come up, though. And Kirk to join us. Hope you don't mind.'

'Of course I mind. Dreadfully. But it's quite all right. Why the awful Bungo?'

'Is he awful? He's a bit cheesy. But he's very clever, Harriet. As he needs to be.'

'Any friend of yours, my lord,' she said. 'Have you told Mrs Trapp about extra people for supper?'

'She said she would contrive. Has it been difficult?'

'Nothing to complain about really. Food has got rather boring. But I have always eaten to live rather than lived to eat. I don't like bananas anyway.'

'I promised myself recently,' he said, 'that if I got home and could be sure of a daily hunk of bread and a glass of clean water I would never complain again.'

'Golly, Peter. You won't be able to keep that one. And was it really that bad? You've no idea what it does to me to think of you hungry . . .'

'Hunger wasn't the worst of it,' he said.

She shuddered, and then braced herself. 'What was the worst?' she asked.

He didn't answer. 'I don't think I have actually thanked you, Harriet, for saving my life.'

'Don't mention it,' she said. 'It was nothing.'

'Good God, Harriet, when I think what an incubus it was when I saved you! What a struggle it was to put that behind us and get on any sort of equal footing! What do you mean, it was nothing? I've been longing to get even with you!'

'Well, there's something about it I hadn't previously realised. It wasn't personal. I would have done as much for absolutely anybody, had I been in a position to. And – I'm right, aren't I – it wasn't personal from you, either. You would have saved any old accused standing in the dock falsely charged.'

'Of course I would. What was personal was seeing you. Seeing at one glance that you *couldn't* have done it. What is personal this time is your knowing what my text must have been. And of course, wanting me back.'

'Yes, my dear,' she said. 'I did want you back.'

They sat in solemn conference in the dining-room. Bunter set a bottle of port on its silver coaster beside Peter at the head of the table.

'Pull up a chair, Bunter,' Peter said. 'You're in on this.'

Superintendent Kirk sat beside Harriet, and Bungo faced them, with his secretary taking minutes.

'This is very serious, Wimsey,' said Bungo. 'I have had to run a security check on everyone present.'

'I thought you would,' said Peter. 'How did we score?'

'Superintendent Kirk is as clean as a whistle,' said Bungo. 'As is Bunter. We have been ignoring your ex-communist sister, Wimsey, as you know, but she is still in the record. Some of your wife's old friends had better be dropped. I have clearance for this discussion, however, among these present, from the highest level. But I must warn you that this is top secret. Breach of confidence might amount to treason.'

'Bungo, I think you and I are the only ones who know what this is about,' said Peter. 'Shall I explain, or will you?'

'Oh, you do the necessary, old man,' said Bungo. 'You're the detective round here.'

'Right,' said Peter, 'here goes. Superintendent, when you turned up to tell Harriet you had found Brinklow—'

'You knew right away he was dead!' exclaimed Kirk. 'Before I told you. And as far as I can see you shouldn't have known, and I haven't had an explanation.'

'I recognised the name,' said Peter. 'It was mentioned to me – as a successful counter-intelligence move – while I was being debriefed from my recent expedition.'

'Keep closely to the point, Wimsey,' said Bungo.

'This is what I think happened,' said Peter. 'Bungo will correct me if my impression is wrong. Alan Brinklow was a reconnaissance pilot, a skilled and brave one. His plane was shot down over the North Sea, and he baled out, but he died of exposure from hours in the water. He was fished out by one of our patrol boats, on a secret mission. All his identity papers were in his pockets, he was as found, downed and drowned, and there was something – don't worry, Bungo, I'm not going to say what – something of very high importance going on over which we wanted to mislead the enemy. The patrol boat captain decided to plant some extra papers in Brinklow's pockets. They weren't very sophisticated, because they had to be mocked up quickly on board ship, so they just took the form of crudely coded letters, instructing Brinklow to parachute into an occupied country, and go somewhere with orders for somebody. Okay so far, Bungo?'

Bungo nodded and Peter went on. 'The patrol boat went close inshore, and pushed the body overboard, hoping it would be washed up on a handy beach. And it worked. The Germans did react to the phoney orders Brinklow was carrying. Everyone congratulated themselves and the patrol boat captain on a nice piece of dirty trickery. And now ... You can see why I was thunderstruck to be told not only that Superintendent Kirk had been looking for Brinklow, but that he had been found interred in Paggleham. You know, Harriet,' he added peevishly, 'I'm afraid we may have to move to a remote island of the Hebrides and live on a solitary rock. We seem to cause our neighbours to be beset by bodies.'

'So let me get this straight,' said Superintendent Kirk. 'You are saying that the fellow who has been living in Paggleham with a broken ankle all this while wasn't the real Brinklow?'

'Can't have been, no,' said Bungo.

'Then would somebody tell me who the hell it was?' cried Kirk. 'I've got the wrong body, is what you're saying. What do I do now?'

'That's what we're here to work out, old chap,' said Peter. 'What happened about his papers?'

'I brought them, as you asked, my lord.' Kirk produced a file from his briefcase, and tipped the little clutch of documents on to the table. 'I must ask you not to touch anything,' he said. 'Fingerprints.'

'Bunter, do we still have a little cache of cotton gloves?' Peter asked.

'I will go and see, my lord. We did before we left.'

They sat round staring at the contents of Brinklow's pockets. Harriet was looking at a little brick-coloured fibreboard disc on a string stamped with name, number and 'RC'. That's why we didn't see him in church, she thought.

There was an identity card of some kind – headed RAF 1250.

Bunter, returning and putting a pair of white gloves on the table, said quietly to Harriet, 'Lord St George has arrived, my lady. Shall I ask him to wait in the study?'

'Yes, he'd better,' said Harriet.

'Where's Brinklow's pay-book?' asked Bungo. 'Where's his ration-book?'

'His ration-book,' said Harriet, 'is on the mantelpiece in his cottage.'

'Yes,' said Kirk. 'He had registered it with the village shop, and with Wagget the butcher.'

'Yes, but who had?' asked Harriet. 'I'm getting confused.

What I meant to say is, surely airmen don't have their ration-books in their pockets when they fly missions?'

'That's a good question,' said Peter. 'Perhaps Jerry can help us after all. Ask him to step in will you, Bunter.'

A burst of laughter from the hall where Jerry was obviously playing with the children was followed swiftly by Lord St George in person, very ruffled, collar undone, and slightly out of breath. 'What's up?' he said pleasantly. Then, as he looked round the table, he said, 'Gosh,' and subsided into the chair that Bunter drew back for him.

'The question is, Jerry, and you are sworn to secrecy – this conversation never took place, and nobody here was here – what papers might we expect to find in an airman's pockets? We need to know if anything that ought to be here is missing.' Peter gestured towards the documents lying on the table. 'Don't touch,' he added as Lord St George bent forward to look.

'Well, this chap's been a bit careless,' said Lord St George.

'What's missing?' asked Kirk.

'Oh, it's the other way round. We're supposed to take the absolute minimum when flying operationally. No papers, nothing, just the dog-tag. But of course it's an awful nuisance; you need the 1250 to go on and off the base, and you would have your pay-book, and you tend to have snapshots and letters from home and stuff in your pockets, and when you scramble suddenly you are probably waiting in the dispersal tents, right down the field, and you can't go back to your lockers and unload everything, so it's easy to have things on you you're not supposed to have.'

By way of demonstration Jerry began unloading his pockets on to the table in front of him. There were several toffee papers stuck to his pay-book. Two snapshots of pretty girls. A lot of betting slips and IOUs. His disc, Harriet noticed, said C of E. He followed her gaze.

'Oh, that, Aunt Harriet,' he said, bestowing one of his most ravishing smiles on her. 'Well, it should say "none" really, but they make such a fuss when you try it. Someone's got to bury you, they say. And "none" would upset the pater fearfully.'

'But so far from there being anything missing from this man's pockets, you think there's a lot too much,' said Peter.

'I suppose the poor devil got pranged,' said Jerry. 'Well, say a prayer for him when you've done picking him over. It's a bit of a warning, I suppose. As you see, if I went into the drink there'd be quite a bit of stuff in my pockets I wouldn't want the pater to see.'

'Shouldn't there be a pay-book?' Kirk asked.

'I'd look in his locker for that,' said Jerry. 'If you're downed it might get incinerated, and it's got a will form in the back. You'd try to leave that in a place of safety, especially if you've got a liaison of some kind your people don't know about. But come to think of it a flight lieutenant wouldn't have a pay-book,' he added. 'Officers are paid directly to their banks by Cox and Kings. RAF agents in London.'

'I take it we can check if any money has been drawn from Brinklow's account in the last three months?' said Peter.

'Yes, I can do that,' said Kirk.

'Is that all you need me for, Uncle Peter?' asked Jerry. 'Only we've got a game of sardines going out there.' He swept his own stuff into his pockets.

'Thanks, Jerry, yes,' said Peter.

'Would you start again,' said Superintendent Kirk. 'Run me through all this again.'

'Well, we know Alan Brinklow was killed in action. Months ago. We know the Germans picked up his body, because they took the misguided action we hoped they would take,' said Bungo. 'But it would seem that there was something we didn't think of: they had got a body with a rank, a uniform, valid papers, a complete identity. I suppose they thought we would not be certain, since he had been lost at sea, what had happened to him. From our point of view Brinklow was posted missing, presumed dead. But sometimes people turn up again. Very occasionally they turn up alive. Taken prisoner, perhaps.'

'So you think,' said Peter, 'that perhaps the German secret service inserted someone into the convenient persona we had presented them with, and sent him over here to impersonate Brinklow.'

'It's a good cover story, really,' said Kirk slowly. 'A man who has baled out and broken an ankle, and recuperating; nobody will have thought to check up on him. I didn't, certainly. It never entered my mind to wonder if he had reported to his base, or anything like that.'

'Peter, he spoke flawless English,' said Harriet.

'That's possible,' said Peter. 'There were some upper-crust Prussian boys at school with me. There are quite a lot of connections between us and Germany.'

'So the long and the short of it is,' said Kirk, 'that you think what I've got in the morgue with its throat cut isn't a British airman, it's a German spy.'

'It seems we can be fairly certain of that,' said Bungo. 'And that leads us into a very great difficulty. Because we don't know what he was doing. We have cottoned on to him too late.'

'What would have happened to him if you had blown his cover in time?' asked Harriet.

'He would have been taken to a certain secret establishment and invited to reveal all, and if he seemed up to it, to "turn" and serve as a double agent.'

'If he wouldn't tell? If he wouldn't turn?'

'Very few people hold out. I'm told we don't touch them; it's all done by cunning. But there are a few steadfast brave ones; and in the end we would hang spies,' said Bungo.

'It would be quite important to find out what he was spying on. Why he was here, you see. And now we can't ask him,' said Peter.

'But even more important,' said Bungo, 'is not to let the enemy know he is dead. If they know he is dead they will replace him on whatever mission it was, and we will be in the dark about it.'

'Well, how can I keep it secret?' Superintendent Kirk cried, dismayed. 'We've got a body come up in George Withers's garden, and he was down the pub like streaked lightning yacking about it all. The whole place is buzzing with it.'

'Do you reckon George Withers recognised the body?' asked Peter.

'I don't think so. He only uncovered the feet, and then he came yelling for us.'

'And after that you screened off the place, and took the body away under a sheet as per usual?'

'Everything done according to the book, my lord.'

'So the only people who know for certain *who* was found are those here present, and your constables? And I take it you can rely on secrecy from them if you solemnly require it?'

'They know it's as good as their job's worth to talk behind their hands,' said Kirk.

'So far, so good,' said Bungo.

'Well it's not very far, though, is it?' cried Kirk. There's got to be an inquest, and I've got to go around asking everybody all about it, and—'

'Exactly. This is a serious problem,' said Bungo. 'I don't suppose the enemy have a spy in the Crown. Of course if he had a local accomplice the report will have been sent back to his controller anyway, but if not we can do something. No detecting, Superintendent. We'll make sure the coroner takes evidence of identification only. An RAF officer will appear to make the identification. The *Paggleham Crier* can report the inquest, but will happen to misspell the name of the deceased. Trinkhough, perhaps. Misheard by the reporter. That can be arranged.'

'Can it indeed?' said Peter.

'In defence of freedom of speech,' said Bungo, 'we have considerable powers to suppress it.'

'I still don't understand,' said Kirk. 'Whoever it was my men have just dug out of George Withers's pile of soil, somebody topped him. Somebody cut his jugular. Are you saying we don't want to know who? If that's the case, gentlemen, I'd like to know how I am supposed to prevent it from happening again. After all, this is the second murder in this out-of-the-way little place in the course of a couple of months. We'll have a bloody massacre going on here if we don't find the killer.'

'Your earlier murder can't have anything to do with this,' said Bungo. 'You detect that one all you like. For this one, we would like you to keep your head well down, and bear in mind that the death has to be kept as quiet as possible.'

Superintendent Kirk rather clearly wasn't taking to Bungo, wasn't liking this.

'I haven't got round to searching the cottage yet,' he said, 'what with being short-handed.'

'Our people are searching it now,' said Bungo.

'And would they tell me what they found?' asked Kirk.

Bungo's silence hung in the air.

'What if my chief is browned off with me for going slow and not getting anywhere?' Kirk asked.

'You won't hear a word of complaint from him,' said Bungo.

'What if I won't lie low like you say?'

'You might find yourself off the case. Working in a different district. Helping to police trawlermen in Hoy.'

'That's enough, Bungo,' said Peter. 'Superintendent Kirk has his feelings. He wants to do his job properly, that's all. You can't blame him.'

'Thank you, my lord,' said Kirk. 'Now if you gentlemen have finished with me, I'll be getting along. I've some fire-watching to do tonight, and a long day tomorrow.'

Peter got up to show the Superintendent out, and Harriet followed him.

'Sorry about this, Kirk,' Peter said. 'But look, your security clearance is better than mine. I'll keep you filled in on what is going on.'

'What's getting overlooked here,' said Kirk, taking his trilby from the hall-stand, 'is that Brinklow was looking as if he had a bit of explaining to do about that other matter. How am I to investigate one without the other, that's what I'd like to know? Because maybe that doesn't have anything to do with this, but this may still have to do with that!'

'What was that about?' asked Peter, as they returned to the dining-room.

'Wendy Percival, I imagine,' said Harriet. 'Two of the three young men who were attached to Wendy Percival threatened openly to kill her murderer if they found out who it was. And we hadn't accounted for Brinklow on the night of the murder. Supposing one of them tumbled to that? Can Kirk even ask them where they were the night Brinklow was killed?'

'Perhaps he'd better not,' said Peter.

Bungo's secretary was gathering his papers, closing his briefcase.

'We'll be off too,' Bungo said, 'and leave you to some well-earned peace. By the way, Flim, it's good to see you. Bit of a close shave getting you back.'

'Luck, mostly. And a neat bit of decipherment,' said Lord Peter.

Twelve

Oh, 'tis my delight of a shiny night,
In the season of the year!
'The Lincolnshire Poacher', Anon c. 1776

The game of sardines seemed to be over, and Jerry was perched on a chair in the living-room, holding forth to an enraptured pair of small boys sitting on the floor in front of him, their arms round their drawn-up knees, composing a scene like Millais's *The Boyhood of Raleigh*. Rather than pointing out to sea, Jerry was flying Charlie's model plane around at arm's length.

'Is it as good as a car?' asked Sam. 'Is it as good as a Bugatti?'

'Much, much better,' Jerry said. His voice took on a tone of reverence, like a boy in love uttering his girl's name. Peter quietly walked round the group, and sat down on the floor behind Charlie and Sam to listen. Smiling, Harriet chose the chair at her desk, set apart from the little tableau, and settled down to overhear.

'Spitfires,' Jerry said, 'are just not like other planes.'

'Are they faster?' asked Sam.

'Fastest kites in the air,' said Jerry. 'And the best

acceleration, and the most manoeuvrable. Make other planes feel like municipal trams. But in a Spit you can out-fly anything.'

'How far will they go?' asked Charlie.

'Ah, there's the rub,' said Jerry. 'You could cruise carefully for maybe two hours – you'd have four hundred miles maximum. But if you got into a fight, Charlie, you'd need all the speed you could get, and you might have only forty-five minutes' flying at combat speed.'

'How do you make the guns go off?' Sam asked.

'There's a neat little button under your right thumb as you hold the joystick,' said Jerry.

'I would of thought you might have had to aim your gun with your right hand, and do the flying with your left,' offered Sam.

'Oh, no, no,' said Jerry. 'To aim the guns you trim the plane itself – that's why it matters so much that she flies like a bird – as though you *were* the bird, as though you *were* the plane. It isn't like riding inside a machine, it's like putting the plane on like an overcoat. Every move you make, every tiny movement of any part of you is connected so that she responds. She'll respond by a fraction or by a big jump, depending on every twitch you make. She's pure joy.'

'Gosh,' said Charlie. 'Gosh!'

'Where's your parachute, Uncle Jerry?' asked Sam.

'You're sitting on it,' said Jerry. 'It's strapped to you, under your bum. It's a tight fit. First time I've been glad not to be tall. Some chaps have to lower their seat right down on to the floor, and even then their heads are jammed against the cockpit cover. But I fit nicely. You've got the joystick between your knees, trimming with every tiny movement, back, forward, left and right; you hold it with your four fingers, and the gun-trigger is under your thumb. Your left hand is on the throttle, and your feet on the rudder pedals, and everything moves like velvet, gives you perfect responses. She's as much under your control as your own body, your own legs and arms. Anything you ask, she delivers. So you soar, and you get between the bastards and the sun, and you dive on them from above, going like a gannet, you put her into a dive and she goes on and on speeding up, she's not like a Hurricane with a maximum speed even when it's falling like a stone.'

He fell silent, shaking his head slightly in amazement at his subject.

'You can see that it's a super shape, even when you can only look at them in the sky,' offered Sam.

'They are beautiful,' said Jerry. 'They have lovely curves. If you stroke one, you can feel little ridges where the plates of the skin overlap each other – and you know what? The lower plate overlaps the upper one, because she was designed by Mitchell and he was a sea-plane fellow.'

'A man in love,' said Peter to Harriet later. 'When he talked about stroking it . . .'

'What he didn't mention,' said Harriet, 'was that his first love was and is danger. Danger and speed. Peter, I wish he were just a little bit frightened.'

'I'm sure he is, really,' said Peter. 'But you can't expect him to say so in front of the children.'

Superintendent Kirk was still rather glum and sulky when he appeared three days later to talk things over. Harriet had forgotten all about it. She had had three whole days of riotous behaviour, joyful children romping around with cousin Jerry and a laughingly indulgent father. There were two picnics, a swim, and a wild and wicked drive to the beach at Frinton. 'A grateful country can spare me the petrol for that,' Peter had said. 'Is my journey really necessary? Let's reason not the need. Let's be superfluous. Children need seaside.'

They were all so light-headed that Polly asked if it was Christmas.

And then reality descended again with Jerry departing for another tour of duty, and the Superintendent standing disconsolately in the drawing-room, declining tea and biscuits.

'What now? Is what I've come to ask you, my lady,' said Superintendent Kirk. 'Well, and Lord Peter too, if, as I suppose, you've filled him in. I've done my best, my lord, to muddy the water by putting it about that the body what we found was a tramp from up Walden way. I don't like being wrong any more than the next man, my lord, and I'll have to admit that I thought that talk of Brinklow being a spy was a load of old cod. In years of police work,' he added, sounding plaintive, 'all the clever ingenious explanations I have dealt with have been wrong. When you uncover it, it's nearly always everyday stuff. Even murder. It's always boring, and often squalid. But I seem to be wrong. The path. report says he has German teeth.'

'What in hell are German teeth?' asked Peter.

'Very elaborate bridge work, with lots of gold, I understand,' said Kirk. 'Much superior to anything you could get done in England, the pathologist says. Well, he thinks you might find a refugee Jewish dentist in London who could do it, but some of the work is ten years old, so it isn't likely.'

'I should rather doubt if a German spy impersonating an RAF officer would like to go to a Jewish dentist,' observed Peter.

'He didn't!' exclaimed Harriet. 'He wouldn't go to a dentist at all; he had terrible toothache, and he said he was afraid of the drill or something. It was the talk of the village.'

'There you are then,' said Peter.

'And something else,' said Harriet. 'There *was* someone who said he was a spy, and that was Mrs Spright, and she's a retired dentist. She even said you could tell he was a spy every time he opened his mouth; and I didn't take any notice because she was saying it about Miss Twitterton and the vicar and various other people as well.'

'We must investigate Miss Twitterton,' said Peter solemnly. 'Is there anything else in the path. report that we ought to know, Superintendent?'

'Deceased had been tied up,' said Kirk.

'Oh ho! Had he now?'

'Weals round the ankles,' said Kirk. 'No swelling, so the pathologist doesn't reckon he was tied for long. Angle of cut to the throat suggests an assailant of short stature, reaching up and from behind to deliver the blow. Hair soaked in blood. Various minor bruises and abrasions. Blood spotting on his uniform—'

'What?' said Peter sharply. 'Spotting?'

'It looks as though the death blow was part of a struggle,' said Kirk.

'You mean there was a second assailant?' said Peter. 'I don't quite see . . .'

'If the cut that killed him was from behind, and he was fighting somebody . . .'

'I would say he had been overpowered in a struggle, and tied up.'

'Hmm,' said Peter. 'It's odd that he didn't defend himself more effectively. Pseudo-Brinklow would certainly have been combat trained.'

'Doesn't that lead to the thought that it was another spy? Someone he trusted, who then ambushed him?' asked Harriet.

Kirk shook his head unhappily. 'Well, if it was our side come to arrest him, it's hard to see—'

'We can rule that out, I think,' said Peter, 'because our side would be so eager to interview him. Of course if someone puts up a very violent struggle I suppose . . .'

'Could he have cut his own throat rather than submit to capture?' asked Harriet.

'We can ask the path. man; but it's not an easy trick;

and it's that blood spotting on the uniform that's worrying me.'

'I can't see why, my lord,' said Kirk. 'If there was a fight . . .'

'A severed jugular?' said Peter. 'Blood-soaked hair? And the uniform not also soaked with blood? Where did the blood go? I mean if a corpse is found like that, there's usually a pool of blood that gets mopped up in the victim's clothing.'

'Well, we think George Withers's garden can't have been the scene of the crime,' said Superintendent Kirk. 'It's overlooked from the road. We've got a time of death around ten in the evening, and there would have been people around. Coming from the Crown, or the choir-practice. I think someone moved the body later, and dropped it into George Withers's handy hole. So if whoever moved it was carrying it over their shoulder, head hanging down, like . . .'

Harriet turned deathly white, and said, 'Oh, my God, Peter.'

And simultaneously Bunter said, 'I might hazard a guess at the scene of the crime, my lord.'

But Harriet couldn't accompany them to the shed, because she was being humiliatingly and violently sick.

She woke from a brief sleep in the aftermath of this seizure, to see Peter sitting in the bedside chair. A glass of brandy stood on her bedside table. She sat up and held out a hand to him.

'Feeling better?' he asked.

'Quite all right now. I'm sorry; the spirit is willing but – the shed?'

'Clean as a whistle. But not cleared of suspicion. John Bateson had sluiced and scrubbed and disinfected it, repaired the rope, checked the pulley, got it all ready for next time. Nobody told him not to, and the idea of leaving it offended him. Not hygienic. He borrowed the key from Constable Baker, who has a bit of explaining to do. Of course the fellow thought he was conniving at covering the traces of unlicensed pig-killing, nothing worse, but Kirk is breathing fire and thunder. Bunter is full of remorse for not voicing his suspicions earlier, but I rather suspect his mind was taken off it by Hope.'

'Not to speak of your return, Peter. Has all the evidence gone, then?'

'Probably not. I've rung Charles and he's sending an expert forensic team. They'll find something. Possibly on that block. Ooops, sorry, Harriet.'

'What for?'

'You turned a rather green shade of white. But the jolly scene in the shed – our shed – makes it much less likely that this is a boy's own spy story. You would have to have local knowledge of that rig-up; very local knowledge. It isn't a bit likely that one of ours or one of theirs could know that. I suppose it's just possible that the shed was chosen because it was secluded and a warm dry meeting place, or hidey-hole.'

'That would still entail local knowledge.'

'Not so much. Only that someone had walked through

the yards and seen the doors. Perhaps actually looking for a hidey-hole. When it comes to knowing that the pig-killing rig is in that particular shed and how to work it, that really is insider knowledge.'

'Well, that isn't impossible, Peter. Perhaps Superintendent Kirk and I were not the only ones to have worked out that pseudo-Brinklow was unaccounted for the night Wendy was murdered. And remember that two of her boyfriends threatened to kill her murderer if they found out who it was.'

'There's a difference between making threats and being able to carry them out.'

'Let me think. Archie Lugg certainly knows about the shed; his family are in the pig club. I'm not so sure about Jake Datchett; I don't see him walking round at our end of the village very much. I think I remember being told that Datchett isn't in the club because he kills his own pigs. But he's a local. They all know everything.'

'So what about Birdlap?'

'Well, he isn't a local man, and he hasn't been here much as far as I know. But when he was here he was making assignations with Wendy Percival, and on at least one night, the night she died, he would have walked through our stable yard to the street. So he certainly passed the pig-shed.'

'Which would have been locked?'

'Which might have been bolted. The bolt is too high to be reached by the younger children, and I don't suppose anybody thought of anything else.'

'There would have been nothing to draw his attention?'

'I don't think so. But of course anyone could have said at some time . . .'

'Well, Superintendent Kirk is playing Pontius Pilate. He has washed his hands of it. He's delegating the task to us. Rather afraid of going anywhere near anything that Bungo warned him off. I thought Bungo came over rather heavy about the poor Superintendent. No wonder his hackles are raised.'

'So where have we got to?' she asked. 'We haven't established where pseudo-Brinklow was the night Wendy was killed. If he was wandering about, anyone could have seen him. Whoever was on fire-watch from the top of the tower, for example, because it was a very bright moon. It's true that Fred Lugg didn't mention – no, wait, he did mention that he hadn't seen his son. But one way or another possibly one of her admirers suspected him, and carried out a threat to kill him.'

'We do rather badly need to know where those young men were, on the night in question.'

'I'm not sure I can see how to find out, Peter. We have to try to find out without letting them guess that the body in George Withers's garden was Brinklow; without letting them know that he isn't accounted for on the night Wendy was killed, and that's why we suspect them of a motive to kill him. I gather that the powers that be think that if any of that got around, the enemy might realise their agent had been silenced.'

'It's a touch delicate, certainly,' he said.

'Just the simple fact that pseudo-Brinklow has disappeared won't surprise anyone,' said Harriet thoughtfully.
'They will assume that he got better and returned to his
unit. People keep coming and going without notice at the
moment. You, for example, my lord.'

'You don't think the village gossip-machine will con-
nect the unannounced disappearance of a resident with
the unexpected appearance of a body? Times must have
changed!'

'Well, all the slogans we have been favoured with, all
the "Be like Dad, Keep Mum" and "Tittle-tattle lost the
battle", are having some effect,' said Harriet. 'It's all a bit
muted, now.'

'Mrs Ruddle is muted?' said Peter. 'You amaze me! Is
Hitler capable of *anything*?'

'Well, she's down a few decibels,' said Harriet, smiling.
'And most of the fuss is going to be about the hypothetical
pork. That's what will be on Mrs Ruddle's mind. But,
Peter, we've only got until the inquest to get on with this.
However distracted villagers are, and however diligently it
has been put around that the body was a tramp, and however creatively the local newshounds mis-spell Brinklow,
the inquest at the Crown will be packed, and then they'll
put two and two together and make fifty-six. This is going
to be another case like the invasion committee for Great
Pagford.'

'What was that?'

'Very sensible arrangements for having emergency food

257

and water, and such like. But a directive came from above to tell everybody about it and keep it strictly secret.'

'Ho, ho,' said Peter. 'But, Harriet, what was that you said about pork?'

'Well, I suppose that most of the village still think that the hoist was used to kill a pig. The hot topic will be: what pig? I gather that at least two unofficial pigs were being kept somewhere in Blackden Wood – our wood – because there was general relief when Sam Bateson found them alive and well. But my guess is that people will be speculating that there was a pig somewhere that wasn't even an unofficial pig, that was a really secret one. And there'll be a good bit of detecting about that, that won't involve Superintendent Kirk or his merry men.'

'Harriet, that's an idea. What if we were to try to buy some blackmarket pork? We would be asking who was around on the very same night . . . I think I might have an appetite for some nice chump chops.'

'Peter, dearest, think of the scandal if you were found out! Famous sleuth breaks the regulations! Greedy aristocrat can't survive on rations like the rest! Twenty-four-point headlines!'

'No, surely, well down the page. Bottom right-hand corner stuff.'

'Well, a woman made headlines the other day, top of the page, across three columns for buying enough sugar for 140 weeks' rations, and driving it home in a Rolls-Royce.'

'What did she get?'

'It's twelve ounces a week. Work it out.'

'I don't mean how much sugar, I mean what sentence was meted out?'

'She was fined. Seventy-five pounds. Don't tell me you could afford it, it's the shame I was thinking of.'

'I am entirely shameless already,' Peter said. 'I shall send Bunter.'

'Supposing, Bunter,' Lord Peter said, 'that a pig had been killed in our outhouse.'

'Unlawful killing, my lord?'

'Oh, quite. Except for this purpose the law is irrelevant. Supposing that we thought there might be some pork around, and we might get a share in it; *when* would we would be asking for it? How long after the event?'

'Well, I believe one would hang the carcass for a day and a half, or two days, my lord. Then the butcher would cut it into joints. Then in a cool pantry, it would keep perhaps two or three days at most. Yes, I think three days in the weather we are having at present.'

'Bother!' said Lord Peter. 'That means we are too late. Another tragedy.'

'Tragedy, Peter?' exclaimed Harriet.

'Thing I heard somewhere: 'A tragedy is a good theory defeated by a fact. In this case a good cover story defeated by a fact.'

'Oh, I see.'

'If I may say so,' offered Bunter, 'the belly and hams of this hypothetical pig would be in brine tubs at the present moment, where they would remain for some three weeks before smoking could begin.'

'So we would *not* be too late to be asking for pork futures – bacon futures, I mean?'

'No, my lord. Assuming that you knew who to ask.'

'We want you to ask Archie Lugg and Jake Datchett,' said Lord Peter. 'We don't expect you to bring home the bacon literally, Bunter. We want you to find out what each of those two young men was doing on the evening of 30th April; and we want them to think you are after something entirely different, like rashers or gammon. You may allege anything you like about the voracious desire of your employers to exceed their rations.'

'Thank you, my lord. If you can dispense with my services this afternoon, my lord, I think I might take a turn round the local lanes.'

'Certainly, Bunter. Certainly,' said Peter cheerfully, with the air of one conferring a favour.

'*More* shelves, is it?' said Archie Lugg. 'Should think they'd be straining their eyes in your household, Mr Bunter, if they've read even the half of them there books.'

'It's more a question of fairness, Mr Lugg,' said Bunter. 'That's a nice piece of work you're on now, if I may say so.'

Archie Lugg was cutting a narrow plank of planed beech at an angle. Two or three sections were cut already, lying on his work bench.

'What is it?' asked Bunter. 'A window-box?'

'No. It's the nearest I can do for a toy bath for dollies,' said Archie, shaking his head. 'I can make it water-tight, but it doesn't look much like a bath.'

'No, it doesn't,' agreed Bunter. 'If you had said it was a feeding trough for a toy donkey I would have been none the wiser.'

'Well, the best I can do has got to be good enough,' said Archie. 'Mrs Simcox has got an evacuee little girl what's breaking her heart over a doll's bath that got left in London, and the little mite's parents seem to have more or less dumped her on the Simcoxes, and don't get in touch, so this is a birthday present.'

'That's very good-hearted of Mrs Simcox,' said Bunter.

'She's gone and got involved,' said Archie. 'I said to her, that's all very well, missus, but what if the parents just turn up out of the blue and take her off of you? But she didn't pay me any mind. Wants the toy bath anyway.'

'I suppose you can put all the off-cuts and shavings to good use,' remarked Bunter.

'Was you wanting kindling?' Archie asked. 'I've got a sack over in the corner I could let you have.'

'I was thinking your workshop sweepings would be good for smoking,' said Bunter.

'They are, yes. Specially the oak shavings.'

'So I thought, if anyone were to be smoking a nice gammon, quietly, somewhere, you might know who.'

'His lordship can't hardly manage on his ration, is it?' said Archie, grinning.

'I mentioned fairness, Mr Lugg,' said Bunter. 'We have

reason to believe that use was made recently of equipment in our sheds, without our knowledge or permission. Naturally it occurs to us that we should be offered a share.'

'Certainly you should,' said Archie cheerfully, fitting the sloping sides of the bath together, and fetching from a little primus stove a pan of hot water, in which was standing a pot of dark brown foul-smelling glue. 'I haven't any problem with that. So long as you didn't react by shopping all concerned to the police.'

'Well, that's exactly the problem,' said Bunter. 'We haven't been offered anything, and we wouldn't know who to "shop" as you put it. I just thought possibly you might know who I should be asking.'

'Sorry,' said Archie. 'I don't know a thing about it. Nobody particular has come asking for wood shavings.'

'And you wouldn't by any chance have been out and about yourself, on the night of the 30th of April, and seen something unusual happening?'

'Who told you that?' exclaimed Archie. 'No, I never! That's to say I was out with a friend that evening, and nowhere near your place, and the first I heard of this bothersome pig it was same time as everybody else.'

'And your friend would gladly confirm that?' asked Bunter.

'No, he wouldn't be glad at all,' said Archie. 'Which is why I aren't a-going to tell you who it was.'

'Well, I can't make you. Thank you for your time, Mr Lugg,' said Bunter pleasantly. 'I'll bid you good afternoon.'

*   *   *

It was the wrong day for talking to Jake Datchett. He was over at Broxford, selling lambs in the market. Roger Datchett greeted Bunter amiably enough, and offered him a seat in the farmhouse kitchen, and a pint from the barrel in the pantry.

'Don't know when the youth will be back, Mr Bunter,' said Roger Datchett. 'Late, if he spots a girl to chat up. There's a dance in the Bull at Broxford after the market is over. Now, you let me know what you want to talk to him about. He got very shirty over being asked about that land-girl.'

'I'll be straight with you, Mr Datchett,' said Bunter, sipping his beer. 'This an excellent brew – your own, I take it?'

'Least said soonest mentioned,' said Mr Datchett.

'His lordship would like to know what became of a certain pig, that made use of our premises for its despatch, in a manner of speaking.'

'That's an interesting question, Mr Bunter. You aren't the only person who has been wondering about that, I can tell you. It wasn't one of ours.'

'No, Mr Datchett. It seems increasingly likely that it wasn't a local pig at all, if I'm to believe all I'm told.'

'So what has my son got to do with it?'

'Very probably nothing, Mr Datchett. But if he were here I would ask him whether by any chance he was out and about the night the pig was killed, and if he saw anything or anyone. Just on the off-chance, you understand.'

Roger Datchett got out of his chair, and went to a Farmers' Calendar that was hanging on the oak beam above the kitchen range. He ran a finger over the squares of days of April. 'When was it?' he asked.

'April the 30th,' said Bunter.

'He was out snaring rabbits that night. It's marked here I was to leave the back door unbolted, and not wait up for him.'

'You don't know where he snares rabbits?'

'Yes. Well, I better ask him where he went. When he gets in I'll ask him. Now, I better get on.'

'Thank you,' said Bunter. 'And thank you for the beer, Mr Datchett.'

It was after supper that evening that Roger Datchett came calling in person at Talboys. Bunter showed him in to the sitting-room while Peter and Harriet were still at the supper table. They finished the pudding, and went through to talk to him. Bunter, responding to a vestigial gesture from Peter, entered the sitting-room a step behind them, and hovered at the door.

'I thought I better deal with this myself, your lordship, if it's all the same to you,' said Roger Datchett. 'My boy's got such a hot tongue he'll talk himself into trouble as soon as talk himself out of it.'

'We shall be grateful for anything you can tell us,' said Peter. 'Sit down. Would you like something to drink?'

'Thank you, no, my lord. I can't stop. I have to get up early. Thing is, I asked Jake where he went on the night of the 30th, and he told me, although I doubt as how he would have told you, or Mr Bunter here.'

'Let me guess,' said Peter. 'He was snaring rabbits in Blackden Wood.'

'Back end of it, yes. On your land.'

'I see.'

'Thing is, your lordship, before the wood was sold to you, everyone used to do it.'

'So I have been told,' said Peter.

'But the boys felt a bit wary about it, like, not knowing what line you might be minded to take, so they kept well the other side of the slope. Down where the wood runs out into the fields at the top of Yew Tree Lane.'

'Where nobody from Talboys would be likely to see them?'

'That's it,' said Roger Datchett. He had not sat down, and was shifting his weight uneasily from one foot to another. 'So naturally they didn't see nothing to do with what might have been a-going on down here.'

'Did they see anyone moving about?' asked Harriet.

'I asked him that. Only that Twitterton woman. She was off up the lane. Jake thought it might have been to feed the other hidden pigs – the ones what survived the night, and lived to see the morning.'

'So the long and the short of this story, Mr Datchett, is that you can't help us?' said Peter.

'I wouldn't say that, my lord,' said Mr Datchett. 'I've brought you a nice side of bacon that I've had smoking in the back of my chimney a good little while, and I'm hoping you will feel that you've had a fair share of anything you should have had, and will say no more about it.'

Peter looked so appalled that Harriet had to button back the urge to laugh. 'But, Mr Datchett,' he said, 'we know that *you* had no hand in killing a pig that night; don't ask me how we know, but we do. You don't owe us anything.'

'Fair exchange for poached rabbits, perhaps?'

'I haven't said I mind the rabbits,' said Peter, almost indignantly. 'As long as your lad knows how to set a snare to kill instantly.'

'He ought to. I showed him often enough,' said Roger Datchett.

A silence fell. Harriet heard the clock ticking. 'I just need to keep the boy out of trouble for another fortnight,' Roger Datchett said. 'His call-up papers have come through, and he'll be gone then. He wants a clean record in the forces. And he says you could ask Archie Lugg. Archie was out with him that night, and he'll tell you where they went.'

'Mr Lugg has already declined to tell my man, here.'

'Oh, that's just sticking by his mate. In case Jake didn't want to say. He'll tell you now Jake has had a word with him.'

'I thought Archie and Jake had fallen out, come to blows, even,' said Harriet.

'Over that land-girl? They was at odds about her, yes. But when the poor girl was killed, that quieted the quarrel. They've known each other from boys, them two, and it doesn't make sense to fall out over a woman. They'll both be taken for soldiers by next month.'

'Heavens, Harriet!' Peter exclaimed as the door closed behind Roger Datchett. 'Of all the wickedly ill-gotten gains I have ever enjoyed, a present of bacon from Farmer Datchett is the most outrageous.'

'Well, you did tell Bunter to purport to be asking for pork!' said Harriet, laughing. 'And I wouldn't like to answer for Mrs Trapp's continued calm of mind if you show her such booty, and then remove it.'

'What shall we do about it?'

'Eat it,' said Harriet.

Thirteen

And take upon 's the mystery of things,
As if we were God's spies . . .
William Shakespeare, *King Lear*, 1608

'That leaves only Roger Birdlap,' remarked Harriet the next morning.

'Sorry, he's in the clear too. I was going to tell you if I hadn't been diverted by Farmer Datchett last night. I rang that Baldock chap at Steen Manor about Birdlap. Incidentally you seem to have made a good impression on him, Harriet—'

'Not reciprocated, I'm afraid.'

'Ah. Perhaps I am not surprised. Stuffed shirts are not much in your line, my dear. But Baldock says he kept Birdlap confined to base, since he had threatened persons unspecified, and that obtained until he was required. Required to be parachuted behind enemy lines, which is where he was on the 30th, and where he now is. So we can cross him off the list.'

'That leaves the list empty.'

'We seem to be on the wrong track. Perhaps after all, as the Superintendent put it, that has nothing to do with this.'

'Speaking as a fiction writer I dislike coincidence,' said Harriet. 'I suspect it of subterfuge.'

'It's odd, isn't it?' said Peter. 'We all encounter coincidences all the time, and never disbelieve them. If a friend tells me he set out impromptu for Timbuktu, and on arriving there bumped into his old school matron's younger son, or whoever, I don't cry, "Ridiculous!" But if I read it in a novel, that's just what I would say. I would know at once it was meant to be comedy. Now, why is that, Harriet?'

'Aristotle again. You were told that the encounter had happened. What has happened is obviously possible, however unlikely it was that it should happen. Coincidence is history, once it has happened. Poetry, the philosopher tells us, is about what might probably or necessarily occur. The underlying logic of the world.'

'But that underlying logic is full of coincidence.'

'But not of any particular coincidence. And coincidence has to be particular; you can't have coincidence in general.'

'One of my commanding officers, when I served in uniform,' remarked Peter, 'had a notice on his office wall that said, "Expect the unexpected."'

'That's probably good advice in war-time. Difficult to do, though.'

'I think that's what I'm saying.'

'I'm sorry, Peter, am I distracting you?'

'Extremely. A room with you in it vibrates with something.'

'No; the subliminal scintillation is caused by you. It

doesn't happen when you are absent. *Revenons à ces moutons.*'

'*Ces cochons* would be more to the point. So where are we? The idea that the man was killed in revenge for the death of Wendy lies in ruins. What is still standing? It must be to do with his mission as a spy. His own side, for purposes we can't at the moment surmise, killed him. Or someone on our side killed him.'

'That at least should be easily found out,' said Harriet. 'Can't Bungo do that between one half of a ham sandwich and another?'

'It would be a process of elimination,' said Peter. 'And there would be a lot of outfits to check up, and most of them would absolutely hate admitting they had done such a thing. The only thing they would dislike worse would be telling someone like Bungo that they hadn't done it, in case there was any credit attached to it.'

'Well, who's in overall charge?' asked Harriet.

'Good question. I don't even know who is supposed to be in overall charge. The thing is, Harriet, that England is full of very senior people, who saw action last time round, and are desperately anxious to enlist, and too old for active service, and they are persecuting the recruitment officers, and pulling every string they can, and busting a gasket at the suggestion that they might like to help with the Home Defence Volunteers . . .'

'Now what does that remind me of?' said Harriet.

'Most of them can't speak a word of a foreign language,' said Peter, smiling. 'But what does one do with them?

Nobody wants to command them; they will clearly be peppery and insubordinate. So each one is given permission to set up something of his own, some fanciful little unit up to something or another. Home-based counter-espionage seems particularly appropriate. You swear them to secrecy, and then you never hear from them again. They're off the backs of Buggins in Whitehall, and God only knows what they may be up to. England is hopping with them. So it is probably just as hard to find out if someone on our side unmasked pseudo-Brinklow and despatched him, as it is to find out if the enemy did it.'

'You know, Peter,' said Harriet. 'I've been thinking. All three of those scenarios involving local lads have him killed for doing something after his death, so to speak. But what about before his death? What if the *real* Alan Brinklow had a mortal enemy in his own right?'

'My God, Harriet – you mean forget about the pretence and look into the real man?'

'Well, there was a real man, I take it. They didn't just make him up from scratch?'

'No, they didn't, and they didn't have time to investigate him. As I understand it they didn't do anything about him at all. It was all fixed up on a ship at sea, that had retrieved a floating body. And to report it in any way might have breached security.'

'So here in England, what would appear to have happened?'

'Something quite ordinary. A Flight Lieutenant takes off

A PRESUMPTION OF DEATH

on a dangerous mission, and doesn't come back. So he's
posted missing.'

'Missing presumed dead?'

'After a few hours, yes. I don't know how long it takes.'

'That message goes up on the board, and his family are
told? And nobody ever told them later that he was known
to be dead?'

'Well, we know, but they don't know,' he said. 'The body
hasn't been recovered. His name won't be on a Red Cross
list of prisoners of war; he won't have written them a letter.
He's just vanished into the blue, like plenty of others.'

'It's absolute hell, you know, Peter. Fearing the worst,
but unable to square up to it because of unquenchable
flickering hope. Just not knowing. Not knowing whether
to brace yourself for a funeral or save rations for a party.
Not having a funeral. It strikes me as very cruel, knowing that someone is dead, and not telling his near and
dear ones.'

'Cruel? Perhaps it is. But necessary. Harriet, keeping
this operation dark saved lives. It diverted German forces
from one place to another, and allowed a crucial exodus
of troops to take place under cover. If it was cruel it was
for more than proportionate gain.'

'I understand that. Can his people be told now?'

'Not yet. We don't want the enemy to guess they have
lost an agent.'

'They'll guess pretty soon, when they lose touch with
him, won't they?'

'Not necessarily. He was almost certainly a "sleeper"

273

lying low until triggered into action by a signal of some kind. If we play our cards right they won't find he's been taken out until they try to activate him. Look, let's follow your hunch. Let's keep our minds on the real Brinklow. We must start by tracing him.'

'Well, what do we know about him?' asked Harriet.

'We know his group and sector if false-Brinklow was using his identity,' said Peter.

'My guess is it won't be anywhere near,' said Harriet. 'There would be too much risk of someone getting to know that false-Brinklow was here. In fact, Peter, the whole thing is appallingly risky. And it's mere chance that that friend of his – who was it? Mike Newcastle – missed him when he turned up visiting. He would have spotted at once that it wasn't the right man, wouldn't he?'

'Yes, it was a risky operation. But no more so than many another. After all, in this case their man would have been carrying genuine papers; mostly they have to make do with forged ones. And spying is always dangerous. There is no shortage of brave men to take the chances.'

'If we found out where Mike Newcastle is based, we could talk to him about the real Brinklow, couldn't we?' said Harriet.

'Well, that shouldn't be too hard,' said Peter. 'I'll get someone on to it.'

'So next we find out where the real Brinklow was based, and then—'

'I've thought of something,' Peter said. 'Didn't Jerry say there was a will form in a pay-book?'

'But officers don't have them, he said.'

'But their wills must be kept somewhere,' said Peter. 'That should lead us to his family. I'll find out.'

Harriet went downstairs to romp with the children and help with tea and bath-time.

Putting his head round the nursery door a half-hour later, Peter said to her triumphantly, 'RAF records, Gloucester. I've got someone on to it,' before dropping on all fours to be a man-eating tiger chasing his son and smallest nephew round the sofa.

'Do you fancy a little trip?' Peter asked. He was walking arm in arm with Harriet up the lane, in a gathering dusk. Bedtime was getting later and later, and seemed, now Peter was home, to be nearly uncontrollable. He was indulging himself in an orgy of childish company. But all was quiet on the home front now, and he was taking the air with his wife. 'Could we leave the nest of monsters for, say, three days, without mutiny in the ranks?' he asked.

'I think we could,' she said. 'Departing with threats and bribes and binding everyone over to be on best behaviour. It sounds wonderful. Where are we going?'

'A long way. Destination unknown, via Gloucester.'

'You wouldn't consider Bannockburn by way of Beachy Head?'

'No. It has to be as I suggest.'

'To do with Brinklow, of course?'

'Of course. But that wouldn't prevent it being fun; it

would just give us a clear conscience about tooling around on the roads, using petrol.'

'I'd love it. When?'

'Day after tomorrow all right? I take it you'd need a day to square Mrs Trapp and Sadie, and Bunter . . .'

'Peter, we couldn't take Bunter, could we? It would be just like our notorious honeymoon. Just like old times.'

'I wasn't thinking of driving gently enough to cradle a case of port in the boot,' he said thoughtfully. 'So it wouldn't be *just* like . . . But would you really like Bunter along?'

'I think I told you once that I love Bunter, and I wish I could have married him. Weren't you listening? But seriously, Peter, Bunter must have had a rough time abroad, too. I expect he would like a break as much as we would.'

'What a scoop this would be for the newshounds that used to chase us of old!' Peter said, laughing. 'Famous sleuth's wife loves another! Lady Peter in love triangle! Seriously, Harriet, I would love to take Bunter. Would the home base run along without him?'

'It has been, for months,' she said serenely. 'I think Hope's parents live in Evesham. Isn't that somewhere near Gloucester?'

'It's in the right general direction.'

'You could give Bunter some leave, and drop him off there on the way, or the way back.'

'As I said before, I have married a practical genius.'

'Didn't you bargain for that?'

'Not specially. Silly of me, really. I thought of you as

slightly elsewhere, very wrapped up in your work. And I don't seem to have had a moment to ask you what you're doing at the moment. Has Robert Templeton got a current case?'

'No,' she said. 'I'm not writing a detective novel, although people keep asking me for one. Somehow with the mayhem going on in Europe a body behind the sofa seems like one too many.'

'Quite apart from two too many here.'

'Exactly. I've been writing articles. Reading for the Le Fanu book. And writing some poems. They seem easier, more in tune with the moment.'

Peter didn't ask to see them. He had a delicate tact with her that spoke eloquently to her.

'May I show you some, some time?' she said.

'Please,' he said. 'Look, here comes Miss Twitterton, as large as life!'

Miss Twitterton seemed, in fact, rather larger than life. She was rosy-cheeked and glowing with her evening walk, and wearing a pretty silk scarf that Harriet didn't remember having seen before. She broke into a trot as soon as she saw them, and closed the distance between them, crying, 'Oh, oh, oh, Lord Peter! Oh, Lord . . . Peter, oh! I am so glad to see you! Oh, I thought we might never . . .'

Peter raised one of her outstretched hands, kissed it theatrically, and said, 'I am just as glad to see you, Miss Twitterton, as you are to see me.'

'Oh, no,' she said, falling in step with them down the lane. 'You really cannot mean that, Lord Peter. I have been safely here with dear Lady Peter and the quiet village society, and you have been in such terrible danger. Such terrible things, such atrocities happening in those poor countries. I just can't bear to think what they do when they capture somebody. We have all been simply *terrified* for you. Every time we have sung *Eternal Father Strong to Save*, you have been the *primary* person I have been thinking of.'

'It's very kind of you, Miss Twitterton,' said Peter. There was not the slightest tremor of amusement in his voice. 'I haven't been in peril on the sea, or at least only for the last six hours of the mission. But it was a touch hazardous. Never mind, here I am you see, as large as life and as odd-looking as ever.'

If Miss Twitterton flushed, as she always used to do when Peter gave her more than a moment's attention, the dusk was now too deep for Harriet to see it. Instead of flustering around the conversation as she would have done only weeks ago, Miss Twitterton said, 'Lord Peter, you are *very nearly* the nicest-looking man I have ever met.'

Peter gave Harriet a gaze of consternation and amazement. 'It's getting rather dark,' he observed. 'And you have a little way to go, Miss Twitterton. May I walk you to your gate?'

'That is most remarkably kind of you, Lord Peter,' Miss Twitterton said. 'But I am quite used to walking round the lanes by myself. There is no need. I was just wondering, Lord Peter, if you have a favourite hymn? Because I thought, to give thanks for your safe return at the morning service next Sunday . . . and if it's a very unusual hymn we would need to learn it at choir-practice tomorrow night.'

'Thank you, Miss Twitterton,' Peter said. 'I have always rather liked the old one hundredth.'

They had reached the bottom of the lane, and their ways home diverged.

'Oh, that's easy!' she cried. 'You shall have it, Lord Peter, you shall indeed. Goodnight to you both.' And she skipped away towards Pagford with a very light step.

'Peter,' said Harriet, in amazement, 'whoever is the *absolutely* nicest-looking man Miss Twitterton has ever met?'

'Whoever he is,' said Peter, 'I owe him a debt of gratitude. He has relieved me of a most onerous and unwelcome role!'

Harriet felt such joy the next morning, waking in Peter's arms, and lying quite still so as not to wake him, that it brought with it also a flicker of guilt. What had *she* done to deserve this, and wasn't it tempting fate; fate that was already rolling towards them, armed and malignant? Yet surely it wasn't a duty to be glum? Wasn't it better to seize the day?

'Why should we rise because 'tis light?' said her husband.

She laughed. 'Did we lie down because 'twas night?' she asked him. 'But, my lord, if we are to pack, and get ourselves on the road for a journey . . .'

'Mmm,' he said, holding her tight enough to prevent her getting up. 'I expect you will find Bunter has seen to the packing. You can have another five minutes abed.'

'Peter,' she said, a little later, 'do you ever feel that you can't possibly deserve happiness – I mean great happiness, like having you home again – when other people can be in such wretchedness?'

He propped himself up on one arm and contemplated her. 'Logically, whether we deserve this morning or not should not be connected to what kind of a morning anyone else is having,' he said.

'I don't think logic has much to do with it,' she said. 'Although I do think Aristotle might cast some light.'

'You keep quoting that pestilential philosopher at me. This time you are speaking of catharsis.'

'Yes, pity and fear. Do you remember what he says: that pity is occasioned by undeserved misfortunes, and fear by that of one like ourselves?'

'And now the world is full of undeserved misfortunes, descending on those just like ourselves?'

'You always understand me so quickly!'

'The Aristotelian emotions were supposed to purify,' he said. 'Can't we feel pure joy?'

'Bought at the expense of other people's suffering?'

'No, bought in the shadow of knowing how we might suffer ourselves. Awareness sharpens joy, don't you think?'

'Sharp joy – that's what I'm feeling!'

'The kind that makes one want to dance at funerals?'

'Now that really is heartless, Peter!'

'I must be rather oddly wired up. But when those great words roll over us – man that is born of a woman hath but a short time; all flesh is as grass; the places where he was known shall see him no more – I always want to rush off and drink champagne, or dance all night, or hear an opera.'

'Or find a lovely woman?'

'That was long ago. Before I became a contented husband.'

'Peter, we surely should be getting up now, even if Bunter is packing for us. We won't have time for breakfast.'

'Good God, woman, why didn't you say?' he said, abruptly sitting up. 'Breakfast is one of the very joys we should wallow in while luck is on our side! Will there be bacon and eggs?'

'If so, don't tell anyone,' she said.

It was only once they were moving, with Peter driving, with Harriet settled back on the deep sensuous leather seat of Mrs Merdle, and Bunter seated in the back holding the road map, that Harriet realised how glad she was of a change of scene. Somehow the idea of moving round England had been expunged almost as thoroughly as the idea of big game hunting in France. 'For the duration' one no longer expected it. The local paper had carried a picture of 'holidays at home' showing a girl in a swimsuit sunbathing on a deckchair in the back garden of a suburban house, and of course a lot of children were happily running wild in woods and fields who would without the war have been in grim urban schools. But grown-up holidays – she had to pinch herself to believe she was awake, and remind herself each hour that a trip with a serious purpose was not made frivolous merely because one enjoyed it.

And although Harriet often travelled with her eyes shut when Peter was driving, it was certainly a lovely treat to reach Oxford in time for a late lunch at the Mitre, and from there to roll gently through the modest but touching beauties of the Cotswolds to reach Gloucester by tea-time. Bunter turned out to have a friend in Gloucester, so he took himself off for an evening visit. Peter and Harriet sat by the fire in the hotel lounge, playing the quotation game.

'Let me not to the marriage of true minds admit impediments,' Harriet offered.

'I will arise and go now, and go to Innisfree,' Peter replied.

'If you have tears, prepare to shed them now.'

'No worst, there is none. Pitched past pitch of grief . . .'

'Go, lovely Rose! Tell her, that wastes her time and me . . .'

'Music hath charms to sooth a savage breast . . .'

'Busy old fool, unruly sunne . . .'

'So sweet, so smooth, so silvery is thy voice . . .'

'V is difficult,' Peter said. Hang on: *Vivre est une chute horizontale.*'

'Is French allowed?'

'Why not? Aren't they our gallant allies, and the pinnacle of civilisation, to boot?'

'Falling over sideways might be all too apt,' said Harriet, suddenly sombre.

Peter regarded her with mute attention. 'Nothing for H?' he said. 'I win then, and you must pay the forfeit.'

'Which is?'

'Being sent to bed early, my dear. Come along, things always look better in the morning.'

Fourteen

Where there's a will there's relations.
Misquoted from the Book of Proverbs

While Peter went off to the RAF records office Harriet spent until noon in the cathedral. One could do the whole history of church architecture here, from the Normans to the Reformation. Harriet lingered most of the time in the cloisters, under the earliest fan vaulting in England, where Peter found her, entranced.

'We've got our lead,' he said. 'Brinklow did make a will and it was a very new one. Changed at the last minute. Everything, which had been to go to Dr Barnardo's, left to a girl called Joan Quarley of Culpits in Northumberland. So off we go.'

'What do we know about Joan Quarley?' Harriet asked Peter as they drove once more through the Cotswolds, this time making north-east.

'Absolutely nothing. Only that he changed his will in her favour.'

'Cutting out his parents?'

'I think the earlier will in favour of Barnardo's might indicate that he was an orphan.'

'Hmm. A young man I knew at college was a Barnardo's boy. He wasn't grateful.'

'I have a feeling, don't you know, that Joan Quarley when we find her will be able to explain it.'

'Peter, how much are you going to be able to explain to her?'

'Depends what sort of a young woman she is,' he said. 'She might be level-headed and reliable. But I expect she's very young.'

'Why do you think so?'

'Because he was.'

'It's interesting, isn't it,' Harriet said a little later, when they were driving again, 'how the word "young" changes as we get older. I would have thought myself completely and fully adult at twenty, and been very offended at being treated as anything less.'

'And now twenty seems green and callow and untried?'

'Well, it does, rather.'

'And yet these children are old enough to die in combat,' he said.

'Bunter, what were you doing at twenty?' Harriet asked the silent rider in the back seat.

'I was in service, my lady, with Sir John Sanderton. I had risen to be head footman.'

'That doesn't sound like a lot of fun, Bunter,' Harriet observed. 'Can one easily misspend one's youth as a footman?'

'You'd be surprised, my lady,' said Bunter, 'at how much misspending of various kinds can go on below stairs in a large establishment. Sir John kept thirty servants indoors and out. And his butler was a vain and inattentive man, who did not run a tight ship, I'm afraid. His lordship's offer to me of respectable service as a gentleman's gentleman after the war came as a most welcome escape.'

'Good lord, Bunter,' said the aforesaid lord, 'I didn't know I was an alternative to assignations in the cellars and propositions in the pantries! Harriet, you have uncovered an aspect of Bunter hitherto completely unknown to me. Amazing.'

Harriet's curiosity about young Bunter seemed likely to be frustrated; it would be very indiscreet to press him further. But he offered a little more unprompted. 'It was difficult, in that household, to maintain a proper formality in dealings with the family,' he said. 'We knew too much about them, and it was hard to regard them with that respect which makes service acceptable with dignity. In particular, when a member of the family gets a young woman servant into difficulty, and abandons her to the harsh judgement of the outside world, it becomes demeaning to assist that person in the conduct of their everyday life. Employment with his lordship, on the other hand, has never given me a moment's concern.'

'For heaven's sake, Bunter!' cried Peter, taking a sharp corner with a squeal of brakes. 'How can I keep my mind on the road, while you chatter like that?'

'If I may make a suggestion, my lord,' said Bunter imperturbably. 'You might find the road less surprising at a more modest speed.'

'You may not make such a suggestion, Bunter,' said Peter, slowing down considerably, and driving very soberly and chastely through back-roads frothing with cow-parsley in bloom till they reached the Fanshaws' little house in Evesham, and left Bunter at the door. In view of the long miles that lay ahead of them they declined offers of tea and biscuits, and Bunter said firmly he would make his own way back to Paggleham when he thought his parents-in-law had had enough of him.

Culpits turned out to be an ordinary enough village with a pretty eighteenth-century inn. Peter booked them in for dinner and bed, and then he and Harriet went for a quiet walk. The High Street rose at a gentle gradient to a modest ridge, with the village houses petering out as the road ascended. Good solid English houses of mellow local brick, with sash windows and fanlights over front doors. The largest of these was the last on the left, and Peter pointed out to Harriet the modest perfections of its proportions, and the old cotton tree growing against the wall. From the ridge they looked down towards the coast on the airfield, which in this case really was an airfield. Within a perimeter fence a dozen Hudsons and an Anson were drawn up on grass, and the runway looked raw and new. A scatter of tents, and some Nissen huts still under construction suggested very rough comfort for the airmen, although there was a smallish hangar on the far side of the field.

As they gazed at this scene they heard a motor vehicle

coming up behind them, and found themselves confronted by a pair of Local Defence Volunteers. One of them carried a lethal-looking, ancient, distinctly unofficial blunderbuss. They were both wearing armbands and tin hats. 'What are you doing here?' demanded one of these.

'Taking the air, and stretching our legs,' said Peter pleasantly. 'We have had a long drive.'

'Identity cards?' the man demanded.

Peter and Harriet meekly produced them. Handing them over, Peter also produced his cigarette case, and offered it, open.

'You look harmless,' the man decided, returning the cards and helping himself to a cigarette. 'You haven't got a camera, or field glasses or anything?'

'Nothing of the kind,' said Peter, offering the cigarettes to the other fellow. 'Just out for a walk. But you are right to be careful.'

'It's just a bit of routine, really,' the officer conceded. 'If the enemy want a look at this they'll take a picture from the air. I expect they already have.'

'Bound to have done,' agreed Peter. 'I say, though, this does look a bit makeshift. Doesn't look as though they've got proper quarters down there, or a canteen or anything. Rough comfort, I would say.'

'Uster be only the local flying club. Gliders and Moths sort of thing,' said the first man. 'It's being used as a forward station. It's taking them one hell of a time to get it organised.'

'How right you are!' said his companion. 'Those poor

blokes get back from a mission and they can't even have a cup of coffee unless they fix it up themselves on a Primus stove. Bloody marvellous! My wife does a bit of helping out down there,' he added.

'So the local people are helpful?' Harriet chipped in.

'Doing our best. A lot of the men are billeted in the village while some huts get built. Bed and breakfast sort of thing. They can't be in a house without a telephone, so they're all with the better sort of people. Got it made.'

'Well, we'll potter along,' said Peter. 'Good luck to you.' And he drew Harriet's arm through his, and began to walk back.

'We didn't get arrested as spies,' Harriet said. 'That's what rank does for you.'

'No; our identity cards give just Christian names and surnames. Not a hint of a title to be found. They must have succumbed to our natural charm.'

'I admit you don't look like a spy,' said Harriet. 'You look far too guileless.'

'English teeth, and all that?'

'And all that, yes.'

'Talking of teeth,' he said thoughtfully, 'I wonder what the landlord will be able to rustle up for supper.'

'Something truly gruesome,' Harriet promised.

'Like what?'

'Turnip tart, followed by spotted dick, with dried-egg custard,' suggested Harriet.

'Devil woman! Fiend!' said Peter. 'It couldn't be as bad as that!'

And it wasn't. The inn rose to a rabbit jugged in cider, and a very nice apple pie.

After dinner Harriet settled by the fire in the residents' lounge. Peter went through to the bar to order a brandy. Harriet could hear voices across the open counter, in the bar, engaging in conversation about the sins and misapprehensions of the Ministry of Instruction and Morale.

Peter was asking the landlord if he knew of a young man called Mike Newcastle. 'Sorry, can't help you there,' said the landlord. 'Anyone know a Mike Newcastle?' he asked his customers, but he drew a blank.

Then what about a friend of a friend; Peter believed she had once lived hereabouts, called Joan Quarley, something like that? He invited the landlord to pour a brandy for himself: 'Be my guest, landlord, what's yours?'

'Whisky and soda, thank you very much, sir,' said the landlord. 'Oh, yes. That young woman is well known in this village. Very well known.'

There was an edge to his voice. 'Gentry, come down in the world, you might say. But still giving themselves airs, oh, yes. But she's a friend of yours, did you say?'

'Oh, not a close friend at all,' said Peter. 'Just someone I have heard about from other friends.'

The landlord visibly relaxed. 'No hard feelings, then,' he said. 'There's a lot of talk about that young woman, though, I can tell you. Mind you, I blame the war.'

'The war has a lot to answer for,' Peter said gravely.

'It's all these young airmen,' the landlord went on. 'Very

good for trade, of course. Seem very thirsty. And there isn't anywhere else for them to go of an evening, till they get a mess for them built. I shouldn't complain, really, but of course it isn't like the old days. Time was when you never saw a stranger in the village from one week's end to the next, and now anything in uniform has the girls all of a dither. And what with them being all up and down the village in digs, and coming and going at all hours and haring around in fast cars, can't see what else we could expect.'

'So you were saying about the Quarleys?'

'Old farming family. Have the best house in the village, so they took in lodgers like everyone else. Now the girl has a bun in the oven and no ring on her finger. Bit of a comedown. It wouldn't be so bad if there weren't lots of people who remember what old man Quarley was like. Her grandfather.'

'What was he like?' asked Peter.

'Quite a martinet, I believe. It's before my time; I took on the licence here in 1923. But he employed a lot of people back then. Big farm, grew lots of vegetables, needed a lot of men. He had cottages everywhere for his labourers; and let there be just a breath of scandal and he'd put the whole family out on the street with one week's pay in the man's pocket. He was hard as nails about it, and people have long memories of that sort of thing.'

'Yes, in many ways the good old days were the bad old days,' said Peter.

'Mind you, if you kept your nose clean, he saw you right,'

said the landlord. 'You wouldn't be in want, working for him, and when the children were sick he'd pay for the doctor. But it's hard not to smirk when you think of his grand-daughter being a common slut like those he put on the parish years ago.'

There was suddenly uproar in the public bar. The sound of an overturned chair, the sound of a glass breaking, and someone shouting, 'I'll knock your teeth down your throat if you talk about her like that!'

'All right, all right, Jeff,' the landlord was saying. 'I'm sorry, I didn't see you was sat over there. Didn't mean any harm.'

'Strewth, Dick, what are you like when you do mean harm?' said a woman's voice. 'Your tongue's so sharp it's a wonder it doesn't cut your mouth sometimes.'

'No offence meant,' the landlord was saying. 'Let's have last orders and change the subject.'

A few minutes later Peter reappeared in the lounge.

'Who was that who got so angry?' Harriet asked him.

'The young lady's brother, I understand,' he told her. 'And a brother is an interesting addition to the cast list, don't you think?'

'This is a bit ticklish,' said Peter the following morning. They were breakfasting in the snug, on porridge and toast, there being neither eggs nor bacon available. Peter, Harriet noticed, took his porridge with only salt and milk, whereas she sugared hers. 'What next, do you think?'

'Why hasn't anyone heard of Mike Newcastle?' Harriet

mused. 'I had thought it would be a good idea to talk to him first.'

'I suppose he could be a friend of Brinklow's without serving in the same unit,' said Peter. 'But it doesn't leave us any option but to interview the young lady herself. She will be found, I imagine, from the landlord's description, at that rather agreeable Georgian farmhouse on the Alnwick road.'

After breakfast therefore, Peter and Harriet went looking for the Quarley farmhouse. It was indeed the one that had caught Peter's eye; a good four-square brick house with a pleasant fanlight over the door, and a look of run-down gentility. Peter knocked and waited. Harriet felt sudden embarrassment. What would he ask? How could he explain himself?

The door was opened by a woman in middle age, wearing a slightly felted twinset and a tweed skirt. She had a pair of secateurs in one hand, and a flower vase in the other. She stared blankly at them. Harriet let Peter do the talking while she observed as closely as she could.

'Can I help you?' the woman said. She sounded as though she thought it unlikely. She had an abstracted look, and that air about her suddenly brought to Harriet's mind various friends of her mother's long ago – a stance of deliberate vulnerability and refinement – a femininity that was a constant unspoken appeal for chivalry in anyone who came within range.

'Mrs Quarley? You might be able to help us,' said Peter. 'We are trying to find out what we can about a young man called Alan Brinklow.'

'Oh,' she said. She glanced rapidly away from Peter and towards Harriet, directing a pallid and anxious gaze on her. 'You'd better come in,' she said.

She led the way through a hall cluttered with a laden coat-stand, – there was a flying jacket hanging on it – and into a pleasant sitting-room. She closed the door behind them. 'Please keep your voices low,' she said. 'My daughter is sleeping in. I don't want her disturbed.'

She did not invite them to sit down, and they stood around uncertainly.

'Alan Brinklow . . .' Peter began.

'They say he's dead,' Mrs Quarley said. 'Have you come for his things?'

'No,' said Peter. 'It is the months before he went missing we would like to know about. Anything you can tell us about him.' There was a gentleness in Peter's voice, Harriet noticed, rather more than would be accounted for by the request not to talk loudly, so that she thought he too had picked up that curious note of fragility about Mrs Quarley.

'He was a lovely young man,' she said shakily. 'Lovely manners. You couldn't ask for a more helpful and considerate person. And always joking; keeping us smiling. And he's very young; only nineteen.'

'You don't happen to know what he did with himself between leaving Barnardo's and joining up?'

'Oh, yes!' she said eagerly, suddenly willing to talk. 'He was in a land surveyor's office. And he had learned to fly as part of the job, because it helps a lot to take pictures from aeroplanes. His boss didn't like the flying part of it, so Alan did all that bit, and when he joined up they promoted him very quickly, because they hadn't got a lot of people who already knew how to fly. That's how he got to know my son – my son Jeff. Jeff brought Alan home with him and said he was a brother officer, and we should treat him as one of the family. And we were glad to.'

'He wasn't a quarrelsome young man? He didn't have enemies?'

'Oh, no, no, not at all. I never heard of anyone he didn't get on with.'

'Or debts? Gambling debts?'

'That wouldn't have been like him.'

'He was very good-looking,' Peter said, picking up one of the silver-framed photographs on the mantelpiece. It showed a young airman, gazing out of the frame with a smiling, candid gaze tinted sepia.

Harriet realised suddenly that the door was standing open, framing a wan-faced young woman with dark red hair, and pale eyes, who said, 'Mother, who are these people? Why are they asking about Alan?'

'I don't know why, Joan,' said Mrs Quarley, almost whispering.

'Alan was an orphan. And he was engaged to marry me,' Joan Quarley said firmly, facing up to Peter. 'Anything you want to know about him, you should ask me.'

'They want to know if he had any enemies,' said Mrs Quarley.

'Ridiculous,' said Joan. 'Everyone loved him. But why do you want to know? And who are you?'

Peter offered his card. The effect on both women was immediate and extraordinary.

'But I've heard of you!' said Mrs Quarley. 'You're a private detective!' All the colour had drained from her face, and the younger woman put her arms round her mother to steady her, and help her sit down. 'It's all right, Mother, it's all right,' said Joan. 'It has nothing to do with us. Nothing. Don't be upset.'

Peter said, 'We do have news for you, Miss Quarley. Bad news, although it can't be unexpected. That notice of missing presumed dead for Alan Brinklow can now be changed to killed in action. I'm so sorry.'

Once again the two women reacted oddly. The mother put her face in her hands; the daughter said quite coldly and calmly, 'I told you so, Mother. Of course he was dead.' She sounded almost triumphant.

Odd, thought Harriet, very odd.

'Why is it you coming to tell us?' Joan demanded. 'What can it have to do with a private detective?'

'There was no official note of your engagement,' said Peter quietly. 'Brinklow seems to have put "none" for next of kin when he joined up. But he had altered his will in your favour, so we have come looking for you.'

'I told you so!' said Joan, turning to her mother. 'I said so.'

'Yes, you did,' said Mrs Quarley. 'I wanted to believe you but—'

Joan Quarley broke into her mother's wavering sentence. 'Can you tell me what happened to Alan?' she asked Peter.

'Shot down over the North Sea,' said Peter. 'He baled out, but the water would have been very cold indeed. His body was recovered by one of our vessels. The vessel was on an extended tour of duty; the news has been a long time being reported.'

Suddenly the young woman's self-control seemed shaken. 'What happened to his body?' she asked.

Peter said, after so brief a pause that surely only Harriet could have noticed it: 'Burial at sea leaves no traces, I'm afraid. No memorial stone. Only his name on a list of honour.'

Mrs Quarley said, 'Please go now. We don't want to talk about it. Please go away.'

'Of course,' said Peter. He stepped across the room, passing Harriet, to replace the photograph on the mantelpiece. Harriet found herself the object of some kind of imploring glance from Joan Quarley.

'We are staying at the Crewe Arms,' she said. 'We shall be there till tomorrow morning.'

'I'll show you out,' said Joan Quarley. Then at the front door she said to Peter, 'There wouldn't be any sort of proof, I suppose? Any sort of document to say what happened?'

'I don't know,' said Peter. 'I'll find out for you.'

Fifteen

On your midnight pallet lying
Listen, and undo the door:
Lads that waste the night in sighing
In the dark should sigh no more:
Night should ease a lover's sorrow,
Therefore since I go tomorrow
Pity me before.

In the land to which I travel,
The far country, let me say
Once, if here the couch is gravel,
In a kinder bed I lay.
And the breast the darnel smothers
Rested once upon another's
When it was not clay.

A.E. Housman, *A Shropshire Lad*, 1896

'Now all that's very strange,' Peter said, as they walked back to the inn. 'Didn't you think so?'

'Why should Mrs Quarley be so frightened at the sight of your card, you mean?'

'Ah, you noticed too. Miss Quarley on the other hand . . .'

'Just as one would expect: very upset, holding hard on to her feelings, but not scared.'

'Not quite as I would expect, I think, Harriet. What was that "I told you so," that slight note of triumph about? And if someone came and told you I was dead, would you ask for documentary proof?'

'I should imagine,' said Harriet, 'just guessing, of course, that people have been smothering her with well-meaning comfort; you know the sort of thing, Peter, telling her all about pilots missing presumed dead who have popped up again alive and well weeks later, and trying to keep her hoping, and not facing the worst. And she on the other hand has been trying to face up to the worst, and so has been saying of course he's dead, don't distract me with silly pretences, and now she says, "I told you so."'

'If you're right,' he said, 'then "missing presumed dead" would be the hardest news of all. Worse in a way than "killed in action".'

'Much worse,' she said. 'I do have to say, Peter, that I think there was considerable cruelty in not letting Brinklow's friends know, once anyone knew, that he had been killed.'

'Hmm,' he said. 'War blunts our feelings, I suppose.'

'It would leave someone who loved him, like that poor young woman tugged towards facing the worst, and pulling back from it, in a pitiable state, Peter. Have you ever had vertigo? You know how the brink almost pulls you over, how you are drawn to it, and shrinking back from it simultaneously? I think it would be like that.'

'That isn't quite how you felt when I was away, though, is it?'

'Yes, it is; oh, yes! The mind has mountains – hold them cheap may who ne'er hung there . . .'

'But you kept clear of the brink; you didn't open my letter.'

'Being married to you, having your sons and your name, having had great happiness with you put me in an infinitely stronger position than that of that unfortunate young woman. She can't have had more than a scrambled week or two with her sweetheart.'

'That's true,' he said. 'I wonder how long they did have? I wonder if that explains things.'

'I tell you something else odd, Peter. I only got a sideways squint at that photograph you remarked on, but I thought it looked a bit like the mysterious Mike Newcastle.'

'Did it, though?' he said. 'Hmm. I rather doubt if we would be welcome making a return visit to the house with auxiliary questions.'

'I think Joan Quarley may come to find us,' said Harriet. 'I got the impression she might want to talk.'

'Well, there was that odd feeling that she and her mother were jumping different ways,' said Peter. 'It all felt pretty tense. If she does make contact, Harriet, I shall make myself scarce, and leave it to you. I think this might be a matter for the National Union of Women.'

Harriet thought about it. There was indeed such a thing; a wide swathe of life that women of every kind had in common. One could always talk to another woman; love, men, rationing, children, running a household, the servant problem, the problem of working as a servant, the list was endless.

'Is there a national union of men?' she asked.

'Oh, yes,' said Peter. 'Cars, horses and guns. I noticed you committed us to staying another night. What shall we do with the afternoon? Shall we find a hill to climb? See the coloured counties?'

Joan Quarley was lingering in the lane as they returned. It was a lovely fine evening, still light. She said to Harriet, 'I wondered if you would like to see the church.'

Peter said, 'You go, Harriet. I've got a thing or two to do before dinner.' And he set off rapidly towards the inn.

The two women crossed the churchyard and entered the church. It was the usual mix, a piecemeal stylistic record of five hundred years or so, nothing extraordinary.

To break the ice, Harriet said, 'I think we may have an acquaintance in common. Mike Newcastle?'

'Sorry, no,' said Joan. 'I don't know anyone of that name.'

Their walk down the nave had brought them to stand in front of a rather fine memorial tablet to an Elizabethan worthy, shown surrounded by kneeling children and the effigies of two wives. The slab declared:

> *His breath's a vapour, and his life's a span*
> *'Tis glorious misery to be born a man.*

'And sometimes it's the misery and sometimes the glory

that we feel,' said Harriet, trying again to make some kind of opening.

'What do I call you?' said Joan Quarley abruptly. 'Lady something?'

'Just Harriet.'

'Harriet, I can't help wondering if you met Alan. If you knew him at all. Otherwise I can't for the life of me see what brings you here. Or perhaps your husband knew him.'

'I'm afraid I didn't know him. And nor did Peter, I think. But something top secret that Peter was doing made him aware of what had happened to your Alan. And that's all I can tell you. As you know, we mustn't ask. I'm so sorry. I suppose you were wanting to talk about him a bit?'

'It's so hard him not having parents. I could have gone and found them.'

'Your own mother must have known him?'

'I don't know what's come over her,' said Joan. 'She was absolutely wonderful to us. Incredible. And very kind to me when the missing notice came through. It was only the next day; and then suddenly weeks later it all seems too much for her, and she's very jumpy, and worried about the disgrace, and she doesn't want me to mention Alan; it makes her jump out of her skin, and I don't know where to turn. So here I am talking to a stranger who didn't even know him.'

'When you said it was only the next day . . . ?'

'After we got engaged. I had known him as one of the crowd for a while; the pilots used to come drinking at the

Crewe Arms, fooling around and sweet-talking the girls. My friend Brenda said it was war work to dance with pilots on Saturday night, when there was a hop in the Village Hall. Alan was rather quiet, so I didn't notice him at first. Then he took a room in our house, and he joined me on a couple of evening walks. And then – it was so sudden, Harriet, it was like being knocked over by a runaway cart or something . . .'

'It's always *falling* in love,' said Harriet gently. 'Never jumping in love, or running, or advancing; it always knocks you over.'

'He just brought me back from a walk, and he said to Mother, "If I come back from the next mission, Mrs Quarley, I'm going to marry your daughter." And Mother looked at me, and I said, "Yes." And he said, "Joan, I haven't asked you directly, because what I have to do is very, very dangerous, and I really might not come back, and I'll ask you properly if I do." And I said, "Never mind about asking properly, it's yes." And then Mother asked him when this dangerous mission was to be, and he said dawn the next day. He was sort of shaking a bit. And Mother said to me, "Come upstairs, Joan." And she took me upstairs and we put the best sheets on the double bed in her room, and she said she was going to sleep in my room instead.'

'What a mother!' said Harriet.

'I said something like that,' Joan remarked. 'I was dazed, really. She said she could see it on my face. She said, "Take your chances, girl." So I took them.'

'I simply cannot imagine my own mother . . .' said Harriet.

'I think she regrets it now,' said Joan Quarley. 'I can't talk to her now. Anyone would think she blames Alan for getting himself killed. Of course I am in a jam. There's the disgrace. Villagers sniggering behind their hands. I don't care about that, but perhaps she does.'

Harriet said, 'Joan, I found that disgrace can be faced down. Even very public disgrace, as long as you don't in any way collaborate with it. As long as you don't flinch. You stand your ground, and stare it down. Then at last it is shamed into looking away, and the shame is not yours.'

'It bides its time to go name-calling after the child,' said Joan bitterly. 'Alan's child.'

'You could put a ring on your finger and go and live somewhere else,' said Harriet. 'There will be a lot of young women in your position; widows and sweethearts, raising children.'

'When Mother calms down perhaps,' said Joan. 'All I can think of is that she thinks this is her fault for helping us. As if that makes sense. Does she think I regret it?'

'I think,' said Harriet, 'one seldom regrets something one has done as much as one regrets what one might have done, and did not.'

'I don't regret anything!' said Joan. 'Look, I brought this to show you: Alan wrote this.' She produced from her bag a carefully folded piece of paper with a few lines on it. Harriet took it, and read:

I'm but the son my mother bore,
A simple man and nothing more
But, God of strength and gentleness,
Be pleased to make me nothing less!

Joan said, 'And I am supposed to believe that the man who wrote that suddenly decided to behave like a cad, a coward and a low seducer?'

'Who asked you to think that of him?' asked Harriet.

Joan said, 'Better not say.'

They had moved out of the church into the grave-yard now. The conversation felt over. Flashes of intimacy between strangers, potent and dangerous as they are, do not bear much extension. Harriet saw a leaning headstone laconically carved, with a memorial date, the words: '*Aet. Sua, 16 ann.*'. And '*Carpe Diem*'.

'That's an eternally good piece of advice,' she said.

'I don't know any Latin. What does it mean?' said her companion.

'Seize the day. I think it covers seizing the night,' said Harriet. 'Look, if you need any help . . .'

'Talking to you has helped. I'll manage.' And she strode away, leaving Harriet looking after her.

'I suppose, as a parent, one might feel one had rather dropped the girl in it, being so co-operative about her ruin,' said Peter musingly. 'I suppose Mrs Quarley might feel guilty. Perhaps when Captain Quarley reappears . . . I don't know, I imagine the wives of merchant seamen get used to taking all the decisions themselves. But why would any of all that make her react badly to my card? Or was it my face? I usually fail to impress on first sight, but I don't usually scare people, do I, Harriet?'

'It wasn't your face that upset her, it was your card. Definitely.'

'She said she had heard of me. So it was my profession. So she has something to hide. But it would hardly be that she had tucked up her unmarried daughter in bed with young Brinklow, would it? I mean you usually need to be married before your behaviour on that front is a matter for a detective.'

'Well, but as it turned out, Peter, since poor Alan Brinklow died, what she had done had dire effects. Even nowadays the world is savage to young women with a child born out of wedlock, and inclined to smile and wink knowingly at the young men involved. Mightn't she regret having helped them for that reason?'

'I suppose she might. But I thought that whole conversation was somehow out of joint. Something was going on that didn't square with what we knew about it. You know, Harriet, by the pricking of my thumb . . .'

'Yes, I felt it too. And something else odd, Peter. I really thought that one of the photographs on the mantelpiece was of Mike Newcastle. After all, I had met him in Paggleham, trying to make contact with Alan Brinklow, and just missing him.'

'Well, it isn't so very odd, is it? With the whole country uprooted and everyone sent hither and yon, one might look up a friend . . . Oh, I see what you mean, Harriet. One doesn't come looking for a friend posted missing.'

'No. But what's really odd is that when I mentioned Mike Newcastle to Joan she denied all knowledge of him.'

'A pseudonym. Someone asking for Brinklow under a pseudonym. Harriet, in view of what we have just learned about the Quarley family, how would it play, do you think, if amidst their tears for the dearly loved Alan, they somehow got to hear a rumour that he was alive and well and lurking in Paggleham instead of returning to claim and marry his Joan?'

'It would play very badly indeed,' said Harriet. 'It would be devastating for them all: mother, daughter, brother – they would think he had deserted her. Seduced her under the excuse that there was no time to marry and he was about to die, and then survived and ratted on her.'

'Don't you think that might be what Joan Quarley meant; saying in effect, I told you he was dead?'

'She meant he had to be dead, or he would have come back to her. Yes, I see. Look, Peter, you're right – it all makes perfect sense; that's why she wanted to know if there was documentary proof of his death; presumed dead leaves it open!'

'Let's go through it one step at a time,' said Peter. 'That rather strange conversation we had with mother and daughter. Daughter now makes perfect sense. Someone has been telling her that Alan is alive and has therefore

308

deserted her – and his unit, by the way – and she has refused to believe it. She is one hundred per cent certain that only death would keep him from returning, so in a way she feels vindicated by the news we bring.'

'Well, that seems understandable enough.'

'So now let's try understanding mother. You think she might simply be regretting her human charity to young Romeo?'

'Well, on reflection I think that's the sort of act one is rather unlikely to regret. But if one had any reason to fear that Romeo is Don Giovanni; that one has pandered one's only daughter into the bed of a philanderer . . .'

'So we think Mrs Quarley must also have heard a rumour about Alan Brinklow in Paggleham. Suppose she did. How would she react?'

'She'd be very angry, I would think. She'd feel she had been made a fool of, and that would sharpen indignation.'

'And if she voiced this anger?'

'Well, Joan would repudiate it and defend her lover. She has perfect trust.'

'We still haven't quite got to the point where we know why the appearance of a detective in the drawing-room so scared her.'

'Unless she knew more than just that Brinklow might be alive in Paggleham; unless she knew that he had met a nasty end . . .'

'And how could she know that?'

'By the same rumour machine that let them know about pseudo-Brinklow in the first place?'

'Perhaps; I wonder what that was. But things are getting clear now, aren't they? The mists are lifting. It's time we talked to Miss Quarley's brother, don't you think?' said Peter. 'Tomorrow morning.'

Talking to Jeff Quarley without further alarming his mother required the consent of his commanding officer. Peter seemed to have an entrée in the form of some kind of document that had the sentries snapping to attention, and secured an interview with Wing-Commander Thompson without delay or ceremony.

Although the Wing-Commander's den was a corner of a very new Nissen hut, behind a plywood partition, still smelling sweetly of new wood, and spartan in the extreme, Harriet was reminded of Steen Manor. The plywood walls were covered with aerial photographs of the Norwegian and Danish coasts; she noticed Lister on one and Narvik on another. There were also aerial pictures of German warships, captioned with their names.

Through the window the airfield could be seen – a wide open grassy space with rows of planes drawn up on it. Several tents and a caravan were spaced out along the perimeter of the field, and the airmen were sitting around outside them. Harriet saw a game of chess being played on an upturned tea-chest outside the nearest tent, and a gramophone was balanced on an orange box. The window was open a crack, and a bar or two of 'A Lovely Day Tomorrow' floated towards her. Beside the gramophone a telephone stood on the grass, at the ready. The whole scene was bathed in a shifting pattern of sunlight and shadow. Harriet felt a sudden constriction of the heart. Very young men, very small aeroplanes, a fragile bulwark made of flesh and bones, made of wood and canvas, against so great a danger. She wrenched her attention away, and turned to the room she was standing in.

The commander was a stiff man, really astonishingly young, it seemed to Harriet, to be in charge of all this. He had a toothbrush moustache, and a rather bad burn scar on his left cheek, still a lurid colour, which made his expressions crooked, half smiling. When Peter asked for Jeff Quarley the commander said, 'He's in the air.' He looked at his watch. 'Should be back in half an hour. Want to wait? What's it about then?'

'Classified,' said Peter.

'Hell,' said Thompson. 'You're not going to nobble him, are you? Some son-of-a-bitch down south isn't pinching him from me? See here, I've only ever had three pilots who can fly our kind of mission with better than twenty to one chance of getting back, and I've lost one of those already. He can't keep track of his boots, but I'd trust him more than most not to lose a plane. Look, Wimsey, I'm responsible for something very important here, and if you take one of my best men I'll have to start raising hell with the High Command and going to the War Office and that sort of thing to get him back.'

'Calm down, Wing-Commander,' said Peter. 'We aren't going to nobble him, as you put it. Just have a quick word with him.'

'Only, I swear to God I can't do without him,' said Thompson. 'Nothing you could want to talk to him about is as important as what he's doing.'

'I believe you.'

'It isn't about a woman, is it? We get that all the time, I'm afraid. If it's just that you can leave it to me, and I'll sort it.'

'I'm sorry, but we can't leave it up to you. This has repercussions. We'll wait to speak to the man himself if you don't mind. What did you mean about his boots?'

'Oh, just that he lost a pair. Had to get issued with new ones.'

'You pay attention to details, Wing-Commander,' said Peter.

'Came to my notice because he got ribbed about it quite a bit. Chaps pointing out to him that the Duke of Marlborough was famous for not needing to take them off. Various suggestions about whose bed to look under. You can imagine the sort of thing.'

'Do your men often come home barefoot?' Peter asked.

'Barefaced is more like it. I expect he sold them for a bit of ready cash for something. It isn't important. Take a seat, and I'll see if anyone can brew up a cuppa.'

Peter and Harriet sat on a pair of wooden chairs, side by side against the wall under the photographs. The commander picked up a winged paper-knife and opened a letter. From next door they could hear voices in little bursts, but the silence in the room grew oppressive.

Suddenly, 'It's such an odd sort of war,' the commander

said. 'I wish they wouldn't get their private lives all snarled up, but I can't blame them. It's so perfectly strange. I mean most wars involve rounding up the troops and marching them off somewhere. The fighting is, you know, *somewhere*. Somewhere else, usually, most of the time. France, Norway, Timbuktu. But at the moment my chaps can be fighting all afternoon, and going down to the local for a pint in the evening. One or two of them can even live at home, we're so short of billets. It's happening, as far as they are concerned, right here. And England doesn't look like a bloody battlefield, does it? It's just puttering along almost like normal, with people living normal lives as though nothing was happening.'

'Something happened to you, Commander,' said Peter quietly.

'Well, that's what I mean, in a way,' the man said. 'I was having hell; struggling to get the plane down without killing myself, cockpit on fire, nasty cross-wind, although it was blowing the flames off my face most of the way down, and as I came in to land there right in front of me, just nicely framed by trees at the end of the runway, there's a cricket match. A damn village cricket match. So my ground crew were pulling me clear, and I said, "Complacent swine, I'd like to rub their smug faces in what I've just been doing." And one of my ground crew said, "Beg pardon, sir, but it's what you're fighting for."'

'And how did you reply?' Harriet asked him.

'Not a word,' he said. 'Plane blew up behind us. I came round on a stretcher. Funny thing though, I've never played the game myself. Cricket, that is.' He looked at his watch. 'Let's see how our man is getting on, shall we?'

He put his head round the door of his room and said to the voices in the next booth, 'Telephone ops and see how fourteen group is doing, will you?'

Then he returned to his desk. 'He's on his way. Do you want to watch them in? I like to watch them in.'

He led the way outside. A group of pilots was standing around, just outside the door, hands in pockets, some of them smoking, one or two with binoculars. Harriet blinked at the warm sunshine. Somewhere overhead a lark was singing, ascending. She could hear its squeaky repetitious trill, but she could not see it. Seeing a lark was always difficult: a tiny backlit vibrating speck against the huge sweep of open sky, it could elude you for many minutes. Scanning for it now she found herself suddenly seeing flashes of silver, shadowy shapes, and hearing beyond the lark-song the sound of engines. At her shoulder she heard a sharp intake of breath from Wing-Commander Thompson. 'Two missing,' he said.

'No, sir, there's another; coming in low. Damaged, maybe.'

Out of all the tents across the field ground crew were now running forward. Excited voices were raised as the pilots clambered out of the planes. The laggard plane landed awkwardly, and everyone's attention was on that one. A fire-truck lumbered away towards it. They watched as someone scrambled on to the wing, and began to drag the pilot out of the cockpit.

A group of the pilots was now coming towards them across the field. They looked exhausted, dispirited.

'Who's missing?' the commander asked.

'Parsons, sir. I saw him go down,' someone answered.

'Did you see him bale out?'

'Afraid not, sir.'

Harriet said to Peter, 'This isn't the time, Peter, is it?'

'I think you're right, Harriet.' Peter gave his card to Wing-Commander Thompson, and said, 'Tell Quarley to come and find us when he's ready, or else we have to come and find him.'

Sixteen

Many would be cowards if they had courage enough.

Thomas Fuller, *Gnomologia*, 1732

'Peter, should we interview Jeff Quarley by ourselves? Is that quite proper?'

'No, Harriet, it isn't really. Strictly speaking we should get a police officer, or an RAF policeman to witness, write down, etc. And he should certainly bring a brother officer, or, better, a solicitor. And then the majesty of the law could roll forward on its inexorable path. But I hope he doesn't bring anyone, and if he doesn't, we won't, because until we hear what he has to say I don't really know what I think we should do about him. I'd like to keep a little freedom of action.'

'So, no witnesses?'

'Well, you are my witness, really. But with any luck he won't see you in that light.'

'Just his lordship's little woman? There's been a very widespread undervaluation of the potential of women going on while you have been abroad, my lord. You should listen to Miss Climpson on the subject.'

'Far from undervaluing you, my lady, I am proposing to

make use of your nimble wits and powers of observation.'

'Well, I have an observation to make before we start on this interview, which is that I entirely agree with Superintendent Kirk that murder is murder, even in war-time.'

'I expect he was provoked. Let's see what he says.'

Jeff Quarley presented himself at five o'clock that afternoon. He came alone, with a bleak and stony expression, and an air of defeat about him. Peter had negotiated the use of a little sitting-room at the back of the inn, where they could talk undisturbed. And Harriet recognised the young airman at once.

'Good evening, Mr Newcastle,' she said.

He gave her a despairing gaze. 'I'm sorry,' he said. 'It seemed a good idea at the time,'

'What did?' asked Peter. 'Giving my wife a false name?'

'That – yes. And other things.'

'Such as killing someone like a pig?' asked Peter.

Quarley returned a terrified expression to the question. 'I don't know what you mean,' he said.

'I think you do,' said Peter quietly. 'What did you do with your boots when you couldn't get the blood off them? What did you tell your mother, that makes her so afraid?'

'I'm getting out of here,' said Quarley. 'You can't make me stay here.'

'No, I can't,' said Peter. 'But look, my wife and I are not the police. We are not the authorities in any shape or form. If we lay our suspicions about you before the authorities, then you are in for a nasty time. But for good and sufficient reasons we haven't yet decided to do that. You don't have to talk to us. But you might very shortly find you had to talk to somebody.'

'Put a noose round my own neck, you mean?'

'You have a right of self-defence,' said Peter.

Quarley said, 'Can I have a drink?'

Peter went to the bar to fetch a whisky.

'You spoke to my mother and sister?' Quarley asked Harriet.

'Yes,' she said.

'How in hell did you find us?'

'Alan Brinklow's will.'

He nodded. 'I just can't get him sorted out,' he said. 'I think he must have been mad, the way he behaved.' Then he said, 'He can't have had much to leave, but of course Joan should have it.'

Peter, returning, waited for the barman to put down the tray of drinks and a bottle of malt, and withdraw before saying, 'Did your sister know what you were going to do?'

'No! Yes, in a way . . . Look, it's all so complicated.' Peter handed Quarley a glass. 'I can't very well say I don't know anything about your beastly village. Never been there in my life.'

'Not really,' said Harriet. 'I saw you there.'

'It's a funny thing, isn't it,' said Quarley bitterly, 'if someone attacks you at five thousand feet, and you kill him you're a hero; if he does it in a shed and you kill him, you're done for.'

'Begin at the beginning,' said Peter gently. 'Take your time.'

Quarley got up and paced about the room. He was having difficulty sitting still. He reminded Harriet of an athlete, running on the spot while waiting for a race. Then suddenly he came to a decision, and sat down again and faced them.

'It was a nightmare,' he said, 'a bloody nightmare. Why did he go for me like that? Do you know why?'

'Yes, I think I do,' said Peter. 'Look, I can guess, roughly, what went on. We haven't read you your rights. Nothing you say to us now is evidence. But you left what they call a smoking gun behind you, and it has to be sorted out. It would be a great help if you would tell us the whole thing, from your point of view.'

'Well, we were pretty upset when we heard that Alan was alive and living in Hertfordshire,' Quarley said, 'as you can imagine.'

'How did you find out?' asked Peter.

'A fluke really; a pure fluke. Some time after we lost him I had to go down to Lopsley to discuss some photos I had taken, and a nice young woman there told me to cheer up. I was brooding a bit, I will admit. So I told her I had lost a friend and she said she thought he was alive and well in Paggleham. She has friends there. I didn't believe her, but I asked about a bit, and found someone who had been at a dance there and thought he had heard the name. I don't have to tell you what it looked like.'

'You didn't think of reporting him to the RAF police?' asked Peter.

'I didn't know why he was hiding out,' said Quarley. 'He was a friend of mine. If he didn't fancy getting back to combat duties right away, I wouldn't have blamed him. I wouldn't have wanted to shop him. I needed to talk to him.'

'But you were pinned down on a tour of duty yourself.'

'Yes. And there was an awful uproar at home. Joan wouldn't hear of it. As far as she was concerned he was dead, or he would have come back to her, and that was that. Mother was afraid she had helped a rotter who was trying to wriggle out of promises. That thought did cross my mind too, along with the thought that he might have had a really nasty scare getting shot down and baling out, and he might just not like the thought of more flying. I needed to see him. So I kept writing to him, and I managed to get down there once or twice, with just an hour or two to spare – it's a hell of a long way on a motor-bike, even a Harley-Davidson. I kept missing him. He was apparently in Cornwall on one occasion I got down there. He never answered my letters. I got pretty angry with him.'

He fell silent. He had knocked back his whisky, and Peter poured him another.

'So what did you do then?'

'I had a weekend leave coming up. So I wrote and told him I was coming to find him, and if he wouldn't state a time and place to meet me I really would tell the group commander he was skiving. And I got this really odd reply.'

'Have you still got it?' asked Peter.

Quarley opened his wallet and took out a folded, typed sheet. He pushed it across the table to Peter, and Peter moved it to his right so that Harriet too could see it. It said:

Nine p.m. Last shed on right in stable yard
between Bateson's farm and the house known
as Talboys.

'I thought it was pretty silly stuff. Boy Scout stuff, but I hadn't been able to find him on my other trips, so I went along with it. I borrowed a torch to go blundering around a farmyard in, and I kept the assignation.'

He fell silent, brooding.

'And then?' Peter asked.

'He didn't come. I sat around on a bale of hay, waiting for him. I switched the torch off after a bit, to save the batteries. The chap I borrowed it from said the batteries were down a bit. There was one of those stable door things where the top and bottom open separately. I left the top half open, to use the moonlight. And I was just about to give up and go home when he came – no, I mean when someone came.'

'You thought it was Brinklow?' said Peter quietly.

'Of course I did. He leaned on the lower door, and he blocked the moonlight so I was sitting in pitch darkness, looking at his outline against the sky. I couldn't see who the hell it was. I said, "Alan?" and he flung the door wide and hurtled in and went for me. I was taken off guard. I was expecting some sort of argument, not hand-to-hand combat. He got me by the hair, and forced my head back, and he was trying to hit me in the throat, and I was kicking and punching all I could. We were both breathing heavily, and blundering about. He forced me right back towards the wall. Then he stood back a bit, catching his breath, or getting his footing or something, and I said, "Joan's pregnant, and what are you going to do about it?" I just blurted it out. And he said . . .'

Quarley's voice began to shake. 'He said, "I don't know what you're talking about. Who is Joan?" And then I really saw red. I went berserk. I drew my knife. He pushed me again, and I fell against something, some bit of wood or something, sticking into my back, and then there was a rumble and a crash, and he barged against me, and I went for him like a rugger tackle, going for him low down, and leaning round him to slash the back of his knees. I thought I'd ham-string him first, and argue later. No, that's not true, I didn't think at all. It was just black anger; I wasn't thinking straight, except perhaps that I thought it was him or me. The enemy is supposed to collapse when you cut his ham-strings. According to survival training. But he didn't. He was still there between me and the door, but he wasn't fighting any more, and he hadn't made a sound except a sort of gurgle. And I went cold. I stood there shaking, and I was saying, "Alan, Alan, are you all right?" Damn silly – how could he be all right? I switched the torch back on, and I could see he was hanging upside down in a noose, and I had cut his throat. There was a lot of blood, pouring down the side of his head, but I could see it wasn't him. It wasn't Alan at all.'

'Nasty moment,' observed Peter.

'Who was it?' Quarley asked him. 'Do you know who it was? Do you know why he went for me like that?'

'Yes, I think I do,' said Peter. 'What I don't understand is why you did what you did next. I suppose you know that on your account so far you would not be at risk of a conviction for murder. It was self-defence. Did you realise that?'

'I suppose I did. I just couldn't understand it. I mean if Alan were really trying to get out of things, to lie low, I could just about understand that he might want to attack me; well, no, really I couldn't get my head around that idea. But why would a perfect stranger do it? Who did he think I was? I was in a hell of a hole.'

'You were. But a jury might think that an honest man in your situation would have called the police and handed himself over. From where we are now, Quarley, it's what you did next that is the source of the trouble.'

'The batteries ran out,' said Quarley. 'I couldn't see a blind thing. I was shaking like a leaf, and I only wanted to run away. I would have done just that if nobody in the village had seen me that evening, but I had a drink in the pub before going to the meeting with Alan. People knew I had been in Paggleham. I had to cover my tracks. So I went and hid out in that wood till first light. Then I walked around a bit. I was in a nightmare, I thought I must have got it all wrong; I must have been dreaming. But when I went back to the shed, of course I found it was true.'

'There's a phone box in the High Street from which you could have called the police,' said Harriet.

'You're not going to believe me,' Quarley said sadly. 'Why should you believe me? But I wasn't thinking of saving my neck. I was thinking of saving the job. I knew you, or someone would catch up with me eventually. But I just couldn't bear to let people down.'

'So what did you do?' asked Peter. His voice was very gentle, unthreatening. But his face was guarded. Harriet found herself looking at the scene as if from outside it; three of them, she the witness whose report would clinch the matter, Peter, cat-like, poised to pounce, Quarley the hapless mouse, hypnotised into offering himself to be devoured . . . she shook the thought off.

'I cut him down,' said Quarley, shuddering. 'I slung him over my shoulder, and carted him a little way down the street, and tipped him into a hole in someone's garden. I spotted it when I was walking around a bit earlier. There it was with a nice pile of earth beside it, all ready to cover him over.'

'Anyone might have seen you carrying the body,' said Peter. 'Did you think of that?'

'Anyone might have,' Quarley said. 'If God were on the side of the enemy, someone would have. That would have stopped me.'

'What do you mean?'

'But the Nazis don't believe in God, do they? And he

didn't help them that morning. Nobody saw me. I shoved enough earth over him to keep him covered for a day or two, and hopped it.'

'You say, for a day or two? You expected discovery?'

'You see,' said Quarley, 'I had a job to do. You might be right that I wouldn't hang – that it would be self-defence and all that. But there would certainly have been hell to pay. I would have been grounded.'

'Indeed you would,' said Peter.

'I had a mission to fly. I only got the leave that let me go down there because the mission was coming up. We had been training for months; and we only had three of us left to do it. The absolute minimum. We lost Alan early on, and poor Bob Fletchling a couple of weeks ago. He flew into a hillside in a spot of mist. So there were – there are, only three of us left. And it takes three. Believe me.'

'We believe you,' said Peter. 'Go on.'

'So I didn't give a damn for what a law-abiding person would have done. I didn't give a damn for the bastard I had done for; after all, he set about me. I didn't start it. I only cared for getting the hell out of there, and getting back on base, and doing my duty by my mates. Flying the mission, as planned. So that's what I did. I just pitched him in a hole, and got on my bike and got the hell out of there.'

'And how was the mission?' Peter asked.

'We made it. We all made it back, what's more.'

'Good. Congratulations. So then you were thinking of facing the music over what you had done?'

'I've torn it now,' Quarley said. 'Made things worse than ever, haven't I? What I didn't know was that the mission was just a warm-up for something else. Something even trickier. So that they were going to say to us: Well done, boys, now you're going to do that every day for months. So it's still just as urgent. Maybe more so. We've lost another good pilot since then, and we're flying with a new boy. He's pretty brilliant, but he's a bit too hot for safety. He's Polish. He doesn't fly technical, if you see what I mean, he flies with murder in his heart. He hates them so much he might risk a mission to down one of theirs. In the heat of the moment. Someone in the formation needs a cool head, and a bit of experience.'

'So what you're telling us is, you do mean to own up, but the moment hasn't come?'

'I suppose it has come,' said Quarley. 'I suppose you're it.'

'Time to go and talk to your commander,' said Wimsey. He was at the door, when he turned suddenly and said to Quarley, 'I say, old man, would you mind lending me that sheath knife of yours?'

Quarley drew it out of his belt, and handed it over. Peter took a handkerchief from his pocket, shook it out and picked up the knife through it. Harriet saw Quarley blanch. She followed Peter out of the room.

'Harriet, I need to go and get a sort of drumhead court martial organised,' he said. 'Would you stay with Quarley here, and not let him out of your sight?'

'If you want me to, of course.'

'This might take a little while.'

'Okay, Peter.'

'I'd like to know what you think.'

She could feel the misery seeping out of him, darkening the gloomy passageway in which they were standing, that feared and now familiar moment when Peter had cornered someone, and his appetite for justice suddenly waned and left him sickened. She had seen him through it before, and expected to see him through it again. But what was he asking her now?

'I'm sorry for him,' she said decisively. 'Are you going to tell him it was a German spy?'

'But it wasn't,' he said. 'As far as he knew when he struck the blow, it was a fellow officer who had been messing with his sister. And there is a chink in his story, Harriet. That knife. Why was he carrying a knife, if he didn't mean murder or mayhem?'

'So you don't feel it would be right to tell him he killed one of the enemy and let him go?' she asked.

'Well, would it?' he asked her.

An image of false-Brinklow, limping along the street, talking to Mrs Maggs, radiating charm at the village dance came to her clearly. Whoever he was. 'No, I don't think it would,' she said. 'But, Peter, it took a bit of inhumanity from high places to bring this about. It took somebody deciding that they didn't need actually to tell a dead man's friends and family that he was definitely dead. It was "missing presumed dead", that did the damage. That caused the misunderstanding. Don't you see?'

'Not entirely,' he said. 'I would say that it was Quarley's knife that did the damage. But look, my dear, it won't be up to us. Too much depends on it. Possibly many lives. I'm sorry to ask this of you, but just stay with him. Make sure he doesn't scarper or string himself up.'

Harriet nodded.

'I'll be as quick as I can,' he said. 'But it's a long way from London here. There might be trains; someone might be able to get a plane, but it might take all night.'

Only a minute after he had gone did she realise, with a lurching heart, how fast he might be going to drive.

The publican made up the fire before going to bed. He brought a mug of cocoa for each of them, and produced a couple of blankets. Quarley played patience for a while. Harriet read some ineffably corny ghost stories from the scant run of books on a shelf. It was an ordeal, no question, sitting with the man. He was in mental agony, and they didn't seem to have anything safe to talk about. Now and then he threw down the cards, got up, paced round the room like one of the big cats in the zoo.

Somewhere round midnight Harriet could bear the over-powering unease in the room no longer. 'Why did you take a knife?' she asked him. 'Do pilots always carry a knife? Is it official issue?'

'It's not official,' he said, turning to her eagerly. 'But we mostly carry them. It can be difficult to get free of a parachute, sometimes. If you're on the ground you can just unbuckle, but if you're caught up in something – if the thing is under tension, you're hanging in a tree or something like that, then it's handy to be able to cut free. Worst of all is if you're down in the water. The parachutes can fill up and drag you under in seconds. So most of us do carry knives. I didn't take it with me specially, if that's what you're thinking. Not at all.'

'It might be worth while to make sure that they know that. It's just a detail, but . . .'

'I can see that it makes a difference. If I had taken a knife deliberately it would look bad, wouldn't it? Premeditated? I wasn't premeditating, Lady Peter, truly I wasn't.'

'I believe you,' said Harriet.

'Look, do you mind if I try to get some sleep? Tomorrow looks pretty bloody, however things work out.'

'Go ahead. I'll try to catnap too. You aren't really going to run off, are you?'

'Not a bit of it,' he said, suddenly smiling at her, and he curled up on the lumpier sofa, punched a cushion to shape up under his head, and fell instantly asleep.

Harriet settled on the opposite sofa, covered her knees with the inn-keeper's blanket and studied the man lying stretched out opposite. She was amazed at his capacity to sleep in such a situation, but he was undoubtedly asleep very deeply. The fire burned down to a glowing pile of ashes, and Harriet got up to put another log on it, and stumbled. She knocked a stool over, but he did not stir. She wondered exactly how old he was – he could easily be younger than Jerry – but his seamless face looked neither young nor old, as though the stresses of his waking life had somehow blurred the fresh and expressionless visage of a very young man, and ripened him, even in sleep. Or perhaps especially in sleep, for she didn't remember thinking him older than his age when he was awake. She had a strong protective feeling about him; someone so young should not have had to cope with all this, should not have to risk his life and that of his companions, should not have killed anyone, should not be on the run; what peace meant, she thought, was that people were free to grow slowly into themselves, like well-lit plants, without this hothouse of distortion and pressure. Then she remembered the pig-shed, and shuddered. What was happening to her judgement? Shouldn't she feel nothing but horror and revulsion at this fellow? And there was a conundrum here: who had he killed? Was Peter right to say he had killed his friend? Or had he killed an enemy? She needed to talk it over with Peter, and he had gone about his business, and she was more than half asleep.

She woke suddenly in a chilly room. The faintest early light was angled through the half-drawn curtains. The fire was cold. Quarley was sitting up opposite her with his head in his hands.

'I've realised something awful. Really awful,' he said to her. 'Can I tell you – you can't think any worse of me than you do now, can you?'

'You can tell me things if you think it will help,' said Harriet.

'I hope they charge me,' he said softly. 'I hope they bang me up out of harm's way, and try me for murder, and take a long time about it. I'm not anything like as scared of that as I am of flying. I'm thinking, well maybe they'll hang me, but at least I won't have to do that again. At least I won't be burned alive.'

'I don't see anything awful in being afraid when you have to do hideously dangerous things,' said Harriet. 'Anyone would be.'

'You can't admit it, though,' he said. 'You've got to be a bloody hero. If anyone cracks it demoralises everyone else. You just keep pretending. You sit around on the ground making tea, and playing cards, and pretending that you hate it, and you just can't wait to be up there in the blue, ducking and weaving while the enemy does his damnedest to down you, and your ground-crew think you're the cat's whiskers, and everyone all round you is showing no fear. All the time it seems that some of them are crazy, plumb crazy. Wild boys, filing the rivets down on their wings to get a little extra speed, playing it like a fantastic game, thinking they're immortal. If they are just pretending too, you'd never know it. But the awful thing is, if I get arrested and locked up the mission plan will be shot to blazes, but I will be relieved, in a way. I am ashamed of myself, but there it is.'

'You don't have to be ashamed of it,' said Harriet.

'Of being a coward?'

'I don't think courage can have anything to do with what one feels inside,' Harriet said. 'I think it has to do with what one does. You haven't funked a mission yet, or "cracked" in front of others, have you?'

'No,' he said.

'As a matter of fact,' Harriet told him, 'I think you might find being locked up awaiting execution asked for a lot of courage; as bad as a flying mission without the excitement.'

'You're probably right,' he said, smiling sheepishly at her.

Heavens! Harriet thought. He hasn't heard of me. Not a word. And, of course, when I stood trial he would have been only a schoolboy . . .

'I won't have a choice, will I?' he asked.

'I don't think you will,' she said.

A dirty grey line had appeared between the curtains of the room. It cast a pencil of ineffectual grey light at an angle across the floor. Then both these apparitions glowed pink. Daylight; dawn. Harriet got up and drew the curtains. Outside it was already quite light, and there was some activity. A farm-worker was walking down the street with a billhook in his hand, and the postman was mounting a bicycle at the other end of the street. Quarley came to stand beside her. His voice had completely changed as he said, 'Thank you for listening to me. You're a real brick. Sorry for inflicting all that tommy-rot on you.'

'That's quite all right,' she said. 'It was nothing.'

'You won't hold it against me? It is a bit off, really. You know, the squadron has the Pole I told you about, and two Czech pilots, and two Canadians who couldn't wait for the official organisation to get them here, and even a Yank. All these people volunteering, and I . . .'

333

'I've forgotten already,' she said, spectacularly untruth-fully. But what does one say to someone who has opened his heart to you, and wishes to close the door again?

Then there was a sound of cars. Three cars drawing up to the building, men in dark overcoats getting out. Peter, Bungo, Sir Impey Biggs, an RAF officer of high degree, Superintendent Kirk, Wing-Commander Thompson: Peter's drumhead court martial, come to try their man. Harriet gazed at them with a spasm of hostility that almost, though not quite, included Peter.

Seventeen

Enough, if something from our hands have power
To live and act and serve the future hour;
And if, as towards the silent tomb we go,
Through love, through hope,
and faith's transcendent dower
We feel that we are greater than we know.
William Wordsworth, *The River Duddon*, 1820

Quarley had to go through it all again. Each detail, each movement, each gesture and blow. Sitting at the back of the room, Harriet listened acutely, attentively for any variation in the tale, any slip that would catch him out; complete consistency is difficult for liars. But he didn't vary his tale by one iota. He forgot to mention the knife; Peter got it out of him with a deftly placed question. He was white-faced, tensed, looking constantly across the table at his Wing-Commander, who sat head down, fiddling with a pen against a note-pad, looking, Harriet thought, black as thunder.

When Quarley had finished, the Wing-Commander said abruptly, 'So where does this leave us?'

Superintendent Kirk said, 'If this was peace-time I would

arrest and charge this man, and the law would take its course. That's what I'd prefer to do now, war or no war.'

Sir Impey Biggs said, 'You wouldn't get murder, Kirk, you know. And I think if you go for manslaughter you still might not get it. If I were defending I'd have a good go at justified homicide. Self-defence. It's nearly watertight. And if the jury knew who the deceased was, you'd never get a conviction.'

'They wouldn't know,' said Bungo. 'We'd make sure of that.'

Quarley said, 'How could I get someone like him defending me? I haven't a penny to my name.'

Peter said, 'If it comes to that, I'll retain Impey.'

'Why?' said Quarley. 'Why should you help me? Look, who the hell was he? He was somebody special, wasn't he?'

'I think in human decency, we have got to tell him,' said Peter quietly.

'He was an enemy agent,' said Bungo.

'But . . .'

'Pretending to be Brinklow,' Peter said. 'You would have known at once. Had you caught sight of him in daylight the game would have been up for him. He had to try to kill you.'

Quarley sat silent for long seconds. 'So when he said he hadn't heard of Joan, he really hadn't,' he said at last. 'That's what got me so blindingly angry. And it was true.'

'Yes, it was,' said Peter.

'So is that it? Can I just go now? I killed a spy, and I'm a sort of hero?'

'You're a damn nuisance,' said Bungo. 'We would have caught up with him in a bit, and found out what he was up to. And if he was acting alone. What he was doing for the enemy. Vital intelligence. Then you come along.'

'I'm sorry.'

'Look, in all the circumstances,' said Thompson, standing up, 'can I have my man back? He's supposed to be airborne in half an hour, and I haven't a substitute who's up to the job.'

'If it was up to me, I'd charge him,' said Kirk. 'But it isn't up to me, I suppose.'

'Look, Commander, Superintendent Kirk has security clearance,' said Peter. 'Couldn't you tell him enough about these missions to convince him that he ought to hold his hand?'

'We need to know where the key German warships are,' said Commander Thompson. 'We need to know if they move out of port. They can hide them in the fjords now they have Norway in their clutches, and it's very hard to fly over a deep fjord between high mountains. The fall of Norway is a disaster. Those ports give them mastery of the northern Atlantic. I know all eyes are on the south, and that's where the battle to get air-cover for an invasion will be. But without supplies from across the Atlantic we're going to be starved out. We must try to protect our shipping, and we must try to sink theirs. The bastards are attacking unarmed trawlers now, as well as neutral shipping. We're flying Hudsons,' he added. 'They aren't as fast as Spitfires, or as manoeuvrable.'

'If it's so important, why don't they give you Spitfires?' asked Kirk.

'Spits haven't got the range. Two hours cruising, or forty-five minutes at combat speeds at most. We've got a lot more in a Hudson. Hamburg and back. Quarley got to Hamburg and back last month.'

'Convinced?' asked Peter.

'All right, all right,' said Kirk. He was glaring wrathfully at Bungo. 'But I have got a body, and you tell me I shan't have either a conviction or an acquittal.'

'Well, you won't have any grieving relatives to nag you,' said Impey Biggs.

'That's something,' admitted Kirk grudgingly.

'What if I insist on making a written statement to this policeman?' asked Quarley. 'Will he arrest me?'

Peter said quietly, 'Everything you have done so far is dependent on your wish to go on flying. To go on fighting. Isn't that so?'

Quarley nodded, mutely. Then he said, 'If I were flying solo, I could find a sort of answer . . .'

Commander Thompson said fiercely, 'No, you don't, laddie. If there's one thing we're shorter of than pilots it's aircraft. I'll ground you if I think you're a risk to your plane, and let these officers of the law take you off my patch.'

Peter said, 'This isn't fair. This is a grim sort of double

jeopardy. Gentlemen,' he added, 'we must leave this up to Quarley himself. He is risking his neck for his country day after day. If he survives, and if he chooses, he can clear things up after the war.'

'You mean I really can go?' said Quarley.

'Get the hell out of here, and get on standby,' said Commander Thompson.

Harriet, standing at the window, saw Quarley emerge on to the street running for his motor-bike, and saw in every step he took, in the set of his shoulders, in the rake of his head as he rode away, what he really wanted, which risk he really preferred.

Behind her Commander Thompson said, 'I wouldn't give much for his chances.'

'What are the odds?' asked Bungo.

'He's good. A good man lasts about eighty hours' flying time in present circumstances. He's done more than forty. But this will get a lot worse before it gets better.'

'I think so, too,' said Peter.

'A chap is old at twenty in this game.'

'Who is going to tell the family?' asked Harriet.

'Tell them what?'

'What they need to know. That Alan Brinklow was not in dereliction of his duty, and that Jeff Quarley is not to be charged with murder. Surely they should know that much.'

'Hmm,' said Bungo. 'Can they keep it to themselves, do you think?'

'Don't underestimate the commonalty, old man,' said

Peter. 'You're not in the Ministry of Instruction and Morale.'

'Thank heaven for that!' said Bungo. 'Well, if you think so, Lady Peter. Perhaps we could leave it to your best judgement.'

'It would come better from you,' said Harriet. 'You look properly official.'

Let this smug and horribly distant man witness some human emotion, she thought. Why should he not see what the consequences of his dirty tricks department might be?

Bungo stood in Mrs Quarley's drawing-room, his immaculately cut black overcoat seeming more impressive than any uniform. Mrs Quarley faced him as though he were a firing squad.

'For complicated reasons which national security forbids me to divulge,' he told her, 'it is proposed that no action be taken against your son as a result of any recent events in which he may have been involved in Hertfordshire. We must ask you to keep anything you may know about this matter entirely to yourself.'

'Oh!' she said. 'Oh, I've been so frightened! When he told me what had happened . . . yes, of course.'

Not quite satisfied, Bungo went on, 'Should any information about the affair begin to circulate the authorities might be forced to initiate the actions which they have decided not to initiate.'

'I understand you very well,' said Mrs Quarley. 'And thank God!'

'Will you tell your daughter,' said Peter, 'that Alan Brinklow died a brave man, and that any impression that he survived and did not act with perfect honesty was produced by the sort of misinformation that can happen in war-time.'

'Oh, I don't have to tell her,' said Mrs Quarley. 'She has never doubted it.' She turned to Peter. 'I think I must have you to thank for this,' she said. 'But it's the right thing. Jeff is a good, brave boy.'

'His courage is not in doubt, Mrs Quarley,' said Peter.

As they walked back down the pleasant street towards their cars, Bungo said, 'If we ever do this again, we'll have to start from scratch. This was too complicated.'

'Start from scratch? Make somebody up out of thin air?' asked Harriet, amazed.

'Well, the real man's only too real connections have caused a lot of bother, wouldn't you say?' said Bungo. 'It would be difficult, of course . . .'

'It would indeed!' said Harriet. 'Bungo, you can have no idea at all how difficult fiction is.'

'The nearly insuperable problem would be finding an available body,' said Peter.

'I'm afraid I don't think there'll be any shortage of bodies,' said Bungo.

'But bodies,' said Peter, 'as my long acquaintance with them has made very clear to me, have histories.'

It was early afternoon before they began the long drive

home. It was raining. The grey ribbon of the A1 unwound interminably in front of them. Peter drove as usual very fast, and very skilfully. Harriet had got so used to this that she no longer needed to ride with her eyes shut. So when he slowed to a modest speed and they began to move gently along a wind-swept stretch, between showers, she said, 'What's up, Peter?'

'We're nearing the turn-off for Peterborough.'

'Are we? How does one tell, with all the signs gone?'

'Long familiarity.'

'A tendency to know everything. Still the wonder grew . . .'

'I accept the implied mockery,' he said.

'Only admiration was implied,' she said dryly. 'Why are we suddenly obeying the speed limit, and the normal need for caution?'

'I was wondering,' he said, 'whether you would consider taking a diversion, and going home via Duke's Denver?'

'Oh, Peter, let's!' said Harriet. 'Your mother hasn't seen you for ages, and she has been so worried about you.'

'You wouldn't mind?'

'I'd love it.'

Peter turned immediately, having reached the corner as they had been speaking, and sped up at once.

Harriet braced herself. Long, straight fenland roads stretched ahead. They ran like demonstrations of vanishing point into the level distances. Occasionally there was a sharp turn, a humped bridge over water, another turn, and the road resumed its set direction on the other bank of a sluice. On one of these sudden switch-backs they became aware of a dog-fight in the air above them. Some miles away a group of planes were catching the golden light of early evening, shining in the air, gleaming, twisting, soaring, diving, four or five of them on the tail of an enemy fighter. They crackled with gunfire, and scrawled vapour trails over the huge overarching dome of the sky.

Peter stopped the car and they watched in silence. If a victory or a defeat was scored they could not decipher it. The planes were moving rapidly southwards, till they diminished to the size of the shower of sparks from a Roman candle.

'Bother!' said Peter, a mile further on.

'What's up?'

'My favourite signpost has gone with all the rest. I wanted to show it to you.'

'What did it say?'

'It said on the right-hand arm "Duke's Denver 7 miles". And on the left-hand arm "Duke's Denver 7 miles". I thought they might have left it. After all, the reason for taking the signs down was to confuse the enemy!'

In fifteen minutes they moved off the fen, and drove through a mile or two of gently rolling, wooded country, to the gates of the house. The lodge was unmanned, the wrought-iron gates had disappeared, and the car rumbled over a cattle grid into the park. Peter said, 'I hope Gerald hasn't sent those gates off for the war effort. They were rather fine.'

'But shouldn't he? If everyone else's railings are to go?'

'There have been a lot of wars and emergencies in the time of a house like this,' said Peter. They had crested a rise and were looking down at the Palladian front. Dusk was gathering, but the great house stood unlit, a brooding mass of stone, and a parade of glass windows in which the last lemony remnant of sunset gleamed, streaked with grey cloud-shadow. No blackout could quench window-glass in this level, late light. Peter stopped the car.

'It looks a bit gloomy like this,' said Harriet. 'Threatening, somehow.'

'I am intolerably threatened by it,' said Peter fiercely.

'I have always supposed that if it came to the point, you would let it claim you, and do your best for it.'

'Did you marry me thinking that?'

'Yes.'

'And prepared to do your best by it too?'

'Yes, Peter. Prepared for anything that being married to you would bring.'

'What we heard about Quarley has a terrible relevance to Jerry.'

'I know. I thought of that too. Did I tell you that Helen wants us to put the boys' names down for some posh boarding school?'

'She would,' he said. 'Harriet, whatever happens to us, we must try to keep the boys out of it. Of course they need a good school, but I would like them to be brought up plainly labelled "Middle class of Paggleham", like "Indignant of Tunbridge Wells". Just look at this! How can this be justified? And it will be even harder in the world after the war. Every living person in these islands will have shared risks and hardship; how will it seem to be claiming privilege? Can we keep the boys modest and ordinary as far as possible?'

'You hate it, Peter, don't you? And I held it against you all those years.'

'It's a quagmire,' he said. 'Because I love it too. All this glory has a lethal charm and majesty. But I do prefer myself now. Peter-after-Harriet is easier to live with than Peter-before-Harriet. That Peter makes me squirm whenever I think of him.'

'Well, don't think of him. He's over and gone. Take me down to the Dower House before we both freeze to the car seats.'

The dowager Duchess flung herself into her son's arms, with cries of delight, while her notorious cat Ahasuerus sunk his claws into Harriet's ankles. Harriet could not remember any arrival at Denver that was not accompanied by the application of Germalene to some part of someone.

'Oh, I am so sorry! Darling Harriet! Ahasuerus isn't at all himself!' cried the Duchess. 'He simply *cannot* understand why there are so few scraps – and of course I can't explain, although of course I do keep telling him about rationing.'

'That dratted cat is actually entirely himself,' said Peter sternly. 'He always scratches someone, rationing or no

345

rationing. We came on impulse, Mother; do we have ration-books, Harriet?'

'Oh, rubbish, Peter, we shall kill the fatted calf and let Hitler choke on it. As a matter of fact you chose just the day; Gerald is coming to supper, and we have a pheasant pie, thanks to Mr Lanson. He's been potting game for us when he isn't teaching the Home Guard how to use firearms. I gather they profit from his teaching by poaching more ruthlessly than ever. Now, come upstairs, dears, and sit by the fire while I get Franklin to make up your room for you.'

'How's the family firm?' asked Peter, when they were settled at the fireside. The Duchess was knitting – she declared it was the only form of war work she was fit for – some remarkably knobbly socks. Ahasuerus kept batting the ball of wool across the floor with a lifted paw, and then flattening himself against the shining parquetry and stalking it into far corners. Harriet kept getting up and retrieving it. She put it back in the Duchess's knitting-bag, from which it would be jerked out as the knitting reached the end of each row, and Ahasuerus would send it rolling away again.

'Rather well, dear, I'm almost afraid to say. It does seem awful when other people are being so discombobulated. Helen was complaining bitterly the other day about the servants and groundsmen all leaving for the forces or war work, or taking leave of absence to fire-watch and train in first-aid. I said to her, "Helen, they are actually *doing* something about the war, and you should be glad to let them." She said she was doing plenty herself, working in London, but I think she's glad of the excuse to be away. Gerald seems a lot more resilient without her. He wouldn't get away with some of the things he's doing if she were around, I think.'

'Like what, Mother?' said Peter.

'Well, he lets our evacuees have the run of the place. I ran into an art lesson the other day, with all of them sitting around that copy of *Apollo Belvedere* that we have in the Long Gallery, and making drawings of it. Our version hasn't even got a fig leaf, you know, Harriet, and you should see some of the works of art those London little ones were making! The girls, too.'

'Shocking,' said Gerald, arriving and bestowing a minimal kiss on his mother's cheek. 'Hallo, Harriet. Peter. Good to see you. How's Hertfordshire?'

'Very nice indeed, after abroad, thank you, Gerald,' said Peter. 'How's Dukedom?'

'Harder than ever,' said Gerald cheerfully. 'I'm letting most of the garden go for pasture. I've only two men left, and they are both getting on. Can't be helped.'

'One can always restore a garden later,' said Peter.

'If things ever get back to normal. Don't suppose a bit of grass and sheep-shit does the flower-beds any harm. But I can't see us setting up anything again that needs so much labour. Hasn't been easy since before the last war, never mind this one.' Gerald poured himself a sherry. 'Thank God the old man isn't around to see it,' he said.

'That's been true for many centuries,' said Peter.

'What has?'

'That there's been an old man who wasn't around to see it, whatever it was.'

'Of course. I see. I don't suppose you've seen anything of that son of mine, have you? Never comes home.'

'Difficult for him, on active duty,' said Harriet.

'Of course it is,' said the Duchess. 'And, Gerald, be fair – he does telephone. He rang me only this morning and sent love to all the family.'

'And it's good of you to be looking after Mary's brats,' said Gerald. 'Lots of work, I should think.'

'Not as children go, really,' said Harriet. 'Besides, once one is looking after one or two, there's nothing left to lose, if you see what I mean.'

'How many have we got here, Mater?' asked Gerald.

'Two hundred and fifty, I think, dear,' said the Duchess. 'With teachers, of course. Weren't you going to ask Peter about one of them?'

'Yes, I was. One of the little perishers has taken a shine to the pictures, and is busy reading up art history and asking me a lot of stuff I don't know about.'

'I'm sure Helen would be outraged if she thought the library was being thrown open to all and sundry,' offered the Duchess gleefully.

Harriet cast a sideways glance at Peter to see if he was outraged himself, but he just said, 'Well the incunabula and the really important books are all in the locked cases, Mother. I don't suppose Gerald's heart has melted enough to offer them the keys.'

'No, of course not. But it's a bit of a poser, don't you know, when a snotty-nosed lad out of the East End starts asking about Caravaggio. Thing is, Peter, what should I do for him? If I wanted to give him a leg up.'

'Are you serious, Gerald? Tell him if he passes the scholarship examination he could get into the Slade and study art. Offer him a fiver for getting into grammar school, and a hundred guineas if he makes it into a history of art course. Then stand back and wait and see. Oh, and leave him with the run of the library.'

'Hmm,' said Gerald. 'I just might. Don't know what Helen would say about the money.'

'Don't tell Helen,' said the Duchess. 'Swear the dear little brute to secrecy.'

'Ah,' said Gerald. 'Look, do you mind if we turn on the news?'

The bulletin announced the fall of the government. Chamberlain had resigned. Winston Churchill was the new Prime Minister. He offered nothing but blood, toil, tears and sweat.

Quietly they listened to his gravelly voice. 'What is our policy? To wage war against a monstrous tyranny, never surpassed in the dark, lamentable catalogue of human crime. What is our aim? Victory, victory at all costs, victory in spite of all terror; victory however hard the road may be, for without victory there is no survival.'

A flustered Franklin in an apron announced that dinner was on the table.

*   *   *

Next morning they set out on the last leg of the journey home. They left mid-morning, with the boot of Mrs Merdle stuffed with game – four pheasants and a hare, which Gerald and Peter had shot before breakfast – a pretty dress for Polly which had belonged to her mother, and which the Duchess had preserved in tissue paper, a battered dog on wheels for Paul, a train for Bredon, a doll for little Harriet, and a model aeroplane for Charlie, all of which had been disgorged from the endless cornucopia of the Denver attics. Somehow it was agreed that there would be no need to hurry, and the journey could take in numerous stops.

As they drove across the fen, under a sunny sky, Harriet felt a strange elated combination of fear and a sort of determined happiness. The enormous arena of light and cloud that spread above the fen was bracing to the spirit.

'Don't drive too fast, Peter.'

'Am I alarming you again?'

'No; not that. It's just that I'd like the journey to go on as long as possible.'

'What dreadful prospect at home makes you wish so? Riotous children? Omnipresent Bunter? The ration-books? The chance of air-raids? Look, Harriet, I really don't think the air-raid risk is very acute. People have to be prepared, of course; but Talboys is three miles from the nearest air-field, and it's those that the enemy is gunning for at the moment. And if they changed tack they wouldn't be dropping expensive bombs, dangerously delivered, on villages in Hertfordshire, it would be to go for militarily significant targets, or large cities where they can terrorise the population.'

'As we were doing raiding Berlin?'

'Yes. I don't like that much, Harriet, but I suppose we have been provoked.'

'Yes indeed. And what puts me off the prospect of arriving home is none of the items on your list, but the depressing prospect of wrestling with that unsolved murder.'

'Odd of you, Harriet. An unsolved murder is just what I like to get my pulses racing. Three before breakfast would suit me best. But I rather think we haven't got even one.'

'What? What are you telling me, Peter?'

'Nothing you don't already know. Wendy Percival: murder method clear from the start. Murder opportunity gradually established by elimination, done mostly by you, Harriet, and very good careful work too. It's only that devil motive that prevented you from arresting Brinklow. The missing motive.'

'And if Kirk had arrested him . . .'

'You would have saved him from a nasty end, by the look of it.'

'But as far as I can see the motive is still missing, Peter.'

'Oh, well, I'm guessing,' said Peter. 'But it's something you said that put me on to it. You said – remember? – didn't the real Brinklow have a life of his own? Couldn't he have had an enemy of his own?'

'And he did, if you would count Quarley as an enemy.'

'So take it one more step: there was, after all, someone real impersonating Brinklow . . .'

'And that real person also had a past! Oh, Peter, how weird! But you must be right!'

'Is it weird?' he asked, turning the car towards March.

'It's a strange inversion, Peter. He tried to kill Quarley, because Quarley would not have recognised him; would have known it wasn't him—'

'And mightn't he have killed Wendy because she *did* recognise him; not as Brinklow, of course, but as Helmut or Hans or Werner or whoever.'

'She had been abroad, quite a bit. Oh, glory, Peter, and one of her friends said that one doesn't get murdered for having a degree in Modern Languages.'

'I've looked at the list of foreign parts she had visited in Miss Climpson's letter to you,' he said. 'It doesn't mention Germany, but if we ask her parents I expect we'll find she was there. It fits beautifully with what the dentist heard.'

'Mrs Spright?'

'At the inquest. Your notes say she said she heard Wendy say, "Great heavens. What are you doing here?" You hardly ask that of a complete stranger. And then what could he do? His cover is blown. He could flee; but if he intends to stay put and do what he came for, he must silence her. Completely. Immediately. He can't risk letting her have a single conversation with another living soul.'

Harriet thought about it. 'Yes,' she said. 'You could be

right. That would make sense. And it would be a relief in a way. That it was, after all, a war-crime.'

'Murders happen, as we both know, in peace-time too,' he said.

'Yes; but somehow a *private* murder in a time of common danger would have seemed particularly foul,' she said. 'A blotch on all we are fighting for.'

'Certainly we are fighting for a young woman's right to walk in safety,' he said. 'But I'm not sure that being killed by an enemy agent ennobles her death, Harriet.'

'It means her death was part of the common danger.'

'Well, yes,' he said. 'I suppose you're right. And it must have been a war-related matter that brought pseudo-Brinklow to Paggleham. I heartily wish we knew what that was.'

Eighteen

The youth of a nation are the trustees of posterity.
Benjamin Disraeli, *Sybil*, 1845

'So what will happen now?' asked Harriet, as they drove through Broxford, and into the familiar, tangled lanes towards Paggleham.

'About what?'

'About pseudo-Brinklow.'

'Kirk will need to get the body out of his morgue. Do you think Fred Lugg could organise a discreet burial?'

'We bury him darkly at dead of night?'

'Something like that.'

'We raise not a stone and we carve not a line?'

'He was a brave, if ruthless man,' said Peter. 'I think after the war I might shell out for a headstone.'

'Peter, are you really going to pay for a headstone for a spy? Spying is so loathsome.'

'Heart's lady, what do you think I was doing, all those weeks abroad?'

'That's different!' she said at once.

'Why?' he asked. His tone was light, but edged.

'Because of the cause being served.'

'I expect the man we are talking about would have said he acted for his country.'

'For his country's ruthless, murderous aggrandisement. We are acting in self-defence. The same argument you applied to Jeff Quarley; they attacked us, and we have a right to defend ourselves by any means available.'

'Yes,' he said. 'They have turned Europe into a pig-shed full of blood in which we will blunder against each other in the dark. But I prefer blood, toil, tears and sweat with Churchill to peace in our time with Chamberlain.'

'So what would a headstone say?'

'You're the writer.'

'Here lies an unknown enemy, who died for the cause he served?'

'That would do nicely.' A mile further down the road he said, 'I *do* wish we knew why it was worth their while to plant a spy in Paggleham. What were they after?'

'I don't suppose we'll ever know, now.'

'That's what's so galling,' said Peter.

A riotous welcome home awaited them at Talboys. The children came running out to greet them, and hung round them all talking at once. Except Charlie, Harriet noticed. As so often he seemed older than his years, and hung back. He looked rather tense.

'So what's the news, tribe?' asked Peter.

'An air-raid!' they cried. 'We had an air-raid! A real one!'

'You were in one of the shelters, I hope?' said Harriet, gathering Bredon and Polly in a two-armed hug.

'We couldn't, Mummy,' said Bredon. 'The siren didn't go!'

'That's bad,' said Peter. 'Is this true, Bunter?' For Bunter had appeared from the house.

'Quite true, my lord. No warning. A single enemy aircraft. It dropped a string of bombs in the field behind the house, my lord, in broad daylight.'

'Any damage, Bunter?'

'I'm afraid so, my lord. It knocked off one of our chimney pots, and broke it on the driveway. And I'm afraid in falling the chimney killed two of Miss Twitterton's hens, that were boarded with us, so to speak, to take advantage of kitchen scraps.'

'Two dead hens?' asked Harriet. 'Dinner?'

'I'm afraid not,' said Bunter mournfully. 'Those wretched evacuee boys arrived before we did. They got the birds.'

'It was Bunter's fault,' said Polly, slipping her hand in Harriet's as they went indoors.

'In my long experience of Bunter,' observed Lord Peter, 'things are seldom his fault, Polly.'

'He wouldn't let us out of the coal cellar for ages!' said Polly. 'He wouldn't let us go and see what was happening. So there was this big crash, and we just waited. And the Marbleham boys got the chickens, and we just saw them running away when we got out.'

'They can't half run!' said Charlie admiringly.

The news took them right through tea-time, and bath-time, to be superseded by joy at the Duchess's presents, and it was nine o'clock before Peter and Harriet could settle in the living-room. Peter was playing to Harriet while she knitted. Something by Bach. 'Do you mind, Harriet?'

'I love to hear you play.'

'I find myself deeply consoled by the continuo,' he said.

They were interrupted. Charlie in his pyjamas stood in the doorway.

'Uncle Peter?'

'Come in and close the door behind you, Charlie, before Bunter or Sadie catches you,' said Peter. 'What is it? Can't you sleep?'

'I need some help, Uncle Peter. It's so *difficult*. And it might be important, and Daddy isn't here!' cried Charlie. 'I haven't seen him for ages!'

'All right, old man. Don't get upset. Let's see what your wicked uncle can do for you.'

'It's all this,' said Charlie, unbuttoning his pyjama jacket and letting reams and reams of paper fall out on to the floor. He picked up a handful and spread it out on the piano. Peter closed the lid on the keyboard and came to look. He put his monocle in his eye and peered closely at Charlie's paperwork.

'What is it, Charlie?' Peter asked. 'It doesn't seem to me to make a lot of sense.'

'That's just it!' cried Charlie, his voice shaking slightly. 'It's just too hard for us! Sam said we mustn't tell any grown-up, because we don't know who is a spy, but *you* couldn't be a spy, Uncle Peter, and I thought if I asked you not to tell . . .'

'Cross my heart and hope to die? I'm not an enemy spy,

Charlie, no. But look here, old chap, you seem a bit upset. Why don't I get Bunter to fix you up a mug of Horlicks, and you sit in that armchair opposite your aunt, and tell us all about it.'

Charlie came across the room, looking anxiously at Harriet, until she smiled at him. 'Would you rather have Bournville?' she asked.

He nodded sadly. 'I know Horlicks is good for you,' he said.

'I don't think it's good enough for you to constitute an excuse for the taste,' said Harriet. Bunter appeared in response to Peter's ring, and the Bournville was duly ordered.

'You see, at first we thought – me and Sam thought – my crystal set wasn't working properly. We kept getting noises instead of the Home Service.'

'They are the devil to tune, those things,' said Peter.

'But it wasn't that. It would go wrong and right and wrong again, and we kept trying and then we realised it wasn't the set. We were picking up something. It was Morse code. So we went and got a book about it. We found out a lot about it.'

'Good for you,' said Peter. 'What did you find out?'

'We found a book about how to read it properly, first,' said Charlie. 'Mr Smith – that's our scout-master, Uncle Peter – was teaching us all wrong. He was making us write it down letter by letter.'

Bunter appeared with his hot drink, and on Peter's eye-signal to him, he stood quietly behind Charlie, listening.

'We were trying to write it down, dah didit dah dah didit,' said Charlie, 'but it was too fast for us. The book said don't write down dah didits, just listen and learn the shape of the letters, and then you would be able to hear sentences and write those down. But we couldn't, because it didn't make sentences.'

'It would have been in code?'

'Must of been. So we had to write down the letters and try to break the code later.'

'I see. So let me have a look at what you've got.' Peter spread out Charlie's jottings on the piano top, and he and Bunter looked at them together.

'This is certainly a bit obscure,' said Peter. But Charlie, having once got launched into his story, was now talking eagerly on.

'We got another book that said if you wound the aerial round a shoe box or something, and turned it round and round you could find the direction the messages were coming from. When they were loudest, you were pointing straight at them.'

'So where were they coming from?'

'From the village. Somewhere by the church,' said Charlie. 'It was quite close. That's why it cut across the National Service.'

The three adults in the room were hanging on his every word. 'So Sam said, we'd got to crack this code and find out who is sending it. And then it stopped. Suddenly we can get Henry Hall and the BBC dance orchestra all the time, and no dahdidits at all. And we just can't understand these letters we wrote down. And when the bomb came I was scared, Uncle Peter, and so I've told you, whatever Sam says. He'll be cross,' added Charlie sorrowfully, 'and he's my best friend ever.'

'When do you reckon it stopped, Charlie?' asked Harriet.

'About three weeks ago. We did wonder if it was a black-marketer. About that unlicensed pig. It went away round about then.'

'Did it, by God?' said Peter.

'If I may say so, my lord,' said Bunter, 'these letters look odd to me. I think they must be a substitution code – not enough Es for English, and too many Zs.'

'It's scrambled German, I think, Bunter,' said Peter. 'But I think there's enough of it to give our wizards a chance at cracking it. However did you have the patience to write down so much of it, Charlie? Weren't you bored?'

'It was exciting when we thought it was spies,' said Charlie. 'But it was boring too. I didn't know things could be boring *and* exciting,' he added plaintively. 'We took turns.'

'Look, Charlie, I'm going to have to tell somebody else about this. May I have your permission?'

Charlie nodded. Peter went to the telephone in the hall, leaving the door ajar, and they heard his voice pitched excitedly. 'Bungo, I think I've got something for you. You won't guess what in a hundred years . . . an intercept. My nephew and his friend. He's ten. Yes, yes, ten years old. Okay, you're the boss.'

Returning to the room Peter said, 'Bungo's getting the

night desk to send a despatch rider to pick this up and take it to Bletchley.'

'Do I have to go to bed now?' asked Charlie.

'No,' said Peter, glancing at Harriet for approval. 'You can hand your stuff over yourself if you would like to. Honour where honour is due.'

'Only it's Sam's stuff too,' said Charlie. 'It's my crystal set but Sam did half the work.'

Harriet said, 'Bunter, would you step across to Bateson's farm, and see if Sam's bedtime can be stretched in a crisis?'

It would later be one of her favourite recollections of the war years at Talboys: two little boys in flannel pyjamas, swaying on their feet with fatigue, handing over a bundle of paper to a despatch rider who saluted them as he took it. Peter, Harriet noticed, was bursting with pride for Charlie. He took the boy up to bed, and she heard him saying as they crossed the landing, 'You ought to have a medal for this, Charles. But the secret service don't get medals in war-time. Obviously. Would you swap a medal after the war for a bicycle now?'

'I'd like the bicycle, please, Uncle Peter, if Sam can have one too.'

'Naturally Sam gets one too. But you are both sworn to secrecy about all this.'

Two days later Mrs Goodacre came to call. 'Have you heard the news, my dears?' she asked. 'The establishment at Steen Manor is moving out! The village is full of trucks and all the young men are going, we mustn't ask where, and ours not to reason why. I'm afraid our land-girls will be rather bereft with only local boys to fraternise with. Everyone and everything is rolling away, down to the station cat.'

'Let me get you a cup of tea?' asked Harriet.

'No, thank you. I can't stop. What I really came over for was to ask if there were any chance . . . if Lord Peter could possibly play the organ for us for a wedding next Tuesday fortnight.'

'At your own risk,' said Peter. 'The piano is my instrument really. But I'll manage something for you. Miss Twitteron can't be there?'

'Oh, she'll be *there*,' said Mrs Goodacre. 'She's the bride!'

'Great heavens!' exclaimed Harriet. 'I'm so glad for her! But what a surprise . . .'

'She's marrying our Polish farmer,' said Mrs Goodacre. 'Such a nice man. He's a widower, we understand, and he knows all about chickens. He's been helping her, and they've been meeting after dark in the lanes, and in the wood; they didn't want anyone to know until they were ready. They had to sort out their religious views, I understand. But after some discussion Jan decided that Common Prayer was just like home only not in Polish.'

'This is really wonderful,' said Harriet. 'I must ask her if she needs clothing coupons.'

'I understand she has a suitable skirt and a resplendent new blouse,' said Mrs Goodacre. 'We are in quest of something to make a veil. All we could say, Simon and I, was "Well I never!" over and over again.'

'So the sudden removal of Steen Manor would be Charlie's doing?' Harriet asked Peter.

'His stuff contained a map reference for it, I understand,' said Peter. 'I suppose pseudo-Brinklow found where it was. He might have been sent to find it. He might have been about to light flares to mark it as a target. Either way Charlie's saved the day, really. Retrieved a blunder, clever little beast. I promised a chocolate cake to go with the bicycles.'

'And what, may I ask, your lordship, will you do if Mrs Trapp's sugar hoards are exhausted, and you cannot make good a promise of chocolate cake?'

'I shall do what many a worser man has done, and buy some on the black market,' said Peter.

'I'm very shocked, Peter. Do you actually know a black-marketer who can oblige us with sugar?'

'I shall send Bunter. Ask me not where. With a couple of bottles of very good port to negotiate with.'

'It's a curious aspect of war,' said Harriet thoughtfully, 'how important it makes food. You can have no idea what it did to my feelings when you said you had been hungry.'

'Do you remember once telling me that although almost everything that had happened to you had been awful, you always knew it was just things that were wrong, not everything? That you never thought of wanting to die, only of getting out of the mess?'

'Yes, I remember. That was about Harriet-before-Peter.

364

Harriet-after-Peter hasn't needed any such stoicism. I'm a different woman now.'

'Well, when I was cold and hungry and more than a bit scared, I remembered what you had said: it was just things that were wrong, not everything, and that I simply had to get out of the mess.'

Harriet thought for a moment. Then she said, 'Peter, will they send you abroad again?'

'Abroad? Possibly. Behind enemy lines? No. They'll find me something at home, I expect.'

'Sure?'

'Pretty sure. I won't volunteer again. I don't trust myself.'

'I don't believe you.'

'It's true. When old . . . when somebody gave me my papers he said, "You've got a wife and children, haven't you?" and I thought he was feeling sorry for me. But I saw a bit later that he was just feeling worried for the safety of his mission.'

'Are you saying that marriage and fatherhood has made you a coward? Peter, how terrible!'

'Love has made me afraid of death,' he said. 'I rather thought it might. Are you surprised?'

'I think I am,' she said. The whole conversation felt dangerous – she could not see how far she might fall if she missed her footing.

'Everyone's afraid of death at one level,' he said. 'There is an animal fear that kicks in and overrides the will. That's why people who have thrown themselves in the Thames to drown struggle in the water. People are afraid of dying in painful and protracted ways. I am too, naturally. But I have never before been afraid of *being dead*.'

'What do you mean, my dear?' She almost whispered it.

'I used to think the world could get along very well without me. A few tears shed for me, and everything would trolley along much as before. And now . . . understand me, Harriet, I don't think you couldn't manage without me, of course you could, but . . .'

'I wouldn't be trolleying along much as before? Too right, I wouldn't. Your being dead is the most terrible state of the world I can imagine.'

'And therefore my being dead is a terrible prospect for me. And do you see how this rabbit runs, Harriet? How we are overstating it? No private grief or horror is now the worst thing imaginable. Once one is afraid of being dead one isn't reliable any more; I mean when that moment of animal fear arrived it would have a collaborator in one's head. There would be a fatal flaw in one's moral fibre; a secret voice that said, "My wife and children need me."'

'We do need you. Terribly. Preferably alive, and here. But most of all we need you to be yourself.'

'And if myself were a poor frightened thing, trying to save its skin no matter what?'

'Do you think I wouldn't love you in that case? Love is not love which alters where it alteration finds; and, Peter, that would be alteration. Whatever you seem like to yourself in black moments, you do not seem frightened and self-preserving to me.'

'You don't know what I may have been up to, just recently,' he said.

'Peter, when you tossed a coin with Bunter to decide who would come home the safer way, which way up did the coin land?'

He gave her suddenly a guilty-looking grin, an expression uncannily like Bredon's, caught taking two biscuits at once from the tin.

'God, Harriet, you're a hard taskmaster,' he said. 'You don't let me get away with much, do you?'

'I know you rather well, by now,' said Harriet.

'You'll love and bear me? You will not change, nor falter, nor repent?'

'Certainly not. But I don't catch the quotation. What is it?'

'Shelley,' said Peter. 'I was reading it the other night, and it seemed extraordinarily apt for the time.'

He brought the book from the shelf, found the place, and laid it open on Harriet's lap. He leaned over her shoulder, his hand resting lightly on hers, and they read it together:

> *To suffer woes which Hope thinks infinite;*
> *To forgive wrongs darker than death or night;*
> *To defy Power which seems omnipotent;*
> *To love, and bear; to hope till Hope creates*
> *From its own wreck the thing it contemplates;*
> *Neither to change, nor falter, nor repent;*
> *This, like thy glory, Titan, is to be*
> *Good, great and joyous, beautiful and free;*
> *This is alone Life, Joy, Empire and Victory.*

Honoria Lucasta, Dowager Duchess of Denver, to her American friend, Cornelia, wife of Lambert B. Vander-Huysen, of New York.

Bredon Hall,   6th June, 1940
Duke's Denver, Norfolk

Dear Cornelia,

Thank you for your kind letter, so full of concern for us. As you will be reading in the papers, the news is dreadful. We have withdrawn from Norway, and now the British Expeditionary Force has pulled out of France. We are all so grateful to have our boys – and a lot of French boys too – back in England, and so proud of all the people in little boats who fetched them home for us, that the mood is nothing like as dark as you might think. There's even an odd sort of relief. People are saying, 'Well, we're on our own now, and it's up to us, so we must just get on with it.' Peter says wars are not won by retreats, however glorious, and my daughter Mary says that the hospital trains bringing the wounded back to hospitals in London were a dreadful sight, and she saw the nurses at

369

Bart's standing in the street crying before going back to the wards. But we all listen to Churchill on the wireless to keep our spirits up.

Now, you are not to worry about us going hungry (although we shall greatly enjoy the food parcel you have sent when it reaches us), because the rationing is quite fair, and quite sufficient. Of course country people have ways and means, but some of the townspeople are better fed than ever before, and we are managing very well at Denver. I tried out, yesterday, a piece of advice from our Ministry of Food (yes, we have such a thing!) that although the butter ration has to be spread pitifully thin, one will be able to taste the butter better, if one eats the bread upside down – butter side against the tongue. I am nearly sure that it makes a difference! We have so many leaflets of advice about everything from growing cabbage to unpicking and remaking clothes, to joining this and that organisation, to what to do if the Germans land, and how to build air-raid shelters that people get quite cross about the waste of paper; we can't get wood pulp from Sweden any more, and The Times *has slimmed down by pages and pages and is a shadow of its former self.*

Meanwhile, taking an interest in our ragamuffin school (they have the whole west wing) is making Denver quite a socialist. He actually said to me the other day that we would have to put things right after the war in respect of education. 'If one has it, all should have it,' he said.

Would you believe, Cornelia, that I have joined the Auxiliary Fire Service myself, and I take my turn standing on the church tower with a tin hat on! Only it's so far from the village for people to walk here at night, and we are so close by. The whole thing was arranged that way, of course, at the whim of an eighteenth-century Duke, who wanted his villagers at a respectful distance, and the church handy on a wet Sunday, but the result is I think I should take my turn. Franklin keeps running up and down the tower steps with blankets and Thermos flasks for me, tut-tutting like mad, silly woman. But as I told her, I have Norman blood.

We are all so heartened at what you tell us about all the organisations in your great country campaigning to per-suade the President to come to our aid. Women's organ-isations, too; but then you and I both know, dear, that women often see what battle will have to be fought while the men are still marching around the parade ground. Peter doesn't think that we could possibly win without you; the most we might manage will be to hang on until you get here; to avoid being engulfed ourselves, so that American aid will be possible. It doesn't seem likely that even the United States could invade Europe across three thousand miles of ocean. So you see, dear, the old country will come in handy as an airfield, and jumping-off base, if only we can hold out long enough. But there will be a terrible battle now that the enemy have all the coastal areas across the Channel, and England is in range for all their fighters and bombers. So we hope it won't take too long for your gallant band of interventionists to succeed, and shut up Lindbergh and people like him who are telling you to stay at home and not get involved. Such an odd line of thinking for a public hero, I think, although perhaps the poor man was unhinged by having his baby kidnapped in that horrible manner.

Talking of babies, we have a visit in prospect next weekend from all the grandchildren at Talboys, and I am cutting up a lovely old lace counterpane to make a wedding veil for a friend of Harriet's. It's eighteenth century – the counterpane, that is – but be bothered to that, there is a good deal of fun to be had in make do and mend! I really don't think we appreciated things half so much when we could just go out and buy them. And Franklin tells me that Gone with the Wind has reached Duke's Denver, and will be showing in the little local cinema next week, which will give us all a treat and take us out of ourselves. So you see, we are keeping cheerful, and getting on with things as best we can. Don't worry about us, Cornelia, the best thing you can do for us is go and throw eggs at your pacifists!

My best love to you and Lambert, and, of course, to John and Margaret and Junior.

Your affectionate old friend,
    Honoria Denver

PS: Can your food parcel really include home-made jelly? However did you wrap it up?

Author's Note

From November 1939 to January 1940 Dorothy L. Sayers made a series of contributions to the *Spectator* magazine, consisting of mock letters to and from various members of the Wimsey family, about war-time conditions like blackout, evacuation, rationing, and the need for the public to take personal responsibility: 'They must not continually ask for leadership – they must lead themselves.'

These contributions, usually now referred to as 'The Wimsey Papers' in effect lay out the characters in the crime novels like pieces on a chess board during the opening moves of a game. They tell us where everyone was. Lord Peter was somewhere abroad, on a secret mission under the direction of the Foreign Office; Bunter was with him; Harriet had taken her own children and those of her sister-in-law to the country, the loathed Helen, Duchess of Denver had joined the Ministry of Instruction and Morale, etc. etc.

The Wimsey Papers are almost, but not quite, the latest information that Dorothy L Sayers provided about her characters. There is also a short story called 'Talboys', contained in the volume 'Striding Folly' which shows Peter and Harriet and their children living in their country farmhouse peacefully together, and which must refer to 1942.

The Wimsey Papers are not fiction, and were not intended to be read in a continuous chunk. Some of them are about details of war-time history that would now require extensive footnotes in explication. But they do afford an authoritative foothold for an account of the Wimsey family in 1940. I have opened this novel with a selection from them, and incorporated insights and information from them in the narrative where I could.

Acknowledgements

I would like to thank Mr Bruce Hunter and the trustees of Anthony Fleming for entrusting to me the continuation of the lives of Lord Peter, Harriet Vane, and their family and friends.

I gratefully acknowledge the indispensable help of Dr Barbara Reynolds, president of the Dorothy L. Sayers Society; the friendly assistance of Mr Christopher Dean, chairman of that society; and of Mr P.J.V. Elliot of the Royal Air Force Museum, Hendon. I thank Mr Christopher Reeves and Mr John Lambert for finding for me a copy of *Norwegian Patrol* by Gron Edwards; Mr John Turner and Mr John Romain for ensuring that I could understand a pilot's-eye view of a Spitfire; Mr Christopher Tanous, for arranging a visit to Chicksands; Mr Malcolm Bishop and Ms Edna Robertson for information about dentistry; and Mr Peter Welton, master butcher with a long memory; Ms Carolyn Caughey, and Ms Hope Dellon for their capable editorial advice, and help received as always and in everything from John Rowe Townsend.

I have been greatly helped and encouraged along the way by the members of the Harriet Vane internet chat-group.

Finally I would like to thank my parents and grand-parents, long after the event, who in my tender years protected me from the times I was living in, and gave me a happy and insouciant early childhood. Reading for this book has engendered in me an immense respect for the courage and sang-froid of those who had to live through those years with adult apprehension of death and danger and adult understanding of what was at stake.

Permissions

Apologies are offered to copyright holders whom it has not been possible to trace.

Lines from *Tommy* by Rudyard Kipling on page 20 are quoted by kind permission of A.P. Watt Ltd on behalf of the National Trust for Places of Historical Interest or Natural Beauty.

Song lines on pages 22/3 quoted by kind permission of Johnny Greenbay & the Dancehall Flourishers.

Extract from *The Diaries of Virginia Woolf* on page 61 published by Hogarth Press. Used by permission of the executors of the Virginia Woolf Estate, the Random House Group Ltd., and Harcourt Inc.

Lines from 'Invitation au Festin' by Aelfrida Tillyard on page 83 from *The Garden and the Fire*, published 1916 by Heffer, Cambridge.

Extract from *The Tale of Pigling Bland* by Beatrix Potter on page 199, Copyright © Frederick Warne & Co. 1913. Reproduced by permission of Frederick Warne & Co.

Poem XL from *A Shropshire Lad* on page 299 by permission of the Society of Authors as the literary representatives of the estate of A.E. Housman.

Lines attributed to Alan Brinklow on page 306 are those of an unknown Second World War soldier, recorded by Mr. Jack Miles.